CRIMINAL IMPULSES

JANIK BRYNN CHRONICLES

SANDY STUCKLESS

Criminal Impulses

Published by: Cloaked Press, LLC
PO Box 341
Suring, WI 54174
Cloakedpress.com

Cover Design by:
Carmilla M. Ravensworth
carmillacreates.carrd.co

ISBN: 978-1-952796-29-6

To my beautiful wife, Heather. I chase dreams while you do the hard stuff. This book is as much yours as it is mine.

To my kids, Dennis and Emmy. The world is yours. All you have to do is take it. Take chances and never give up.

To my mom and dad. I wish more than anything that you could've been here to see this.

I love you all.

Contents

CHAPTER 1:
THE PROMENADE

For Janik Brynn, it was a terrible day to steal a Bentley. Well, any car for that matter. If anyone caught him, they'd never find his body. Not that anyone would miss a lowlife thief anyway.

The Promenade was packed on this busy midmorning Tuesday. Janik counted the data recorders he could see hanging from the billboards. Every one of them had facial recognition tech. He should know. He helped develop the software for it. This job could've been so much easier on a darkened residential street where people didn't appreciate constant surveillance.

He pulled the charcoal-colored fedora low over his face, blocking out the early September San Francisco sun. The fewer people that saw his face, the better. The absence of the Judiciary's uniformed goons here didn't make Janik feel any better. The security arm of the Consortium had eyes and ears all over the city.

Janik thought about the Promenade, back when it was still Hallidie Plaza. Mothers shopping with children in tow, teenagers enjoying bright summer days, old men in the back left corner playing chess. Janik used to come here with his kid sister Patricia to play. He was good. She was the best. Really, it was just an excuse to ride the Powell Street cable car. Those were the good old days. Before the Great Quake, before the Consortium stepped in to revitalize it. Before his sister hated his guts.

A well-dressed figure descended the stairs from the parking lot on the far side of the Promenade, joining the morning crowd.

Janik's stomach sank. His mark was William McIntosh…

Kirox didn't tell him his mark was a McIntosh. Janik would've never agreed to this had he known. He swore once he got away from them, he'd never go back. Janik hated the McIntoshes and they were only family by marriage anyway. But if Patricia found out, any chance at reconciliation with his sister was gone. He should've guessed when Kirox's mission file said Bentley. Even in a rich city like this one, there weren't many of those to go around.

Bigshot Bill shoved his way through the crowd, watching the screen in his hand more than where he walked. Business never stopped for that crowd. They were heavily involved with the Pharmacy. Like the Judiciary, Infrastructure, and the rest of the city's top industries, the Consortium owned them, ruling each one with an iron fist. Only the Underground Network gave them something to think about. The Consortium may have come together to rebuild the city after the Great Quake, but saviors they were not.

They hadn't been since the Consortium Executive Order started calling the shots. The only problem was, no one knew who they were. That's who his friends with the UN had really been after. With every strike, they hoped to draw them out. Janik hoped that wasn't what this was about. He didn't want his last job to be pissing off the biggest crime syndicate in the city.

Bigshot Bill took his coffee and joined another well-dressed man at a nearby table. At first, Janik didn't understand why he'd pick the most public place in the city to have a secret meeting, but then it dawned on him that anything important would be transferred electronically.

Leaving his spot against the railing, he crossed the Promenade. Janik would never call it Brynn Square. That represented a part of his family's legacy he wanted no part of. A vane reward for playing the game of corruption so well.

He passed close enough behind Bigshot Bill's table to establish a link to his phone. Whatever data he was sharing with his coffee date, would be shared with Janik as well. He winked at a kid playing chess with his mother as he passed.

This place was the convergence of the whole Consortium machine. Ads pasted the side of every building from food to pharmaceuticals to cybernetics. What most people didn't realize were these billboards were full surveillance systems. Everything in the Promenade, including faces, was recorded. It's how the Consortium maintained control. They knew what everyone was doing all the time.

Breakfast was still in full swing, but the synth burger stand had already fired up in anticipation of the lunch rush. The searing stench nearly made Janik retch. Meatless synth patties grilled on either side for a couple minutes to make it look like a real burger. *More flavor in one of my worn-out shoes.*

The Bentley sat at the back of the lot by itself. There's my break for the day.

He checked his watch. Ten minutes. He had ten minutes before Bigshot Bill returned. He shook his head. Insanity, that's what this was. Pure insanity. The busiest time of day, in the middle of the Consortium's crown jewel. Insanity.

This should've really been a three-person job. One to boost the car, one to keep watch, and one to distract the owner, if it came to that. Janik always worked alone, relying on his hacking skills to get him out of situations. With a little more prep time, he could've hacked the city's earthquake early warning system to give the marshals something else to think about. Or, at least knock out the cameras.

A deep breath did nothing to ease his edginess. The aroma of fresh cinnamon rolls made his stomach growl. Great. Hungry and nervous. Better than the stench from synth burger stand. Beauty day this was shaping up to be. He hadn't felt like this since his first job. That one hadn't gone exactly as planned either.

Janik had grown tired of a game that had become harder to play. The Consortium would cut shipments to the southern districts and the UN would raid a warehouse. The UN would hijack a shipment of meds and the Consortium would close a clinic. No one gaining ground in a war that had been going on since about two years after the quake that changed San Francisco's landscape in every sense of the word.

The mission had changed somewhere along the way, the mission the whole UN had been founded on. Before, the proceeds from every car he stole, minus his fee of course, ended up funneled back into the districts neglected by the city's power brokers. Now, the street crews had gone from hitting loads of medical supplies to hitting warehouses full of weapons. Janik had no interest in any of that. He told Kirox as much before this mission even came across the wire.

Helping those who couldn't help themselves no longer mattered. Greed had become the name of the game on both sides of the line. He was no different. He wouldn't have even taken this job if Kirox hadn't begged. A couple of neighborhoods needed a new generator. A favor for a friend, he said. Janik had already announced his retirement quietly and he surely didn't need the money, but he never could say no to Kirox.

Janik lifted the fedora from his eyes as he approached the car. Focus, you idiot. The descrambler plugged into the car's security panel usually made quick work of the systems, as long as there were no upgrades. Another sign to call it quits. The job had become way riskier.

Another check of his watch. Eight and a half minutes left. Ninety seconds gone without so much as a bloody door open yet.

Janik glanced toward the lower level of the Promenade. The quiet thrum had become load and frantic. He listened a little closer, hearing something about the video board and no network connection.

He briefly considering making a run for it. Maybe the commotion would buy him an extra couple of minutes. Or, on the other hand, if Bigshot Bill came back early… He wiped his sweaty palms on his pants. What the hell. This is why I'm paid the big bucks.

Another glance at his watch. Seven minutes left. Janik tapped his fingers against the car door. Hurry up, you stupid hunk of junk. Finally, it trilled. Janik checked his watch yet again. Four minutes.

Almost six minutes to descramble the locking sequence. Didn't leave much time to find the ignition sequence. Janik swung the gull-wing door up. Despite his time constraints, he paused to admire the interior. Soft, black real leather seats, polished chrome, state-of-the-art electronics. A VIP's ride. The only thing missing was the auto driver. So, Bigshot Bill liked a little old school control. Relatable. The commotion below had grown more frantic. Janik pushed it away. There were still obstacles to getting this baby running. The thumbprint scanner and voice activation system.

A deafening roar slammed into him an instant before the cloud of hot debris engulfed the car. Janik dove onto the Bentley's floor, screaming as he wrenched his knee.

He lay motionless, trying to determine if he was dead or not. Waves of pain and nausea shot through him with every movement. Okay, so not dead. He suspected many on the Promenade's lower level weren't so lucky.

Janik squeezed his eyes shut against the choking dust and smoke. He rolled out of the car onto all fours, fighting to keep his Non-Synth bacon and eggs down. A high-pitched squeal rang in his ears. Pressing his palm to his temple, he staggered to his feet. What the actual hell? Did he miss one of the Bentley's upgrades?

The back of his trembling hand came away red after swiping it across his forehead. Bleeding wasn't on his 'to-do' list when he left the house this morning. Janik inspected his condition.

Bleeding *and* his favorite suit ruined. Car theft was supposed to be a non-contact sport. Yet another notch in the 'pro' side of quitting for good.

Panicked screams from the Promenade replaced the ringing in his ears. An explosion, not a Bentley security measure, had rocked the middle of the Promenade. What the hell were the baristas putting in the lattes?

Janik grimaced at the mess of shattered glass and twisted metal of the ruined Bentley. So much for one last easy payday. Someone had some explaining to do. He liked to avoid violence usually. Today, he might make an exception.

Steadily thickening black smoke billowed across the parking lot. He should scram while he still had the chance. Enough other people were on the way to handle the situation. He hesitated. There were kids down there.

Leaning against the wall for support, Janik staggered to the lower level, waving his hand trying to disperse some of the stinging cloud. He tripped over something solid. Too soft to be a rock, he almost threw up again when his eyes locked onto the body.

The billboard that only minutes earlier played Consortium sponsored advertisements burned in the middle of the Promenade. A motionless hand stuck out from beneath it.

Sirens grew louder. Janik had minutes before marshals crawled all over this place. Every marshal in San Francisco knew to watch for him. Hell, they likely had his picture pinned to the bulletin board at the station.

He wove his way through the debris. A few others that had escaped major injury, miraculously, had found their way to their feet and were assisting. The lifeless eyes of the boy who'd been playing chess with his mother stared up at him. Janik fell to his knees, overcome by the emotional punch to the gut. An innocent kid. He didn't deserve this. No one did.

Janik had been prepared to walk away. He didn't want to waste the rest of his time trying to save a city that didn't want to be saved. Now, he wasn't so sure. How many explosions would he be walking away from? How much danger would countless others be in? He became sick to his stomach at the thought.

An obsidian chess piece, a knight, a dark hero fallen in battle, sat a few feet away smeared with blood. What happened here wasn't a battle. An ambush, maybe. Janik scooped up the piece, wiping some of the blood away with the cuff of his ruined jacket.

Off to his left, someone moaned. Through the haze Janik spotted the boy's mother, covered in blood, stirring. Panic stole Janik's breath. He couldn't let her see her boy. Not like this. He stuck the knight in his pocket and rushed over to her. "Don't move. You're hurt. Help is on the way." Janik checked her over quickly. She appeared to have escaped major injury. The blood had to be someone else's.

"My son," she mumbled. "Where's my son?"

Janik's voice hitched in his throat. Delivering devastating news wasn't something he wanted to do so he pretended not to hear. "I'm going to check on others. Stay still, okay."

People thought being a thief made him a cold heartless killer. He tried to avoid all that. Some people in the Underground Network thrived on it. That was, if all the rumors about the hits on Consortium assets were to be believed.

The crumpled form of Bigshot Bill lay next to the blasted remains of the coffee hut, a blackened half-melted coffee cup next to him. Janik only recognized him because of the swatches of expensive cloth that used to make up his suit. No big loss. One less power-hungry elitist manipulating the system. Not that there weren't others waiting in line to take his place.

A frightening realization dawned on him as the sirens screamed closer. He'd be blamed for this. The Consortium didn't take kindly to people blowing up their property, especially when

VIPs died in the process. He thought of Patricia's family. Though they wanted nothing to do with him, he had to protect them. To do that, he had to have never been here in the first place.

Janik picked up his pace, as much as his battered body allowed, up the stairs to the Market Street Boulevard. He turned east, away from the chaos. A vehicle screeched to a halt in front of him, blue and red lights flashing. The hatches flung open and two marshals jumped out, pistols drawn.

The San Francisco Marshals Service - the long arm of the law. Janik almost laughed. Funded entirely by the families and competing corporations who routinely circumvented those laws for their own benefit. Unfortunately, San Fransico knew no other police force. Not since the Great Quake.

"You in some kind of hurry, pal?"

As a matter of fact, yes. And he'd kindly thank them to get the hell out of his way. He didn't want to be here when the Consortium showed up. They wouldn't leave something this public to the marshals.

"Turn around. On your knees," the marshal on the left commanded. "Don't do anything stupid."

Maybe he wasn't in that much of a hurry. "There's a kid with his mother down there. The kid is dead, but the mother needs help."

"We'll get to them, don't worry. Right now, we're looking after you."

"How sweet. I'm sure they'll give you a nice shiny medal." He figured attempting to leave the scene of an explosion marked you more as criminal than victim. Doing something stupid wouldn't get him far. Getting shot in the back wasn't his idea of a good time. He locked his fingers together behind his head. Turning his back to the marshals, he knelt, crossed his ankles, and waited for his next instruction. Maybe there was still a chance to talk his way out of this.

"You've done this before, I see," one marshal told him as he wrenched Janik's wrist none too gently behind his back.

He had. It hadn't been much fun then, either.

The other marshal spoke next, a hint of surprise in his voice. "I recognize this guy. This is Janik Brynn, Scriber to his friends. A lot of people have been looking for him. We've caught one of the UN's big fish. Better call Renaude."

Janik's heart sank. That was the last name he wanted to hear.

CHAPTER 2: TRANSPORT

The marshals shoved Janik, hands secured behind his back, through waves of people into the Hall of Justice. That was just the name on the side of the building. Justice was the one thing that didn't happen here.

They removed the mag-cuffs to take fingerprint scans, retinal scans, and mugshots. The marshal jabbed a meaty finger with increasing force onto the console. He threw his hands up when it still wouldn't work. "What the hell?"

"Problems?" Janik said with a smirk. "Oh well. I guess you'll have to let me go. I promise to be a good boy."

"Shut up. The network is down. We'll have to upload this later."

Janik's bravado faltered. Central Booking was on the main city network. That never went down. A major expedition and a network failure at the same time? That was no coincidence.

They dumped him in a cramped cell at the far end of the block. Janik wasn't the neighborly type anyway. His only furniture consisted of a sink, toilet, and cot. He tried breathing through his mouth as much as possible. Smelling his own stink was bad enough.

"Don't you go anywhere, now," they mocked.

Janik limped around the cell, ignoring their receding laughter. He shook his head at the flickering lights. Odd that this place didn't have reliable power. Now they had some idea of what the Mission District had struggled with for decades. Of course, none of that mattered to these cretins. The people north of Market Street were oblivious to everything going on in the rest of the world.

Janik stripped off his jacket and shirt. His whole body shook as he washed away some of the dried blood. Now that the adrenaline had worn off, he was crashing hard. He tried easing himself down onto the cot, but flopped as his legs gave out beneath him.

He tried not to think about the Promenade explosion. Unfortunately, his analytical mind had other ideas. His UN connections made him a prime suspect. Or a scapegoat to ease public panic. The Consortium had the ability and motivation to make people disappear. He'd heard more than one horror story of street crews vanishing, never to be heard from again.

It had to be the UN. No one from the Consortium would be dumb enough to launch such an open attack, unless this was a power move from within. Janik flopped back onto the cot. He was loath to consider the possibility his family and their allies set this up to bring him down. How many hitmen did he have looking for him? More than a few, he figured. No, though while possible, he didn't think this was about him. There were far more subtle ways to get rid of him.

Before he left the family business, he cost some people a lot of money and likely a few prominent positions. He still smiled seeing those McIntosh bribery photos in the Chronicle. Something like that wasn't easily forgotten. Kirox would've known. He knew everything. A voice in the back of Janik's head screamed setup. Hard to believe Kirox would sell him out like that though.

Either way, he was a sitting duck in here. An easy payday for a Consortium guard with some type of sharp implement or another. If they took him to the rumored torture chambers in the bowels of this place, it was game over. Hopefully the Consortium puppets in the uniforms were too concerned with the blackouts to worry about him.

He pulled his jacket, stinking of smoke, and sweat over his head, trying to shut out the whining from the other prisoners. Most likely guilty of nothing more than jaywalking. He shifted on the lumpy mattress, hoping for a short nap before his doom arrived. Instead of falling asleep, images of the bodies strewn over the Promenade hit him like a hard left hook. The boy and the chess piece. Renaude pointing a stubby finger at him.

You did this. This is your doing. Child killer!

No! No, I'm not. I didn't do this. Please, let them not be dead.

Janik bolted upright in a cold sweat. His chest tightened with dread. He pressed his back against the wall and drew his knees up to his chest. Slowly, the panic eased, and his vision cleared, bringing his prison cell back into focus. He wiped the moisture from his face. The patrolling guard stopped at his cell, snickering as he raked his persuasion stick across the bars, every clank stabbing like a dagger to Janik's temple.

"Where's Renaude?" Janik demanded. "Get me Renaude." He wasn't a child killer, no matter what the dream said. Somehow, some way he'd prove that. Janik rested his head back against the wall once the guard had passed without a response.

Footsteps down the corridor followed the heavy steel cellblock door retracting into the wall. Other prisoners banged on the bars and shouted to be released. "You're a dead man, Thiraro," one shouted. The guard stalked down the hallway and jammed his persuasion stick between the bars.

Renaude stopped at Janik's cell, regarding him for a long while with an arrogant smile. Janik was used to being the one wearing that grin. *Karma's finally catching up to me.* "There's the man I wanted to see. Expected to see you sooner, Renaude. Another lunchtime visit with your wife? Oh wait…" Janik shrugged. "Sorry."

"Go to hell, Janik. You're the reason she left. Now that you're behind bars, perhaps she'll see reason and come back."

"Don't hold your breath. I'm no expert, but raving lunatic isn't exactly a quality women go for."

"Neither is heartless criminal. At least there's hope for me."

That jab struck a nerve. Janik was lonely. Partly by choice, partly as a byproduct of his profession. He wanted an opportunity to change that. He limped from the cot to the front of the cell. "Feel good having me in here, Renaude?"

Renaude removed a pill bottle from his pocket and popped one of the tablets into his mouth. "I must admit, there is some measure of satisfaction. The past seven years have been pure agony because of you."

"You should talk to someone about that," Janik mocked. "Get your brain reprogrammed or something. I'm sure the Pharmacy has a list of experts you can choose from. Maybe there's a pill you can take."

Renaude's face turned a deep shade of red. If not for the bars between them, Janik was sure the marshal would've strangled him. "I don't need more pills."

"You sure?" Janik replied with mock seriousness. "Looks like you're hurting a little bit."

"My pain is nothing compared to the pain you've caused. Hundreds dead; thousands displaced."

Janik's brain spun. He registered the words from Renaude's mouth, but they made no sense, as if they were in another language. "Thousands? What are you talking about?"

Renaude tugged at his sleeves and scowled. "I don't have time for games, Janik. You're going for a little ride. Save yourself some trouble by telling me about the bombings and the cyber-attack. How do I shut it down?"

Janik gripped the steel bars, more to keep himself upright than anything else. "Bombings? As in more than one? What cyber-attack?"

"Play dumb if you wish." Renaude stepped in closer to the cell door. "We both know you're as guilty as sin."

Janik slammed his hand against the bars. "I didn't kill those people. Check the damn data streams if you don't believe me."

Renaude's arrogant smirk returned. "That won't be necessary. You were arrested fleeing the scene. What type of explosives did you use? How many more bombs are there?"

Janik couldn't breathe. This couldn't be happening. This had to be a play by the McIntoshes to get rid of him. But the, why take out one of their own? He had to stall Renaude long enough to work this out. "I didn't plant any bombs."

"You're lying. Maybe if you cooperate, we can come to some sort of arrangement."

Yeah, one that sees me buried in a shallow hole. "Maybe you should take a closer look at your bosses. Someone's after a bigger share, I'd say. I'd suggest someone grew a conscience, but I don't think that's possible in the Consortium."

Renaude shook his head. chuckling. "Don't be ridiculous, Janik. You still believe the Consortium Executive Order is some evil shadow corporation controlling the city? You're living in a fantasy land."

"I've seen the evidence." The McIntosh servers were full of it. And theirs weren't the only ones. The city had festered a poison of the elite. An infection of the privileged. This was nothing like the city he knew as a kid.

"For argument's sake, say your claims are valid. Why blow up their own city? They're not that dumb. They still need the resources."

It was a good question. One for which he didn't have an answer. He wouldn't find it stuck in here either. "Well, it wasn't me. These bars are my alibi. I didn't kill those people." He wished he sounded more convincing.

"You could've planted the bombs before your arrest. Did your UN friends put you up to this?"

"Don't be ridiculous, Renaude. You still believe there's some underground network undermining the city's leaders?"

"I can have your life spared if you tell me where to find them."

Rumors of that Ice Water heist were a little more unnerving now. That truck had enough Synthetic Liquid to level the city. He returned to sit on the edge of the cot. "I don't have any friends, Renaude. Thought you knew that."

Renaude paced in front of Janik's cell. "You know, I never really understood the purpose of the UN. Why do you people have to disrupt the lives of honest citizens? Can you at least tell me that much?"

"I know you're not that naïve, Renaude. The Consortium turned their position of power into a major extortion ring." Janik held up his hand. "Don't try to deny it. You may not see it from the safety of your high perch, but you know I used to work on your side of the line. You want the UN gone? Dismantle the Consortium and return the city to free government. Stop letting the corporations make decisions that only make the rich richer and the poor poorer."

"I guess it makes sense that you'd fall in with the criminal element given your disgraceful family history. Who is your contact? Maybe you finally decided to take out your revenge on your former employers."

"I'm not stupid enough to poke a sleeping bear, Renaude. Going after them now makes no sense."

"How much did they pay you? Why did you do it?"

Janik wasn't playing this game anymore. He'd already lost any way he rolled it. Particularly because Janik was the reason they were disgraced in the first place. "No idea what you're talking about. I'd ask for a lawyer, but we both know they ain't any cleaner than the rest of your corporate buddies."

He needed to talk to Kirox. Where did the intel for the Promenade mission come from? Who was paying for it and why did they insist on him?

Renaude's lip curled into a disgusted sneer. "You're pathetic."

Janik locked eyes with Renaude. "I did not do this." Why couldn't they check the data stream? "You have to protect me, Renaude. Once your Consortium friends connect me with the bombings, I'm as good as dead. I'm surprised it hasn't happened already."

Renaude crossed his arms. "So, you admit to the bombing then?"

"No, but confession isn't a requirement to make someone disappear. How long have you been chasing me, Renaude? How many years watching me? As much as you hate me for our little run-in, you know this isn't something I'd do. Someone is setting me up."

"I can't help you if you don't tell me what you know. I am a man of some influence. What's so important about the District?"

Every bit of Kirox's business came out of that club. The marshals likely already knew that. But Kirox was no dummy. They'd have better luck finding the Templar treasure on that property than any trace of the UN. Kirox kept those secrets to himself. "I don't know anything."

Renaude rubbed the back of his hand, his patience seemingly running thin. "Why were you in the Promenade this morning?"

Janik hesitated. "The Coffee Hut has good coffee. The cute barista puts real cream in mine."

"That they do. So much so that William McIntosh, the Vice President of Experimental Treatments for McIntosh Corp picks his up every morning promptly at 10 o'clock."

Janik swallowed the lump in his throat. "Is that so? Didn't know that."

"Lying to me is not a good way to get into my good graces.

Some friends of mine are very upset at his passing."

It was those friends Janik truly feared. "I doubt your graces are anywhere near good. Do me a favor. Make sure the hole you bury me in is deep enough."

"You're a piece of scum, Janik. I'm going to see you burn for this." He motioned for the guard to open the cell door. "Your ride is here."

Mag-cuffs were snapped onto his wrists before they led him out the back door to a waiting prisoner transport. At least they didn't take him to the basement. Renaude shoved him. "Inside."

The back of the transport reminded Janik of a coffin, with the low ceiling he had to duck to avoid, and the narrow aisle down the center. Seven other prisoners had the pleasure of riding with him. By the smell of things, they hadn't been allowed a shower either.

"Sit here," the guard ordered, pushing down on Janik's shoulder.

They secured his ankles and wrists with mag-cuffs connected to the floor by a stiff metal cable, limiting his range of motion to five degrees in any direction.

Determined to shut out everything around him, he leaned back. Except, closing his eyes renewed the assault of devastating images. Janik resigned himself to the fact he wasn't getting any sleep back here. He shifted uncomfortably, trying to ease some of his numbness.

The transport lurched forward. To where, he had no idea. The possibilities ranged from anywhere between the bottom of the harbor along the north shore to a shallow hole somewhere in the Old Sierra Nevada.

His eyes slid shut. The low thrum of the transport combined with the lack of sleep was catching up to him. Janik tried to sit up on the hard, metal bench, but his whole body felt heavy, like someone pushed down on his shoulders. He couldn't let himself fall asleep until he knew where they were going.

His eyes grew heavy again and his head drooped. Something was wrong. Why couldn't he keep his eyes open? He hadn't been this sleepy in the cell. Through the thickening fog of drowsiness, he saw the issue. Every passenger in the compartment slumped over unconscious.

Panic set in. He struggled against his bonds, but his arms wouldn't work. Janik couldn't see the driver. He had no idea if they were suffering the same effects as everyone else. As he continued to lose consciousness, the transport jerked from side to side, tires squealing before slamming into something and coming to an abrupt stop.

His last thought before his eyes slid shut was that he was about to die and he wouldn't even be awake to witness it.

CHAPTER 3: SHUTDOWN

Serena sat in her office of the surveillance division of Marks Risk Assessment and Management three floors beneath the Pyramid. Horrific images streamed across her tablet, dredging up memories she'd rather forget. Her chest felt tight, like body armor that was too small.

Rubble and burning debris. Bodies, always the bodies. No eleven-year-old should see so many bodies. Especially not that of her father. Serena glanced at the picture of her mother on her desk. She hadn't just lost her father the day of the quake, she lost her hero. Her mother lost her best friend. His friends lost a kind soul. The Latin community in the Mission District lost a champion. San Francisco hadn't seen a darker day. Until today.

She clutched the rosery beads around her neck and uttered a silent prayer for the victims.

"Serena," someone barked, pulling her back to the present. Her boss, Logan Marks sat across from her, annoyance chiseled on his face.

Logan wasn't a patient man, or a compassionate one, it seemed. The images on her monitor could've been a new strawberry flavored synth formula for all the reaction it garnered. Unsurprising for the former Fed Sec product. That crowd tended to beat the emotions out of their operatives.

She regained her composure. "Sorry. What did you say?"

Logan blew out a long breath through his nose as he tapped a finger on the desk. "Is this the Underground Network?"

Serena spun her chair to a monitor on the wall behind her. Everything her analysts picked up filtered into this one terminal. Nothing caught her attention today though. She turned back to Logan. "It's possible. Morning rush in a crowded plaza. It's an attractive target, that's for sure, but it feels off. This goes against everything we know about the UN. They're cowards who operate from the shadows. Hijackings, sure. Muggings. Again, not out of the question. Outright terrorism seems too high profile. I'll know more when the marshals' reports start rolling in."

"Who else could it be? I'm sure they hijacked the Synthetic Liquid shipment. Something must've changed for them to up the ante like this. What are your people in the Mission District saying?"

Serena hadn't had a chance to reach out to her few contacts yet. She had to be careful. Those willing to talk to her, did so at great personal risk. "None of the chatter indicates they had a bigger target in mind. Why was the Consortium moving that much explosive anyway? You never did fill me in on that."

"It was need-to-know. The bigger question is how did the hijackers find out about it?"

She still had to answer that one. So far, none of her 'friends' were saying. Infiltrating a major UN cell had proven difficult. A mole inside the Consortium was bad news for San Francisco. She checked the data streaming into her tablet. "Someone has to help those people."

"Always the humanitarian, Serena. The only way to help them is to put a stop to the UN once and for all. Their black-market activities are completely undermining everything our clients are working to accomplish. The more they disrupt us, the less comfortable people are. I don't have to tell you the scars of the Great Quake still run deep."

He had a point there. She hadn't been able to pinpoint where the stolen food and medicine ended up. Yet. The UN loved to boast they were helping the under privileged. Except, all they were doing was driving prices up. Basic supply and demand economics. The lesser the supply, the greater the demand, the higher the price. Never mind trying to recruit young girls into prostitution. "Give me an hour for my team to work and to make some calls. We'll figure it out."

"Fine. I have to go upstairs to get my bosses to start locking down their servers and backing up their data. They won't be happy if their servers are breached."

Logan left and Serena dug into her morning reports. She scrolled through the data on her tablet, very little of it from the Mission District. A little odd, but not overly so. A major disaster had struck the city. Their attention was likely elsewhere.

She keyed in Bruno's number on a communicator that only she and the person on the other end knew existed. It beeped a couple times then went dead. *Mierda*. He usually answered.

She went out to the control room, where three analysts poured over streams of data, both from the news and private sources. They were looking for patterns and keywords. "Tell me you have something."

Nelson, her lead analyst, and all-around computer genius sat with his head in his hands. "Does a bad case of indigestion count?"

"Logan swears this is the UN. He'll kill us both if we don't find him something."

"It'd take days to filter through all data."

"We have about forty-five minutes. Maybe this is nothing more than an old-fashioned heist and the bombing is a mere distraction to keep us busy."

Nelson hammered on his keyboard. "Checking the banks and depositories now. There isn't a lot of physical money to steal. Everything is digital."

"Maybe it's not money they're after. Can you see who's

transferring a lot of data right now? Especially the people upstairs."

Serena had requested several times, unsuccessfully, for access to the client servers. She didn't have the proper clearance, they said. They didn't realize or didn't care that something on those servers might help track the UN. Perhaps now they'll listen.

"They're moving a lot to an offsite location, but I can't tell what."

"What location?"

"Your guess is as good as mine. I'm coming up against a bunch of shadow servers. It's like being stuck in a house of mirrors. Every time you think you hit something real, it turns into an illusion. I can tell you though, it is in San Francisco."

Clever bastards. Hard to steal data when you didn't know which server to hack. "Run facial req on the images from the Promenade. Maybe we'll get lucky. I need to call Logan. Keep me posted."

Serena sat quietly behind her desk for a few minutes before punching in Logan's number. She had to slow down, think about this logically. She thought about her time as a young marshal going through archived case files. She needed that attention to detail now.

A couple deep breaths calmed her thumping heart. Logan's theory of this being a UN op held merit. All of her contacts had gone silent and the Promenade had to be a distraction. She hit the button for Logan's personal communicator.

"Talk to me."

"I have a working theory. What if the Promenade wasn't a statement, but a distraction? Whoever is behind this needed us occupied long enough to acquire whatever it is they're after."

"It's a wasted play. The UN has no shot of infiltrating our systems."

"Unless it's not the UN." Her internal communicator beeped.

She hit another button. Nelson appeared on her monitor. "What is it?"

"Problems, that's what."

"You better get down here, Logan. Things are heating up again."

"On my way."

Alarm bells and flashing lights greeted them when she entered the small ops center. Every one of the giant monitors on the wall displayed 'No Signal' Serena raked her hand through her hair. "What's happening, Nelson? Where are my data feeds? Where's my video?"

He hunched over his monitor. "It's a DoS attack. We're losing critical systems."

Screens popped up and closed down in a flurry. Serena couldn't follow it all. "Slow down. Who managed to get a denial-of-service attack past our security?"

"Excellent question." Nelson's fingers flew over the keyboard. "Whoever it is, they're good. They used a remote access Trojan we couldn't detect. They busted down our door and shut us down. We're offline. Our backup systems can't keep up."

Logan entered the control room looking like a volcano ready to erupt. Serena put herself between him and Nelson. This situation was challenging enough already.

"Are they getting our intel?"

Nelson shrugged. "Probably."

Serena leaned over Nelson's shoulder. "Can you trace it?"

"With difficulty. They're bouncing all over the globe. I've managed to isolate it to somewhere in the city. No exact location yet. Phantom servers are popping up all over the place." Nelson glanced up reticently at Serena from his terminal. "This could take a while."

Logan slammed his hand down on the desk. "Not good enough."

Nelson shied away, sweat sliding down his temple. "I'm doing my best, Sir. We're dealing with pros here."

"How long? Can you give me a number?"

Nelson threw up his hands. "I don't know. They'll know as soon as I get close. We could be here all night."

"What good are you then?" Logan sneered. "Maybe I should find someone who does know."

Serena wheeled on him, her own anger flaring. "You are not helping." She patted Nelson on the back. "Keep at it."

Logan paced Ops, hands folded behind his back. His face betrayed the intensity his body hid. "It has to be the UN," he mumbled. "Those bastards have been far too quiet lately. Now, in one morning, we've lost the Promenade, the power grid, and our network."

Serena rolled her eyes. Now he was talking to himself. This business with the UN had him riled. She related to a certain degree. Two years with no major breaks in the case. She thought bringing down Harlon's cell would open the flood gates. No such luck.

That didn't give Logan leave to harass her people though. Nelson was one of the good ones. Serena knew it when she saw him at the university testing. That kid was going places. "Let's go back to my office and let these guys work."

Once the door closed, she unleashed on him. She kept her hands clenched on top of her desk. Breaking his nose wasn't an option either. "Jumping down the throats of my staff isn't going to produce answers any faster. If anything, it's going to cause mistakes."

Logan grunted. "I have no use for people who can't handle a little pressure."

Serena crossed her arms over her chest. "Do you want me to run this department or not? I can't do it if you're always in the way. It's bad enough you won't give me access to the servers."

"That's not my decision. Our clients are not willing to risk compromising their data."

"Then you need to be patient. My people are pretty smart. They'll figure it out. We won't have enough power to run the water cooler unless you get those backup generators humming."

"Once I've taken care of our primary benefactors, I'll handle it."

Nelson's face popped up on her tablet screen. "I've narrowed it down to the northwest sector. Most of the city's essential services have switched to reserves, but they won't last long."

"That doesn't make any sense," Logan said. "The UN doesn't operate out of there."

"Face it, Logan. This may not be the UN. Like you said, they don't have this type of capability. There aren't enough power or network resources in the Mission District to run a laptop, never mind a full-blown cyber-attack."

"So far, we've lost communications, public transit, traffic cams, and certain parts of the power grid. It's probably going to get worse."

"They're targeting infrastructure to keep the marshals and emergency management busy," Serena said. "This isn't over yet."

"Media assets are still online though," Nelson added.

"Sounds like someone still has a message to deliver."

"Maybe they're running it from a secret facility somewhere up there to siphon our resources," Logan replied.

"If that's the case, it's bad news for the Consortium. It means someone here is helping them."

Logan tapped a finger on the desk and chewed his lower lip. "We need eyes out there. Go to the Mission District. See what you can dig up. Cash in every marker you have if necessary. I'll handle things here while you're gone. I promise to play nice with the weenies."

Serena's eyes bulged. "Are you crazy? I'm a data analyst, not a field operative." She wasn't keen on going back there anyway. They'd likely shoot her on sight, and she risked discovery every time she contacted one of her informants. They were sympathetic to the Consortium, but still had families to protect.

"We can't move until we know where the attack is coming from. I'll send a team with you in case things heat up."

Serena shook her head emphatically. "Call the marshals, Logan. They're better equipped. Isn't this why you pay them?"

Saying it out loud reinforced the bitter truth. A few weeks working the streets with them had shown her that. The few good ones weren't enough to overcome all the dirt. Serena should've listened to her mother all along. She'd seen the marshals' intimidation firsthand.

The first time she went into the Mission District as a marshal horrified her. Higher ranked officers mag-cuffed and harassed citizens for just being on the street. As a rookie, she couldn't say anything. Stop lying to yourself, Serena. You were angry at those who supported the UN. You wanted to see them suffer.

She used her mother's medicine to justify her actions. Getting back at Harlon Cruz and the UN only added to the satisfaction. In the end, it didn't matter. Her mother died anyway.

Logan linked his hands behind his head. "They have their hands full with the Promenade and traffic control. This is the best option. People in this city have forgotten their place. We saved them after the Great Quake. We rebuilt this city from the ground up. They'd still be picking up the scraps from the rubble if not for us. They should be thanking us, not attacking us."

And you make sure people know it every chance you get. Serena dropped her head into her hands. Arguing was pointless. "What happens if I get caught snooping around?"

"Use your imagination or the gun in your desk drawer for all I care. Use your head for something other than coming up with excuses. You belong to us. No one would dare touch you unless they wanted to start a war."

Serena's jaw tightened. She belonged to no man. Not that it mattered to Logan. He had no concept of mutual respect, only master and servant. She seethed, trying not to dwell on things too long. She had to focus. "I want you to understand I seriously disagree with this. I'm going out there with no plan. If things go bad, I'm hung out to dry."

Logan headed for the office door. "Be ready in ten minutes."

Serena sat back and rubbed her face. Was Logan's insistence punishment she hadn't shut down the UN yet? She told him when she accepted the job that beyond Harlon's cell, which had already been dismantled, she didn't know anything. Everything she had on the UN she'd gathered after accessing this little room.

He completely overlooked the time and effort it took to cultivate her current sources. All those hours in Mission Dolores Basilica praying with those who only wanted a better life. It hadn't been easy convincing them they weren't abandoning the Mission District but charting its way forward. In the end, her bank account did more convincing than her words.

She reached into her desk drawer for her sidearm, brushing the King James bible that sat next to it. Serena wished she had a few more minutes to pray on it, but Logan would be angry if she kept him waiting. She clipped the gun to her belt and grabbed her tablet. Her stomach churned as she left her office. She wouldn't give Logan the satisfaction of thinking her weak. She'd prove she could do it. "I'm going to the northwest sector," she said to Nelson as she walked by. "Send me everything you have."

Logan handed her a keycard when she exited the elevator on the ground level. "This'll give you access to the residences we have around the city. There's one at Stanyan and Frederick. Call me if there's trouble. I'll extract you when I can. If you pinpoint the attack, I'll send in the cavalry. I'll make sure they don't ever think about trying this again."

Serena accepted the card with hesitation, seeing right through the charming smile. "Are you sure about this? Why not send in the strike teams? There has to be someone better."

"Don't worry, you'll be fine," he replied before walking away.

CHAPTER 4:
INFILTRATION

The transport flew in low between the buildings. Serena clutched the sides of the jump seat behind the pilot as she tracked a strong signal with her tablet. She tried to focus on that instead of her flip-flopping stomach. Farther back in the cabin, one of Logan's heavily armed strike teams sat quiet, yet jittery. They were ready for a fight.

"Head for Land's End," she called into her mic. Her foot bounced as she waited for ops center to update her.

"Roger," came the reply. "We're three mikes out."

The comms link in her other ear chirped. About damn time.

At least Logan was smart enough to set his operations comms up on their own secure network. Whatever was happening in the city wouldn't affect it and they could still talk to each other. It was also encrypted six ways from Sunday so no one could listen in.

"Your options are Land's End or Golden Gate Park." Nelson had calmed significantly from earlier. Logan must not be around. "They're throwing up phantom servers faster than I can eliminate them. These guys are using scripts I've never seen before."

Serena pressed her fingers to her eyes. There was nothing up there. Not necessarily a rundown neighborhood, but perhaps a forgotten one. Certainly no attractive Consortium target. "Underground material?"

"Probably, but high-level stuff. Security firms, intelligence gathering, that kind of thing. Similar to what we're using, actually."

"You can bet your ass they didn't get them at a local computer shop." None of the dossiers she had on suspected UN operatives fit this M.O. They were street thugs. They may have acted like Robin Hood to some, focusing on food and medical shipments, but street thugs, nonetheless. Serena discovered the truth of it after the way her mother died. So what changed? Why the sudden escalation, change in tactics? Was she witnessing the start of a full-blown revolution? Too bad she wasn't back in her quiet office to think about it.

"Yeah- Wait, what the hell!" Nelson disappeared from the screen. "Goddamn it," he swore. Sounds of frantic typing came through the comms link.

"What's going on? Talk to me."

"We're done," Nelson huffed. "Locked out. I can't even run the chilling towers anymore. I'm shutting down the servers or we're going to lose them permanently."

Serena had spent years gathering the intel on those servers. Every bit of UN dirt she had housed in one place. Hopefully, they managed to back up some of it offline before the servers shut down. "How the hell did they infiltrate our systems?"

"Someone had to let them in. The only problem is it's not happening here. It's external."

"Can you reverse it?"

"No. The algorithms are constantly changing. I can't pin it down. Not until I find out how they gained access in the first place. Finding the source would be really helpful."

"Hey, we've got a problem here," the pilot called in her other ear.

Serena muted him. She had her own issues. "Give me something, Nelson. I'm lost out here."

"There are still a few private servers online near your current position. That won't last when the power runs out."

The transport pitched forward, for a landing, she figured. Her heart sped up when the pitch angle steepened. "Alright, I'll check it out. Keep working and tell Logan to stay by his tablet. I have to go."

She unmuted the pilot's comms in time to hear him shouting. "We're going down. Brace for impact. Brace for impact."

Serena secured her tablet beneath the jump seat harness against her chest and clamped onto the hand grips. Her stomach flipped again. This was why she preferred to stay out of the field. Crashing tended to hurt.

The transport hit the ground with a teeth-rattling jolt despite the pilot's best efforts. The straps digging into her shoulders kept her from slamming into the ceiling. "*Hijo de puto*, that hurt," she muttered. She hoped God would forgive her vulgarity due to circumstances. She traced the cross over her chest just to be sure.

She inspected herself and her equipment for damage and flashed the strike team commander a thumbs up as he rushed forward to check on the pilot. They returned a few seconds later, the pilot with a cut over his eyebrow where his combat helmet dug in. "What happened?"

"No clue," he replied caustically. "We were doing fine until our systems shut down. We were basically a flying brick."

Serena tapped a few buttons on her tablet touchscreen. "Had to be a remotely transmitted computer virus." Hopefully, Nelson could trace the source.

"No way. Not possible," the pilot insisted. "These birds are protected six ways from Sunday."

"Right," Serena replied. "And there's no way for them to shut down an entire city either, is there?"

"That's not my area, Miss. I just know that it would take something pretty powerful to break into our systems."

"Rest assured they have it." Every event solidified Serena's belief that this wasn't a UN op. They were likely involved. She just didn't think they were running it. Of course, there was always the chance she was wrong. The cells had likely gotten much more sophisticated since Harlon's day of bolt cutters and getaway cars.

"What's the game plan, Commander?" one of the commandos asked. "We're exposed here."

The commander donned his helmet and slung his weapon over his shoulder. "Set up a perimeter and await further instructions. I'm sure Mister Marks will be in touch soon."

Serena scrolled through the data on her screen. They were close. "That's not going to work, Commander. The signal that's shutting everything down is somewhere in this sector."

"Damn techies," he muttered. "Listen to me good, lady. We're not walking all over this place. Whoever downed the bird is probably on their way here to say hello. We're going to hunker down and wait for word from command. End of story."

"'Fraid not, Commander. My orders come directly from Logan. Hide if you want. I've got a signal to find."

"Goddammit, lady. You're going to get us all killed."

He probably wasn't wrong. "Talk to Logan. This was his idea."

The commander harrumphed. "Alright, here's the plan." He pointed at the pilot. "Damage report and working comms on the double. Davies, you're with me. Never mind that everyone from here to Oakland probably saw us go down. Hopefully, the bad guys already have their hands full."

Davies slung his rifle over his shoulder and stomped to the back of the transport. "Be nice to know who the bad guys are."

That's what she was here to find out.

Serena exited the back of the transport to a hazy midday sun. The transport had gone down on Geary, near 28th Avenue, not far from the old cathedral. Serena hadn't been to a mass there since she was a little girl. The streets were otherwise deserted. No traffic lights blinked, no lights in any of the buildings. Distant car alarms and sirens broke up the uncomfortable silence.

"Keep your head down," the commander warned. "This area is a prime spot for snipers." He tapped Davies's shoulder. "Set up a sniper nest on one of these roofs and start clearing these buildings. I'm going for a nice stroll down the block with our little techie friend here. Hopefully we don't eat a bullet for our troubles."

They jogged down the left side of Geary towards Nash Industries. The landscape had changed a lot since the Great Quake. The tiring hills remained, but many of the houses and shops still showed the scars of the rumbling. Nash Industries no longer resembled the VA hospital it had been at one time.

Serena counted twelve security officers out front, but she likely missed some. Only a few skinny cypress trees blocked their approach to the complex. No doubt there were other unseen security measures. "The signal is definitely coming from inside that complex."

"We have the best signal jammers available. If they can't shut it down, nothing will."

"Worth a shot, I guess."

"Can I ask you something personal?" the commander asked out of the blue. He gave her an instant to answer, then continued. "Why are you fighting for us and not the UN? Forgive me for saying, but you don't look like you belong on this side."

Serena let the sideways insult go. She didn't think he meant it that way anyway. "Because the UN take and take, and never give. They use people and discard them without a second thought. At least up here, I have a purpose."

"Fair enough," he replied and started back toward the transport.

They double-timed it back to the bird, where Davies was waiting outside. "Status report."

"Minimal damage sustained, Sir. She'll fly again with a full system reboot. Comms are coming up now. You'll have to make it quick. It won't take them long to track us."

"Unpack the jammers. We're gonna need 'em."

Serena joined the commander inside hunching over the small LCD monitor. Logan's tired face, with his disheveled hair stared back at them. His monochrome tie hung loosely around his neck. He rarely let his appearance go like that.

"What happened? We had you on radar, then you disappeared."

"We were hit with some kind of electronic attack," the commander said. "The transport is in one piece, but offline. We'll only have comms for a few more minutes. No doubt the bad guys saw us go down, but we haven't hit any resistance yet."

Logan rubbed his brow. "Have you accomplished anything useful?"

"The signal is coming from Nash Industries," Serena replied. "The building is huge and there's a small army roaming around out here. Fed Sec wouldn't be able to storm this place."

"That doesn't make any sense. Felix Nash work for us."

"It has to be him. Everything else out here is dark. You must have done a background check on him. What do we know? Does he have any connections to the UN?"

"He's supposed to be some super engineer. No link to the UN, only to his work in other quake zones. He's squeaky clean. No finger or retinal scans, no facial shots. Nothing."

"Sounds like a false identity to me. Unusual for a legit businessman, don't you think?"

Logan tapped his finger on his desk. "That answer, among others, is probably inside his system."

Serena snorted. "It's not like I can just walk up and say hello. It won't take much for them to connect me with the downed transport. They'll shoot me to save the hassle."

"She's not wrong, Sir," the commander said. "You're sending her on a suicide mission."

"Give me something I can relate to him with," Serena added. "How does he unwind after a long day of terrorist activity?"

"He has a soft spot for homeless shelters. I can't imagine why."

"He probably spent time in one after the quake. Not everyone had rich parents to put them up in fancy hotels after the shaking stopped."

"Tell him the shelters have been overrun since the blackout. See if he'll bite. If not, walk away and I'll shove a couple bunker busters down his throat."

"What about us, sir?" the commander asked. "We could use an ex-fil from here after we deploy the signal jammers. We won't stand much of a chance in a firefight."

"Find some cover. Support Serena any way you can. We'll extract you when we can." Logan paused, his attention drawn away from the screen. "Sonofabitch…"

"What is it? What's wrong?"

The scene of a burning building popped up on the right side of the screen. "The Van Ness metro station just blew."

"They're taking out the infrastructure, isolating us from any sort of help."

"Why blow it now?" Logan muttered. "Why not this morning when the Promenade went?"

Serena's mind went to the unthinkable. "He wanted to make sure it was full. It's another valuable high-profile target."

"It was full four hours ago. Has to be something else."

Serena's heart dropped. "Oh mother. He wanted to wait until the marshals went in to rescue people. This is personal for him. He'll probably be coming after you too."

Logan snickered. "He'd regret that for the rest of his very short life. Remember your cover story. You're a disgraced marshal named Olivia Benitez. Go to one of the safe houses if you're compromised. That's the best I can do for now." He hung up without waiting for a response.

Great. Stuck in a hostile environment with little support and a flimsy cover story. And expected to deliver. Piece of cake.

"Okay, boys. Wish me luck," she said as she moved towards the transport door. "Stay close by. You'll likely be recovering my body in an hour or so."

"Keep your head in there," the commander said. "You seem like a smart girl. You'll be all right."

She shuffled back towards the complex, feeling exposed. She hadn't felt like this since leaving the Mission District for the first time. Felix had a soft spot for homeless shelters, Logan said. Certainly relatable for her. She ripped her sleeve from cuff to elbow before rubbing dirt on her face and arms. She rubbed more dirt on her pants and practiced scuffling like a vagrant. It wasn't difficult. She'd done it before. She crossed the road in front of the complex's main gate.

Two sec officers cut her off. One was a tall brute with wide shoulders. Someone who'd tackle you to the ground and keep you there. The other wasn't much shorter, but he was slimmer, with thicker legs. A runner, probably trained in some kind of martial art. Each had an assault rifle slung over their shoulder.

"Where do you think you're going?" the wide one demanded.

"I was hoping to find a hot meal. Maybe a bed for the night."

The sec officer's face never twitched. "Does this look like a shelter?"

Serena's stomach dropped when his gun came up. "Come on, friend." She hugged herself. "This is the only place with power. I haven't eaten for days. I'm so hungry."

A red targeting dot painted her chest. "I don't care."

Serena collapsed to her knees and buried her hands in her face, sobbing loudly. "No, please," she wailed. "Don't kill me. I'm not trying to cause trouble."

Slim grabbed the gun wielder's arm. "Wait a minute. What if she saw something with that transport? Ivan will want to question her. Besides, we can't do it in the open like this and I don't feel like dragging a body all the way around back."

The brute's gun barrel dipped. "You have a point. Ivan'll skin us alive if we're away from our post for too long."

"Call it in?"

"Nah. You stay here. I'll take her inside. Ivan can figure out what to do with her. They're not paying me enough to babysit street rats." He hauled Serena up by her collar. "Let's go, you."

Serena didn't resist. She wanted to go inside. She hadn't figured out how to keep them from killing her yet. Her eyes shifted left, then right, seeking a place to run. The sec officer shoved her constantly on the back, keeping her off-balance. Once she passed through the double doors, her whole perception changed.

She stood in an expansive lobby with high ceilings and marble floors. Expensive taste for a man who cared about the homeless. Refinement, right down to the ornate detail on the receptionist's desk.

Footsteps echoing from the corridor on the right grabbed her attention. A man in a midnight-colored suit that matched his slicked back hair walked towards them. His closely cropped goatee had a certain satanic look to it. His hands were clasped behind his back and he moved with purpose. "Is there a problem here?"

"It's nothing serious, Mister Nash," the sec officer stammered. "Just some homeless drifter looking for a hole to crawl into. I was hoping to hand her off to another officer so I could man my post. Ivan won't be happy if I'm out of position for too long."

Nash? Serena couldn't believe her luck. She never expected to succeed in the first place, but the chances of meeting Felix Nash directly were astronomical.

"I'm not a drifter," Serena blurted. She cowered away, surprised how easy it was to fall back into the homeless mentality. It scared the hell out of her.

CHAPTER 5:
CONTROL SLIPPING

Renaude leaned back in his office chair and popped another little red symmetrically formed chunk of hell into his mouth. He massaged his sore knee as he waited for the meds to kick in. The urges were becoming harder to control. For the sake of the city, he had no choice.

Images of a burning city flashed through his mind. Over and over again. During his every waking minute, like a glitch video stuck in a loop. It was too much. Every path he sought through the chaos only led him farther astray. Cars, buildings. Homes. All consumed by fire.

Memories of the Great Quake's massive destruction turned to something entirely different. A need for cleansing, purification, wiping away history's painful scars. To see a new city, one to be proud of, rise from the ashes of despair. It was like someone who constantly washed their hands, unable to rid themselves of the dirt. Renaude wanted to wash the city in fire.

Renaude shook his head forcefully. No! I can't think like that. I'd be better off dead. People swarmed outside City Hall. He had to maintain control — for them.

It never used to be like this. Things were normal before the Great Quake. Almost five years of working the traffic beat, making a difference. Renaude relished the street-level contact he had with citizens. Then it all went to hell in about ten minutes of the worst shaking he'd ever experienced. The aftershocks lasted for days.

After things settled, people became desperate. They resorted to theft and assault. Renaude was having none of that. When they announced the creation of a new team to combat the issue, he signed up. He didn't know then he was witnessing the birth of the Underground Network.

None of this would be necessary if not for Janik and his outlaw UN friends. Not the pills, not the anxiety, not the cleansing fire. But there were too many like him, willing to run anyone down to maintain their criminal enterprise. Renaude rubbed the scar on his knee again, the remnant of one such encounter. Renaude fought to return to his place of balance. No matter how hard he tried, the screams of the dying in an inferno remained. Renaude popped another pill and closed his eyes. One breath. Two breaths.

The violent images faded to the background as the medication kicked in. The throbbing in his knee eased. He went back to the computer logs on his screen. He'd have to deal with the prisoner transport logs sooner or later. Before people started asking too many questions. He didn't think anyone would miss a bunch of lowlifes, but stranger things had happened.

He tapped a button on his desk communicator, connecting him with the Pit four floors beneath his office. If he slacked, the Almighty Mayor Rhea Waters wouldn't be pleased. As long as her 'donors' didn't start calling. If he were to scorch the city, he'd start with her office. "Frank, please tell me all you have to do to restore power is flip a switch."

"I wish, Sir. Our units are tapped out right now pulling people from the subways and stopping the looting. Once we have a handle on that, we'll deal with the roving blackouts."

Renaude pursed his lips. They hadn't been able to pin down the next neighborhood to be hit. Marshals were running around discombobulated. "Has everyone checked in yet?"

"Almost, Sir, but there's a lot of ground to cover. The drones will be airborne within ten minutes."

"Okay. Post patrols on the ground floor and in the parking garage. I want building sweeps every hour and snipers on the roof. We're going to have to defend ourselves."

"We don't have the manpower for that, Sir. Everyone is mobile."

"Recall a couple units. The looting can wait. Hopefully everyone can go home soon to working lights." And I can finally get rid of these blasted pills.

His office door slid open, and Mayor Waters strolled in as if she owned the place. Renaude jerked at the cuffs of his uniform sleeves. He didn't have time for this. He wasn't due to give an update yet. He had nothing to tell her anyway. "I'll call you back, Frank. I have company."

He wished he could get rid of her, but like she inherited him, he inherited her when she won the election. Not that elections mattered much. The Consortium bought whatever government they wanted. Her first surprise move was to announce that he'd be retained as Chief Marshal.

"You look like hell, Renaude. Are you taking your pills? Now's not a good time to be coming off the rails."

He clenched his hand on top of his desk, resisting the urge to retrieve the pistol from his desk drawer and put a bullet in her forehead. "I assure you, Mayor. I am quite capable. My medication is as effective as ever. If you must know, I'm seeing a new doctor who is trying some fascinating new techniques. The results are promising."

"Good. What's our status?"

"The Promenade survivors have been rescued. People have been ordered back to the safety of their homes. The roads will be jammed for hours while we clear them out. All marshals have been recalled, but it will take some time for them to mobilize."

"Anyone claim responsibility?"

"Not yet, but we both know there's only one group capable

of carrying this out."

"That doesn't make any sense. The UN is only interested in shutting down the Consortium. Why kill all these people? It's excessive."

"The UN is nothing more than a band of ruthless criminals, Madam Mayor. The why of their actions don't have to make sense."

The mayor chewed her lower lip for a second. "Every convoy, every warehouse the UN hits only pisses the Consortium off more, making my job harder. I can't even get the local leaders in the Mission District to take my calls anymore. I wish they'd all just go away."

Renaude shared her frustration. The marshals had made no real progress in shutting down the black-market runners. Until now. "We may now have the evidence to eliminate them for good. We think we've recovered fragments of a metal case used to transport the device. Based on the blast pattern, we think the explosion originated from a table near the coffee hut. The power outages are making it difficult to identify the explosive."

"Didn't you investigate a hijacking of a shipment of Synthetic Liquid recently?"

"That investigation is still ongoing. Our friends at the Pyramid have been less than forthcoming with information and every search warrant we execute comes up empty."

Mayor Waters glanced up at him. "Surveillance?"

"The power outage has knocked large sections of the city offline. Our cyber-crimes unit is working the problem as we speak. As soon as I have something, I'll let you know."

"Let's cut to the chase, Renaude. How do we keep it from escalating?"

"I have a team on their way into the Mission District. If the UN is responsible, we may be able to cut them off at the knees."

"And if they're not?"

"Then I have no idea who's behind this and our day gets a whole lot worse."

She strode to the monitor mounted on the far wall showing the body bags in the still-smoldering Promenade. "Heartbreaking. How are we supposed to talk to the families about this? It's too much."

Renaude didn't answer. Today, that was her problem. He had a terrorist to deal with. "The victim list isn't complete yet. Identifying everyone may take weeks. Where are we with public services?"

"Water, power, and public transit is down. Thousands are trapped in the trains. It won't take long for carbon dioxide poisoning to become a problem. The financial system is down. People cannot access their money. All non-essential personnel have been sent home."

"I must warn you, Mayor. If this continues, it may end up worse than the Great Quake."

The mayor pressed her fingers to her forehead. "We've ordered the depots to ration remaining stores. The Emergency Management office is helping rescue people from the trains. Focus on getting the systems back online before the violence escalates."

"My team is working on it. They assure me cracking our servers would require some robust software and a significant amount of time. Our data is safe."

Renaude's desk communicator chirped and Frank's face appeared on the screen. "There's been more bombings."

The image on the monitor shifted to show sections of highway heaved and cracked, almost like crumpled paper. Vehicles lay all over the place, tossed like pebbles. His city had descended into a war zone.

A mass of people, many of them children, covered in blood and dirt moved about in a daze.

"...crews are still working to save as many as possible," a

reporter explained, "the number of dead is expected to eclipse the Promenade bombing as many were attempting to leave the city at the time of detonation."

Renaude's hand went for the pocket with the pill bottle. He clenched his fingers shut and pulled back. They weren't the answer to his problems. They only dulled the edge a little. "There's your answer on escalation, Madam Mayor."

"They're cutting us off from outside help," the mayor gasped. "They're taking the infrastructure down little by little. Better post a watch on the bridges. I've had enough of these bastards trying to run my city."

"Of course, Mayor. We will see it done, but if it creates another problem. With every event, our resources are stretched thinner. It won't be long before we won't be able to respond."

"We'll have to make it work, Renaude. We don't have a choice."

Renaude's communicator chirped again, this time with an external call. Funny how the phones still worked when nothing else did. He exchanged a knowing glance with the mayor. They were bound to hear from the Judiciary sooner or later. "This is Chief Marshal Thiraro. I'm here with Mayor Waters."

"This is Logan Marks, Chief Marshal. Our corporate partners require an explanation if you please."

The menacing undertone in Mister Marks' voice stole his breath for a moment and set his stomach fluttering. "We are working to ascertain the source of these attacks as quickly as possible."

"An explosion at the Promenade is a black eye for the Consortium, Chief Marshal. And a black eye for the Consortium is a major migraine for the city. How are we supposed to provide for the citizens when our resources are being attacked?"

"As I said, we are working as quickly as possible. Our first priority is getting people to safety."

"We lost a trusted Pharmacy colleague, the Vice President of Experimental Treatments, if I'm not mistaken, in that explosion. We are very interested in bringing the full weight of the Judiciary against the perpetrators. Do you understand me?"

Renaude shivered. He knew exactly the sort of justice the legal branch of the Consortium meted out. He'd seen the bodies personally. "Of course, but we don't have any suspect information as of yet."

"What of the reports of an arrest at the scene? Who is this person? I should very much like to talk to him."

Renaude's face screwed into deep contempt. "Yes, we arrested someone. A thief with UN ties that, I'm sorry to say, I have some history with from my time in Traffic Services. So far, he is denying involvement. I'm moving him to a more secure location to try to reason with him again, though I'm not confident."

"You will send me your location, Chief Marshal. I will speak to him myself."

"Once I have questioned him, I will make him available. However, it may take some time. As you said, our hands are quite full."

"What of the power outage? My clients cannot conduct their business without the grid."

"Again, it's early yet. We're awaiting word from the power centers. This is still a very fluid situation. We don't know how many more lives are at risk. As soon as I have answers, you'll have them."

"Be sure that we do. Our resources are at your disposal." The call ended.

The mayor sneered at the communicator. "They're like a virus running rampant through the city. Them and the UN. Why can't they just kill each other and leave the rest of us alone?"

"With respect, Madam Mayor. The Consortium is the only reason either of us have jobs. When they own the judges, lawyers, and the cops, they can do whatever they want."

The mayor harrumphed. "Doesn't mean we have to like it."

The building shook violently, and the lights flickered. Dust showered down from the ceiling. Renaude rushed to the window to see a plum of smoke rising from the Van Ness metro station. "The subway…" he stammered. "Thousands buried alive."

Panicked citizens scurried away from the downtown station as thick black smoke coiled into the air. Just like the Promenade and the overpass. Images of a destroyed metro station already filtered into his office across the monitor on the wall. He returned to his desk and hit the button for the Pit. "Coordinate rescue efforts, Frank. Save as many as you can."

Renaude shook with a rage he'd never felt before as he watched the video feed of his city under attack, helpless to stop it.

The screen blanked and a single ominous message appeared.

THIS IS JUST THE BEGINNING…

CHAPTER 6:
FELIX

Serena found herself taken by Felix's warm, charming smile. Almost as if he really did care where she spent the night. She clenched her jaw, shoving the odd tingle away. She wasn't interested in a date. He'd only try to use her like Harlon and the UN did, like Logan currently was.

"She arrived not long after the transport crashed," the sec officer said. "Thought she might know something."

Felix eyed her. "Do you?"

"I saw it go down, but I was several blocks away. I wasn't going anywhere near it. Who knows what that thing was carrying?"

Felix studied her face for the lie. "What brought you out here?"

Serena drew in a deep breath. She had to be convincing. "I went to a shelter when the power went out. I saw you there once. You were handing out sandwiches to people in need. I thought you might be able to help me."

"Even without power the shelter is better suited to offer assistance."

Serena stared at the floor, appropriately embarrassed. "They've been overrun. The stronger ones were fighting each other for the beds. The rioting makes it dangerous to move around. Not to mention the marshals think everyone using the shelters are black market traders."

Serena threw that last bit in herself. Some of the stolen drugs had surfaced at a few of the local shelters, but no one could tell them where they came from. They just arrived with the regular shipments with no way to trace them. Logan had his ass handed to him by William McIntosh over that little debacle.

"I'm sure things will improve soon." Felix smiled, but his eyes held an edge of anger. "Perhaps we can find a plate and a bed for you here somewhere."

The sec officer snorted. "Clean her up a bit and she can bunk with me."

Felix wheeled on him, grabbing him by the front of his jacket. "Watch your tongue or I'll cut it out. We're not soulless criminals."

Felix was well spoken, composed. Obviously an educated man. Smart criminals made her job much harder. She thought back to a couple of the most recent UN heist jobs. None of this fit that M.O. The violence was too public, too widespread. Even the uniforms on the sec officers didn't line up. It wasn't enough to convince Logan, but Serena had a feeling they were dealing with a whole new threat.

He turned back to Serena. "Come with me, Miss- I'm afraid I didn't get your name."

Serena stammered over her alias, almost blurting out her real name instead. *Jesus, woman. Get a grip,* she told herself. "Olivia, Sir. Olivia Benitez."

"Such a lovely name." He glared at the guard again. "Return to your post."

That was way too easy. No way he believed the downed transport story. She almost felt the vice tightening around her. She had no choice though. Backing out now would only confirm her guilt.

Felix led her down a hallway to the left, past several offices, to a closed door with thumbprint scanner next to it. Data recorders were spaced every fifteen feet along the ceiling. They were probably already searching their database for information on her face right now. Hopefully Logan made that cover story airtight.

"What do you do here?" she asked.

"It's my engineering firm, specializing in earthquake readiness. Used to be a VA hospital before the Great Quake. Surprisingly, much of the building survived. I only needed to make a few renovations. We have full manufacturing facilities on site. In fact, we're almost completely self-sufficient."

Renovations meant permits. She'd have Logan check with his contacts in the City Management office once she was able to make contact again. They had to be able to track this guy's history somehow.

"Where are we going?" she asked as Felix pressed his thumb to the scanner.

He grinned at her from the side of his face. "The cafeteria. Would you like some coffee? It's Non-Synth."

More luxury. Not everyone in San Francisco enjoyed Non-Synth coffee, or Non-Synth anything, for that matter. Serena preferred tea. She accepted, not wanting to push his generosity. He hadn't shot her yet so that was a plus.

Felix spoke to a lady behind the counter before showing her to a table at the back of the room away from everyone else. "Food will be along shortly."

A monitor mounted on the far wall replayed the gruesome images of the bombings. The overpass and the metro station still teemed with rescue crews, though it was more recovery at this point. The reports said the marshals had arrested someone fleeing the Promenade bombing. With luck, Logan would have information from them in a few hours. The man was efficient, if nothing else.

Serena looked away, unable to stomach the images any longer. Instead, she focused on the cafeteria with as many data recorders as there were in the hallway. Well-dressed, well-armed sec officers surveilled from the corners. A lot of firepower for a simple engineering firm.

Data was her real weapon. Her father always told her with information she could dictate any situation. Particularly important when dealing with people in positions of power. The more you knew, the more you can use against them and right now, she didn't have enough.

"Tell me a bit about yourself. How did you become homeless?" He held up his hand. "You know what, never mind. That's none of my business. I'm sorry."

Serena remained silent for a while. The question wasn't totally unexpected. How much did she want to tell him though? "You're taking me in," she said finally, "you have a right to know why."

"It's curiosity on my part, that's all. I understand if you're uncomfortable."

She rubbed a finger over the handle of her coffee cup, wiping away a stain that wasn't there. "I was fired from the marshal's service after an incident… We were in the Mission District investigating some UN hijacking or another. Things were going okay until one of my colleagues harassed an innocent old man. Apparently, they don't like marshals breaking the noses of other marshals."

Felix's eyes narrowed, smoldering with anger. Like the metro explosion, the marshals triggered something within him. "Yes, I have some experience with people in positions of authority abusing their station. They rely on fear and intimidation to keep people from fighting back." He leaned back and his smile returned. "That was a long time ago. We all must learn the harsh realities of the world sooner or later."

A woman in an apron brought her a plate with a sandwich and some celery. Serena remembered she was supposed to be starving. Not a difficult job since she hadn't eaten since this morning. She chomped two huge bites off before grinning at Felix sheepishly.

"I lost everything," she said around a mouthful of ham and whole wheat bread. "No, those bastards stole everything." Her emotions were genuine. She really did hate the marshals. She thought she'd pissed them off by joining the people who controlled them. The only one she made miserable was herself. "I'm sorry. The way they treat people upsets me."

"Don't be sorry. Yours is not the only life they have ruined. Their pandering to the Consortium is as sickening as it is obvious. As long as they continue to be bought off, nothing will change."

There it was. Felix blamed the marshals and the Consortium for ruining his life. Logan wouldn't be too happy to find out what his new friend really thought of him. A fair bit of the blame deserved to go south of Market Street. Everything her father fought to keep, Harlon Cruz and the UN destroyed. The last she heard, he was dead. Served the cold, heartless bastard right. "I guess someone finally decided to change it."

"Yes," Felix replied eagerly. "It's sad innocent lives had to be sacrificed to affect it."

"Wars usually are." She smiled. "But occasionally they are necessary and I, for one, am glad someone decided to start it. Hopefully things will be better after this." Her voice held a certain conviction. No one else should have to die because they couldn't afford necessary medication.

"I'm convinced they will be." Felix leaned forward with his chin in his hand, studying her. "I like your passion. A useful trait, particularly around here." There was no escaping those eyes drilling deep inside her. Could he see her lies?

"I was doing okay until the power went out. Not sure what to do now. I'll be dead in a week if it doesn't come back." Or within the hour if you find out who I am, she finished silently.

"I'm sure we can prevent that. Now that you've eaten, a proper shower will help you feel better. We'll see where things go from there."

They left the cafeteria, turning right, towards a heavy steel door on the back wall. Felix punched a code into the control panel and pressed his thumb against a scanner. The door opened to an elevator. "After you."

Six buttons on the control panel meant six levels, only one above ground and biometric security locking everything down. It'd take forever for her to find her evidence. Felix pressed his thumb against another scanner and the door slid shut.

They exited the elevator on Level One. Narrow aisles stretched to the left, right, and ahead. Light tubes stretched along the ceiling from one end to the other. For a moment, Serena saw herself back at the academy. "This is the barracks level. I'm sure there's an empty one around here somewhere. We've had a few recent terminations, unfortunately."

"Barracks level?" Was this some kind of military complex? Seemed a little overkill for an end of the world bunker. "What else is there?"

"Don't worry about any of that for now."

Abandoning her common sense, she pushed her luck. "Your facilities need a heavy steel door and a small army roaming the grounds? I understand operational security, but Fed Sec doesn't have this much firepower."

Felix took the question in stride, but she got the sense his patience was running thin. "Some of our technology is proprietary and you can never tell when someone means you harm." He stopped in front of a plain gray door. "Ah yes, here we are."

The small apartment had a bed, a closet, a bathroom, and nothing else. "How many people do you have here?"

"You're a very curious girl," Felix replied as he pulled a charcoal colored security uniform from the closet. "I'm sorry. I don't have any dresses."

He sounded disappointed. Serena bit her lip against the giggle that bubbled in her throat. Typical man. He probably thought she belonged in a kitchen too. "I'm not much of a dress girl anyway.

They're impractical. My mother stopped putting them on me after I refused to keep them clean." She glanced down at the clothes on the bed. If this was an engineering firm, she was a fairy godmother. "Why all this? What's its purpose?"

"It's complicated." Felix folded his hands behind his back. "You know, thinking on it, there may be more I can do for you. How badly do you want to get back at the marshals?"

Serena sat on the edge of the cot. "It isn't so much about me anymore. I've accepted my fate. Others shouldn't have to suffer. The Consortium should be stopped." She'd be telling the truth if they'd been discussing the UN.

"What if I told you stopping them would change your fate?"

"Sign me up," she replied without hesitation.

CHAPTER 7:
IN DEEPER

Serena regretted those three words the instant they left her mouth. She had no idea how deep the rabbit hole went. Her job was to get in, confirm Felix was behind the attacks, and get out. That's it. They never intended this to be a prolonged undercover op.

Felix turned back on his way out of the apartment. "I strongly suggest you not go below this floor. For your own safety, you understand."

Serena refocused on Felix, almost completely missing that he'd spoken. "What about outside? Is it okay if I go for a walk? I'm not used to staying in confined spaces for too long."

"You'll be fine if you stay to the main courtyard. I'll let the security detail know not to harass you."

Better than nothing, she thought. Hopefully Logan's goon squad hadn't bailed on her. She found nothing incriminating when she checked the other doors on the level. They all belonged to apartments except one that was locked. Outside offered little else. A power generator and the loading dock was all she found.

She returned to the elevator, debating her next move. Disobey Felix or go back to the apartment. She could always blame a wrong turn if she were caught. The sixth-floor button was the only one that worked without a thumbprint scan. *Was that a mistake?* If he thought she was a spy this may be bait, making the elevator ride a one-way trip.

Serena hit the button. *Only one way to find out.*

Cool air washed over her when the elevator door opened. Bluish light similar to the barracks level illuminated the hallway. Serena swallowed the lump in her throat, trying to slow her pounding heart. Go back upstairs. Forget you ever found this place. As her brain told her to leave, her feet carried her forward out of the elevator.

Her stomach dropped when she rounded the corner at the end of the corridor. A brute of a man, a head taller than her, stood with his arms folded across his chest and his feet slightly apart. Short-cropped hair and clean shaven. Former military, surely. Not someone Serena wanted to mess with, except, the elevator had already returned to the surface.

She cursed her stupidity. Stupid for letting Logan talk her into this, stupid for coming down here, stupid for getting caught. Serena steadied herself, lifted her chin and pulled her shoulders back exactly as her mother had taught her.

Never let a man see your fear, she always said.

The man smiled coldly. "Miss Benitez, I believe it is."

"Who are you?" she demanded, somewhat uneasily. Her brave face somewhat masked her trembling. She'd give anything for a weapon right about now.

Keeping a lock on his eyes, she failed to notice the pistol in his hand until he jammed it into her stomach. "I'm Ivan, head of security. You have some explaining to do."

Her plan to feign losing her way sounded absurd in the face of this man. No doubt he'd see right through it. She raised her hands, cursing herself for yet another mistake. Ivan directed her down the hallway into an office. Felix's office.

"I found this little mouse roaming the halls," he announced as he shoved her through the door.

Serena glared back at him. Didn't his mother ever teach him how to treat a lady? His face didn't change, except to curl into a bit of an arrogant smirk.

Felix sat behind his desk, poring over something on his tablet. No anger, no disappointment. Not a sliver of frustration. She inched closer to the desk, catching the words 'dross lakes' on the screen. His lack of surprise reinforced her belief that he had left this floor open on purpose.

A monitor mounted on the right-hand wall streamed news of the bombings. Other than Felix's desk and chair, a black leather sofa against the left-hand wall made up the office's furniture. A door in the back right corner was closed.

How am I getting out of this one? Running wasn't an option. Neither was trying to overpower two strong men, one of them armed.

Felix glared up at her as he slid the tablet to one side. *Probably thinks he's scaring me. Okay maybe he is a little.* Deep breaths did nothing to calm her nerves.

He sidled around to sit on the front edge of his desk, arms crossed. "I see you've met Ivan. Quite imposing, isn't he? Fed Sec does grow them big."

Serena crossed her arms. "I'm not that impressed." Logan was former Fed Sec. Maybe they knew each other.

Felix laughed. "I'm not surprised." He leaned back. "You seem nervous."

"Being escorted around at gunpoint tends to do that." She winced a little at her acidic tone. Provoking either one of these men probably wasn't the best idea. "I appreciate you taking me in, but I won't be held prisoner. If this is your idea of help, I'm not interested."

"Yes, I see your point," Felix replied. "Though, I specifically remember telling you not to go below the barracks level."

"Yet you gave me access to this level and no other. Why is that, I wonder? Maybe you wanted me to find this place."

Felix scowled. "An oversight that does not excuse your actions. I told you we take security here very seriously. If it had been anyone other than the magnificently composed Ivan you'd likely be dead. Not the help you were after, I think."

Her knees weakened and she strained to remain standing. "You're absolutely right. I apologize. My curiosity got the better of me." She stepped back.

The barrel of Ivan's pistol jabbed into the small of her back. "Don't move."

Her mind raced. This wasn't an office with a computer screen to hide behind. These were real bad guys, with real guns, that fired real bullets. Serena had miscalculated. She'd underestimated Felix. His charm was a mask, a shield to protect himself. He was a ruthless man who wouldn't hesitate to kill her to protect his interests. For the second time today, Serena prayed for safety. This time her own.

Felix nodded, accepting her admission. "Be that as it may, it is unacceptable. It promotes a lack of trust. It makes me question everything about you. Are you really homeless?"

Serena's chest tightened. "I wasn't lying. The marshals destroyed my life. But you're right. I took advantage of your kindness. I'm sorry. I'll leave. Maybe the shelters are in better shape by now. I'm sure I can find help elsewhere. If I stay alive long enough."

Felix's silence felt like it lasted hours. "There is a protocol we follow here, an order to things. When we don't follow it, chaos ensues. I have too much at stake to allow chaos."

Ivan's gun still pressed into her back. "So, are you going to kill me now?" she sneered. "Big man with his little guns."

"Kill you?" Felix chuckled. "No, no, my dear. I'm not that hasty. I must admit, I'm more curious than angry. You have a certain gumption I find in short supply around here. Not many would disregard a direct order from me." He went to his side stand to pour a cup of tea. "To be honest, I'd like to know more about your experiences with the marshals."

Serena was more than a little confused. Her marshals experience amounted to a forgettable steaming pile of crap. She'd only ever been a low-level street cop with limited clearance. "What would you like to know?"

"We can discuss that later, among other things. I will chalk your severe lack of judgment up to eagerness- this time. This is not to be repeated. Understand? If you go below the barracks level without permission again, I will not be responsible for the consequences. And there will be consequences."

Ivan stepped around her, his musky odor filling her nostrils. "This is not a good idea, Felix. You're introducing a new variable. We can't trust her. She knows your face."

Felix held up a hand stopping a full-blown diatribe. "Everybody knows my face. She's a homeless girl of no threat to me. She is the type of person I'm trying to save. Not to mention the potentially useful information she might have."

"Unless she's not who she says she is. I heard about the downed transport. You can't be that dense, can you?"

"Be careful, Ivan. My tolerance only goes so far."

The former Fed Sec mercenary seemed unbothered by the threat. "Don't you think it's odd that she showed up right after all the fun started? Let me deal with her so you can get back to work."

"I will handle this personally, Ivan. Tell me of the deliveries."

"Some of them have encountered complications. I told you this-" He glanced at Serena, "method was unreliable. We should rethink this."

"Every new system goes through its bugs. Re-issue the orders. See to them personally. Now, if you will excuse me, I have a lot of work to do."

Serena turned to follow as Ivan stormed out. She had to get out of here before she threw up on Felix's expensive shoes.

"Before you go, Olivia, I have to say I admire your ambition, misguided though it might be. You remind me a little of myself when I first started out. So full of vigor and eagerness. I hope you have the stomach for what's coming."

"Thank you. I'm sorry I caused problems for everyone." She started for the door, properly chastised.

"Have dinner with me. We'll see if we can focus your energies in the proper direction."

Serena stopped and chuckled nervously. "I'm not sure that's such a good idea. I'm grateful, but I don't want to be a distraction. It is better to keep things professional."

"I understand. I'm of the same mind. You can tell me about the marshals and perhaps I can tell you more of what's happening around here." Still, she hesitated. "It's just dinner."

"What about Ivan? He's obviously not happy you're keeping me around. I'm sure he would've pulled the trigger here if you'd given him the word."

"Yes, well. That wasn't going to happen. I abhor the sight of blood. Ivan is an exceptional sec chief, though a little dramatic at times. He takes his Fed Sec training too far sometimes. I'm sure I'm perfectly safe."

Logan told her to get close to Felix. She'd get no better chance. "I'd love to."

CHAPTER 8: MISSING TIME

Janik regained consciousness more than he woke up. Waking up usually happened pleasantly in a bed. This was no bed. His body screamed in agony as he rolled onto his back and spit out a mouthful of dirt. In a way, he welcomed his throbbing head. Pain meant he wasn't dead. Small victories, Janik. Small victories.

Sunlight filtered down through Cypress trees, casting broken, asymmetrical shadows. The sun's position put it at around three in the afternoon. The day? Now, that was anyone's guess.

Hard ground dug into his back. A chilly wind cutting across exposed skin made him shiver. The aroma of sea salt accompanied the sound of crashing waves. A shoreline, but not the beachfront property of his dreams.

Janik's head spun when he knelt up. Squeezing his eyes shut, he drew in sharp breaths, trying to ease the raging tempest in his stomach. What the hell had happened? He felt like he'd been on an all-night bender before going three rounds in a no-holds-barred death match. Trying to remember was like trying to steal a car with no wheels. All he came up with was an explosion and a boy's face. An explosion? Janik didn't know anything about explosives…did he?

No, stupid. Stay alive first. Then figure things out. That meant finding his way out of here. Fresh waves of nausea clutched his stomach as he stood. While he waited for his stomach to settle, Janik considered his options. If he followed the shoreline, he'd eventually hit civilization. He had to chance it. What did it matter if he died here or halfway down the beach?

Trying to pull his jacket closed around him revealed that he wore only a flimsy hospital gown. No wonder he was cold. Half-naked and alone in the woods. Story of my life.

No strange cuts though. He still had all of his organs. Circular burn marks on his temples and chest added to a growing list of mysteries. A hot shower should help piece together some answers. Provided he made it home to take one.

His feet hurt on the uneven ground as he stumbled from tree to tree, holding on for support. He found the shoreline when he almost tumbled over a cliff. Probably best to avoid that. Why couldn't whoever dumped here at least leave him with shoes?

The path cut left, following the shoreline closely. Some of the fuzziness in his head dissipated allowing him to form a complete thought. Janik still had no idea what had happened, but finding some familiarity should be easier.

He found it in the parking lot of the filthiest of steamy cesspools. The Sutro Baths. A bustling tourist attraction before the Great Quake, it was now *the* place to make a body disappear. That cleared things up somewhat. Someone tried to make him disappear permanently. Sloppy work though, not finishing the job by throwing him over the cliff. What the sharks didn't eat would've been washed out to sea.

He tried to think back to every step he'd taken, every job he'd done. Someone from his past, probably someone from his estranged family had caught up to him. He didn't think Patricia had it in her to come after him. Her husband, Stephen, though. He was a piece of work, a McIntosh through and through. He'd kill Janik in a heartbeat and spit on the corpse. The fact that Janik woke up in a hospital gown supported his theory they were somehow involved. The McIntoshes worked heavily with the medical industry, including some programs involving human experimentation that weren't exactly on the level.

Janik dismissed all the questions that revelation generated. He wasn't out of the woods yet. Literally and figuratively. Most of the vehicles here were burnt out husks, torched after being used in some nefarious deed or another. A couple were still drivable. Boosted rides street crews couldn't sell.

He picked the vehicle closest to the tree line and farthest from the building. It still had all of its wheels. Bonus points for no bodies in the back seat. He'd check the trunk in a minute. Even though this was an older model with an outdated security system, he had no way to bypass the locked doors. He spotted a fist-sized stone in the short brush nearby. Well, except that one.

A few seconds, and his best fastball later, he turned on the cabin lights from the front seat. He pressed his fingers to his eyes as he tried to access some deep seeded memory about a vehicle he knew little about to begin with. Janik found the VIN number plate near the bottom of the open door. One thing the car companies didn't tell people, the factory override codes were usually some combination of the first six digits of the VIN number. A failsafe in case some dumbass locked himself out of the security system.

Three attempts failed to start the engine. Two more and he'd be completely locked out, forcing him to move on. His head slumped forward, his glimmer of hope of making it out of this alive beginning to fade.

Janik faced the panel again, as if it would magically reveal the code. This would be so much easier if he had his equipment. He focused on the numbers. One more time, with feeling:

546328

ENTER

Nothing.

Janik slammed his fist against the dashboard, and then again, for good measure. In the end, it didn't help. Now, on top of the still-dead engine, his hand hurt. Those had to be the numbers. He ran through them again, digit by digit. Then he had it. They were the right numbers in the wrong order. He reached for the keypad again. Last shot.

563428

ENTER

. . .

. . .

The engine sputtered to life. "Hell yeah!" he screamed. Finally, a break his way.

Slamming the car into gear, he sped south away from the Baths towards his house. He raced through intersections with blinking traffic lights without a second thought. One of the few times the marshals weren't chasing him. They were all likely dealing with the source of the oily smoke and ominous orange glow in the sky to the east.

How long had he been at the Baths? He remembered nothing beyond a prisoner transport in the morning. But what morning and why was he prisoner in the first place? Being arrested was something he probably should've remembered.

Janik winced as fragments of explosions and dead faces flared in his head. The Promenade? The marshal's headquarters? Both bombed? Were they memories or nightmares? *I didn't kill anyone. Did I?* He rubbed the back of his head, fighting off the confusion. Sounds of explosions and sirens drifted in over the growl of the engine. War was coming to San Francisco. If it wasn't already here.

That much destruction made Janik rethink his theory. Too much collateral damage for simple revenge, no matter how much money he cost his enemies. This felt like something bigger, but he'd know more when he accessed his network.

Less than an hour after leaving the Baths, Janik left the car at the Eureka Square shopping center. He wasn't sure he'd be able to return to it so he wiped down the steering wheel and door handle with his sleeve. Fingerprints weren't a good thing in his line of work.

No one moved through the darkened street except him, but he cased everything as he approached the house. The shadows, other houses, even the parked cars were a threat. He couldn't rule out that someone from his past had found him.

Janik entered through the back door and flipped the switches for the backup batteries. He held his breath as he stalked through the kitchen. Only silence answered. His bare feet slapped on the marble floor as he crept down the corridor lined with artwork he really ought to sell.

The rest of the house was empty. Either his family wasn't involved, or everyone thought he was dead. No, that didn't make sense either. Killing him wasn't enough. They'd have cleaned him out, taken everything and left him in despair before ending his life. The third option was they just hadn't found his house yet.

He showered in the upstairs bathroom, staying under the hot water a few minutes longer than usual to help soothe his beat-up body. He should lie down, but he was too keyed up to sleep. Questions needed answers first. Let's work out the timeline and see where things go from there.

Servers lined one whole wall of the office while monitors lined another. In the center sat a desk with a smaller monitor, several tablets, and a communicator with only one message from Kirox.

'Bentley

Promenade parking lot

Sept. 16th, 10am

Don't be late.'

Next to it was a tablet with a picture Janik was all too familiar with. He thought he'd gotten clear of William McIntosh, but it seemed that wasn't the case. The note below the picture said:

'McIntosh moving something big. Hack his phone to find out what.'

Janik remembered being in the Promenade recently. But stealing a car from there, especially a Bentley? Stupidity at its finest. The Consortium watched that place like a hawk. From the rest of the conversation on the communicator, Janik had made that observation clear. To no avail, Kirox insisted, saying he'd trust only his best thief with such a tough job.

He turned on the local news, surprised they were still broadcasting. The caption showed 'Updates from September 16th'. At least this nightmare was only a few hours old. He still had a chance to escape this without too much more damage.

A solemn-faced reporter gave a rundown of recent events. "Marshals have made little headway in the cyber-attack crippling the city, stating a motive for the attack is still unclear, though, they believe this is a direct strike by the shadow organization the Underground Network. Sources tell us a daytime raid into the Mission District, a known UN stronghold, yielded little information."

"Explains the blackouts," Janik mumbled. He hoped no one in the Mission District was too badly hurt. The marshals weren't known for their gentility.

"In other news," the reporter continued, "authorities are no closer to answers regarding this morning's deadly bombings. The bomber, a suspected car thief, is believed to have been killed in a prisoner transport crash after being arrested at the Promenade. So far, no further threats have been detected, though marshals continue to search for additional devices. They're scrambling to find answers before the body count climbs any higher.

Meanwhile, families of the victims are demanding answers and asking for federal intervention. While Fed Sec has been notified, they have not been requested to intervene. Neither the Mayor's office nor the Chief Marshal offered further comment."

"Jesus Christ." Everything he saw in his head was real. No mention of the marshal's building, though. If it hadn't happened, why did he remember it? He switched off the monitor and rubbed the back of his head. He had a lot of whys. Why bomb a bunch of places just to steal a car? Why the cyber-attack? Why do any of this? This had to be way bigger than his family's plot for revenge.

Hopefully, this other equipment on the desk would help him piece some things together. If he could hack into the Promenade cameras, they'd tell him exactly what happened. They'd prove he had nothing to do with any of this.

Everything came rushing back with the first button he hit. This is what he really was. A code scriber. And now, one with a mission. He opened his main laptop and checked his systems. Nothing had been compromised. All of his ghost servers were still locked and the data intact. If he'd been the primary target, he'd have nothing left.

Janik entered the encryption key that unlocked those servers. It had been some time since he'd looked at the data here. It was all part of a painful past he'd rather forget, but somehow knew he couldn't.

He clicked on the folder called 'McIntosh'. Several files appeared on the screen, one of the called 'Eldridge Row'. William McIntosh's former personal assistant was dead the last Janik heard. Killed in prison after Janik put him there.

Gina Hendrix was another name that popped up. The only other person he knew who could rival him with a computer. She was dead too. People who messed with him tended to end up that way.

Rolling blackouts wouldn't stop him. Most of the city's critical servers had backup power. He only needed one open port to get past their paper-thin security. Except there were none. No network access anywhere. Not the prisoner database, not the city's traffic management system. Even listening to the marshals' comms chatter was out. Janik wasn't used to being completely shut out. He rubbed his palms together. Challenge accepted.

He launched a *sniffer* to pick up cross talk on any network. No dice. The only thing he saw was outgoing data from City Hall. Figures the government still had juice. Bunch of blood sucking vampires.

Nothing displayed on the screen made any sense. The answers were in there. All he had to do was find them. He had to think it through logically. Like a code scriber. He didn't want to believe he did any of this. Hopefully, Kirox could help him prove it.

Kirox rarely did favors though. Janik would have to bring something to trade. Maybe Kirox would take one of those paintings on the wall downstairs. He'd definitely get a good price for it on the market.

He stopped as he reached for the communicator. Something else was going on here. Right now, he'd trust only himself. No, he'd make his visit to Kirox a surprise. The reaction to his visit would tell Janik a lot.

For now, Janik needed a few hours of proper sleep. He wouldn't find Kirox until after dark anyway. The good news was everyone thought he was dead so his rest should be peaceful. He set the alarm for four hours and flopped onto his bed. He'd have preferred eight hours, but there was that whole beggars can't be choosers thing.

CHAPTER 9:
MORE QUESTIONS

Janik packed his best laptop, two tablets, and two wrist computers into a briefcase. No network was secure with this equipment, including the McIntosh Corporation. The hard drives with the incriminating evidence he left. He couldn't risk losing it if he ran into trouble. Not that it mattered much. Everyone who'd been involved with Gina and Eldridge were either dead or in prison. At least, that's what he thought.

Janik stopped on his way to the garage. The Porsche would stick out like a sore thumb where he was going. He'd take the boosted ride instead.

The deeper he drove into the city; the worse things were. Burning cars lined almost every street. Looters emerged from abandoned shops with arms loaded down with stuff. No one stopped them.

As he neared Valencia and Sixteenth Streets his senses sharpened and he became more alert to anything out of the ordinary. Besides his house, this was the only place that truly felt like home. He understood the people here, related to them more than anyone else in the city.

A few people hanging out in front of rundown buildings eyeballed him as he passed. Normally, Janik didn't walk around armed. Given recent events, he would've welcomed a stun gun or something.

He left the car on the corner, taking only his briefcase. Knowing this neighborhood, it'd be stripped down like every other unattended car, the valuable stuff destined for one of the many district UN chop shops.

People here didn't have much. What they did have, they took without apology. Their survival depended on it. Generators or other neighborhoods provided the only available power. Stolen in both cases. Unregulated power had caused more than one fire around here over the years.

The UN was supposed to fix all this. Instead, the power and corruption that had taken the Consortium entrapped them. Janik helped where possible, but he was only one person.

His eyes searched the shadows for danger. He should feel safe here. Except for the overwhelming sense of dread. An amber light over the door marked the District's entrance. The nightclub was a known stronghold of the Underground Network, but Mission District folks knew to keep their mouths shut when they came here.

Everything within ten feet of him stopped when he walked through the door. The shocked expressions were almost amusing. Most of these people recognized him but weren't used to seeing his face on the news. "Kirox?" he said to the bouncer.

The black clad bouncer tilted his head towards a bar in the darkened corner near the stage. A skinny Latina beauty with barely enough clothes on to make a handkerchief danced to a ferocious Latin beat. Kirox's trademark ponytail bounced as he kept time to the music. His arm rested on the chair back while his other hand held a glass of amber bourbon.

Fighting his way to the stage, Janik sat next to the black-market trader. "The bouncer's nervous," he shouted over the din. "What'd you do to him?"

Kirox smiled knowingly. "You know, I don't normally believe in ghosts. Seeing your ugly mug in here might change my mind. Word through the circuits is you were pinched for the Promenade bombing."

Janik waved to a waitress roaming the floor, taking a moment to scan the rest of the club. No one paid them any obvious attention. "You mean my face on the news didn't give it away?"

Kirox traced his finger over the rim of his whiskey glass. "Everyone thinks you're dead."

"I'm not that easy to kill. I'd like a word. Privately."

Kirox spread his arms, offended by the notion. "Hey, come on. We're all family here."

Someone tried to kill him. When they learned they'd failed, they'd try again. "I'm not playing, Kirox. Besides, my head is pounding harder than it did after the Tenderloin job." Tequila shots until three in the morning didn't feel so good after the buzz wore off.

Kirox's grin faded. "I think the office is free."

Janik accepted the shot of whiskey from the waitress before following Kirox into the back room. There wasn't much here. Bathrooms to the right and Kirox's office straight ahead right before the emergency exit.

The walls cut the music somewhat. Kirox leaned against the wall and folded his arms, unimpressed that he had to give up his front row seat. "So what gives?"

Janik downed the whiskey in one gulp, grimacing against the fiery track it cut down his throat. He slammed the shot glass on the table as he shuddered. He wasn't an accomplished drinker, tequila shots aside, but the past twelve or so hours called for an exception. "Tell me what you know. And don't say nothing. You had something to do with what went down at the Promenade. I should charge you double for pain and suffering."

Kirox put on a fake pout. "Hey, I'm offended. I had no idea the job would go sideways."

Janik didn't twitch. "Somebody tried to take me out. I woke up out near the Sutro Baths in a hospital gown half-dead. Any idea what that's about?"

Kirox's face turned angry, his playfulness blowing out like a storm in the bay. "Of course not. What, you think I set you up?"

Janik didn't like crossing Kirox. They'd built a pretty good gig here. But someone decided to make it personal. He wasn't letting that go. "Did you? Did someone from my family get to you? You know my history with Bill McIntosh. My departure from that company wasn't exactly amicable. I know why I even took the damn job."

"The paycheck, that's why. In fact, if I remember correctly, I tripled your fee. I needed my best man on the job. I needed someone I could trust. My sources were telling me the Consortium Executive Order was planning something big and McIntosh was right in the middle of it."

That made his heart skip. He'd been targeted after all. "Who's the source? I want to talk to them."

"You know that's not happening, Janik. I like you, man, but business is business." That was the truth. Kirox would sell out his own mother to turn a profit. "Speaking of business. Did you get the intel?"

"I got something, but didn't have a chance to go through it. The cops took everything when I was arrested. Don't worry. It's all encrypted. They can't read any of it."

"Damn… It'd be really helpful if you found a way to get it back. My source is paying premium money for it."

"Are you serious right now? How the hell would you like me to do that?"

"I'm sure you'll figure something out. I'm withholding your fee until you do. Call it a security deposit."

"You son-of-a-bitch. I should bury you."

"You can try. Look, Janik. I don't like playing it like this, but I have people I answer to as well. They're not happy this whole thing went south."

That part was understandable. Any intel the UN had was

ammo to use against the Consortium. The Pharmacy, with the weight of the McIntoshes behind them, was the biggest bunch of drug dealers in the city. Almost everyone in the northern districts had a pill to pop. God knows what else they were experimenting with in their labs. The exec's death would put a dent into business.

Janik was hesitant to reveal anything else about his past. Perhaps he'd made a mistake telling Kirox about his connections to the Consortium when they first got together. Kirox loved to exploit any small detail others considered insignificant. Nothing kept him from burning Janik now that he had announced his retirement. "I heard about the raid earlier today. I see you escaped unscathed."

Kirox retrieved a bottle of bourbon from the cabinet on the back wall, poured two shots, and handed one to Janik. Was that a slight tremble in his hand? "Lucky. That's the second one this month. They're after info on the cyber-attack. The Consortium's nervous."

"Maybe they're looking for me, considering they think I'm a cold-blooded killer."

Kirox's dismissive shrug hurt. "They won't find anything here. Though, you probably shouldn't have come here. No doubt this place is being watched." He downed another shot and refilled his glass. "What do you remember?"

"Nonsensical fragments, mostly. The Promenade exploded. I think I tried to help before being arrested. Everything afterward is a blur. The last thing I remember clearly is a prisoner transport."

"I saw some images of the burnt-out transport. A bunch of rioters swarmed it or something. It's not hard to believe. Everything north of Market Street is in chaos."

Janik waved Kirox off as he offered another pour from the bottle. His brain was addled enough already. "What about the marshal's building?"

"Still intact as far as I know but information down here is sketchy at best."

Horseshit, Janik thought. Kirox always knew more than he let on. The real question was why he remembered something that never happened? "Feels like someone stuck a spoon up my nose to scramble my brain."

"Sounds like the celebration after one of our jobs."

Janik had the cold feeling someone didn't like the idea of him retiring. "Who tried to take me out? Who wants me gone?" *Besides everyone who shares my DNA,* he finished silently.

"No one that I'm hearing. Being a bit paranoid, aren't you?"

"No one in the UN can do what I do. It's why my fee is so high. It's why I normally work on my own terms."

"Everyone can be replaced."

"Somebody's got a grudge. Is it Benny? My fee is enough to pay his whole crew."

Kirox laughed. "Benny couldn't steal a bicycle from a schoolyard. It's astounding he hasn't been crimped yet."

"If you believed that, he'd be dead already. His crew's good. It's no secret he's after a big score. What else have you heard?"

"They think you used a stolen car in the bomb. They had images."

"Any idiot with a tablet and rendering software can fabricate those images," Janik growled. "The bomb went off on the lower level, right in the middle of the morning rush. Probably in a briefcase or something on a timer." *How the hell did I know that?* He dismissed the question without a second thought. He had bigger problems.

"What are the others in the Underground saying?"

"Not much. They're distancing themselves. They're not ready for a war with the Consortium."

"Not ready for a war, yet they keep hitting warehouses and supply lines. I bet you don't know anything about that either, do you? Wasn't there a truck of Ice Water hit a while back? Not exactly the humanitarian targets the UN used to stick to. Be curious to know what kind of explosives were used in these attacks."

"Hey, that's just business, the price of operation." Kirox returned the whiskey bottle to the cupboard. "Kids died in the Promenade bombing. It's annoying, really. I have unfinished business with the UN."

Janik needed no reminding of the kids. He saw that boy's face every time he closed his eyes. It reminded him of Javier's kid the night Javier died. "Why would I blow up the Promenade?" Rubbing his face again didn't wipe away the memories. "I was retiring. I had no reason to jeopardize that."

"How can I help? Though, I'm not sure I can. I'm staying off the grid until things cool down. Every Consortium agent with an itchy trigger finger is going to be on the lookout. It'll be a city full of bounty hunters. I've spread the word that business is closed until this blows over."

"The Promenade data stream has my proof." He hoped. "Ask around. Call in some favors if you have to. After everything I've done for you, you owe me."

Kirox scowled. "I make no promises. The Consortium is keeping a pretty tight lid on this one. Nothing is being leaked. Hang tight here for a while."

"Bring me back a couple of bacon cheeseburgers from Bruno's. Non-Synth, none of that other synth crap the Sustainers peddle. Those idiots wouldn't know a decent meal if it smacked them in the face. And some coffee. I could really use some coffee."

Kirox returned less than an hour later with a grease-stained paper bag and a styrofoam cup with steam billowing out of the top. Janik nodded approvingly. Even the wrapping was old school. He expected nothing less from Bruno. "Nothing else shook loose. Just asking the questions cost me a couple large markers."

Janik stopped midway through opening the bag. His mouth watered over aromas of medium rare beef and real bacon. "Sorry to inconvenience you. I'm supposed to be a dead bomber remember? Never mind that my head is no better than scrambled eggs."

"I'm just telling you the score. You'd be wise to finish your meal and make yourself scarce. You don't have many friends around here right now. Dead kids don't sit well with the UN."

"How the hell do you think they sit with me?"

"I don't know what else to say, Janik. I've gone as far as I'm willing to go. Don't be here when I come back."

Kirox went back to his belly dancer while Janik finished his burgers. His next play had to be logical, one step at a time. He snorted. Think like a marshal. Visiting the crime scene would be the first thing on any marshal's list. That scared the hell out of Janik, but he had no choice if he wanted to spark his memory. He should probably pay a visit to McIntosh's offices too. He liked that idea even less than going back to the Promenade.

He left the District feeling no better about his situation. Kirox's cold reception, and the fact no one told him about the attack only hardened his belief someone had tried to end him. He wouldn't put it on the UN yet. Kirox was right about one thing. They didn't condone killing kids.

The car door closing was his first indication of trouble. Two figures in dark jackets stalked towards him, both hiding weapons behind their legs. Operation Kill Janik: Take Two.

Janik spun back towards the club. He'd die before he let them take him again. He'd lose them inside and slip out the back. He sprinted, slipping more than once. Leather shoes weren't exactly made for running.

"There's nowhere for you to go, Janik," one of them shouted.

We'll see about that. He made it past the bouncer at the front door, fighting his way through the crowd to the back door. His heart sank as he neared the front of the alley. Three more thugs stood at the end of the street, pistols leveled at him and smug grins on their faces. One of the thugs came up behind him. "I told you there was nowhere to go."

Pain erupted in the back of his head. He collapsed to the ground. Everything went black.

CHAPTER 10: THE TRUTH WITHIN THE LIE

Serena fell against the apartment door, exhaling with puffed out cheeks. Her heart pounded as she pushed off the door and paced in front of the small bed. She'd gotten away with one. If not for Felix, Ivan would've killed her. And she still had no answers. This wasn't like a computer where changing a few parameters fixed everything. Failing here meant more people dead.

Serena sat on the edge of the bed, head in her hands. She tried to picture it logically, like her father used to do. How many times had she watched him sitting at the splintered kitchen table with his eyes closed? He usually came up with the answers too.

She had to find a way to tell Logan about this place. Felix sure as hell wasn't going to let her access a computer. Maybe he didn't have to. One of the sec officers or other workers would have network access. Still not an easy job though.

Serena returned to the main level, hoping the cafeteria still had some tea. Sipping on a warm cup helped her focus. Another thing she inherited from her father. Neither of the sec officers roaming the corridor acknowledged her. Serena turned in the opposite direction towards the main exit. If they weren't going to stop her, she might be able to make a run for it. Logan can bring in the cavalry.

She passed the unmanned desk and out the front door. Smoke wafted over the city, bringing the stench of burning rubber and metal with every breath. The rolling blackouts accentuated the glowing orange sky as San Francisco burned.

Serena questioned the necessity of all this. Sure, there was corruption, some price gouging, but the Consortium investment meant more people had food, more had clothing, more had housing. What more did they want?

Three sec officers patrolled the grounds between the front door and the security gate. There were likely others. The deep darkness off to her right seemed her best chance to sneak away. She could escape through the woods behind the complex and find her way back to the downed transport. Logan's strike team had the firepower to make short work of the mercenaries here.

She *should* go to tell Logan what she'd learned, but would he listen? He'd more likely bitch that she hadn't shut down the whole attack by now. She went back inside to find that cup of tea. She had an angle to work now that she knew what drove Felix. When you stripped away the finer detail, they were both the same. Hurt by the people in power and wanting to make sure no one else suffered that fate. Ivan worried her the most. He didn't trust her. Not one iota.

Serena stirred a spoonful of sugar into the black liquid. *How do I reach Logan?* Until she gained some credentials, her options were limited.

"I thought I'd find you up here," Felix announced behind her as she pulled the spoon from the cup.

Serena gripped the edge of the counter to keep from jumping out of her skin. She faced him once she regained her composure. "Couldn't sit still." Her voice squeaked like a frightened mouse. She cleared her throat. "Strange places make me nervous. Shelters were the worst. Wish I still had my harp to play. Used to always relax me."

"Perhaps I can show you a little of what we do here. I think a little perspective will help put you at ease."

"I'd like that," Serena replied. I'd like you to show me everything.

She didn't expect him to show her anything on the locked levels, but to stop him, she had to understand him. He took her behind the offices to the expansive factory floor. It had to be thirty feet from floor to ceiling. Cranes, and hoists, and conveyor belts dotted different parts of the floor. Her footfalls echoed as she walked.

Felix waved a hand before him, thrusting his chest out a little more. "This is where the magic happens. We build everything from emergency shelters to base isolation systems."

They weaved their way around stacks of building materials and pre-fabricated sections. "Base isolation?"

"Right. You're not an engineer. It's a design method that allows more movement in a building during a quake, making it easier to withstand the shaking."

"That sounds pretty useful."

Felix's eyes bulged. "Useful? This will mean the difference between unchecked destruction and countless homes being saved. Imagine how many families won't be forced out of their homes because some clueless bureaucrat decides it's not safe."

They entered another section of the factory where several single-room structures stood in a row. "What are these for?"

"There are still parts of the city that have not recovered from the quake. My hope is these shelters will help address that."

Serena clenched her jaw, suddenly enraged. The Mission District had been lying in ruins for years. Where was this guy when her father lay beneath the smoking rubble of his music shop? Where was he when they had been forced to live in half-collapsed, unstable shelters? Where was he when her mother lay dying in the back of Bruno's restaurant?

No, that wasn't fair. Many would've still perished. Felix didn't sound like a madman blowing the city to kingdom come. He sounded like he really cared. It was more than she could say for Harlon Cruz and his UN masters. "I wish this technology existed twenty years ago."

"Me too" His voice had a slight tremor to it, a genuine pain impossible to fake. "I can't change the past, but I sure as hell can help ensure a brighter future."

They circled the building, all the way to the back near the loading docks. Behind a sectioned off part, there were several drones, along with crates labeled 'Brynn AI'. Why was an earthquake engineer doing business with a company specializing in unmanned weapons systems? What else did Felix have planned for the city? One thing was certain. Logan wouldn't be happy to learn one of the Consortium's biggest partners was selling weapons to the person trying to take them down. "Why are you helping me? Why not let your guard or Ivan kill me? I'm not all that significant in the grand scheme of things."

"I know what it's like to be alone and helpless. I know what it's like to be forgotten while others deemed more important get the help you deserve. What's happening here is meant to remove the corruption, not destroy the city. It's hard to see now but will be obvious soon."

That sounded a lot like a confession, but Serena needed more. She needed the why. "How did you get into all of this? If you don't mind me asking."

"I guess it's only fair you know a bit more about who you're trusting. You're right. I had some help with the complex. I worked in heavy tech before this. Construction mostly. I thought it logical to employ the technology that created the mess to clean it up."

Heavy tech and construction. That sounded like security protocols and people with access to high explosives. "Sometimes our best intentions cause the most damage."

"San Francisco used to mean everything to me. Everything I ever wanted was here. It was my home in every sense. The Great

Quake ripped it all away. I don't want anyone to ever feel that same hopelessness again."

"I bet people are feeling pretty hopeless right now. What's happening out there is almost as bad as the quake."

"This will pass, like all storms do. We must focus on the rebuild."

Again, Serena bit her tongue. *A storm from which you stand to make a great deal of money, I'd imagine.* He wanted to put down the Consortium in order to take its place. Felix, the UN, the Consortium. None of them cared about helping people. Greed drove them all. It was disgusting.

Serena noted possible breach points as they strolled towards the back of the factory. The offices back here would have computer terminals she could use to send a message to Logan.

"Forgive me for prying, but your accent leads me to believe you're from the Mission District. A tough neighborhood in which to grow up."

Serena stopped walking and gazed around the room, looking anywhere except at Felix. "I haven't been back in some time. I doubt it looks anything like it did when I left."

Felix leaned against a stack of steel girders. "You have no family left there?"

"I have no family left period. Those the Great Quake didn't kill, the aftermath did."

"Is that why you joined the marshals. Not exactly an upstanding organization to those south of Market Street."

Serena didn't answer right away. "It's complicated." That wasn't necessarily a lie. Her true life mixed with the cover story made the drama genuine.

"I'm a good listener."

His disarming voice drew her in like a siren's call. *Remember why you're here*, she reminded herself. "My mother became ill not long after the quake killed my father. I couldn't afford the medicine to help her. I'd heard stories about the UN, but they only agreed to help if I did them… ummm… favors. My mother didn't want me to sell my soul for her sake. I went anyway. I refused to watch her die like I watched my father die. I can still see the disappointment on her face. She died before I got the medicine."

She wandered away from him, towards one of the half-finished shelters. Why was he so easy to talk to? She spilled her guts like some love-struck schoolgirl. "I promised myself that I'd never let another person go without essential things. I joined the marshals, hoping to end the corruption, not realizing at the time they were the most corrupt of all. Every street-level drug dealer we arrested, every Pharmacy suit we exposed, ended up back on the street the next day. The charges never stuck. Evidence disappeared, witnesses recanted. Never mind that the UN black market only drove prices higher."

Felix wrapped his arm around her shoulder. This time, she didn't shy away. "I'm sorry. There's no shame in doing what you believed was right."

She found it difficult not to take comfort from his touch. She missed the feel of another human being more than she realized. "It has been some years. The pain is not so great anymore." The ease of her lies disturbed her.

Felix directed them back toward the offices at the front of the complex. "The loss of one's mother never really leaves. Trust me, I speak from experience."

"How did she die?" Serena asked, since they were being personal. Her chest tightened when he didn't answer right away. Had she crossed another line?

Felix's smile disappeared. "She was killed. Brutally. I've been on my own ever since."

Sensing he didn't want to discuss it, Serena redirected the conversation. "Is that how you became involved with the homeless shelters?"

His face lit up again, the darkness that had befallen him gone. "If my resources can ease their suffering, it'd be irresponsible for me not to try."

"I'm not the only one the Consortium hurt. I'm sure they'd like to see the score settled as much as I do. Even before the quake, my father and other community leaders saw the corporations for what they were. Opportunists trying to take what others worked for. His death, along with many of the other loudest voices gave rise to the early forms of the Consortium."

Serena felt his eyes studying her, wondering if she was telling the truth. Hopefully, she'd done enough convincing.

"Have faith, my dear. Change is coming."

"I like to think my time on the street made me a pretty good people reader. You seem to have few troubles of your own for someone with so much going on."

"My burdens are for me to bear," he said politely. "Like you, the marshals and the Consortium are in no small part responsible for them."

Yes, but why, Serena questioned silently. She didn't push it. One step at a time. "Perhaps you're right. My mother always told me though, that a friend to talk to is one's most valuable possession."

"Your mother, rest her soul, was a wise woman."

Serena nodded. "It's too bad I realized it too late. I thought I could be different, but the people I tried to help resented me because I was a marshal and the marshals resented me because I refused to play their games. In the end, I failed to make any sort of difference."

"Would you like to go home eventually, Olivia? I mean to the Mission District?"

"There's nothing back there for me anymore, except bad memories," she replied. "Did you know that there hasn't even been a Carnival since before the quake? My mom used to dress us up in these colorful outfits and we'd parade through the streets playing our instruments. Used to be the biggest one around. Now, we can't even hear the echoes."

"Truly a tragedy that cannot continue. Maybe one day soon we'll hear the music again."

"Most girls there work for the UN. I'm sure I don't have to explain in what capacity. Can't say I blame them. They're trying to survive like everyone else. I refuse to be used like that."

"The Underground Network means well, but they are largely ineffective. They lack the resources to take on the Consortium alone."

"They don't mean well," Serena snapped. "Maybe at first they did. Now greed drives them like it does everyone else. Those who can't fend for themselves are left to suffer."

His cold grin returned. "If I could help you make the difference you desire, would you consider it?"

"What do you mean?"

"I will explain more at dinner. For now, I have some business requiring my attention."

CHAPTER 11: A DEVIL'S OFFER

Janik woke with a pounding headache in a holding cell. Flickering fluorescent light stabbed his eyes like daggers. He moved his head slightly, hissing at the pain. He lay back with his eyes closed, waiting for some of the agony to pass.

Everything in his head jumbled together like a tangled ball of string. What had happened? The last thing he remembered was… a burger? That didn't seem right, but it had to be. Janik tried searching his memory for specifics, but came up with only vague feelings, intuitions that he could neither confirm, nor deny. His head continued to pound, and pressing his fingers to his eyes didn't help.

He dragged his feet to the front of the cell and pressed his head against the bars. Maybe whoever was on the other side could shed some like into what happened. Dingy walls flanking empty cells greeted him. *Not even a window to highlight my natural complexion.* This wasn't the marshals' building downtown. Probably one of the Consortium's 'black sites'. Made sense. Easier to make him disappear that way.

A marshal strolled by, a powerful taser inches from his left hand. Janik snorted. He reminded Janik of one of those cowboys from the Wild West ready for a quick draw. He wasn't about to give this idiot a reason to light him up.

The comedy aside, the sight presented another question Janik had no answer for. Marshals meant he'd been arrested, but from what he could tell, no one thought he was alive.

He worked his mouth, trying to get any sort of moisture in there. "Can I get some water?" His voice sounded like he smoked two packs a day.

Quick Draw McToughGuy stood outside the cell, hands on his hips and a judgmental sneer screwing up his face. "About time you woke up. Must be nice to be able to sleep all day."

Janik should've faked being unconscious a while longer. A couple more hours of shut-eye would've gone a long way. "Sorry to inconvenience you. I'll try harder to stay awake next time. How about that water?"

The marshal pulled the cell door open. "Turn around." Cold metal mag-cuffs snapped around his wrists. "Someone wants to see you."

"Is that right?" Janik replied. "Any chance you can enlighten me a bit more? Like who that is, or maybe we can start with where the hell I am and how I got here."

The marshal yanked him away from the wall and shoved him out of the cell. A foul stench followed them down a narrow, dimly lit hall to an interrogation room. *That's probably me. Or it could be Quick Draw.*

The clock over the door outside said 20:00. Only eight o'clock. Janik had been out for about an hour. No wonder Quick Draw was so cranky. He likely missed his afternoon nap. Janik glanced back toward his cell longingly.

The guard retreated to the back corner of the room after shackling him to the table. All very spy-like. Janik half expected James Bond to walk in. Instead, his head dropped forward when Renaude entered instead. *Why am I not surprised?* This had his greasy touch all over it.

Janik felt the knot on the back of his head and things began to take focus again. He'd gone to see Kirox and before he could get away, the marshals found him, and none too gently had taken him into custody.

Renaude eased the door closed with barely a click. He set a dark tablet on the table and slipped into the chair across from Janik. He stared for a while, a smug smirk on his face. "You look like hell chewed you up and spat you out."

Janik snickered. "Close. Seems hell isn't quite done with me yet. I wish you would've told me we had an appointment. I would've at least changed my socks." Sweat gleaned on Renaude's forehead and his hands trembled. "Not looking so hot yourself."

"I must say," the chief marshal replied, forcing his voice to remain even. "I am a bit surprised to see you. I thought I'd seen the last of you when I put you on that transport."

"Sorry to disappoint. Speaking of the transport, I didn't think they made deliveries to the Sutro Baths? Did the driver get lost? Or, maybe he was paid to get lost. You know, if you're going to hire someone to dump a body, you should at least ensure they know what they're doing."

"I don't know what you're talking about. I did not handle the transport crash directly. As you can imagine, other matters demanded my attention." Renaude maintained an outward calm. "At any rate, the transport is not your most pressing concern."

"Just tell me one thing. Did you dump me yourself or did you have one of your scumbag Consortium friends do it? We all know how you don't like to get your hands dirty."

Quick Draw darted forward and jabbed the thick end of his 'persuasion stick' into Janik's side. His whole body convulsed as a painful jolt of electricity coursed through it. "Show some respect."

Janik slumped to one side. If he hadn't been shackled to the table, he'd be twitching on the floor in a puddle of his own urine. The guard yanked up him upright by the collar. Renaude had a satisfied grin pasted on his face.

Renaude shook his head disgustedly. He stood and paced behind his chair, his polished shoes clicking on the tiled floor.

"You think so little of me. All I'm trying to do is put the city back on the right track. I see an opportunity here. For both of us."

"What are you talking about?" Janik demanded through clenched teeth. His kidneys no longer throbbed, but they probably wouldn't work right for a while. "Last I checked, you weren't the charitable type. Especially towards me."

Renaude slid the tablet on the table over to him. "Shut it down. Then we'll talk."

Janik arched his back in an effort to ease a little more of the discomfort. "Come again?"

"The cyber-attack. Shut it down. Turn the lights back on."

Janik laughed, then stiffened as fresh jolts of pain stabbed his back. He was going to need a year's worth of acupuncture to get the kinks out. Things were a little clearer now though. "Two things. First, I'm mag-cuffed to a table. In my line of work, hands are kind of a necessity. Secondly, I vaguely recall telling you I don't know how."

"Yes, you did. I didn't believe you then either." Renaude leaned forward. "If I remove your restraints, you'll behave, yes?"

Janik shot a wary glance at Quick Draw. "You have your little puppy with his devil stick. What do you think I'm going to do?" Renaude nodded and Quick Draw released him. Janik pulled the tablet towards him. "I don't know what you expect me to do with this little trinket. Probably doesn't have enough processing power to turn on the coffee maker."

"Give it a shot anyway," Renaude encouraged.

Janik tapped the screen. What came up wasn't a string of programming code. He tried not to let his shock show. He recognized the file and was kind of surprised it was complete. "What the hell is this?"

Renaude motioned to the guard. "Leave us."

Janik's hand clenched on the table. What game was Renaude playing here? "Are you sure that's a good idea? He might pee on the floor."

"Don't be childish, Janik. I'm here to make you an offer."

"Does it include a sandwich and a glass of water?"

Renaude stopped the guard briefly. "Please fetch Mister Brynn some refreshment." Once Quick Draw pulled the door closed behind him, Renaude leaned across the table. "Now, shall we chat?"

Janik sat up a little straighter, though his unease continued. A bullet to the chest was far more likely from this maniac. "I'm listening. Start with this here file."

"These are all vehicles you are suspected of stealing, many of them high-end from high profile citizens." He pointed at the third one on the list. A Porsche. "Recognize this one? You nearly killed me with that vehicle. We were lucky to recover it at all." Renaude held up the bottle with the tiny red capsules. "These pills are a direct result of that encounter."

"Sorry. Don't recall. I'd never harm a fine upstanding lawman such as yourself. Perhaps if you had some video evidence of this alleged assault it might jog my memory." Janik hadn't meant to run him down. The idiot jumped onto the hood of the car as Janik hit the accelerator. They usually didn't put handholds on the hoods of high-end sports cars. That Nob Hill job was the closest he'd ever come to ending up behind bars. Or worse.

Heir McIntosh paid a pretty penny for the return of that car, especially since a certain video file depicting him in a compromising position with an unknown female accompanied it. Janik's hacking before he switched sides wasn't completely useless.

As it turned out, the unknown female ended up being Gina Hendrix, long thought to be the founder of the Consortium. It was more complicated than that, but Janik had no desire to revisit that particularly painful part of his life.

"We both know you did every one of those jobs. Earn yourself some leniency by helping me neutralize these attacks."

Janik's voice squeaked. "Your puppet masters aren't known for leniency. They'll go after the families of people who've pissed them off. Helping you puts people I care about in danger."

Renaude sat back and crossed his arms. "I didn't think you had any family."

Touche. Score one for Renaude. Still, he didn't want anyone else getting hurt because of lies told about him. "If you had enough to bury me, you'd have done it by now."

Renaude let out a sigh of frustration. "Be reasonable, Janik. The scripts the attackers are using are so complex my people are having issues figuring them out. We both know you have the skills to shut down the city's power grid. Consider it a part of your debt to society."

"You mean a society that preys on the weak and extorts their friends without a second thought? How many times do you look the other way in exchange for all that shiny gear you people use?"

"I have neither the time nor the patience for your conspiracy theories, Janik."

If only they were theories. He had the data to prove every one of his claims. Anyone with the power to stop it was bought and paid for with dirty Consortium money. It wasn't just McIntosh Corp either. Every one of these companies fed the beast of corruption. They invaded people's privacy, found their weaknesses, and fed on them.

He shifted in his seat, wishing he could rub the knot out of his sore back. "What's your game, Renaude? Why me? Why not ask your puppet masters for help? I know some of their scripters. Went to university with them." He went head-to-head with some of them during his time at the McIntosh Corp. Sometimes, he missed those cat-and-mouse games. "A little cyber-attack shouldn't be a problem for the all-powerful Consortium."

Renaude grinned. "How about this? Help me or I'll hand you over to those puppet masters. In fact, I hear they are most eager to speak with you."

Janik squirmed. Renaude hated him more than anything. What would make him desperate enough to blackmail him for help?

"A simple yes or no will suffice," Renaude pressed.

He'd probably regret this, but Janik didn't have the cards to call Renaude's bluff. People on both sides wanted Janik dead. He didn't have much time to prove he wasn't a killer. "I'll help you under a few conditions."

Renaude snorted. "I have already outlined what's in it for you."

Janik shrugged. "Now who's being unreasonable? All I want is a little information. I'm sure I can convince your Consortium friends I'm not the one behind this. I wonder what they'd think of you asking for help from someone suspected of UN associations. I don't think they'd be giving you a medal."

"Your vileness knows no bounds, Janik."

"Criminal, remember? Like you, I do what's necessary to finish the job. Kind of ironic, don't you think? The person you hate the most is more like you than you care to admit."

Veins popped out of Renaude's neck. His hands clenched on the table. "What do you want?"

"First of all, any backlash from this ends with me. No more innocent people die." Renaude may be a puppet, but he had some authority. Janik would make damn sure no one went after his sister. Despite their involvement with the McIntosh Corp and their refusal to believe their friends weren't actual friends, Janik didn't want to see them harmed. Next, he pointed at the tablet. "That file right there disappears completely. Without a trace. None of it proves I did anything, but I know how you people like to twist info. I want the data stream and the victim list from the Promenade bombing, and you're going to return the belongings taken from me at the Promenade. There is an item of particular interest among them. You're also going to answer my questions."

"The Promenade data stream is evidence. I'm not about to

give you a list of survivors to terrorize."

"Non-negotiable, Renaude." Janik had to give the mother of the boy he watched die the chess piece. Hopefully, it offered her a little bit of closure. It was more than he got when Javier died. "It's up to you. We can leave it in the hands of your code scribers if you want. I'm not sure there will be much left to your precious city by the time they figure it out. I'm not sure there's much left now."

Renaude clenched his fists and huffed. "Very well. The truth of the matter is the Promenade footage is corrupted. We lost the feed when the power went out about ten minutes before the explosion. We have no idea what the footage shows."

Janik spread his hands. "All the more reason to give it to me. I can figure it out." It also meant there'd be no footage of him stealing the Bentley. Win, win.

"I'll see what I can do. Ask your questions."

Janik rubbed his eyes. Where to start? "How did the marshals find me at the nightclub?"

"We had eyes on it, but an anonymous tip called in on a burner. They hung up before the dispatcher traced it."

Someone from the District wanted him out of the way. Kirox, that son-of-a-bitch, probably knew who. "I want the recording of that call. I may recognize the voice of whoever sold me out. Might also lead to whoever is behind the attack."

Renaude sneered. "Sounds like your list of friends is pretty short."

And getting shorter. The question was why. He set that mystery aside for now. He had more questions. "Who's really behind all this, Renaude?"

"You tell me. We suspect you're working with the UN."

Kirox said the same. The problem was there was no upside for him to pull a job like this. He had nothing to gain. Renaude believed this was revenge against McIntosh Corp. If that were true, Janik wouldn't use a bunch of explosives to do it. "I guess real investigative work isn't a requirement for the marshals. Did anyone find any trace of explosive on me? Did anyone figure out my motive? Did anyone wonder why I stayed after the bomb exploded? If I planted it, why wasn't I halfway to the Golden Gate Bridge?"

"All part of the investigation. The current power situation has limited our abilities."

"The way I see it, we both need answers. What about my memory? I haven't been able to think straight since this morning. I remember something then five minutes later, my mind is blank. That's not natural." He still hadn't figured out why he was remembering the marshals' building exploding. "The last thing I remember clearly is you shoving me into the back of a prisoner transport."

A split second of fear flashed across Renaude's arrogant face. "It was a pretty traumatic accident. You were exposed to the harsh elements for an extended period. Some amnesia should be expected."

No friggin way. Renaude knew something, but proving it meant cooperating for the time being. "Okay, Renaude. If I'm going to do this, I need some gear and a quiet place to work."

Renaude called Quick Draw back. "You can use the offices upstairs. I brought your personal effects taken at the Promenade along with the briefcase found with you at the District."

Good. He needed to get a look at the intel he downloaded from Bill McIntosh's phone. He still hadn't completely ruled out their involvement. Someone lured him to the Promenade. They were the only ones he knew besides Renaude with a grudge. "Do you have the access protocols for the power centers? Maybe I can find a backdoor in and trace it back to the source."

Renaude hesitated before nodding to the guard. "Everything is there except for the video footage. It's locked up in evidence.

I have to get back to ops." Renaude half stood. "One more thing, Janik. If you double-cross me, all bets are off."

"You should know by now, Renaude, I never gamble."

CHAPTER 12:
TRACED

The empty third floor office space reminded Janik of a hospital ward, complete with images of him strapped to a gurney. This felt like a trap. As a thief, he knew about such things.

Renaude handed him a data stick. "This is everything my code scribers have compiled, including some of the power center access codes. It isn't much." Next, he handed Janik a communicator. "It's not coded. You'll only be able to reach me so don't think you can call in a bunch of your friends. I expect regular updates." Renaude grabbed Janik's arm. "Our arrangement remains discrete. If not, all deals are off."

Janik stared at Renaude for a minute. *Easier for you to renege that way, hey chief marshal?* Renaude was never going to wipe his record clean. As soon as Janik ended the cyber-attack, he was a dead man.

He stripped off his torn jacket and fired it onto the plain brown sofa, causing fresh waves of agony through his body. Flopping down next to his jacket, he closed his eyes. He longed for a deep sleep in a city far from San Francisco. The Promenade was supposed to be the end, his exit plan. Not just the end of a career, the end of a lifestyle. Instead, it became a steady descent into a nightmare. He shook off his despair. He had to do the work if he wanted to escape.

He jolted upright when the guard kicked his foot hard. "You're not up here to sleep. Get to work."

Janik pushed himself up off the couch slowly. *Weren't you*

supposed to get me a sandwich or something? Hard to work on an empty stomach."

The guard glowered and disappeared into the small kitchen. Janik took a minute to really see his surroundings for the first time. The bright white walls and large windows made the room seem big. Janik closed the shutters, and kept the lights low. Not that anyone could see him on the third floor.

The Pyramid, two blocks northeast and reflecting the setting sun, dwarfed everything around it. The heads of the corporations, including McIntosh Corp holed up in there like a bunch of moles. The heart of Consortium territory, here long before the Great Quake and its current tenants. The perfect symbol for their arrogance. One of these days, maybe he'd see what really went on inside.

This is so screwed up. *The government losing control and me helping the marshals by choice.* His mind was fragmented, like a screen with half the pixels blown.

The bombings, the cyber-attack, his arrest at the District, making things right with the woman and her dead child. So many problems to solve. So many things going against him. Still, he clung to a little bit of hope. Things were obviously connected. Unraveling one problem unraveled them all.

Janik prioritized things in his mind, like debugging a string of code. Each fix should make things clearer. Of course, the flipside of that coin was each fix might reveal a larger corruption. *No sense worrying about that until I know what I'm dealing with.* The first thing he had to do was look at the data he stole from William McIntosh. Maybe there was something in there that would tell him what the hell this was all about.

The monitor on the wall showed only a solid blue screen. So the failure at home wasn't entirely him. The entire network was down. Now, with a clearer head, he might be able to do something about it.

"Here's your damn food," the guard announced. "Now, can we move this thing along?"

Everything he had when he was arrested at the Promenade, including the chess piece, sat on the desk in the corner. Patricia's face flashed through his mind. That could've been them sitting there playing chess when the bomb went off. He wiped the last bits of blood from it. He couldn't let that mother's last memory of her son be a bomb. He had to find a way to give this to her.

Janik secured the chess piece in his pocket and rubbed his hands together in anticipation. Time to get to work. He found his phone in the pile of gear Renaude left him and plugged it into the laptop. It only took a minute for the encryption program to decrypt the data he'd downloaded from Bill McIntosh's phone.

It was a waste of time.

There was nothing on McIntosh's phone to indicate some grand scheme. Not to say he wasn't having any grand schemes, but he was smart enough not to carry it around with him. Janik leaned back and linked his hands behind his head. That presented two possibilities. Either Kirox received some bad intel, or they had been set up. The gurgling in his stomach said it was the latter.

He launched a passive eavesdropping attack on the Chronicles internal server. A steady stream of buildings burning and marshals struggling scrolled across the screen. The people behind this wanted everyone to see it. Janik was wrong. The whole network wasn't down, it was being controlled.

Janik played a bit of a hunch and launched another tracer script on several public service networks. If whoever was behind this could control one network, they could probably control others. The question was why. His answer came less than a minute later.

He sat back and munched on his sandwich absently as he considered what this meant. The people behind this were siphoning data, not only from the active server, but from the archives as well. They were after something specific. Janik was a little impressed. He kicked himself for not seeing it sooner. The bombings, the rolling blackouts. They were nothing more than distractions to steal the city's data.

This kind of thing was right up McIntosh Corp's lane, but still something felt off. They couldn't be going after the data he stole. They didn't know he had it. At some point, he had to lose the meathead in the other room and make it back home to scan through those hard drives.

Images hit one right after another—buildings burning, bodies lying on the ground, emergency crews rushing about trying to save as many as possible. And that was just the Promenade. Unfortunately, none of it exonerated him.

The next sequence showed the overpass. Tons of rock and concrete and twisted metal buried cars with caved-in roofs. Red stained glass littered the ground. Janik's stomach heaved at the thought of the bodies underneath that. The last series showed the metro station. He switched off the monitor. He'd seen enough. *How can they believe I did this?* Whatever else happened to him, he'd prove this wasn't him.

Janik activated another tablet. Lines of code scrolled on one monitor and a virtual map of San Francisco popped up on another. *Let's see what's working.* It quickly filled with red dots. He initiated another script and more dots, green this time, appeared. Most of the servers still online were in the Financial District, along with some news agencies, City Hall, the hospitals, the marshals building.

The marshals building? Another indication it hadn't been bombed. Yet another mystery to unravel. All of the data from the Financial District was streaming out. If McIntosh was behind these attacks, it'd be the other way around.

Janik keyed in on a server in Land's End that linked into the Chronicle. Enormous amounts of data streamed in and out of it.

Janik tapped a few keys, bring up some of the stream. *Damn it! All encrypted.* He didn't have computing power or the time to strip away the layers right now. All of that stuff was at home. "What are you doing all the way up there?"

A few seconds of digging through Renaude's data proved the chief marshal was right. There wasn't much there. Janik dry washed his face in frustration. Despite his disdain for the marshal's code scribers, they weren't stupid.

He launched a tracer script hoping to map where the lockouts originated. It was a bit more robust than its older phishing script cousin. To shut down the attack, he first had to isolate its origin. Blue lines connected the green dots from his location. But the tracer bounced between four irrelevant servers in a continuous loop. "Sneaky bastards," Janik grunted.

Renaude's code scribers would've seen that. Had they seen where the loop started? Janik worked on the tablet methodically, isolating one of the servers and finding a way out of the loop. *You want to play rough, do you?*

Janik launched attack after attack against the Land's End servers. SQL injections, cross-script attacks, polymorphic viruses. Everything he had, he threw it. Someone else saw the attack and joined the fun. It had to be Renaude's scribers. Maybe Janik had underestimated them a little. He'd gotten through the outer layers of security, almost to the good stuff.

Then he hit a brick wall. His best worms were useless against the inner firewalls. Something about the code struck Janik as familiar. He'd seen this somewhere before.

One of his tablets beeped loudly. His poking around caught someone's attention. Within seconds, they'd narrowed down his location. *Just a bit longer to find the back door.* He swiped his arm across his sweating forehead before going back to the keyboard.

Servers dropped out as Janik closed in. Almost there. Then the spam hit. Ads for anti-aging procedures, augmentation surgeries- of all the anatomy. And the medications that went with it. Abominations, every last one of them. In desperation, he plugged a thumb drive into the tablet and introduced another subroutine that overwhelmed their connection with spam and three-way porn. A crude, but effective attack. "We've got a problem here."

Quick Draw burst into the room, gun drawn. "What did you do?"

"What Renaude told me to. Whoever is out there has eyes in the sky. They pegged me pretty quickly. They'll be on us in minutes and I doubt they'll be the cheerleading squad."

Quick Draw headed for the door, his weapon drawn. "Pack it up. Follow me when you're done. I'm going to buy us some time."

Gunfire rang out at street level not five minutes after the guard left. *That was quick!* They must have already been in the area. Janik peeked around the curtain. Two figures crouched behind a vehicle shooting towards the main entrance. Muzzle flashes erupted from their guns.

Janik scrambled back to the table and threw equipment into the case. Living took priority over being gentle. He called Renaude on the coded communicator. "Someone noticed my snooping. Your little guard dog is entertaining them as we speak. We need a way out of here."

"Briefcase on the top shelf of the closet. There are ignition codes, and other things, for vehicles in the parking garage. They'll be in a locked cage in the back right corner of the garage. Call me when you're clear."

Janik ran from the office and down the back stairwell, taking the steps in twos. The gunfire echoing through the main lobby sounded like the Fourth of July. Back when there was a Fourth of July...

Quick Draw ducked behind the far corner of the reception desk. Janik whistled, drawing his attention. There was no way either of them crossed the lobby without catching a bullet or two.

The guard shot behind him as a bullet struck his shoulder, spinning him to the ground mere feet from the door. Several more shots hit as he pulled himself to cover. Blood seeped onto the floor as Janik stared on in horror. Quick Draw shoved the gun across the floor at him. "Run."

Janik hesitated before grabbing the gun and bolting into the stairwell for the parking garage. Bullets tore chunks of plaster from the wall over his head. His heart pounded as he tried to keep his momentum from throwing him down the stairs. He'd never been shot at before and he had to admit. He didn't much care for the experience. *Don't look back. Don't look back.* He had to make it to the garage.

Heavy footfalls echoing above drove him faster. His lungs burned as they cried out for oxygen. How many more damn stairs were there?

"Stop right there," someone shouted. Janik kept running. He zigzagged the width of the stairwell, keeping his shoulders low. No sense making it easy for them.

Flickering emergency lights assaulted his eyes when he entered the parking garage. The short stroll to the vehicle cage in the lot's back corner would feel like a mile-long trek. Janik cut to the right away from the door.

Seconds later, the stairwell door crashed open. "Let's make this quick," one of the thugs ordered. "Ivan wants us back on schedule ASAP."

"Take the right. I got the left." Several more steps down the corridor. "You might as well come out." His voice echoed, masking his location. "There's nowhere for you to go."

That's what you think. Janik followed the aisle toward the far side of the lot, staying low and tight against the wall. This wasn't the way he worked. Obscurity seemed more his style.

The gun tucked into his waistband pressed against the small

of his back. He hated guns. Seeing Quick Draw's dying eyes staring up at him reminded him why.

Sweat poured down Janik's face as he shuffled into the center of the lot, still dragging his cases of equipment with him. He passed several high-end luxury cars, stopping at a polished Lexus to catch his breath. He was a sitting duck out in the main corridors. He had to get between the cars, where he at least had a bit of cover.

He pressed his back against the front grill and pulled at his collar, hoping to get a little more of the hot, stifling air. He'd take the Lexus if he had more time to boost it. His pursuers didn't seem like the patient type. He bolted across the lot, unable to do anything about his heavy footfalls.

The thug scrambled towards him. "Over here."

Janik ducked behind a delivery truck as gunfire pinged off the front fender. Acrid smoke soon replaced the small amount of breathable air. Janik held in the building cough until it passed. He wasn't cut out for this. This wasn't his environment. His was a broom closet office with blacked out windows and candy wrappers littering the floor. He assaulted broken lines of code, not trained killers.

The gunfire stopped. "If you come out now, I promise to only break one of your arms."

Not the best offer he'd received so far today. He was rather fond of *two* working arms. He pulled the gun from behind his back. He didn't want to shoot the nice people threatening to hurt him, but they started it. Somehow, he didn't think a timeout in the corner would help.

Janik laughed, letting his head fall back against the vehicle's bumper. Getting out of here was damn near impossible. Getting out of this whole goddamn mess alive was impossible. He glanced around the corner. The thugs inched their way closer, leading with the cocked pistol and checking around each car. He shifted his gaze in the other direction and spotted the corral.

Freedom was less than a hundred feet away, but it might as well have been a country mile. The second he moved, they'd know. Ah well, he thought. Life's a bitch, then you die.

Janik sprinted from his cover, weaving from car to car until he reached the vehicle corral in the back corner. Thankfully, the apartment keycard also granted him access here.

"Over here!" the searching thug shouted.

Janik managed to open the door of the closest car. He dove inside the cab as gunfire slammed into the wall behind him. The windshield shattered. The side mirror followed it into oblivion. His hands shook so hard he had to force himself to slow down as he entered the ignition code.

He'd never been so happy to hear an engine roar to life. The tires squealed as he slammed the car into gear and hit the accelerator.

Janik hit the exit ramp with a jarring bang. In the rearview camera, he saw the two thugs chasing after him. Twice he went seeking answers and twice someone showed up to take him out. He couldn't trust anyone at this point.

He kept checking behind him as he drove north on Montgomery, trying to figure out what just happened. That had been some next-level mercenary assassin stuff. No one followed him. Who did those goons work for? UN? Consortium? Or someone Janik hadn't seem coming? There seemed to be no shortage of people wanting to get rid of him.

It didn't help that he was in the heart of their territory. No one would bat an eyelash if someone whipped out a gun and shot him. He hung a right on Broadway and headed for the piers. Another place that elicited fond memories. Especially in the summer when all the college girls were studying. It was all from another lifetime. He pulled the car to the back of the lot at the corner of Broadway and Davis. He rested his head back against the seat. His eyes drifted closed.

The images of death hit him immediately. The Promenade, the overpass, Quick Draw, all the way back to Javier. He was the first to die because of Janik's actions, back in the days of Gina Hendrix and Eldridge Row.

What a nightmare.

Of all the questions he had, one pushed to the front. Why wouldn't Kirox help him? It was odd that the trader wouldn't know about a UN op. The only person in the city willing to help him wasn't exactly his best friend and had his own agenda. But what choice did he have?

CHAPTER 13: DINNER PLANS

Serena saw the emerald green spaghetti strapped dress on the bed as soon as she entered the apartment. Matching shoes sat on the floor. A note accompanied it. Felix must've dropped it off before meeting her in the cafeteria.

'I managed to find you something a little more womanly to wear. I hope you like it.' – Felix -

Serena frowned. It wasn't that she didn't like it. The dress was beautiful. Just not her. Not anymore. She pushed away the echo of her mother's voice telling her how pretty she looked in her Carnival dress. The last time she wore anything like it, she'd changed into slacks and plain white blouse as soon as formalities had ended. The Great Quake stole any joy she used to feel.

She showered and reluctantly put on the dress. She ran her hands down across her belly and over her hips. It fit her well, hugging her figure in all the right places to help loosen Felix's tongue. She normally wore her hair in a loose ponytail, but this time, she wrapped it in a bun behind her head. Butterflies fluttered her stomach at the unfamiliar woman in the mirror. It had been a long time since she'd attracted a man's attention. Much to her own design.

Serena hugged her shoulders against the chill of the air conditioning as she went to the elevator. She felt naked. Her hand brushed her upper thigh. Another downside to dresses. No quick access slit up the side.

Serena shuffled through Felix's empty office towards the open door in the back corner. This had to be a test to see how far she'd go. She figured that's why he left Level Six unlocked. *Keep your guard up, Serena.* Felix wasn't some dumb UN criminal. As long as Ivan didn't show up with his gun, she'd be okay.

A high-pitched squeak escaped her throat when Felix materialized in the doorway. Serena fell back, her hand over her racing heart.

"I'm sorry," he said, grinning mischievously. "I thought I heard someone."

Serena brushed aside a wisp of hair, taking a moment to calm the growing heat in her face. "It's my own fault. I should've knocked."

Felix waved his hand dismissively. "It's no trouble. Come in. You look lovely, by the way. Dresses suit you."

She rubbed the back of her neck. The last person to pay her this much attention tried to recruit her into the UN. Harlon's plan had always been for her to trade certain 'favors' for intel on the Consortium. He dumped her to the side like a trash bag when she refused. If Felix tried the same thing, she'd bury her dinner knife into his spleen. "Thank you. Not too many opportunities to wear them in the gutter."

"Of course," Felix replied sheepishly.

The room was nothing like she'd expected. The bluish glow of the artificial lights, dimmed slightly, and the whirr of the climate control fans overhead made it feel like the marshal's academy barracks.

She expected a sprawling, lavish complex. Instead, a bedroom and bathroom on one side and a tiny kitchenette on the other flanked a small common area. Not an ounce of opulence anywhere. The furniture consisted of a cushioned sofa and a small dining table. Not a single item was out of place. Weren't all megalomaniacs supposed to live like kings? "This is cozy."

"I'm a simple person," he replied. "Please, make yourself comfortable."

Bullshit, she thought. And it's my job to strip away the layers to find the truth. I just don't know how I'm going to do it.

Serena shuffled around the apartment, reconning everything. Logan taught her that much. Nothing was a coincidence. Everything had a purpose. She'd always been observant. He just taught her how to focus it. Four deactivated video monitors hung on the left-hand wall. "That's a lot of monitors for such a small apartment."

"I run a large operation. I can't be everywhere at once. This way, I can keep an eye on things. Perhaps I will show you them after dinner."

Felix disappeared into the kitchen and the sound of dishes being arranged came shortly after. Serena tried not to let her growling stomach and the succulent aroma of roasting chicken distract her. She continued searching for anything to use to her advantage. She found nothing.

Felix emerged from the kitchen carrying two glasses of white wine. She accepted one clumsily, sloshing some onto her hand. "Oh gosh, I'm such a klutz."

Felix handed her the towel he had draped over his shoulder. "Don't worry about it."

They sat on the couch and she shied away from his gentle touch on her knee. A slight smile of hurt twitched the corners of his mouth. "It has been a long while since I've felt someone else's touch." She had no time for romantic entanglements. Having someone else to care about only complicated her life and made her vulnerable. "As you can imagine, having to scrounge for your next meal doesn't leave much time for a love life."

Felix set his wine glass on the table next to the sofa. "I didn't mean to be so forward. It has been some time since I've enjoyed real companionship as well."

"I have to be honest, Felix," Serena began cautiously. "I'm more interested in reclaiming my life than pursuing any personal relationships right now. With the power the marshals and the Consortium have, I'd hoped for some help."

Felix retrieved his wine glass and sat back. "They only have power because we give it to them. If we want it back, all we have to do is take it. The shadow networks, the hidden funds, the intimidation exists because we are too scared to fight. I've given the process a small shove."

He made it sound so simple. She tried to take her own power back when she joined Logan's firm, but it was like water slipping through your fingers. She thought she'd use her position as a data analyst to track where the meds were going. She'd had no luck to this point. "Blowing up half the city is a small shove? A dangerous way to get someone's attention, isn't it? What if they retaliate?"

"There is risk in crossing the street. It's unavoidable. Are you familiar with the term Consortium Executive Order? As in a secret group. They're the ones with the real power in the city."

Serena sat up a little straighter. She hadn't expected the conspiracy theories to drop. Was the UN involved and how much did Logan know about it? Not that he'd tell her. He still had plenty of secrets. How many of his clients were legitimate businesspeople? She bit back the flood of questions threatening to burst from her mouth. "Can't say that I have. Who are they?"

"That, my dear, is the million-dollar question." Felix stood. "I believe dinner is ready. Shall we?"

Serena sat at the table as Felix retrieved two plates of golden-brown chicken and steaming vegetables from the kitchen. "As a matter of principle, everything is Non-Synth."

She resisted the urge to tear into the meal with her hands. The sandwich in the cafeteria had been some time ago. "Your principles smell really good."

"Hopefully one day soon, fake food will no longer be

necessary. There's real food outside the San Francisco Zone. I've seen it. There's no reason for it not to be here."

Serena had heard about the Federal Farms on the Old American Mainland. Every time they made overtures to come here, the Sustainers shut them down. People like Bruno only got stuff here because they had contacts outside. "I have to ask. How are you sitting comfortably here when the rest of the city is in darkness?"

"The power for the complex is independent of the city's power grid. We can survive down here for months."

Serena digested the information as she ate. It confirmed her suspicions earlier about the buildings out back. Now she had a few more options for shutting down the attack. "Sounds like you're prepared for the power to be out a long time."

"One can never be too prepared, but it's more than that. I take good care of the people that work for me. Without them, I'm nothing. Any competent leader would think the same. We've had a void in that area since the quake."

Serena set her fork on the side of her plate. She wiped her mouth with the cloth napkin slowly, deliberately, before setting it next to the plate. "May I ask you something?"

"Please do."

"Are you testing me? You're detail-oriented. No way you left this level unlocked by accident. You tell me enough to whet my interest, but hold back the good stuff. Why."

"Perceptive and intelligent," he replied. "I knew there was something I liked about you."

Serena leaned forward. "Did I pass?"

Felix gazed at her over the rim of his wine glass. "You're still alive, aren't you?"

A knock on the door kept her from processing that statement. Felix wiped his mouth and threw his napkin onto the table, nearly knocking over his glass. "Come in."

"Apologies for the disturbance, Mister Nash," the unknown man stammered.

"What is it?" He tapped a finger on the table. "Be quick. I'm in the middle of dinner."

"There has been an assault on the network, sir. Your presence is being requested in the control room."

Felix's jaw tightened. "The marshals are probably trying to crack our firewall again. Have Ivan handle it."

"He sent me for you, sir. He said to tell you this one wasn't from the marshals."

Felix drew in a long breath through his nose. "Is everything else on schedule?"

"Yes sir. We are well into Phase Two. The first packet is ready to be released."

"Very well," Felix replied. "Tell Ivan I will meet him in the control room shortly."

"Of course, Sir." The man backed out of the room.

Serena held back her flood of questions, not wanting to seem too eager. If she played it right, Felix would tell her everything. The 'first packet' reference concerned her. Was it biological? Chemical? Or worse, nuclear? None of that seemed like Felix's style though. Not if saving the city was his goal.

"I apologize for that," he said, returning to his meal, although noticeably more distracted. "Unfortunately, we don't keep normal business hours. Interruptions happen from time to time."

"No problem. Sounds like you're having network troubles."

Felix shrugged. "When you're involved with a group such as this, people are always trying to infiltrate your systems. Our security is not so easily defeated."

"You must have some pretty smart people working for you."

"Smart and motivated. We all believe in the same thing. I happen to have the resources to see it through."

"All of these people have a grudge against the marshals?"

"Not directly, no, but they are sick of the oppression. They're sick of the rich one percent having control over everything. Once you've been here a while, you'll understand. Our fight is about equality. Nothing more."

Equality? If everything were equal, Logan would be here instead of her and she'd still be in her office feeding him intel. She was a goddamn analyst, not a field operative. She held up her wine glass in a toast. "Here's to your- to our success."

Felix topped up their wine glasses, though Serena had been resisting drinking too much. This whole setup was likely intended to loosen her lips to reveal her true intentions. She wet her lips enough so as not to arouse suspicion. It wasn't enough.

"You don't like the wine?" he said.

Serena set her glass down gingerly. "It's not that. I'm not much of a drinker. I don't want to put either of us in a compromising position."

He leaned back in his chair and drank shakily from his wine glass. Redness crept up his neck from beneath his pressed collar. "I'd never do something like that, Olivia. My goal is to help people, not take advantage of them."

Her face heated. "I'm sorry. I didn't mean to imply. This is all new to me. Honestly, I'm not sure how to behave."

"Just relax. You have nothing to fear here."

A ringing communicator in one of Felix's jacket pockets saved her. Checking the caller ID tag, he pushed his chair from the table. "Excuse me for a moment. I have to take this." He disappeared into his office, closing the door behind him.

Serena let out the breath she'd been holding and set the utensils she held in a death grip down on the plate. Her stomach had been in such knots, she was surprised she actually tasted the meal. She stood from the table, holding onto the edge of the polished wood until her wobbly legs stabilized beneath her. Now was her chance to check those monitors. The first one showed the public data stream. Not unusual. Most people were probably following the news closely right now, although they warned they'd be going offline soon due to waning resources.

The second one, a live stream of the city's power centers and water collectors, disturbed her a little more. She'd been under the mistaken assumption that like the power grid the surveillance network was down. Felix had commandeered it. No wonder Logan was in a pissy mood. He'd lost complete control.

Serena checked the office door again before moving to the third monitor. This one showed traffic streams downtown near city hall as well as the marshals' headquarters. Smoke still rose from the metro station, but the others were still intact. For how long, though?

The images on the screen cycled. A small whimper escaped Serena's throat. Nob Hill and the Tenderloin. Her home and neighbors were up there. Regular people that weren't a part of the Consortium. The university was up there along with several community leaders. Why would Felix be watching it? Thankfully, they weren't burning. Yet.

If the locations shown on these cameras were targets, why hadn't he hit them yet? Unless he was waiting for confirmation they were part of this Consortium Executive Group… or whatever he called them.

The last screen showed communication links to the control room, Ivan, and several field teams. Teams for what? Each link had a location tag. Ivan closed in on Land's End and the teams were spread out in several neighborhoods along the northern shore.

She clicked on the link for one of the north shore teams. "We're on location. There's no one here."

"Figures they've all gone into hiding." That was Ivan's voice. "Burn the house and move on to the next one."

Serena turned off the monitor and went to the kitchen for a

glass of water. Her hand shook violently, spilling water down her front. She sipped a little slower the second time, though it didn't help calm her. Felix was just getting started and she had no idea where he was going next. She had to get out of here to warn them. Either that, or find some way to get word to Logan.

"Olivia?" Felix called from the sitting room.

She almost spat water all over the back wall. She coughed and choked, gasping for air. She dragged her arm across her mouth, wiping away the remaining spillage.

Felix appeared at the door and Serena held up the glass of water, offering him a disarming smile. If only she could slow her racing heart. "The wine hit me a little harder than I expected. I hope you don't mind."

Felix smiled. "Of course not."

She pushed past him and retook her seat at the table. She kept her hands in her lap to hide their trembling. "Is everything alright?"

His eyes narrowed. "I'm sorry?"

"I'm assuming that was Ivan. Has he shot anyone over this latest episode?"

Felix laughed. "That wasn't Ivan. Update from a supplier. The power outage is affecting shipping schedules." Felix's gaze lingered on his half-eaten chicken breast, though she doubted his focus was anywhere near the food. That call had nothing to do with shipment schedules. "But you're probably right. I better go find him before he does something foolish. Return to the apartment. I will find you in the morning when perhaps you can become a little more involved."

Serena did return to the apartment, but only to change into more practical clothes. She had to get this information to Logan and try to find out who tried to hack Felix's system. Hopefully, Nelson was around to help her.

CHAPTER 14: ENCOUNTER

Janik yawned into the back of his hand as he pulled out of the parking lot. Clear his name first, then sleep. Hopefully, it wouldn't take all night. The information on the hard drives at home should help, but first, he had to make a detour.

Darkness had completely fallen by the time he crossed into Land's End. Concrete and technology gave way to cypress trees. Houses sat farther apart, reminding Janik of a time before the Great Quake.

He didn't think McIntosh Corp had purchased any properties here, but then again, he wasn't following the real estate listings. Truth be told, none that lived up here could claim total innocence.

He shut off the headlights and guided the car down one of the empty residential streets south of the Nash Industries complex. Many had already fled the city or hunkered down to wait out the disaster. Looters had no interest in residential addresses. They were after the expensive downtown department stores.

Janik activated the tracer script on his tablet again, careful not to set off any alarms. He was a lot closer to the hornet's nest this time around. Whatever was going on definitely centered around Nash Industries and city hall. Now all he had to do was figure out what they were after.

He scrolled across the screen, searching for any small bit of advantage. He stopped over a small router node still transmitting a block to the east. Probably his only shot at unraveling some of the mystery.

Janik kept his head on a swivel as he approached the conduit box tucked into the side of the hill, tablet in hand. The electronic lock normally securing the cover had already been busted and the cover sat askew on the node. Someone had already tampered with it. He wrested the cover off, exposing the equipment beneath.

Janik plugged into an open port and tapped into the data stream. Too bad his decryption program would take too long to go through the files one by one. Part of him didn't want to see what the files contained. He'd gotten his share of the filth working for the McIntoshes.

Janik accessed the utilities by piggybacking on the signal going into the Nash Industries complex. *Time to give you clowns a toothache.* Over near the complex, panic rose. People barked orders. That should buy him enough time to sneak a peek at some of these files.

Janik clicked on one of the files and his eyes bulged a little. Housing contracts? Land deeds? Earthquake readiness? Not exactly the damning evidence he expected. There had to be more to this than real estate. Several more folders scrolled by, mostly government type. There was one called Pharmacy Files, but Janik didn't have time to read it. One thing was certain. Nothing had changed in the five years since he went rogue.

Most of the commotion at the complex had died down. Janik expected a car to be pulling down the street any minute. But he wasn't done just yet. He resisted launching another script that would've dumped all of the encrypted files onto his tablet. He had a better idea. Janik hadn't met a single scriber yet with the skill to defeat his own encryption program. He uploaded the program to Nash Industries network, locking down those city hall files tighter than a Consortium bank account. Whoever wanted those files would pay handsomely to get them back. Janik may have caught his first real break.

He called Renaude. Smoke and dust swirled around Renaude's

head, coating it in a thin layer of grey. He was at one of the bombing sites. "I see you made it out alive."

Janik hesitated. "Barely. Your guard wasn't so lucky though. He died saving my life."

When Renaude spoke, sadness tinged his voice. "Did your hack turn up anything?"

"I pinged a server in Land's End that made some people real upset. How come you didn't tell me about it? Your boys had to have picked it up."

"There was nothing to tell. We couldn't crack its high-level security. How did you manage it?"

Janik hated having to tell Renaude as much as he did. Janik didn't trust him, but right now, Renaude was the only one who could help him. Their little alliance wouldn't last forever though. "I didn't get all the way in. Even with the extra hand from your boys. There's a lot of activity between them and City Hall. I imagine the marshals' secure networks would be a high-valued target as well. You might want to check your servers."

Janik had tried to break into the City Hall servers himself back in the day, before he got into stealing cars. Not the public ones everyone knew about. The juicy stuff was on the shadow servers. The ones with all the dirt on Consortium's shadow network and government officials. The ones that linked right into the Pyramid.

When he first joined the UN, he'd heard rumors of some kind of Consortium shadow council that called the shots on everything. Janik always figured it was a load of crap to drum up sympathy for the UN. The Consortium was definitely corrupt, but a secret council was some next-level conspiracy bullshit. Thinking back on it, some of the things McIntosh Corp had been involved in leant credence to the theory.

"Where are you now?"

"An area node up near Nash Industries that they're using to funnel the data."

"Are you able to access it?'"

Janik clenched his jaw. He hated admitting failure. It wasn't in his nature. "Unfortunately no. Everything is encrypted. It'd take more time than I have to unlock the files. The thugs are probably already onto me. I did manage to stir up some excitement at Nash Industries though."

"The whole city's infrastructure is on those servers."

"Already working on it. What do you know about it? Who is Nash Industries? Don't lie to me, Renaude."

Renaude moved away from the commotion behind him. Now, Janik didn't have to watch firefighters pull mangled bodies from the rubble. "A corporation owned by Felix Nash, an earthquake freak who thinks he can save us from the next big one."

"Assuming he's the one behind this, if he's trying to save the city, why is trying to tear it down first?" That sounded like something out of the UN's playbook, but Janik hadn't heard Felix's name come up from any of his contacts, and as far as he knew, Felix had no connection to Gina Hendrix or any of that business from five years ago. "No doubt your friends in the Pyramid have checked him out. What are they saying? Who's he in business with? He can't be doing this on his own."

Janik hoped to God the connection didn't tie back to Patricia. Her marrying a McIntosh was bad enough. He'd almost ended up in a similar spot with Stephen's sister. A fleeting romance that would've spiced up the family dinners, that's for sure.

"If they have, they haven't passed that information onto me. Those conversations are above my pay grade. Our people are working on a file now."

Either Renaude was lying, or this Felix Nash wasn't associated with the Consortium or the UN, and that made no sense at all. "A little suspicious, don't you think."

"He is a person of interest. As I said, the security is high. They're blocking everything we throw at them. I'm surprised you had problems though?"

Janik laughed at the implication. "Give me a break, Renaude. You sound like your vocal chords are stuck on repeat. You should have that checked out. I recall asking you earlier for the Promenade footage. It's a condition of our arrangement."

"I'm still working on it. You have more pressing matters like the power and the city hall servers."

Renaude was stalling. He didn't want to give Janik the footage to exonerate him. "Work harder, Renaude. I've encrypted those files with my own special brand. The footage in exchange for the decryption key. Make it happen."

"I warned you about double-crossing me, Janik."

"I'm not double-crossing you. Let's call it an insurance policy. Now we both have something the other wants."

"I'll get you the damn footage. Hurry up and fix my city."

Janik held back perhaps the most important reason for wanting the Promenade footage. He remembered almost nothing about it. He didn't care what Renaude said. His malfunctioning memory wasn't from being outside all night.

He had vague memories of growing up, but not the neighborhoods in which he'd grown. The way things were going, he was lucky he remembered Patricia and her family. Maybe he should go see them. *They'd likely shoot me on sight.*

First things first. Stop the attack, then go see his sister. Perhaps if he proved he saved the city she'd let him leave still breathing. Now he had a name to work with. Soon he'd have a face and other pieces to fill in the blanks.

"Whatever they're doing, they're not done. They also mentioned a guy named Ivan. Sounds like he's calling the shots. Ring any bells?"

Renaude shook his head. "Names rarely do. The reports might say something about him. Did they say anything else?"

"No, but they found me fast, which means they were already

close by. Whatever they're doing is in the Financial District. I'm surprised your people haven't clued in that certain neighborhoods up there still have power. Someone should check on your Consortium benefactors."

"They'll have to get by on their own for a while. We're still rescuing bombing victims. You need to work faster, Janik. Before they have our whole city held for ransom."

"Little late for that, I think. I'll be in touch."

Janik closed up the conduit box, the hard part done. He jogged back to the car to drop off his gear. If he was smart, he'd drive away, go home where it was safe. But home wasn't where his evidence was.

That brought him back to Renaude. Why risk everything keeping a thief he hated above all others happy? They were all working to restore the power. So why short circuit his handlers to do it? What meant more to Renaude than Janik in a prison cell? Janik squeezed his eyes shut against the confusion. Piecing together the rest of this story would be a nightmare.

He crept his way to a copse of trees a short distance from the complex's western entrance. He counted a dozen of the sec officers Renaude mentioned. Who knew how many more were inside? Ringing the doorbell might be somewhat of a challenge.

If they were smart, and Janik had little doubt they were, they'd have sensor nets and other countermeasures buried in the ground. Activating one of those would definitely add some excitement to his day.

A sec officer started toward him, carrying a high-powered assault rifle. Fed Sec mercenaries carried similar weapons. He'd want to avoid the business end of that. He pressed his back tight against a wide cypress and held his breath as he checked the path behind him. In the failing light, the path's terrain had become treacherous. *I'm either going to break an ankle or end up shot. Or end up shot after breaking an ankle...*

Janik eased away from the tree while the sec officer swept his flashlight across the ground. Janik would have to chance the long way through the thick brush. His stomach clenched when his foot snapped a dry twig.

"Hey," the officer shouted and sent a burst of rifle fire zipping past his head. "Contact rear," he called into his radio. "Single subject. In pursuit."

Janik slipped on a wet patch of earth sprinting for the tree line. Pain exploded in his rolled ankle, echoed by pain in his knee as it slammed off a jutting rock. The sec officer hovered over him, rifle barrel aimed at his forehead. "Sorry, buddy. Didn't think anyone else was back here."

The officer pulled him roughly to his feet and punched him hard in the ribs. "What are you doing back here?"

Janik growled through clenched teeth. That was going to leave a mark. "Hiding. Got interrupted trying to acquire a new ride, if you catch my meaning."

"You're a scumbag car thief?"

"Hey, now. Sounds bad when you put it that way. I'm just taking advantage of the current climate, so to speak. These Consortium clowns can afford it."

The thug's communicator squawked. "Intruder alert. Intruder alert. Initiate full sweep protocols."

The sec officer looked at him with a mixture of shock and suspicion. "Is that you? Did you set off those alarms?"

"I'm a car thief, not a Consortium hacker," Janik replied. "Never really got the hang of computers."

"Filthy thief and a liar. Ivan can figure out what to do with you. Let's go."

Janik couldn't let him take him inside. It had been stupid to come here. *Why didn't I go straight home?* As the guard shifted to one side to let him pass, Janik stumbled forward feigning a trip and punched him in the face. Both went down hard, struggling for the rifle. Janik managed to wrap his hand around the grip and pulled the trigger without thinking. The gun bucked and danced, spraying bullets all over the place. The sec officer convulsed momentarily and went limp.

Janik wheezed and then threw up. He'd never killed anyone before. That's not how he operated. He'd seen it done. Working with Kirox had its disadvantages, but he was a computer nerd, not a murderer. Blood dripped down his face. *I had no choice*, he told himself. *They were going to kill me.* Janik tried to push the dead man's face from his mind as he ran back through the trees towards Veteran's Drive and his escape car.

CHAPTER 15: UNRAVELING

Ivan entered the control room seconds before his boss. Felix's neck practically glowed a bright red above his pressed collar and his nostrils flared. He was a geyser about to go off. Ivan had to regain control of this situation. A commander that let emotion drive their actions usually made mistakes. Ivan's tactical brain hated mistakes.

"Update." Felix kept his voice even, but it held a razor's edge.

Ivan stood outside of Felix's considerable reach. "Someone infiltrated our utilities. They set off a bunch of alarms. Nothing we can't handle."

"Was it the marshals?"

"I don't know yet. Your scribers are still tracking its source. The attackers threw up a bunch of roadblocks. The marshals will likely take advantage of our vulnerability though. A direct assault would be damaging."

"We have provisions, but it won't matter. The hammer of change has already fallen. There is nothing they can do. That idiot McIntosh this morning in the Promenade was just the first. Their whole world is about to come crashing down around them. They are too stupid to realize the bombings are nothing more than a distraction. Once I decrypt the files and the Consortium Executive Order is dead, people here will realize how much they've been fooled."

"Yeah, your little revolution is all great. As long as I'm paid on time. I know a nice little beach in the middle of nowhere with my name on it."

Felix sneered at him a little bit. "You have no worries about that. The Consortium has no idea they're financing their own downfall. Tell me about the utilities."

"The marshals have everything locked down, but there is nothing they can do. Their guns are useless with no one to shoot at."

Felix stroked his chin. Stubble on his cheeks had joined the thick goatee. "Our assets are protected?"

"The marshals don't even know they're there. Of course, the marshals wouldn't be a problem if their facilities had been destroyed as planned. We only managed to trap a fraction of them in the subway tunnels. What happened to the subject tasked with taking out the marshal's building?"

"Thank one of the doctor's failed experiments for that," Felix replied. "By the time we realized the upload to the brain didn't take, it was too late for a second attempt. The marshals will have to be dealt with the same way as the Consortium Executive Order."

Ivan took a deep breath, feeling the rug come more unraveled. This was what usually happened when non-military people led military ops. The whole mind programming thing was an unexpected wildcard. He liked things under control. He couldn't control this. "Yet more deviation from the plan."

"Every great venture has setbacks. We have adjusted well."

"We've traced the source of the hack to an area node not far from here, sir," one of the techies announced. "The data download is streaming directly through it."

The red in Felix's neck deepened. "Why wasn't someone watching it?"

Ivan counted to five in his head and pulled in a deep breath. How much longer did he have to suffer this idiot? "There are a lot of nodes, Felix. We're not an army. We can't be everywhere. I had no idea the data was coming through that one or it would've been guarded."

"It's probably the same one from the Financial District," Felix spat. "He's here. I thought you said you had him cornered."

"I sent a team to deal with him after he tried to hack our network the first time. They lost him in the parking garage."

"I thought your men were professionals. I'm paying them enough to be."

The techie spun his chair to face them. "With respect, you two should know something. If this guy is who I think it is, you have a big problem."

"What are you talking about?" Felix demanded. "Elaborate."

"His name is Janik Brynn, also known as Scriber. He's the best car thief in the city and an even better code scriber. A lot of these algorithms are his. The only reason he didn't gain access is because I know his work. We've put up enough roadblocks to slow him down. Eventually though, if you don't eliminate him, he'll wreck your whole setup."

"How do you know this?" Felix demanded. "And if he's so good, why isn't he working for me?"

"If you're anywhere near this business you've heard of Scriber. We've had run-ins with him back when he worked for McIntosh Corp. You should look up the name Gina Hendrix. Her and Janik had more than one run-in when she was around. She's practically the reason the Consortium exists. We're pretty sure Scriber's accessed sensitive information from just about every major player in this city. What you did to McIntosh this morning with the bomb, he did it five years ago with a laptop. He's the reason behind much of the security that's in place now. Hell, the Consortium trained him. I don't know why he's not working for you, sir."

"How come your UN contact didn't tell you any of this?" Ivan demanded. "We used him as bait when he could've had this whole network shut down and your data decrypted by now."

Felix's neck was bright red and he trembled visibly. "You can be sure I'll ask him. It'll be the last time he ever speaks."

Ivan laid a hand on Felix's arm. "We're mission critical here. This guy is a grenade with the pin pulled. He'll leave us in a smoking crater unless we deal with it."

"There's another problem, sir," the tech said. "He's added another level of encryption to the files. We can't crack it without his codes and the device he used."

Felix screamed and tore at his hair. He'd have thrown a chair if one was near. There was the meltdown Ivan expected. He had to find some way to calm this simmering volcano. "You better decrypt those files," Ivan told the techie. "For your own sake."

"Yes sir. On it."

Outside the control room, Felix rounded on him. "Find him and bring him to me, Ivan. Alive. Without those files I can't expose the Consortium or access the money you so covet."

Ivan keyed a button on his communicator. "Intruder alert. Intruder alert. Initiate full sweep protocols."

The communicator crackled again. "Shots fired. Shots fired. Southwest sector. Units responding."

Felix glared at him. "How hard can it be to catch one unarmed thief?"

"Stay here," Ivan told him. "I'll deal with this."

"No," Felix replied. "I'm going to wring the decryption codes from him, and then I'm going to put a bullet in his skull."

Ivan huffed, but didn't argue. It would've been pointless. He really wished Felix would get out of the way and let him do his job.

The commotion had died down by the time they reached ground level. The techies in the control room had gotten the alarms turned off and the lights to stay on. Ivan pointed at three sec officers standing off to the side. "You three, with me. If

Mister Nash so much as gets a splinter, I'll kill you."

They found the location of the disturbance behind the complex with little difficulty. Two sec officers surrounded their fallen comrade. Anger creased their chiseled jaws. "He was already dead when we found him, sir. Footprints lead through the woods out back."

Ivan's own anger rose. He didn't pick just anyone for these jobs. He only used guys he knew, guys he trusted. It was like losing a family member. "Go. Find out where he went. Don't kill him. We need him alive."

"How did a single thief overcome one of your expert mercenaries, Ivan?" Felix demanded.

"He's obviously more capable than we anticipated."

"Or he had help," the remaining sec officer finished.

Ivan's hands clenched as he shook his head. "I suggest you make another call to your UN friend, Felix." One loose thread had the potential to unravel the whole damn rug. Ivan indicated to the men around the body. "Deal with him, then search every inch of these grounds. I want every door in this place watched. Report anything, and I mean anything out of the ordinary."

The sec officer returned, sweat coating his face. "He's gone, sir. He must've had a car stashed somewhere behind the complex."

"We can use the traffic cams to track him," Felix said. "He can't have gone far."

Ivan escorted Felix back towards the complex, holding his tongue until after they were out of earshot of the sec officer. "How did this thief survive in the first place? I thought the procedure was supposed to be foolproof."

"An unreliable process. Sloppy work from the doctor. I've been assured it won't happen again."

"We should kill the incompetent fool. He has fulfilled his part. We have enough soldiers. Once your Consortium Order is eliminated, their usefulness is over."

"No. I have grand visions for this program and others he was involved with."

Ivan didn't like the sound of that. "Such as?"

Felix grinned broadly. "Imagine an assassin who had no memory of the mission after carrying it out. Even with the amount of surveillance in this city, there'd be no way to implicate you. It's the perfect failsafe."

"That's why you have me."

"Everyone has a price, Ivan, even the most loyal. Remember that should you be approached. Besides, your role in this operation was only ever meant to be temporary. Once you are paid, your contract will be at an end."

Ivan cringed, but having his loyalty questioned was the least of his problems. "I don't like any of this, Felix. First the girl, now the doctor and the thief. There are too many variables."

Felix waved his hand, dismissing his concern. "Don't worry about the girl. I have her under control. Dispose of the thief once he has decrypted the files."

"You have her under control for now. What happens if she bolts? What happens if she's not who she says she is? What if she's working with the thief?"

"There is nothing anyone can do now. If she's involved with the Consortium, she may have information the files don't. We can use her connections against them. That organization will burn for the way they treated my family."

Ivan couldn't believe Felix was actually defending a woman he'd met less than twelve hours ago. "Hand her over to me. I'll find out what she knows."

"I said I have her under control." Felix's expression softened a second later. "You can't solve every problem with violence. In certain occasions, finesse is required. By the time I'm finished with her she'll tell me everything willingly. You have other tasks to complete."

They didn't have time for finesse. If she were hiding something, he'd find out. Then he'd enjoy what happened next. "Understand, Felix, I'm not trying to defy you, but you have to trust me. You have a goal. I have the operational knowledge to make it happen. Let me do my job."

"She's from the Mission District. Ask around. She's not at all enamored with the UN. I'll have to deal with that lot sooner or later as well."

"I'll take care of it."

"Make it quick. We are in a delicate phase. The transfer isn't finished yet. Further delays affect the schedule. Everything must be in place when resources start to run out. Desperate people are much easier to control."

"My teams are ready to move when you give the order."

They were almost back to the complex when Ivan's communicator chirped. "What is it?"

"Sir, calls coming in from the Financial District. Our teams are taking fire from some kind of private security force. Casualties reported."

"Goddammit," he bellowed. What else could go wrong today?

"I should've expected the Consortium to not rely wholly on the marshals for their protection," Felix said. "They're nothing but a bunch of cowards."

"There's more, sir. The warehouses you put tabs on are being looted. These guys look like pros though."

"Sounds like your UN friends are taking advantage of the situation."

"That wasn't part of the deal. I will handle this one personally."

"What do you want me to do about the Financial District?"

"Give them something to draw their attention. Keep them occupied." Felix grinned at him. "Level their fortress and release the first media packet. It's time for the citizens to see whose thumb they've been living under." Felix handed him a data wafer. "Here is the first batch of names. They are not the Consortium Executive Order, but it is a start. You know what to do."

CHAPTER 16: LOOSE CONNECTION

Renaude leaned against his police vehicle for a brief respite. He rubbed his aching knee, wincing at the throbbing, constant agony. Sweat poured down the side of his face. With everything going on, and in his haste, he left his pills at the office. He had no idea when he'd get back there to retrieve them.

He surveyed the scene around him one more time. It was a chaos of burning rubble and rescuers running around shouting orders. Another three ambulances screamed away from the scene, sirens blaring. It seemed a steady stream. If the hospitals weren't overrun before, they would be soon. Even with the number of survivors found, the hospitals wouldn't be as busy as the morgues.

Renaude stayed back, letting his field commander work. Renaude wasn't really needed here. His job was in the command center overseeing the whole operation, but he couldn't stay in that claustrophobic room any longer, feeling useless. He had to get out into the field, right in the middle of the action, like he used to when he was a spry new marshal. Back when walking didn't hurt.

That thought brought him back to Janik. The little bastard had made progress, but it wasn't happening fast enough. Renaude needed him to figure out what was happening so he could return to his medical research. Janik had no proof but guessed Renaude had volunteered him for the program without his knowledge. The procedure should've killed him. A little detail he'd have to reconcile sooner or later.

His secure comms link chirped in his ear. At least the terrorists hadn't been able to hack that network yet. Consortium tech really was the best on the market, even if they had to sell their souls to get it. He moved away from the noise of the rescue operations going on behind him. "Go for Renaude."

"Mayor Waters for you, Sir. Standby."

Goddamn it. Couldn't he escape that insufferable woman for a little while? She was like a rash no salve could eradicate.

"Where are you, Renaude?" Her shrill voice stabbed his ear like a dagger.

"Madam mayor," he said through gritted teeth. "How nice to hear your voice again. I'm at the overpass bombing site. I felt the rescuers would benefit from my presence here and I needed to see the damage for myself."

There was a short intake of breath and a pause on the other end of the line. "What's it like down there?"

"Living hell, Madam Mayor. It's like a living hell."

"I need you back at the office, Renaude. We're initiating evacuation plans, and I need real time updates on the situation."

Initiating evacuations now would only stretch already thin resources thinner. Halting the attack quickly should be their focus. On the other hand, if he let her run with it, she'd be out of his hair. "I'll be back in a little while, Madam Mayor. I'm following up on a couple of leads that I will fill you in on later."

"You have teams for that, Renaude. You're not a field marshal anymore."

She had no idea how much of an insult that was. His physical limitations were a constant dagger twisting every time he tried to push himself. The mayor's constant reminders only added to the pain.

Renaude pushed the self-loathing aside and focused once again on the current conversation. Should he tell the mayor about the data breach inside City Hall? No, he'd keep it to himself for now. If there was a mole inside the government, it could tip them off. "I need to handle this personally, Mayor. I will be in touch." He killed the link as she launched into another diatribe.

Renaude called the Ops center and thankfully, Frank answered. "Frank, I need the cyber guys to check our servers, and get them looking at city hall too. This is priority one. I'll be in the Nob Hill if you need me."

Renaude hung up and grabbed two marshals carrying assault rifles. "You two, with me. We're going on a field trip."

"Sir? We're supposed to be working perimeter security."

"I'm changing your orders. Get in the car."

The two marshals exchanged apprehensive glances but complied with the order.

Renaude sped north on Van Ness toward Nob Hill. At least most people were smart enough to stay off the roads. Darkness enveloped everything. None of the streetlights worked and all the high rises were dark. Until he crossed into the Nob Hill.

Several buildings had lights on, but the glow was muted by thick smoke hanging in the air. It resembled a thick fog rolling in off the bay, but this one stank of death and destruction.

They weren't the only vehicle on the road and gunshots rang out in the distance. Renaude knew people who lived up here. He rubbed elbows with them at some public event or another. They didn't take kindly to aggressors causing trouble at their homes. He turned east on Broadway toward the thickest of fire and smoke. There were no fire rescue crews up here yet. They were all still down at the overpass.

Renaude pulled over to the side of the street, a scary realization dawning on him. Maybe that was the whole point of all the bombings. Keep emergency services busy while they execute an attack in a completely different part of the city.s

Everything Janik said was true.

His communicator chirped again. "Go for Renaude."

"Chief marshal, it's Frank. We checked into the servers like you asked. I don't know how you knew, sir, but everything's being downloaded, and the drives wiped clean. We can't stop it."

"What if you cut the power?"

"We do that, sir, and we lose everything. We'd be sitting ducks."

They were that anyway, but he took Frank's point. They had no choice but to keep the power on. "Can you tell what they're getting?"

"A lot of stuff from the Department of Housing, sir. More besides from the Department of Infrastructure and City Planning."

Renaude wracked his brain trying to remember if anyone from those departments lived up here. It was possible, but nothing came to him at the moment. "Find out if any of those people live in Nob Hill or close by. And tell the geeks to search the names Felix Nash and Nash Industries. Let me know what you find."

"Will do, sir. Frank out."

Renaude turned south again. He thought it was onto Hyde Street, but with the smoke, he couldn't be sure. If he thought the overpass was a war zone, this was the apocalypse. Glass and twisted metal littered the street. Everything burned. Cars, houses, even parts of the street itself. Renaude found another patrol unit holding a defensive position in a plaza on the edge of the neighborhood. "What's happening here?"

One of the marshals left his observation post and came back to Renaude. He drank deeply from a water bottle before speaking. "Looters, sir. Going house to house and torching what they can't steal."

"That makes no sense," Renaude replied. "Looters usually hit department stores and expensive boutiques."

"Yes, sir. Maybe they think there's too much going on downtown right now."

Fair point, but something still didn't add up. Looters were

opportunists, taking advantage of situations to get in and get out. They didn't waste time shooting things and setting fires. It presented another question. Who were they shooting at? Renaude hadn't sent any other units up here. It had to be that idiot Logan Marks, sticking his nose where it didn't belong. "Alright, we're going to check this out."

"Sir, there are only five of us and we counted at least fifteen. There's probably more."

"I hear you, Sergeant. We're strictly reconnaissance. If things heat up, we pull back to a defensible position."

They crept along the street with Renaude in the lead, and the others flanked out to either side of him. They kept to the darkness the best they could, but patches of light still exposed them occasionally. They used parked vehicles for cover where available.

Up ahead, several apartments burned. Nothing was savable, even if there were fire resources available, they were already too far gone.

They continued up the street and Renaude caught his first sight of movement. He raised his fist, halting their advance, and motioned for them to take cover behind a truck. He pointed at one of the marshals he'd brought with him. "You're with me. The rest of you wait here."

They went from vehicle to vehicle until they spotted heavily armed mercenaries going from house to house in well-organized teams, torching as they went. They made no moves to actually enter the homes.

Muzzle flashes pierced the darkness as they engaged another unknown force on the far end of the street. "Safe to say these aren't your run-of-the-mill looters."

Nothing marked them as working for Felix Nash, but it was clear the explosions and the cyber attack were connected. But what was the endgame? What was Felix after? Renaude needed to find out what data he was stealing for that answer.

There was one other route Renaude could take. Logan would have information on Felix, but Renaude hated dealing with that heartless man. Logan didn't care about the city the way Renaude did. The former Fed Sec operator was a shoot first, ask questions later kind of guy.

"How do you want to play this, sir?"

"We're severely outgunned. There isn't much we can do. We'll retreat and send in the heavy artillery. They're equipped to handle situations like this."

"What if there are people in those houses, sir? We can't just leave them."

"If I know the type of people who live in those houses, they've already moved their families into hiding. These mercenaries are wasting their time and their bullets. If there are people there, then I'm sorry to say, they're on their own for now. Let's go, before our own luck runs out."

Renaude went to stand, but his knee buckled, and he collapsed hard into a pile of trash bins next to the curb. He pulled his head down against his shoulders as the bins went crashing down the street.

Seconds later, the bullets flew.

His companion returned fire as he helped Renaude limp to his feet. Renaude doubted he hit anything, but it didn't matter. It bought them enough time to get away.

They were almost back to the others when his companion went down with a grunt. Renaude went back to him as projectiles flew overhead. He'd taken three rounds in the back and was already dead.

Renaude grabbed him under the arms and tried to pull his fallen comrade back to cover. His damaged and weakened knee wouldn't allow him to find purchase. *Goddamn you, Janik. When this is all over, I'm going to choke the life out of you personally.*

Renaude let his hand rest on the marshal's back for a moment.

Car windows exploded around him, high-velocity rounds pierced sheet metal. He hated leaving a fallen comrade behind, but he was dead too if he stayed here.

Keeping his head low, he darted back to the others. "Fall back. Find a defensible position and take cover."

"What about Pepe?" one asked.

"He's dead. I'm sorry." Renaude bolted past him and back to his waiting vehicle.

CHAPTER 17: LEADS

The first thing Janik did when he got home was strap ice packs to his bruised ribs. Then, he poured himself a drink. He grabbed the half a plate of beef Pad Thai left over from his dinner last night and brought it to the couch in the sitting room.

Janik sat on the couch, motionless. Breathing, the only energy he spent. These few minutes here of not being beaten, chased, or having electrified batons jabbed into his kidney were paradise.

Closing his eyes, he pictured himself next to Gina on a beach sipping a cocktail, or better still, in a mountain cabin sitting in front of a roaring fire.

That name. Gina… Something. It meant something to him, but he couldn't remember what, or where he knew it from. From his past, for sure. But when? Everything that came to him now was more feeling than memory. An empty feeling took his stomach, and tears spilled from his eyes. What if he never remembered?

He opened his eyes and struggled to sit up. He still had too many unanswered questions and now, the bad guys knew he was alive. He devoured the Pad Thai cold as he trudged up to his office. A heated meal was a luxury he didn't have time for.

The encrypted hard drives came out of the briefcase and plugged into his laptop. He hoped the data shed some light on this whole mess. His memory was behaving like a loose connection in a circuit board, or worse yet, a corrupted file. What data he could remember, he couldn't trust.

As Janik clicked on files and folders, things started to come back to him. There were still gaps, but he had rough big picture to go on. Gina was a girl, a fellow hacker who Bill McIntosh had Janik chasing. Over the course of their electronic sparring, Janik collected all sorts of data on Bill McIntosh and those he'd paid off. And he'd fallen in love with Gina.

A lot of this data came from Gina the night she'd died. He'd been sitting on it for a long time, unsure of what to do. Releasing it to the world would've made life very uncomfortable for Patricia.

Janik didn't have a choice now. He had to prove he didn't kill those kids. He opened a few files he'd downloaded from McIntosh Corp. Those low-life scum were slimy enough to drive a plot that killed kids.

None of these files targeted Nash Industries. They targeted GenPulse, one of McIntosh Corp's chief competitors. They had as many medical shops and pharmacy services as anyone and used their clout to undercut everyone else. From what Janik had heard, they weren't hesitant to have someone whacked if it suited their purpose. Probably explained why Heir McIntosh always had an armed protection detail around.

The McIntoshes were trying to leverage Genpulse at the time. It's why he was stealing their files. They all had one hand in the same cookie jar while the other held a stabbing dagger. They were all glorified mobsters fighting over the same turf.

Hospital and private clinic contracts, research contracts, pharmaceutical contracts. Even some defense contracts. Everyone wanted a piece of a very small pie. He hadn't expected Gina to come into his life and turn everything upside down. He'll never forget her terrified face and the blood pouring from her chest as she died in his arms. Or, that he was the one who caused it.

Janik needed to figure out how it all connected to the crazies in Land's End. If these files were to be believed, there were a bunch of shadow servers suggesting the existence of a secret network used to funnel money and other resources. The Consortium Executive Order, the McIntoshes called it. Janik's job when he worked for them had been to trace the money to see where it all went. McIntosh wanted in and never got an invitation.

He opened several video files of Eldridge Row exchanging data wafers with various people, including government types. McIntosh Corp had moles all over the city feeding them information. He wondered if those wafers contained names of members of this secret network. Where were those wafers now? He'd ask Eldridge himself if the man hadn't died in the same confrontation that killed Gina. Maybe that weasel Stephen knew but going to see him meant implicating Patricia.

Felix Nash had to be looking for these shadow servers and the money. Stealing everything wasn't very smart though. It'd take years to filter through it all to find the juicy stuff. Another potential advantage to exploit. Either Felix or the McIntoshes would tell him anything in exchange for this information. Not to mention others equally as eager to never let it see the light of day. There'd be some uncomfortable questions for a lot of people.

Janik clicked on another file that caught his eye. Cerebral Impulse Transplant. That sounded an awful lot like memory manipulation. Janik scanned the small amount of available information. Experimental treatment to repair or restart a brain that had suffered a catastrophic brain injury, often by implanting the synapses of another subject. Promising research, but inconsistent results. Program recommended for decommission.

Janik sat back in his chair for a minute and sipped his drink. He remembered Gina saying something about having a specific goal in mind. Something that would make a lot of people unhappy. Janik wondered if this was it. Five years was a long time to try to remember details. Especially since he'd spent those five years trying to forget.

Another attached video showed several people in immense pain, many not surviving to the end of the experiment. Those were the lucky ones. Others roamed the rooms in a fog or were driven insane by the pain.

Was this what happened to him? It might explain why he remembered an explosion that hadn't happened. When and how though? He couldn't remember anything clearly after the ride in the back of a prison transp- *Son-of-a-bitch. Renaude.* The prisoner transport crash had been a set up all along. He'd been trying to end Janik for years. Janik had been gassed and dumped in a lab with scrambled eggs for brains. No wonder Renaude was pushing him to resolve this off the books.

Janik doubted they ever intended him to survive the procedure. Nothing to tie it back to Renaude that way. Janik still wasn't convinced he had survived. He probably wasn't the only prisoner transport victim to end up at the Sutro Baths. They'd just done a better job of disposing of the other bodies. McIntosh Corp had their own little test subject supply line.

It was public record that the esteemed chief marshal suffered from some sort of mental malady. Janik wondered if it linked to that cerebral impulse transplant thingy. A search of his hard drives yielded no mention of Renaude, or any other names associated with the program. No files or names associated with the program.

Janik's stomach dropped at the sight of a familiar face on one of the photos that did pop up. Bigshot Bill exchanged a data wafer with a mystery man. Janik tapped into the news streams again and searched the name Felix Nash. The face came back a match to the one accepting the data wafer earlier. Bill McIntosh gave Nash Industries the data on Cerebral Impulse Transplant and they used it against him. Karma was a bitch.

He needed to access McIntosh Corps current files, but how the hell was he going to accomplish that? Going to their offices was pointless. They'd have the data locked down like everyone else. Never mind that it meant leaving the safety of his house again. All this imminent danger stuff was bad for his complexion.

There were rumblings of a secret server farm where all the big Consortium corporations store their sensitive data, included those on the fabled Consortium Executive Order. Janik grinned when it clicked. Felix was a man after his own heart. Felix wasn't stealing all of the data. He was forcing the Consortium out of hiding, forcing them to reveal their corrupt network. His head start likely put him much closer to finding that server than Janik. There was a last resort for him to catch up. A trip he didn't want to make. Unless…

Janik tapped a few buttons on his laptop. The Financial District still had power and several of their servers were being pinged like crazy. Rich and corrupt executives still trying to access their money, but unable to do so. Payoffs, most likely. He shifted his search towards the northern shore and the headquarters of Brynn AI Solutions. As expected, their servers were locked out. He tried old access codes on the off chance they'd still work but no luck. Patricia had completely wiped him from their systems.

This exercise didn't tell him which server held the pot of gold. Only the district. As soon as he started poking around, they'd find him. If he removed his encryption, he'd lose his advantage. No matter what he did, he put himself in danger. Janik clutched his head in his hands. He couldn't keep going like this. He was heading full steam ahead towards a full mental breakdown.

He drew in a deep breath. His scrambled brain was making him act dumb. He had to slow down and attack the problem one bit at a time. Everything was connected. He only had to uncover the path. He had to go from 'Janik the Car Thief' to 'Janik the Code Scriber' and take another crack at the city's network. From here, he had more options for defense and counterattack in the eventuality he was discovered.

He started with the prisoner transport. San Francisco Corrections, a division of the Hall of Justice ran them. There should be some evidence of who ordered the transports and where the rest of the prisoners ended up.

Janik launched his phantom network. It wasn't impervious, but it'd buy enough time to poke around. After ten minutes of coming up empty Janik slammed his hand down on the desk. He was completely locked out of the servers.

Something was way off here. The Consortium had top of the line tech and protections, making it damn near impossible to crack their network. Janik should know. He'd tried several times. Felix had to have someone on the inside. There weren't too many scribers around better than Janik. Not since Gina. Unless there was a new kid on the block.

Janik cycled through several other files on his encrypted hard drives, searching for any familiar face. Nothing. He let out a sigh of relief that Patricia nor anyone else from his family popped up in the compromising images.

He'd have to go down there. Linking directly into the Hall of Justice was the only way to see those transport logs without exposing himself to further retaliation. The longer he stayed off the grid, the better.

Janik sat back and linked his hands behind his head. He knew what he had to do. It'd be about as enjoyable as a night in one of Renaude's cells. In fact, he'd probably pick the cell. Unfortunately, his answers weren't in a cell.

The one thing Janik had going for him was leverage. He figured Stephen would help him just to recover the data on these hard drives. He left his office for his bedroom. His pounding head stole his focus. Nothing a few hours sleep couldn't cure. That was until his perimeter alarm went off.

CHAPTER 18: IMPRESSIONS

Serena exited the elevator at the ground floor, moving quickly, but methodically. She couldn't afford any more impulsive decisions that usually led to mistakes. *I'm lucky to have escaped my last ones.*

The commotion with the alarms provided the perfect opportunity to slip away. Felix and Ivan would be hours dealing with the mess. She shivered as she inched her way across the parking lot, past the west wing beyond the street lamps, and into the trees. A faint orange glow hanging on the western horizon over Point Lobos was all that remained of the daylight.

She would've preferred to go to Level Two. Difficult without proper access. Patience, she told herself. *Prove to Felix you can be trusted first.*

Felix was intelligent. He dealt with threats as they appeared. Right now, he didn't perceive her as a threat. Serena wasn't stupid either. Felix had to have suspected her of something, which meant he was playing her. Probably had something to do with this Consortium Executive Order he mentioned. He'd be disappointed though. She knew nothing about it.

Ivan worried her the most. He'd have killed her already if Felix had let him. He might regardless. Forgiveness was easier to obtain than permission. With her mother it was anyway. Their battles had been ones for the ages, but her mother had always been there to lend a shoulder. She'd give anything for that now.

Part of her wondered if Felix's fight for change was necessary.

The Mission District still needed help. For that to work though, she'd have to stop the UN from taking advantage of the people there.

Movement to the right caught her eye. An unknown, yet familiar man in a torn and dirty suit crept from the bushes towards the back of the complex. She tracked him as he half-decently tried to stay hidden. Her jaw dropped. It was the thief everyone thought responsible for the attacks. He looked pretty good for a dead guy.

His presence here made no sense. Was he working for Felix? The reports said he was arrested at the Promenade. No evidence had been released actually proving he planted the device. Wrong place, wrong time perhaps?

He circled the complex, searching for a way inside. Not the actions of someone working on the inside. The news said he had ties to the UN. Maybe Logan's assertion that they were moving to shut down the Consortium had merit.

One of Felix's sec officers intercepted him and bloodied him up a bit. The two struggled on the ground and the gun went off. Serena dived to the ground as bullets sailed over her head. The struggle ended with the sec officer dead, and the thief stumbling back through the woods.

She shouldn't be surprised. Murder wasn't much of a step up from stealing cars. Serena set aside her disgust temporarily. He probably hacked the network earlier. *What did you find?*

Serena followed him as he staggered to a car parked on a side street not far from her downed transport. She detoured to the crash site only to find it abandoned. It figured that Logan would leave her in the middle of hostile territory alone. She did find a pistol and a communicator on her jump seat. Better than nothing. She keyed in Logan's number, his face flickering onto the small screen seconds later.

"Where are you?" he demanded frantically. "You were

supposed to check in hours ago."

"I'm following the thief from the news. He showed up at Land's End."

"The dead one? What happened? Were you made?"

"In a manner of speaking. The thief hacked into the complex's systems. He took a beating for his efforts though. I really appreciate you leaving the strike team here to support me."

"I had to redeploy them to the Financial District. Our clients have to come first. Our warehouses are being overrun. You seem to be doing all right."

"I don't have a lot of time, Logan. The thief is getting away."

"I didn't leave you completely empty handed. I left you a car in place of the strike team in case you had to make a run for it. There are also a few goodies in the trunk."

Maybe the man wasn't a complete idiot after all. She found the car a few yards behind the transport. The engine roared to life, and she sped off after the thief.

"Where's Felix now?" Logan asked.

"In the control room with a former Fed Sec brute named Ivan, who by the way, didn't buy my homeless person story. I think the thief pissed them off."

"That name sounds familiar. I still have a few Fed Sec friends who might know something about him. What are our other options?"

She caught up to the thief on the Great Highway, south of Golden Gate Park. Much of the heavy traffic headed in the opposite direction, north toward the bridge. "There's a massive underground complex here. Six levels, the first being barracks. Felix's office is on the sixth level. I have no idea what's on the rest. He's locked in there pretty tight. As far as I know, there's only one way down into the complex. I don't think we'd have enough time to override the security."

"Anything we can do from out here?"

"I'd suggest surveillance on the loading dock and the power generator out back. Do it quietly though. I'm sure there are other security measures around the grounds."

"Any idea on motive?"

Serena let out a slow breath through her nose. "He has a personal grudge against the marshals and the Consortium. Does the phrase Consortium Executive Order mean anything to you?"

"Should it?"

The lack of denial was telling. "I don't know. Thought one of your connections might know what he's talking about. Felix says he's fighting for equality. The metro station was only the beginning."

"He's got some pretty big balls if he's executing an attack on the Consortium."

"He doesn't care, and I don't think he's done. He was looking at something about the dross lakes on his tablet when I walked in."

"Those lakes were formed when we rebuilt the city. There used to be neighborhoods up there. I'll check it out. What else?"

"Felix is watching everything via monitors in his apartment. The power centers, the water collectors, the marshals' building. All high-value targets. Hitting any one of those would cripple the city. Hitting all of them would be as bad, if not worse than the Great Quake."

"You've been in his apartment," Logan said, sounding somewhat amused. "There's a story I'd like to hear eventually."

"Let's focus, Logan. I'm not out here putting my ass on the line for your dirty fantasies."

Logan's smirk faltered. "Maybe this big reset is what he wants. Wipe everything out and assume control."

"If the mayor doesn't evacuate those areas, a lot more people will die."

"I'll see what I can do. We have to be careful. We don't want to tip Felix off. If we start pulling people out, he'll suspect something. Let's let this play out a little bit longer."

"We can't leave those people to fend for themselves. I'll get them out myself if I have to."

"Those people are not important to me," Logan snapped. "Besides, we don't know that they are rigged to blow. He's probably watching those places to make sure nothing happens to them. I have some assets in place. We'll check it out discreetly."

Serena clenched the steering wheel, resisting the urge to smash the screen with Logan's face on it. *They're important to me, you son-of-a-bitch.* One way or another, she'd find a way to help those people. "What do you want me to do about the thief? What do you know of him anyway?"

"Give me a minute."

Darkness pressed down on her. She kept one eye on the area outside her car. There were enough other lowlifes that'd see her as an easy target.

Logan's voice snapped her out of her brooding. "You've got to be kidding me. I thought he was dead."

"Wait, what?" Serena demanded. "You know this guy? Why the hell didn't you tell me?"

"I had no idea he was the one behind this. He crossed one of my previous employers. There was confrontation and I thought he was dead. I was wrong."

That was the first time Serena had ever heard Logan say those words, but there was more to that story. "How does that affect what's happening now?"

"Obviously, he's back to finish what he started." Logan's voice trailed off for a moment. "I can't believe we trained him…"

"Excuse me."

"He spent four years at the university. Computer science, programming, network analysis. If anyone has the skill to hack our system, it's this guy."

Serena shook her head. "Great. My only hope of infiltrating deeper into Felix's network is as bad as them. I don't know who to trust."

"Listen, Serena. This guy is dangerous. Find out what he knows. Make him stop the attack. By any means necessary. If he can't, he's of no use to us. At that point, a covert assault might be our only option."

She'd gone from analyst to spy to interrogator all in a matter of a few hours. If she kept this up, she'd be mayor by morning. "I'll check back in when I know more."

"You do that."

Logan's voice faded, leaving her with her thoughts. Why bother fighting off the attack if it wasn't to protect the people caught in the middle? Serena shook her head. That was it. These weren't people to Logan or the Consortium. They were assets to be used. They were the UN with a different name. Maybe that's how she had to approach this. Make Logan understand that he's losing assets with every minute he delayed.

The thief pulled into the Eureka Square Shopping Center parking lot in upscale Pacifica. He circled around the back of the building and parked out of sight. What could he possibly want down here? Unless he was here to meet his UN contacts. Serena parked a block south on Pacific Avenue behind a giant Land Rover. With luck, she'd be gone before anyone noticed it was there.

She backtracked along the deserted street to the shopping center, keeping no clear line of sight from the parking lot to her position. The thief still sat in his car, probably checking for a tail. Her hand found the pistol tucked inside her jacket. *I'm probably walking into a trap.*

After a while, the thief left his car and marched to the northeast side of the neighborhood. Serena stayed far enough back to avoid detection. Her eyes flicked to a few of the other houses but saw no other signs of life. The ravine to the north offered her a quick means of escape if necessary. They came to a house on a corner, a solid eight-foot stone fence surrounding it.

The house towered over the fence and spanned the equivalent of two, maybe three Mission District lots. She'd only seen such opulence after joining the Consortium. It turned her stomach. Especially since it had been acquired at the expense of others.

At least Felix was trying to help people. Thieves stole only for themselves. Most people in the Mission District would give everything for a fraction of what this speck of dirt had. The amount of medicine she could buy from the value of his home alone was astronomical. Anger welled up inside her. *I'm going to enjoy teaching him a lesson.*

Instead of going to the front door, the thief went around back. Serena approached carefully, aided by the obstructed sight lines. She watched from the end of the street for a while. No one else came or went. The fence line curved right towards the back of the property. Data recorders stared down every twenty feet or so along the top edge. Serena kept her face low in case they were active. She checked her six.

The steep terrain blocked her view over the fence. A max sec cell didn't have as much security. Serena ran her hand through her clumpy, oily hair and fell back against the fence. *I need a better vantage point.* As soon as she planted her foot in the short grass to head back toward the road, floodlights flared to life. The data recorders on top of the wall swiveled her way. From somewhere inside the fence an alarm claxon squawked.

Serena's chest clenched tight. She cut away from the fence towards the trees between this house and his next-door neighbor, heading for the ravine she passed earlier. *Hopefully he hasn't seen my face.*

Her second mistake of the day endangered her life and her mission. Again. The potential return wasn't worth it. She stopped.

Logan said to find out what this cretin knew. Running guaranteed her failure. The thief had the advantage of environment, but he was a criminal. Criminals were dumb.

Serena cut back towards the front of the house, no longer hiding her face. Let him see her coming. He was beat up pretty good. She'd have no trouble subduing him if things got out of hand.

Serena crept underneath a low-hanging balcony, that was still too high to reach, towards the door. *There has to be another way inside.* A low window or something. She crossed in front of the door just as it opened a crack. Without thinking, Serena bowled her way through into the house. The thief writhed in pain on the floor. Serena aimed her pistol at his forehead. "Let's chat, you and I."

CHAPTER 19: INTRODUCTIONS

Janik clutched his throbbing ribs. Every breath burned. After a moment, the dizzying pain subsided enough to see through the shadowy darkness. A strange woman dressed similar to Felix's guard dog stood in his front hall pointing a gun at him. *Should've put pants on before answering the door.* He slid backwards deeper into the house. "Who are you?"

The woman slammed the door shut and locked it. "Who else is in the house?" she demanded. "Do you have any weapons?"

Janik struggled to keep up with the rapid-fire questions in the thick Latin accent. "Who? What? Weapons? What are you talking about, lady? I've had a pretty rotten day so if you're going to kill me, make it quick."

The woman motioned with the gun. "Stand up. No sudden moves."

Sudden moves? Planned ones were a challenge. Janik hauled himself up by the wall. His ankle still throbbed, and his ribs felt like they were on fire.

"Face the wall. Hands behind your back."

Janik glanced over his shoulder as she snapped a pair of mag-cuffs on his wrists, slightly confused. "Aren't you here to kill me? You followed me here from Land's End to finish what Felix's thug started, right?"

The woman hesitated. "First, you're going to tell me what you know."

Janik's shoulders slumped. For a brief moment, he let his

hopes rise. "You're wasting your time. I don't know anything. In fact, I've never been more confused in my life."

It wasn't all a lie. The data he'd uncovered on McIntosh Corp, Felix, and cerebral impulse transplant didn't supply any new answers. Only new leads to follow.

She shoved him into the kitchen and motioned with the gun for him to sit. "You are going to tell me what I want to know, *Ladron*, or I'm going to shoot you."

Janik cocked an eyebrow. "What the hell is *Ladron*?"

"It means 'thief'. I'd heard you were smart. I guess not all rumors are true."

Janik tensed. So much for maintaining a bit of anonymity. "You know who I am. Can't say the same about you, I'm afraid."

"Everyone knows who you are. Your face is all over the news." The woman tilted his head to one side with her finger. "That sec officer really did a number on you. Your own fault. What were you doing at Land's End?"

Janik cleared his throat, taking a minute to process what was happening. *She saw his beating. That was a bit embarrassing. He usually tried to impress the ladies.* "Did you set him on me?"

"If it had been Felix or Ivan, you'd be dead."

"So, Felix sent you to find out what I knew, then kill me." The woman kept the gun trained on him. "You won't shoot me if I make myself a drink, will you? Consider it my last request."

She studied him for a moment before removing the cuffs. "Try anything and I *will* kill you."

"So you keep saying." He poured a double shot of whiskey over some ice. He wrapped some more in a towel for his damaged cheek. "Can I get you anything? Soda? Water? A happy thought?"

"This isn't a social call," she spat. "You're going to tell me what you know, including where you got your information."

Janik sat on the opposite side of the island, rested the towel on his swollen cheek, and sipped his drink. The situation called for an operational assessment. The outlook was grim. "I wasn't lying. I don't know anything. Why do you think I went to Land's End? I'm after answers, too."

She thrust the gun at him. "Don't play games with me." The way she emphasized that last word made him seem like the devil. "You were at the Promenade. Now everyone is after you."

Janik didn't look away, though his heart pounded. "Popular, I guess." The ice clinked inside the glass as he swirled it.

"Are you hacking networks for Felix? Did you cause the cyber-attack? Did you plant those bombs?"

Janik laughed causing a fresh wave of pain in his face. "You're kidding, right? You think I'm working for Felix? And you said I was the dumb one. I barely escaped Land's End with my life. Breathing hurts. I woke up this morning in a nice little shady spot at the Sutro Baths wearing nothing but a flimsy hospital gown. I'm being set up."

"You're nothing but a UN scumbag. Why would someone set you up?" The strange crazy lady wasn't wrong. "Is one of your contacts running Felix?"

She wasn't listening. Maybe if he spoke Spanish she'd understand. He wished he knew Spanish. "Listen, lady, you're running on some bad info. I'm not working for Felix or the Underground. Someone made sure I'd be at the Promenade when it blew. One of Felix's merry men beat the crap out of me, and the marshals want me in a deep hole, too. I don't exactly have too many friends."

"Tell me what you know. I might be able to protect you."

"How stupid do you think I am?" Janik sneered. "Did you know one of McIntosh's top execs died at the Promenade this morning? So guess what, I'm in for it from all sides. The minute I tell you anything, you put a hole in my chest. I'll pass, thanks." Janik didn't flinch when she brought the gun up again. He sipped his drink then placed the chilled glass on his swollen cheek. It felt better than the towel. "You're not going to shoot me."

The woman stared at him incredulously. "Oh no? Why is that?"

"Everyone thinks I have something of value. My guess is if you go back to Felix without me or the information in my head, things aren't going to go well for you." She'd have killed him by now if that was her intent. Assassins weren't known for their small talk.

"I have other methods of getting what I want."

"I'm not interested in your bedroom proclivities. I have bigger concerns."

Her face turned a deep scarlet. "I'm not a hooker."

Janik shrugged. "Whatever you say, I'm not judgmental. You still haven't given me a reason to tell you anything."

Doubt crossed her face. "Okay, what do you want?"

"Proof I didn't plant any bombs or launch the cyber-attack for starters. I want to know who set me up." He downed the rest of his drink to hide his quivering lip. "I want proof I'm not a child killer."

Her gun dipped. "I don't have it."

"I guess we're done here then." Janik spread his arms presenting a large target. "Try not to get blood on the countertop. It's real marble."

The woman didn't move. "I didn't say I didn't know where to find it."

Janik poured another drink. This woman was testing his last nerve. "I'm listening. You don't like games. Neither do I. Either say something useful or pull the trigger."

"Your evidence is on Felix's network. It's yours if you help me shut it down."

Whiskey sloshed onto his wrist as he stopped swirling it abruptly. His initial assumption had been wrong. She wasn't working for Felix. She was an undercover marshal. No, the infinitely more dangerous likelihood was she worked for the Consortium. He definitely couldn't trust anything she said now. Still, he couldn't pass up this slim opportunity. "Let's start with baby steps. How about you put up that gun and we'll talk. All your twitching is making me nervous."

The crazy woman holstered her weapon but didn't take her hand from the grip. "Satisfied?"

"It'll have to do, I suppose. The limited amount of information I garnered came from trying to hack Felix's network."

"How did you know to go after Felix in the first place?"

"His server is one of the few still active. All hell broke loose when I pinged it." He did a little more than that, but what she didn't know wouldn't hurt her. He sure as hell wasn't going to tell her about the encrypted files Felix was stealing. Not yet anyway.

"He knows it was you."

Janik's eyes narrowed. "How do you know that?"

"It's not important," she replied much too quickly for his liking. "You have to try again."

Janik shook his head. "It won't do any good. If you'll follow me to my office upstairs, I'll show you why. Besides, I feel kind of awkward sitting here in nothing but my underwear and bandages." Janik led her to his office door. "Don't touch anything. My pants are in the other room."

The woman blocked his path into the bedroom. "I don't think so. I don't trust criminals, especially UN ones. I'm not letting you out of my sight."

Janik smirked. "Yeah, I get that a lot. Occupational hazard." What did she think would happen in a bedroom? He had a few ideas, but they'd just met. He'd have to buy her dinner first. "Well, I'm not bashful. After you."

Janik dressed in a charcoal-grey pinstriped suit and tucked his fedora under his arm while the woman watched from the door. He pulled in a refreshing breath. Being properly dressed renewed his sense of purpose. Now, he could get to work.

"Expensive taste," the woman said. "Not what I expected."

"Oh really. What did you expect?"

"I don't know. Tattoos and scars, maybe. Definitely not banker."

Janik paused in buttoning his jacket. "Sorry to disappoint. I have money, might as well look the part."

"I'm disgusted, not disappointed. There are people in this city with nothing, who need medicine to survive. Why not use your wealth to help them?"

"Oh, you mean like your Consortium friends? I'm sure they're doing everything they can for the people in the Mission District. Your friends in the Pyramid have done far more to destroy people's lives than I ever will."

"How can you say that? The Consortium trained you. They taught you every skill you have."

That she knew that only reinforced his belief she worked for them. "Exactly the reason why I don't play for them anymore. You think what I do now is bad. I've been on the other side. The grass ain't any greener."

The flicker in her face said he'd struck a nerve. "Your mother must be so proud. What does she think of your career choice?"

"None of your business. My family has nothing to do with this." He couldn't even say for sure if his parents were still alive. No way they'd speak to him if they were. "If any of your goons go after them, I'll kill you all."

"They're the smart ones. Too bad your money can't buy you the same intelligence."

Janik bit his tongue. Trading insults with this crazy woman solved nothing. He motioned her into his office. "Feel free to leave at any time. The way I see it, you need me more than I need you. Besides, my wealth is because of my intelligence. Why do you think I've never been convicted?"

Janik sat at his desk while the woman roamed the room. "This is a lot of computer equipment for a UN lowlife. I thought the Consortium were the only ones to run such sophisticated gear."

"Yeah well, every man's gotta have his toys." The three tablets embedded in the desktop bloomed to life and a holographic screen materialized in front of him. "You know an awful lot about me. Seems hardly fair that I can't say the same thing." He hated thinking of her as 'the woman'. Most pretty girls he knew had a name. Of course, most weren't threatening to kill him. "If we're going to be working together, I should know your name."

"We're not working together. Show me Felix's network."

Janik spread his hands out to his sides. "Sorry, can't remember the password. Took a nasty bump on the head. Memory's a little shoddy. Two plus two is still four, right?"

The woman pressed the gun against the back of his head. "Does this help?"

Janik didn't budge, though for an instant, he thought she'd call his bluff. "Nope, guess you'll have to shoot me."

The woman rubbed her eyes. "Fine, my name is Olivia, now show me."

As if that's your real name, he thought. "I'm not going to show you Felix's network because I'd rather not have a team of blood thirsty killers show up at my front door. They weren't very nice last time. Here's what I can show you." He loaded two files, one on the left screen, and one on the right. They were almost identical except for the lines of code locking out control.

"What am I looking at?"

"This," he pointed at the left screen, "is original code from the power center operating system." He tapped a few more buttons. "This is what's running now. See the differences? Felix is controlling which neighborhoods have power and which ones don't. The minute I attack it, I'm shot down. It's like a perimeter defense system."

Janik loaded a mapping script to identify the differences between the two. He had no hope of fixing it if he didn't know the good code from the bad. Renaude said that the original code became corrupted as soon as it was loaded onto the system. Someone had to be monitoring an open port somewhere.

"They used a RAT here too," she mumbled. "How did you get this?"

Janik grunted, impressed she knew about Random Access Trojans. Maybe she wasn't *all* bad. "You're not the only one with resources."

"Can you shut it down?"

Janik shook his head. "The RAT intertwined with the original code, changing some of it. We don't have time to study it. Oh shit. That's a problem."

"What?"

"You see these lines of code," he said, pointing at the screen on the right. "They're logic bombs. Nasty little bastards usually set to go off at certain times or when certain conditions are met. The digital version of the trigger on your gun."

"I know what a logic bomb is," she snapped. "What are they triggering?"

"Good question. Alarms or security measures, maybe. They may still have uses for it or, they're not ready for that part yet. I did overhear Felix's thugs say they still had a lot of work to do so I'm betting on the former. I know one thing. I can't do anything from here. We have to shut it down from the source and I doubt I'm on Felix's VIP list."

"What if the goal of the attack wasn't to shut down the power grid? What if it was to wrest control away from the Consortium? Felix could turn the power back on any time he wanted."

Explains why he's stealing the files, he thought. "It makes sense if he's trying to protect those assets."

The monitor switched on and flashed a special bulletin. "We're coming to you live for breaking news. The San Francisco marshals' building is burning."

CHAPTER 20: ESCAPE

Serena froze, her gaze fixed on the monitor. Orange flames and billowing black smoke filled the screen. The building had been reduced to six floors of burning rubble. Emergency crews maintained a perimeter, helpless to do anything more. As the camera panned, the scope of the destruction became clearer. More dead because she wasn't working fast enough.

"I'm going to be blamed for this," the thief muttered.

She spun him around by his fancy jacket. "So find a shred of decency in your pathetic body and help me. All your evidence is in a place only you can access."

He didn't fight her. He stared at the monitor, fear and doubt burning in his eyes. Seeing his cocksure attitude stripped bare satisfied her a little. "I can't," he said finally. "You saw what happened with the power center code. Felix is watching. He's already tried to kill me twice."

Serena let him go. "My friends can help."

He laughed. "I've seen the help your friends offer. I'm not interested."

"Don't be stupid, Janik. They have resources you don't. Let me take you to them."

"Do they have access to the Promenade footage from this morning's bombing? That might be worth a little cooperation."

Nelson could probably help her with that if he could regain control of the surveillance network. "I'll see what I can do."

Serena tuned out the reporter until Janik's face appeared on the right side of the screen. "Marshals are seeking this man, Janik Brynn, for questioning in the string of deadly attacks. Original reports of his death in a prisoner transport crash were inaccurate. He escaped custody a short time after being arrested in the Mission District. Marshals are urging the public not to approach him if spotted. He is considered dangerous and mentally unstable."

"I'm not mentally unstable," he mumbled.

"They know you're not dead. How did you escape?" He fidgeted with his hands, refusing to make eye contact. "Don't lie to me or I'll turn you in myself."

"It's complicated," he said finally.

"So uncomplicate it. People are dying out there."

"You think I don't know that?" he screamed. "Every move I've made has been anticipated, intercepted. I can't trust anyone, least of all someone I met an hour ago who introduced herself with a gun. There are people out there actually putting in the effort to kill me. So forgive me if I opt for a little self-preservation." Silence filled the room like a bad smell. "Believe it or not, there are other people I'm trying to protect."

Harlon fed her the same lines. They were always doing bad stuff to protect others. In the end, it was nothing more than crap wrapped up in a pretty bow, and those people they claimed to be protecting were the ones who ultimately got hurt. She wouldn't let this one manipulate her into deviating from her path.

Serena turned back to the monitor. "He isn't going to stop, you know. He has some sort of grudge against the marshals and the Consortium that has to do with the dross lakes. By the time he satisfies it, it will be too late for either of us."

"Then let's ensure he doesn't succeed."

The sound of an approaching car got their their attention. They rushed to the window to see a car with no headlights making its way slowly down Talbot Street.

Janik grabbed the briefcase. "That's our cue. Wasn't expecting them quite this quickly. I guess the beauty sleep will have to wait."

"Felix has control of the traffic cams. He probably tracked you here using them."

They left through the back door, towards the ravine. I have no choice but to trust him for now, she thought. I'm dead if Felix's men catch me.

"Come on, the terrain down here will make us harder to follow. Watch your footing."

The warning came too late. Her foot slipped on a patch of loose gravel. She slid, squealing as she fell. Janik caught her as she slid past him into the ravine. Her momentum pulled him down with her. They came to rest a little farther down the hill with him on top of her.

Serena caught a whiff of the thief's natural odor as she pulled him in close. Dizzying memories assaulted her mind. Her father, Harlon, Bruno. Memories of a time she thought she'd left behind.

"Told you to watch your footing," he said with a grin. "Are you hurt?"

She shoved the memories, and Janik off of her, ignoring the heat in her face. "I'm fine." On the road above them, a vehicle passed.

"We can't outrun them."

"I left my ride at the plaza."

Her fingers hooked in a small tear that ran down the outside of her knee. She must've caught it on a jagged stone. Blood coated the edges. Something else to explain to Felix. Or worse, Ivan. "If we make it. You said they tried to kill you once. They probably sent more this time."

"Now would be a good time to use that gun you brought."

The car stopped on the road at the top of the ravine. A few seconds later, a door opened. Serena craned her neck towards the top of the ravine but couldn't see anything.

"Check the ravine," someone said. "I'll drive around."

They jumped at a communicator going off in Janik's pocket. Serena stared at him as he fumbled for it. By the time he shut it off, it was too late. The thugs had closed in on their position.

"So much for stealth," he said with an apologetic grin. "Time to make a run for it."

Janik grabbed her arm and pulled her along. She couldn't find enough footing to pull free. Falling rock and dirt behind them announced their pursuers had entered the ravine. Serena stopped resisting Janik and bolted past him.

Janik stopped at the intersection, panting heavily. A thin sheen of sweat glistened on his forehead. Behind them, flashlight beams slashed the darkness. Serena had no idea where the hell they were. "How far to the plaza?"

"Not far. There'll be places to hide inside."

Serena drew her gun. *Just in case.*

Sprawling multi-story homes blurred as they sped past. Serena's lungs burned, and she wasn't sure how much longer her legs would hold her up. The three silhouettes gained on them. Being shot was less appealing than being winded. *Please, God. Don't let them recognize me.*

The plaza was teasingly close. Just one more wide street to go. Almost free. Serena hated 'almost'. She dealt in absolutes. Like, this was the absolute worst idea she'd ever had. She wouldn't allow herself to feel relief until she was absolutely inside the complex - perhaps not even then. She was absolutely sure Ivan was going to kill her.

Headlights bathed her and her stomach roiled in dread. She shoved the thief onward. "Go." She weaved and bobbed as bullets flew over her shoulder. *This is intolerable.* "We have to find some cover."

"Inside the shopping center will do. Maybe I'll have time to pick out a new hat."

"Eventually, we'll have to escape the group of killers chasing us.

They dashed the last few feet to the closest door inside the plaza. Janik grabbed a rock and threw it through the glass paned door. So much for subtlety.

Not even emergency lighting illuminated the main mall concourse. Serena followed Janik. He seemed to know where he was going, and even though he was a despicable criminal, he was far less threatening than the thugs chasing them.

Footfalls and flashlight beams followed them across the smooth tiles. "They're in here somewhere," one of the thugs said. "Spread out."

She shoved Janik in the middle of the back. "Move faster, *ladron.*"

"Not if you don't stop calling me that," he replied.

"You'll never be anything more than a thief to me. Now, hurry up, or we're both dead."

"Well, when you put it that way."

"Cut off the far side," another thug ordered. "Don't let them out. Don't kill the thief. Ivan wants him alive."

Serena stared at him, mouth hanging open. "Why does Ivan want you alive?" she hissed, straining with considerable effort to keep her voice low.

"You'll have to ask him. I don't even know who Ivan is."

Serena's left hand tracing along the wall provided her only orientation. "Isn't there anything in that blasted case that can help us? If not, why the hell are you dragging it around?"

"We're not far from the server room. I have an idea that might work. In theory. Hopefully, there's enough power left in the reserves to create a diversion."

The corridor angled left, and the bright flashes of red emergency light stabbed her eyes. Janik led them down a short access corridor, past the security office, to the server room at the end. Serena cut back to the security office to find a couple flashlights left behind by the rent-a-cops. Why Janik didn't have one in that bulky case of his, she didn't know.

"You must feel at home in here," Serena said, "surrounded by darkness."

Janik ignored her, instead going to work at the control terminal with all of its blinking lights. Tablets came out of the briefcase and cables were connected. "The fire suppression system is likely on an uninterruptable power source. I can access their triggering subroutines without too much trouble. The goons will probably thank me for the bath."

Serena checked the hall again. The thugs were still at the far end of the mall and had not clued in on their position yet. She sank to the floor and hugged her knees. The adrenaline from the chase through the ravine had worn off a bit and now the trembling started. Or, maybe she was just cold. One thing was for sure. She was confused.

She took a brief moment to refocus her thoughts. Easier said than done. *How much farther do I take this? Do I stay, or do I go?* Janik had proven useful, but risky. Never mind the matter of the information he had. She felt like she was diving headlong off a cliff in the dark. Eventually she'd hit bottom.

She raked her hand through her hair and huffed. *Maybe I should leave him.* She could probably convince Felix's men she'd been kidnapped without giving up the thief's location. "What's the plan after you create your little diversion? Felix's men are not stupid. They'll see it for what it is."

Janik's shadowy outline turned towards her. He appeared amused. "You've been threatening to shoot me all night. Instead of talking about it, why don't you actually follow through on that with those guys out there?"

"I already told you. They don't know about me. I'm not about to give up that advantage." If Janik couldn't access the network, she'd need Felix's trust more than ever.

She stood outside the office clutching her gun. Janik typed furiously on his tablet's virtual keys, seemingly in his own little world. *Go on. Slip away. Melt into the darkness.* She stopped before reaching the corridor's exit. Why the indecision? Let Janik figure things out on his own. He'd likely leave her in the gutter if their positions were reversed. He was just another Harlon Cruz in different wrapping.

Janik materialized beside her a few minutes later. "We have about fifteen seconds before the sprinkler triggers."

Right on queue, alarms blared from one end to the other. Bright orange lights flashed. Torrents of water cascaded down from sprinkler heads in the ceiling. Serena bit her lower lip to keep from screaming as ice cold water ran down her back.

"Not yet," Janik warned, placing a hand on her arm.

Then she saw them. Six separate flashlight beams all focusing at the far end of the corridor to their right. The noise of the rushing water drowned out everything they shouted. The thugs bolted towards one of the far exits. Apparently, they didn't like the water either.

"That's our cue," Janik said and ran into the main corridor in the opposite direction.

They made it out of the drowning torrent. Serena shivered as Janik led them across the parking lot to a dark corner against the building, a space much too wide open for her liking, to the car he arrived in. Serena hesitated. *I can't believe I'm about to get into a stolen car.*

Janik stopped halfway to sitting in the driver's seat when he saw she moving around to the passenger seat. "We can't outrun a half dozen armed sec officers. My diversion will only slow them down for so long. If you have any interest in living past the next few minutes, you'll get in."

One of Felix's sec officers popped around the corner. Serena's stomach leaped into her throat. She shot him. Her mouth hung open, and her breath stopped momentarily. A bullet hitting a body sounded a lot different than hitting a metal target. Now she knew what both sounded like…

"Nice shot," Janik said.

Serena spun and slapped him across the face. "This is not a contest. I killed a man. I'm a goddamn computer analyst."

Janik rubbed his reddening cheek, his features sympathetic. "Earlier tonight, I gunned down a stranger without a second thought. Then I threw up. Believe me, I know this isn't a contest. We're in survival mode now. Things are going to be even less pleasant from here on out."

Serena grabbed his arm when he started towards the corpse. "What are you doing?"

"His tech can likely provide a few answers."

Janik returned a minute later with the goon's weapon, a communicator, and a keycard for the Land's End complex. Maybe that would get her onto the operational levels.

"We should go now," he said as he dumped the gear into the back seat. For once, Serena didn't argue.

They spent the next hour driving south almost all the way to the dross lakes before turning back. The sky had taken on the early morning orange. Serena blew into her hands, trying to bring back some of the feeling. "I have to get out of these clothes."

"I'm flattered," Janik said, "but how about we lose the armed killers chasing us before snuggling?"

"That's not what I mean, you idiot." It'd be so easy to shoot him and forget this whole episode. To hell with what Logan wanted. Nothing since she'd walked out of Felix's complex had gone as expected. She'd lost control. Story of her life, if she was being honest with herself.

Who had been on the other end of that communicator? The marshals were the only ones who'd have working comms. A thief working with the marshals was like oil and water.

Serena intended to go her own way when Janik dropped her off at her car. Hopefully she could convince Felix that Janik killed the sec officer. "Give me the thug's gear, and I'll be on my way."

He cocked an eyebrow. "Just like that, hey? And here I was, almost ready to meet your mom."

Serena's throat constricted. She wouldn't give this callous piece of filth the satisfaction of knowing he'd gotten under her skin. "Unless you have more to say that will help me, like why Ivan wants you alive, I see no reason to continue this relationship."

"Who said I couldn't help you? We haven't even checked out his communicator yet."

"I'm in no mood for games, *Ladron*. I'm tired, I'm beat up, I'm soaking wet, and I'm about ready to snap. Tell me what you know, or I'm going to kill you and take the gear anyway."

"First a little bargain. I've answered your questions, under duress, I might add. I have a few of my own. Pretty sure I've earned some answers. And maybe, just maybe, mind you, I might be inclined to give you the stuff."

Serena growled under her breath. She'd put up with this imp a little longer if it got her the keycard and communicator. "Fine, ask your questions."

He stuck his head out the window, presumably checking for trailing headlights. "No, we're not safe here. Follow me. I know a place we can go."

"And follow you right into a trap? Not likely."

"Oh, come on, why help you escape only to kill you somewhere else? I have no desire to see any more dead bodies. Besides, you're the one with the gun."

She blew a frustrated breath out through her nose. "If you so much as twitch the wrong way, you're a dead man."

"You got it. Oh, and before you go. You know my name. Use it."

CHAPTER 21:
MEMORY AND SORROW

The sinking feeling grew the farther Serena followed him. Nothing had changed in the Mission District since her mother died. Buildings still fell around rusted and burned-out cars. Only a few windows, those that weren't broken or boarded over, had a dim light glowing in them. This had been her home once. Denying it did no good. *Nothing I've done has changed it*, she thought. It deserved better.

She blamed the UN for much of it. Perhaps she'd been naïve to think working for the Consortium would be any better. They had the money and the means to fix everything. They chose not to. Both organizations deserved their fair share of blame laid at their feet.

Familiarity twisted her gut, wrenching her back to a time when the shaking had started. Falling brick and concrete, shattering glass, her father's unmoving hand sticking out from beneath the pile. Her mother's screams. She heard them as if she were sitting beside her now. Her own screams and nightmares followed. Nightmares she still had occasionally. *Time definitely doesn't heal all wounds.*

Janik pulled farther ahead as her foot came off the accelerator. It wasn't too late to turn away. Take the next right and melt into the darkness. She tried to convince herself she didn't need the keycard. She couldn't.

Janik pulled over near the Mission San Francisco de Asis. Cracks from the Great Quake still snaked along the lower walls of the foundation and several windows were boarded up where stained glass had been. San Francisco's oldest building, and one central to her childhood before her world was shattered, didn't warrant restoration, apparently.

She climbed into the passenger seat next to Janik but refused to look at him. "What are we doing here?"

"Pretty sure many of my answers originate in a club not far from here," he replied.

She cracked a window for some air and caught a whiff of searing meat. Bruno's wasn't far from here, but the risk of being recognized was too great.

He glanced sideways at her. "You okay? You look like this is the last place in the world you want to be."

She squirmed in the seat. Her breath caught in her throat. Serena wouldn't admit how right he was. She felt sick to her stomach that her parents rested in the cemetery mere steps away. She hadn't had the heart to visit in some time. "Fitting I suppose that you'd expect to find answers from your own kind, in a den of thieves and liars."

"I'm not all that enthralled with the idea either, but it's all I've got. I hope I still have a few friends here."

"I doubt anyone here is smart enough to help Felix conduct such a complex attack. Most are too worried about exploiting another young girl."

Janik glanced askance at her. "That sounded personal."

Serena turned away. She didn't want pity from the likes of him. "Ask your questions."

Slinking lower in his seat, he pulled his fedora down over his eyes. "What did you mean when you said Felix thought it was the marshals after I told you I tried to hack his system? You had to have been with him to know that."

Serena held her breath for an instant. She'd hoped he'd forgotten that. "I can't tell you."

"Why not? What's the point of me asking questions if you won't answer them?"

"It's complicated. Next question."

"Why do all this? Why blow up the Promenade, the roads, and the marshals' building? Who's he targeting?"

Serena paused, wondering if this was a ploy to confirm something he already knew. She didn't believe for a second he'd told her everything. "It's a direct assault on the Consortium. He's trying to isolate the city, eliminate its dependence on technology. He's trying to save us."

"Yeah, but why? No one goes after the Consortium just because. This is somehow personal for him."

"Why don't you ask the person on the other end of that communicator that almost got us killed?" She spun toward him then. "How do I know if you have spoken any truth? You still haven't convinced me you're not working with Felix."

The surprise on his face was almost comical. "Are you serious? In case you hadn't noticed, they were shooting at me, too."

"It's easy to shoot someone without killing them. Are they trying to bring you in?"

He stared out the window. "Believe what you want. I don't care. You'll never trust anything I say anyway. You haven't exactly given me much reason to trust you either."

Serena rubbed the back of her hand. He was right about that. "You're working for someone. If it's not Felix, then it's the marshals. They're the only other people with comms tech like that. I should know. The Consortium gave it to them. The people that run this city have infinite resources at their disposal. Why would they get a scummy UN thief to help them?"

"I told you why I'm doing this," he said. "Everyone thinks I killed a bunch of people, including kids. That's not okay with me. I'm not blind, either. You're connected to the Mission District somehow. Well, so am I, and I don't want to see any more of my friends hurt."

"There has to be more. Are they holding your family? I can help free them."

Janik scoffed, but in the darkness, she saw the conflict on his face. "I don't have any family," he said finally.

She didn't blame him for this lie. "Then what is it, some big payday? Is it always about money with you?"

"You saw my house. Does it look like I need any more money?"

"Want and need are two different things," she replied with a sneer. "People need medicine to survive. They don't want to have to sell their souls for it."

"I don't know anything about that. Wanting a bit of luxury isn't a terrible thing."

"It is when it's obtained at the expense of others."

"Everything in life is at the expense of someone else. Do you think what your pal Felix is doing isn't costing someone else, someone who doesn't deserve to be caught up in this?"

"He isn't my pal, but I understand his motives. In his mind, he's helping the city."

"I'm not against paying it forward, once you look out for number one. I guarantee the people you work for don't have a shred more virtue than I do. Do you think the Consortium cares when they're robbing the Mission District blind? Tell me something. How much do you really know about the people you work for? I'd wager it's barely a fraction of what you think you do."

"What do you know about the Mission District?" she sneered. "You're a spoiled little rich boy with no conscience. You have no idea how hard the people here have had it."

"I know more about this place than you think. I know the people. I've seen them struggle. I've seen them die. Most here are honest, despite what they have to do to survive. They don't deserve to be caught in the middle of a war the Consortium started."

On that, he wasn't wrong. In all her conversations with Bruno, she gathered one thing. They just wanted to be treated fairly. Nothing more. "The UN isn't full of saints. They hold resources hostage in their little black market unless you have something they want."

"No doubts there. It's one of the reasons I tried to retire. But ask yourself why the UN is around in the first place. After the quake, the Consortium were in a position to completely rebuild this city, except they only helped those with money or some skill they could extort. Everything you accuse the UN of being, the Consortium got there first. Tell me you'd never think of stealing food or medicine in desperation."

She had thought about it. More than once. Harlon wouldn't let her out of his sight though. Perhaps if she had tried harder, she'd still have her mother.

"I don't expect you to understand. You hate me. That's fine. I can live with my choices. But it seems we're both after the same thing. So, let's take each other on a little faith, shall we?"

Faith in others had only hurt her. "I can't afford faith."

"Okay then. Leave. I'd rather take my chances on my own then listen to any more of this high-and-mighty crap. You're not leaving here with any of this gear though."

"Excuse me?"

"You heard me. I'll clear my name on my own. This is going to be hard enough without the extra baggage. Good luck shutting down Felix's network. I almost guarantee his code scribers are good enough to keep you people chasing your tails for days."

She drew in through her nose and released through her mouth. *Calm down, Serena,* she told herself. She'd never find her answers if she kept losing her temper. As much as she hated admitting it, this thief had some useful skills. "You'll never find out what happened without me."

"You'd be surprised what I'm capable of, sweetheart."

She shot him an ice-cold glare. *I'm no one's sweetheart.* "Fine," she said finally. She only had to put up with him for a short time.

The communicator crackled with static when Janik switched it on. "It's likely encrypted." He rubbed his hands together in anticipation. "I can work with that."

"Ivan wouldn't give his people unsecured comms gear. I'd be impressed if you actually cracked it."

He grinned childishly at her. "Challenge accepted." He set the communicator on the dash and retrieved his case from the other car. Yet another opportunity for her to leave him behind. Again, she stayed. She wished she could shake whatever was drawing her to this fiend.

A tablet came out of the case, and he connected the communicator to it. "These things usually have a back door through the encryption software. Finding it is the tricky part."

Serena recognized some of the decryption scripts scrolling across the screen, but she'd never seen this level of sophistication. What the hell did the university teach this guy?

"You must be wondering why the fine upstanding citizens at the university would be teaching someone how to crack secure networks and defeat encrypted comms gear."

Serena had assumed they were training the next wave to go after the real criminals. Turns out it was the criminals they trained. Or, maybe she was being naïve again.

Janik tapped at his keyboard, his brow furled, and his jaw tightened. Serena watched their surroundings with her gun clutched in her hand. She tracked a few shadowy figures as they moved along the near pitch-black street. They either didn't see them here or didn't consider them worth the trouble. *Hurry up, thief,* she begged silently. *They won't ignore us forever.*

"I'm in," he announced, punching his fist into the air. He

grinned arrogantly at her. "Impressed yet?"

"Turn on the communicator," she growled.

"You're impressed," he teased. "I can tell. It's okay, I won't tell anyone."

"I am running out of patience, thief." *And nerves*, she finished silently.

The communicator crackled again. This time, voices replaced the static. The first one didn't sound happy. "Chasing this hacker has put us behind schedule. Ivan is pissed."

"Not as pissed as he's going to be when he finds out Vaslo is dead, and his gear is gone."

"You two morons can't get anything right. This is the second time you've let him get away. Find him and get him here soon for when the transfer is complete. We have to finish up the raids. As soon as the files are decrypted, we're moving on the Pyramid. The Consortium won't be able to hide behind their firewalls anymore."

"Those are the same guys that chased me from the apartment," Janik mumbled.

Serena glared at him confused. "That's why Ivan wants you. You're helping them decrypt stolen information. I'm taking you in." Why did she even think she could trust anything he said?

Janik threw up his hands. "It's not what you think."

The communicator crackled again. "Hopefully the doctor has the kinks worked out. We can't afford another one of his experiments going berserk. It's bad enough we have to babysit these clowns when they first wake up."

"Hey, better they get ten thousand volts shot through their brains than us. I don't fancy becoming a vegetable."

Ten thousand volts? Doctor? Experiments? A chill ran up her spine. What the hell was Felix into? "Do you know what he's talking about?"

"I was hoping you did," Janik replied.

The second sec officer snorted. "I don't know why Felix keeps him around. That dude creeps me out. I won't be sorry when all the bombs are planted so we can get rid of him."

Serena's stomach turned. The car felt like a coffin. She gasped and cracked her door open. Despite the sickly stench of oil and smoke, the cool night air eased her nausea a little. Nothing in the city would be left untouched once Felix was done. Would any of them survive? She closed the door and pressed her fingers to her eyes. It didn't help. "He's crazy if he thinks they're getting anywhere near the Pyramid. That place is a fortress."

"He's got a lot of firepower."

"I'm not worried about the Pyramid. I'm more interested in the files he's referring to and the experiments. Why does he need you to decrypt them?"

"When I pinged Felix's network, I noticed they were transferring a lot of files from city hall and the Financial District. I added my own encryption as an insurance policy in case they caught me. Without me, they can't open them." He took a breath. "So, you see, if you take me in, we're both back on the grid and lose any chance of figuring out what's happening."

"What's in the files?" It had to be something to do with the Consortium Executive Order. *There's no way Logan doesn't know about it.*

"I don't know. They were already encrypted when I intercepted them. I didn't have time to crack them open. I'd put money on them containing names, locations, accounts. The whole Consortium network. One thing is for sure. He had to be fairly certain of success if he was going this far. This isn't something you play the percentages on."

Serena suspected he still held something back. She admitted, begrudgingly, it was a smart play. They had a long way to go before either trusted the other. "Give me your encryption keys so I can unlock those files."

Janik laughed and shook his head. "You don't negotiate very

often, do you? I'm not giving up the one thing keeping me alive. I'll promise you this instead. I want no part of whatever game Felix and the UN are playing. Help me prove I'm not a killer and I'll disappear. I don't want any money or reward. I only want vindication and a clean break."

There was no debating the man was a lowlife, but he didn't deserve to be crucified for killing all those people if he didn't. The Promenade, the overpass. That blood was on Felix's hands. And perhaps by extension, the Consortium. None of this would be happening if they had an ounce of virtue.

Her hands were no less stained. She worked for them after all. "I'll help you clear your name." Serena looked him square in the eye then. "If I find out you're in any way involved, I will bury you."

He nodded, without the arrogant grin this time. "I believe you."

"What did our friend Vaslo have access to?" Serena asked.

He plugged the keycard into a card reader from the case. Again, the screen filled with more code. Then it changed to a layout map. "Only a couple of levels by the look of things."

"That's the complex." Serena pointed at the top left corner of the screen. "That's the loading dock."

Janik shifted the screen to show the 3D layout. "There's a stairwell down to the other levels. Felix left himself a little escape hatch."

"That has to be how they're moving the bombs."

Janik pointed at a wide open area. "I bet this is where they're building them."

"Those smaller sections lined up in rows are apartments. Felix's whole force stays on site."

Janik scrolled through the code. "He's got an armory and storage on Level Two, a bunch of server rooms, and control center on Level Three." That was her way into the network.

"There's some kind of lab on Level Four, and there doesn't seem to be much on this last level."

He tapped a few keys on his tablet, unplugged the keycard, and handed it to her. "I've removed all access restrictions. You can go anywhere in the complex. Once your friends have control of the complex, I'll bring the decryption codes."

"Aren't you coming with me?"

"I wasn't at the Promenade by accident, which means someone set me up. I have to deal with that one on my own."

He handed her the communicator as well, but she didn't take it. "You keep that. Use it to stay ahead of Ivan and his goons."

He turned back as he reached for the door handle. "Here's a piece of advice you probably don't want, especially from me. People aren't always as bad as you think they are."

"But they're never as good as you want them to be," she replied without hesitation.

"There's more than a little truth to that."

Janik got out of the car and began walking away. Seconds later, Serena followed, closing the distance between them. Despite their 'understanding', she couldn't trust a thief. She would never trust a thief. If he was caught, she couldn't have him telling Felix where she went. "I'm sorry," she whispered as she brought the butt of her gun down on the back of his head.

CHAPTER 22: VISITATIONS

Janik rubbed the back of his head as he stumbled to his feet, the tender knot a painful reminder never to turn his back on that woman again. That was, if he ever saw her again. Part of him wished he did so he could return the favor.

Who am I kidding? I've never hit a woman in my life. Not about to start now.

The thought of her suffering a small bit of misery offered a little satisfaction. Other than being easy on the eyes, she didn't have much going for her. Smooth, light brown skin, slender with long black hair. He felt the back of his head again. Her caress was a little rough though.

Janik chuckled. *Forget about her and head south.* He knew enough places on Federal land to buy a new identity. He was pretty good at disappearing when necessary.

No, not until that little boy got some justice. Olivia said he'd find everything on Felix's network. Every time he tried to gain access, thugs with guns showed up. That or Latina girls with a sharp tongue and heavy fists. That girl intrigued him more than a little.

Her Consortium friends might help him if he restored the power. If only it were that simple. Going to the Consortium meant turning his back on the UN. He'd never be able to set foot in the Mission District again. He'd only miss a few like Bruno. Especially on prime rib night.

I have to see this through. That meant hacking Felix's network again. Third time's the charm. Someone to keep the wolves at bay while he worked would help. Perhaps one of the utilities would mask his identity and location. Renaude said to be discrete. An engineer troubleshooting the problem wouldn't draw much attention. Not the best laid plan, but better than nothing.

Janik slipped into the driver's seat of his surprisingly intact car. Must've only been out a few minutes. His case sat open on the back seat, but nothing was missing. His tablet with the decryption program sat on top, the password screen glowing in the darkened cabin. Janik grinned as he picked it up. 'Bring to Land's End Unlocked,' the screen read. He should've known she'd try to take the encryption keys.

The communicator Renaude gave him chirped again. Janik's shoulders slumped as he hit the 'Connect' button "What are you doing in the Mission District?"

Janik should've expected a tracking device in the communicator. Setting him up for weird brain experiments was only part of what Renaude did for fun. "Ordering tacos. Had a craving for spicy meat." Actually, that wasn't such a bad idea at the moment.

"You're leaving a trail of destruction in your wake. Bodies are piling up behind you."

"The marshals' building wasn't me," Janik protested, "but that's not important right now. More bombs are coming, and Felix is planning an assault on the Pyramid. Probably within the next few hours."

Renaude went quiet for a moment. "How credible is your intel?"

"I heard it over the communicator I lifted from one of Felix's dead sec officers." Janik stopped Renaude's obvious question. "It was a traumatizing experience. Oh, and by the way, the looters you're fighting are really strike teams targeting major Consortium players for Felix."

"Yes, I figured that part out for myself. They were much too organized for random desperate citizens. I believe they are hunting specific people. How close are you to restoring the power?"

"Not close, unfortunately. I've been traced both times I've tried. I barely escaped with my life. Speaking of which, your little phone call almost got me killed. A bunch of thugs were right on top of us when the communicator went off."

"Us?"

Janik winced. Too late to take that little slip back now. "There's a woman working some kind of angle. She followed me from Land's End. I think she's in bed with Felix, but it goes farther than that."

"What do you mean?"

"I mean Consortium, Renaude. Use your head. You think the marshals are the only ones trying to shut this down? The corporations didn't build their little empire just to let some maniac with a cause tear it down."

"Get rid of her before she blows this whole operation. I don't care how. I will not have the Consortium interfering with my business."

"I'm not going to kill her, if that's what you're suggesting."

"I don't care how," Renaude repeated more forcefully. "Remember what's at stake for you, Janik. Finish this and you walk away a free man."

"There are enough bodies on my tab already. I'm not adding more. On top of that, I'm at the limit of how far I can go with Felix. There are logic bombs embedded in his code. I don't know what they're for. My guess is anyone messing with it is in for a nasty surprise."

"Can you defeat them?"

"Not without accessing it from a source. Can you get me access to the city hall servers?"

Renaude shook his head. "Too risky. If you're recognized, it's game over for both of us."

"Do you want this fixed or not? I can't do it any other way. Dress me up like one of your cyber cops if you have to."

Renaude sighed. "Alright Janik, but if you're discovered I'll kill you. Do you understand?"

"Get in line, Renaude."

"Give me an hour. I'll bring you some gear."

That gave him enough time to go see Patricia. Now that rumors of his death had been debunked, they'd be targets. And though he'd hate every second of it, he needed a word with Stephen. Bill McIntosh and Cerebral Impulse Transplant required an explanation. If nothing else, Janik could warn them to get out of sight.

He weaved his way back north to where he'd escaped Felix's thugs the first time. The streets were mostly deserted at this point. Those not trying to flee the city were riding it out in their homes. Flaming cars and rubble blocked a few, and that made him a little nervous. He pictured dead bodies lying on his sister's living room floor. Janik hoped he wasn't too late.

He parked one street over from Patricia's. Everything seemed oddly unfamiliar, as if someone had thrown a veil over his memory. Patricia's house sat halfway down the street. Instead of walking through the front door, he snuck through the backyard. He slung his laptop bag over his shoulder and climbed the wall vines to the second-floor balcony. The study window swung in silently when he pushed it. *What the hell Patricia? Lock the damn window.*

Patricia sat hunched over her laptop at her desk, probably poring over some AI project or another. Not what he was after tonight. He clamped one hand over her mouth and held a finger to his lips with the other. "Don't scream. I'm not here for a fight."

He removed his hand from her mouth, and she slapped him

across the face. He rubbed the sting as he probed the inside of his cheek with his tongue. *I deserve that one.* He intercepted her other hand as it came in for a repeat performance. Once was enough.

"What are you doing here?" she growled as she ripped her arm away. "I told you I never wanted to see you again."

He backed away, out of the reach of her fist. "I came to warn you. The explosions, the blackout, it's a direct attack on the Consortium and the people behind it are good."

She crossed her arms over her chest and tapped her foot the way his mother did when she was angry. "I don't believe you."

"Fine, don't believe me. Believe the chaos that's almost on your doorstep. Frankly, I'm surprised your house is still in one piece."

"What did you do?" she demanded. "Don't lie to me. Your face is all over the news."

Janik let out a long, slow breath. Keeping his patience with her was hard sometimes. *Exactly like mom.* "I know you hate me, and I deserve it, but this isn't about me. I'm being set up and I think someone from McIntosh Corp is involved. I'm not stopping until I find the ones behind it. I don't want to see you get hurt."

"Serves you right. Your helping Gina Hendrix costed us millions in lost defense contracts. All because you're a coward who wouldn't get his hands dirty. Mom and dad had no choice but to step aside and leave everything to me. They couldn't show their faces around town."

"You still believe I left because I didn't want to build weapons. News flash, little sister. I was the weapon."

The door burst open, and Stephen stood there holding a pistol out in front of him. "What's going on here?" His eyes bulged when he saw Janik. He raised the gun a little higher and cocked the hammer. "What the hell are you doing here?"

"Dropped in to say hello," Janik replied with a grin.

Stephen pushed his shoulders back and leveled the pistol at

Janik's forehead. "You have five seconds to get out of my house or the marshals will be here picking up a body."

Janik sauntered forward. "Relax, tough guy. You sure you even know how to use that thing?"

Stephen trembled as he tried to contain his rage. "The only reason you're not already dead is because you're her brother."

Patricia placed a hand on her husband's arm. "He's no brother of mine," she spat. "He turned his back on us when he decided to run with thieves and murderers. The Consortium gave you everything, Janik. Your education, a secure place to work, freedom to do what you want. You threw it in their face."

"If that's what you believe, you're as blind as the rest of them. Wake up and smell the coffee, Patricia. The Consortium doesn't have people. They have assets, slaves. You're expendable. Once you die, they'll tap someone else on the shoulder. Your dear in-laws used me like a tool."

Stephen turned to Patricia. "What's he talking about? What did he say to you?"

"He said this is a direct attack on the Consortium and that your family is somehow involved." She hesitated for a moment. She wanted to believe him, but she wouldn't defy her husband.

Stephen snorted. "You're a lunatic, Janik, and you don't know a fraction of what the Consortium is capable of."

Janik shrugged. "I know the kind of people doing this. They're relentless. They won't stop until every trace of the Consortium is wiped out. The Pharmacy, The Profiteers, the Sustainers. They will all fall to this new threat. The Judiciary will fall the hardest of them all."

Patricia found her confidence standing next to her husband. "You're nothing but a liar, Janik. Get out of my house."

"Goddamn it, Patricia," he shouted. He regained his calm with a deep breath. "Please listen. The people behind this will hurt you to get to me."

"No," she growled back, "The Consortium will fix whatever it is you've done. Now, get out."

"I expected this sort of reception, so I came prepared to appeal to you on a different level. A business one." He opened his laptop and called up a couple specific files. "Recognize anyone?"

Patricia gasped. "That's your uncle, Stephen."

"Uncle Bill was my father's righthand man. They were practically inseparable. Where did you get this?"

"He died in the Promenade this morning," Janik pressed on. He didn't have time for compassionate sensibilities at the moment. "Want to know who the other guy is? His name is Felix Nash, who happens to be terrorizing the city right now."

"I don't understand," Stephen stammered. "What exactly am I looking at?"

"Kind of obvious, isn't it? Dear Uncle Bill, a Consortium partner, was accepting bribes from someone trying to bring down the Consortium."

"That's a filthy lie. My uncle was a loyal company man. He helped my father make McIntosh Corp what it is today."

Janik hit another button, bringing up another video. This one showed Bill McIntosh standing in an observation room watching several people thrashing about on gurneys and surrounded by medical personnel. "Believe that if you want, but the vids don't lie. Your precious uncle was financing human experimentation."

"It's fabricated," Stephen insisted, though the gun had dipped a little. "It has to be." His eyes betrayed his true thoughts.

"Where did you get this, Janik?" Patricia repeated.

"Remember when I said I was the weapon. This is what McIntosh Corp had me doing for them. A little more than setting up networks and fixing computers, wouldn't you say?"

"You were a spy hacking competitor networks."

Janik kept an eye on Stephen the whole time. "McIntosh was willing to do anything to bury them. I mean anything. People died because of them. People I cared about."

"What are you talking about?" Stephen demanded.

Anger flared in Janik's stomach. "What do you think the business with Gina Hendrix was all about? She knew and was trying to stop it. Peyton's bribery, Eldridge Row, and my friend Javier. All that was your uncle. Call me a liar all you want but your uncle was the biggest criminal of us all."

Patricia glared at Stephen. "Did you know about any of this?"

"Of course not. I worked in marketing, public relations. My father and uncle handled special projects on their own. They didn't trust anyone else."

"Come on now, Stevey. We were just starting to get somewhere. No more crap. Forget our history for a minute. Just straight answers. Fair?"

Stephen huffed. "I saw some of the drug recipes and human experiments they were cooking up, but I had no idea they were using it in blackmail."

"I was protecting Patricia. I wanted to shut it all down, but was told to back off. I'm sure I don't have to tell you what it feels like when your own family threatens you."

"What do they have on you? Any skeletons in your closet?"

"No, nothing. That's why they put me in there. I'm not an attractive target."

"No gambling debts or late-night peeks at dirty holos that can be traced?"

"I resent the implication. I love your sister."

"No doubts there, Stephen, but you wouldn't be the first man to stray."

"Well, I haven't and that's the end of this discussion."

"Do the phrases ten thousand volts through the brain and Cerebral Impulse Transplant mean anything to you?"

Stephen's head snapped up; his eyes as big as saucers. "It's an experimental treatment for cognitive disorders. It was cancelled due to unreliability. Why?"

Janik thrust a finger at the computer. "Does that look canceled to you? Now Felix has found a way to weaponize it and I was a test subject. I suspect that's what Bill gave to him. There are other players, but those files would really help."

"That's crazy," Patricia said. "Why would they do something like that?"

"Janik is right," Stephen replied. "They want more people indebted to them. They want more slaves."

"It's more than that," Janik said. "Your AI, their mind control, and who knows what other secret tech, all controlled by one person. Felix will be virtually invincible."

"You've had this the whole time, Janik," Patricia said. "You could've buried us with it. Why didn't you?"

"Because despite what you think of me, I still care about you. As long as you left me alone I had no reason to use it. Until I was lured to the Promenade right before it blew. I was there to steal your uncle's Bentley. I should've seen the trap for what it was."

"That's why you're here," Stephen said. "You want something. You wouldn't be playing this card otherwise."

"You're smarter than you look, Stevey. I'd like to look at McIntosh's current project files. I need to know exactly what Bill gave Felix."

"You're crazy, Janik. That's never going to happen."

"I have no interest in becoming involved with McIntosh business again. I'm out for good. You let me see those files and this-" He gestured at the laptop. "Along with everything else I have is yours. I don't want it anymore. You don't have to let me touch anything. Just show me. If Bill really did give Felix CIT, you and everyone you're associated with is in a lot of danger."

On the street in front of the house, several vehicle doors slammed shut. Speak of the devil.

They left the study for the top of the stairs at the front of the house. Shadows and flashlight beams crept up the front walkway.

"That'll be our escort arriving," Stephen said arrogantly. "They'll kill you if they find you here."

Something didn't feel right about this. "Make sure the safety's off that pistol, Stevey."

"What are you talking about? We're safe now."

"No, I don't think so." The first bullet shattering the window confirmed it. "Get to your car and get out of here."

Stephen dragged Patricia down the stairs and through the front hall, with Janik behind him. Glass shattered behind him them. Bullets tore chunks from the walls.

"You brought them here," Stephen accused.

"Don't be stupid," Janik said. "They were already doing raids in the area. I told you. They're after anyone that can tie them to your company. Give me the gun. Find some place to hide until I draw them away. The bridges are still your best way out of the city. You better hurry though. I have a feeling they're planning to blow those too."

Stephen handed him the gun, grip first. "Everything you need to exploit them is at Coit Tower. Everyone thinks the Pyramid is their seat of power, but everything is backed up at the Coit Tower security hub, including our company files." He handed Janik his security card. "All of my clearances are on there. They should still work."

Janik poked his head out the door in time to see a grenade arching towards the front door. "Move!" he bellowed and dove deeper into the house.

The explosion whipped hot dirt and concrete across his skin. Patricia and the Stephen were on the floor next to the kitchen. Blood dripped from Patricia's forehead. Janik lifted his head to see three mercenaries working their way towards the hole where the front of the house used to be. He pounded his fist against the floor.

He rolled onto his stomach and spotted Stephen's gun near the now-ruined closet. Stephen stared at him, wide-eyed with fear. Grabbing the gun, Janik scrambled to his hands and knees.

"What are you doing?" Patricia wailed.

Janik grabbed Stephen by his shirt and shoved him towards his sister. "Get out of here now!"

Patricia crawled over to him, pulling on his arm. "You can't do this. They'll kill you."

Janik gently pulled free. "That should make you happy." She didn't answer. He wrapped her in a tight hug. She didn't resist. "I'm sorry I hurt you. I'm sorry you hate me so much. I can't change the past, but I'm going to try to fix this so you have a future."

"She still asks about you, you know. Mom. She wonders if you're still alive."

"Tell her I'm dead. It's easier for everyone that way. If I never see you again, just know I never stopped caring. Now, go."

Stephen pulled her towards the back door. Janik didn't wait for her to say anything else. The time for talking had ended. He raised the gun and pulled the trigger.

CHAPTER 23: SERENA'S DECEPTION

erena left Janik and the Mission District behind, but didn't call Logan. She didn't care what he said. She had to check on her home and neighbors. She approached Lower Nob Hill and saw the flame and smoke billowing into the air. They destroyed everything. She swallowed the lump choking her throat as she drove past her street. People gathered in clusters outside, supporting each other the best they could. Serena almost turned around to go to them, to lend her hand to the effort. In reality, she was as helpless as the rest of them.

Serena turned north, towards the university as it was designated a disaster relief location. They'd have the hospital and supplies there for the survivors. Dread grew in the pit of her stomach and she had to bite back the scream when she saw the flaming pile of rubble that used to be the north wing. The pharmaceutical school was there, as were the law and citizenship schools. Felix was striking at the heart of Consortium control.

Everything he'd done up to now seemed surgical, precise. There had to be more to this alleged Consortium Executive Order. It was time for Logan to come clean on the matter. If he wanted her to stop the attack, he had to tell her everything.

Serena continued north, toward the glow of flood lights and the distant groan of the generators. She pulled into the parking lot, but only made it past the front gate.

The explosion rocked her car, pummeling her car with gritty concrete and glass. The roar swallowed all other sound. She jammed on the brakes, her knuckles white around the steering wheel. When the wave cleared, the front of the community center was gone. People ran, screaming from the burning wreckage, covered in blood and dirt. Serena left the safety of her vehicle. The stampede of panicked people pushed her back.

Time slowed down for Serena as she struggled to process what was happening. It didn't make sense. It didn't compute. She shook her head, bringing her focus back to the community center. The whole front was gone, and the rest of the windows were blown out. Anger replaced her sadness.

She returned to the car and called Logan. She stammered to get her words out. "Felix just bombed the community center, along with the university. So many dead, Logan."

"What are you doing down there? I told you not to worry about it."

"Shut up and listen to me," she screamed. "For once in your goddamn miserable arrogant life, shut up and listen. These people were my friends, my family. They've done nothing to anyone. This is your fault. You knew this was going to happen and you did nothing."

"Serena-"

"Shut up! You're going to do everything to save them or I disappear right now, taking everything I've learned with me. Good luck stopping Felix on your own."

A long silence came through the communicator. "All right. I have a team responding. We'll deal with the survivors. Can we get back on track now? Meet me in Buena Vista Park in thirty minutes. We'll talk."

Serena slumped back in the seat. The stream of people from the ruined building had slowed to a trickle. She prayed for those left inside. Felix would pay for this, right after she dealt with Logan. She left the parking lot, her tires squealing as she stomped the accelerator.

Serena hid her car amongst the few trees left on the south side of Old Buena Vista Park. She refused Logan's demands to tell him everything. She had to look him in the eye, to see how much he cared. His reaction would determine her next move.

She walked north on Buena Vista Avenue almost to Frederick, leaving everything in the car. She may never be back for it. She hid in one of the darkened bus shelters to wait for Logan and let her head fall back against the shelter wall. Public transport had been shut down so there was no worry of anyone coming by. Everything had been shut down.

The faces of the community center victims haunted her. She should've been there to protect them instead of chasing Felix. But then, she'd be dead too and that helped no one. Somewhere in the distance a car alarm sounded. Another thief at work. Probably not much left of the city to steal. If it were up to her, she'd bury every criminal in a deep, unmarked hole. A proper grave was too good for them.

Serena's head drooped forward and she snapped it up with a sharp breath. She rubbed her face trying to wake herself up a little. She checked the street again and huffed. *Hurry up, Logan.*

She couldn't keep this up much longer. *How did I make such a disastrous miscalculation?* She tried telling herself she was referring to her encounter with the thief, but was it really? Her entire life since she'd turned her back on Harlon had been one big miscalculation. Her return there tonight only reinforced those feelings.

She expected joining the Consortium to make a bigger difference. It hadn't. It only made her feel guilty. Then there were those people tonight. No matter which side of the line she was on, it made no difference. Her father would not have let things get this far. He always knew how to direct her focus properly. *Serena,* he'd say. *You know what to do. You only have to decide to do it.*

Serena tensed as a vehicle approached. She swiped the wetness from her cheeks as it pulled to stop and Logan climbed out. She wouldn't let him see her in a moment of weakness. She was a survivor and she'd survive this.

Serena would do it on her own, though, instead of counting on a thief or a madman leveling the city one bomb at a time. Or Logan for that matter. People like them were only interested in themselves. She was resourceful enough to salvage this. She could convince Felix and Ivan her disappearance had been a kidnapping. Not an easy task though. She'd given him more than enough reason not to trust her.

"You okay?" Logan asked as he got out of the car.

"What do you think?" she snapped. "I've been shot at, almost run over, and now Felix probably thinks I'm working with the thief. I'm just peachy."

"We have to keep going. We can't let these people dictate to us. This is our goddamn city. We built it from the ground up. No one is going to take it from us."

Was Janik really that smart and she that naïve? The more she thought about it, the more she doubted. "Easy for you to say. You're tucked away safely in your office with your Consortium pals. I'm the one getting mixed up with thieves and homicidal maniacs. Now I have to convince a terrorist that I'm not a spy, and that it'd be really nice if he didn't kill me."

Logan glared at her. "I haven't been behind a desk. I've been dealing with the looting teams in the north. So far, I've been able to keep them away from the major assets. I am also dealing with reports of UN crews hitting our warehouses. They're robbing us blind, Serena. I've had to call in some Fed Sec favors. They'll be touching down within the hour."

"Oh right. You mean the strike teams Felix has out hunting for Consortium members. Like the one that blew the fuck out of Nob Hill." She was almost screaming now. She clamped her mouth shut, allowing the moment of burning rage to simmer down. "I'm going to ask you a simple question and I demand a straight answer. Does the Consortium Executive Order exist?"

"Officially no, but there are some who want to have more say than others."

"Who are they? Are you protecting them inside the Pyramid? Is that why I don't have clearance above the tenth floor?"

"No. I don't know who they are. Listen Serena, I'm not sure what you've heard, but this shadow council business is mostly propaganda and rumor started by the UN to gain sympathy. There's nothing there."

She didn't believe him. Not one little bit. "I told you this was too much for me, Logan. I can't do it anymore."

"You signed up for this, remember. Maybe I was wrong thinking you could handle it."

"Go to hell," she shouted. "You insisted even after I told you I had no undercover experience. This is all on you." The tears spilled over now. "Take me back to Felix. Whatever else he is, he at least has a bit of sympathy. Who knows? Maybe he'll make my death quick."

She got into the car and slammed the door. He avoided looking at her as he climbed behind the wheel. He took a wrapped piece of food from the dashboard and held it out to her. The aroma of roast beef overruled her anger and desire to accept anything from him. She grabbed the sandwich and devoured half of it before taking a breath. Neither spoke for a long while as they drove back towards Land's End. Perhaps he felt guilty. No, she doubted Logan had a guilty bone in his body.

"Where is the thief now?" he asked finally. "Does he know about us?"

"He knows I work for the Consortium. Someone called him while we were running from Felix's men. Probably a marshal. I left him in the Mission District with a nasty headache."

Logan's eyes narrowed at the revelations. "Interesting. What else did you learn?"

Serena stared out the window, chewing on her lower lip. "They're stealing all of your data and planning an assault on the Pyramid sometime within the next twenty-four hours. I don't think they'll wait that long though. They'll strike as soon as they find your little boy's club."

"How do you know that?"

"One of the sec officers dropped his communicator after I shot him. We only heard a few seconds of the transmission before the encryption kicked in."

"They're not getting inside the Pyramid. No one gets inside the Pyramid."

"They will if they have all the access codes and override protocols. That's part of the reason they're after Janik. He's supposed to help decrypt the files."

Logan punched the steering wheel several times. "Make sure they don't get him. Kill him if you have to. Have you figured out who his Mission District contacts are yet?"

Serena choked back the sour tang in her mouth. It was always about the advantage for Logan, no matter who he used. "No, and I doubt I'll see him again. I imagine he's not pleased about how our encounter ended."

"Find him and figure it out," Logan growled. "I want names. I'm going to shut them down permanently. Bring him to me if he won't cooperate. I'll get the information out of him myself."

She let out a slow, deliberate breath. Trying to reason with the man was pointless. "Is Nelson still online?"

"I have no idea. I haven't been back to ops all day. Why?"

"He's going to help me convince the thief to cooperate. I need the Promenade bombing footage."

"Do whatever you have to. Was there anything else on the dead guy?"

She hesitated. Should she tell him about the keycard? "Just his weapon. I guess Felix doesn't even trust his own people."

"With good reason." Logan let out a frustrated sigh, but he was no more frustrated than her. "Figure out how to access Felix's network. Soon."

Serena regarded Logan from the corner of her eye. *I guess that answers the question about how much he cares.* Logan Marks only gave a damn about himself and the people who paid him. Those people would likely find themselves on the wrong side of his pistol if it benefited him.

"Be honest, Logan. Why is it that the Mission District never received help after the Great Quake? The Consortium had the money and the resources to ensure no one went cold and hungry. They were ignored."

"They didn't want to participate in their own survival, so we left them to their misery."

"What does that mean? Didn't want to participate in their own survival? Makes no sense."

"They refused to help rebuild unless certain guarantees were made. My superiors wouldn't give them."

"So you abandoned good people when they refused to be used as slaves."

"It had nothing to do with me. The decision was out of my hands, but why should the Consortium provide handouts? We're not running a charity. Pay up or get lost."

"Because it was the right thing to do," she mumbled. "Greed killed way more people than the quake."

Logan snickered and shook his head. "I didn't think you were so altruistic. It's a trait not helpful to the world we live in."

"Perhaps the world we live in is because we lack that trait."

"I'm beginning to worry about you, Serena. Can I trust you to see this through? I've invested a lot in you. Don't disappoint me."

"I'll do what I have to. Mainly because what Felix is doing isn't making things any better."

Logan dropped her near the Sutro Baths. "I'll leave the car at the corner of Prado and Cervantes. Report back in two hours. If you're not dead."

CHAPTER 24: STRIPPED BARE

Serena dragged her feet towards Land's End, Logan's last words echoing in her ears. *If you're not dead.* He may have been facetious, but Ivan and Felix were no fools. Her lifespan now probably measured in minutes. Her heart sped up, and her palms became clammy. Her legs felt like cement blocks. A terrified whine escaped her throat as the Nash Industries complex came into view.

Ivan leaned against the side of the building, arms crossed. His oily grin unnerved her. "I should've put a bullet in your chest when I caught you outside Felix's office. The aggravation it would've saved me." He had that look in his eyes, like he would enjoy hurting her. He shifted his position and massaged massive hands as if preparing them to do their painful work.

She swallowed her fear. *You've been in situations like this before.* She'd confronted criminals, taken down dangerous UN operatives. All with ice cold calm. This was no different. "Felix will want the information I have."

Ivan snorted. Felix was perhaps the one person on the planet he wouldn't cross. "Felix wants you dead. Lucky for you, he wants to talk first."

Serena had never been on death row, but she imagined the trek feeling this way. The result would likely be the same.

In the elevator, Ivan leaned in close, breathing hot air into her ear. "Tell me what you're really doing here, and I'll make your death quick."

Serena held still for a moment, tilting her head slightly toward Ivan's raspy mouth. "I will tell you one thing, Ivan. Something very useful to you. Consider switching mouthwash." She smirked to herself as Ivan growled and backed off. He wanted so bad to hurt her. Hopefully, Felix's protection would last a bit longer.

Felix shared a brief glance with Ivan as they walked into the office. Ivan's rage was far more comforting than the passive calm etched on Felix's features. He revealed nothing. He could be picturing a thousand ways to flay the skin from her flesh or deciding what to have for breakfast.

Finally, the uncomfortable silence pushed her over the edge. "I'm sorry. I didn't mean to get kidnapped. The thief grabbed me when I went to see what the alarms were about. He had a gun."

Ivan stared at her. "He kidnapped you, drove you all the way to Pacifica, then all the way back, and what, just let you go? Is that how it really happened? Don't lie. Felix doesn't like liars. Neither do I."

Serena's mind raced. "He had a gun. He grabbed me from the path. What was I supposed to do? I told him if he wanted to live, he'd better bring me back to Felix."

Felix studied her, his eyes drilling deep inside her soul. "What did you tell him?"

Standing up to him was the only way to get him to trust her enough to let her in. Or it would get her killed. "Nothing. I don't know anything. He kept asking about your network. He asked if there were any back doors. I have no idea what he's talking about."

Ivan crossed his arms, not buying her story. "Why didn't you scream for help when my officers showed up in Pacifica?"

Serena rubbed her face tiredly. "I panicked. They were shooting at us. I didn't think they'd stop because I told them I was Felix's new girl. After we got out of range, I told him I didn't know anything."

"Who killed my officer?" Felix asked.

"He was the one with the gun."

"Did he take anything from the body?"

"Not that I saw." She applauded herself for having the sense to leave the keycard in the car.

Felix sat back, tapping his finger on his desk. "Where is the thief now?"

One dead sec officer didn't seem to bother him. "I don't know. He disappeared after dumping me at the Sutro Baths." Serena pointedly ignored Ivan, "I know I screwed up, Felix. I want to repay the help you've given me. I know I can."

"What can you do to help Felix?" Ivan demanded.

Serena kept her eyes locked on Felix. "I know people. You know who I used to work for. They can get you leads to the Consortium you don't have now. Don't throw that away because of one stupid mistake." She hoped Nelson could drop a couple false trails to keep Ivan busy until she figured out her next move.

"You could've compromised me, Olivia, but you seemed to have handled the situation coolly. A useful trait."

Serena bit her lip and let out a quiet exhale. "I'll try to be more aware of my surroundings next time. This won't happen again, although it wasn't completely without reward."

Felix cocked an eyebrow and smirked. "Is that so?

"During our escape from Ivan's men, someone called him on a communicator exactly like the ones the marshals use. It nearly got us killed. If I ever see that little bastard again, I'm going to strangle him."

"Interesting," Felix said. "Perhaps there's a future for you in covert ops. Maybe I should send you back out with a weapon. Who knows what other valuable tidbits you'd learn?"

I'd settle for access to the files you're stealing. With those and the decryption keys Janik had, she'd take down both the UN and the Consortium. No more manipulation, no more greed, no more extortion. If she couldn't help anyone on either side of the line, she'd erase the line.

"Felix," Ivan protested. "You're not actually buying this crap, are you? This is the second time she's crossed the line. I warned you about this. Let me get rid of her."

"I'll decide who I get rid of," Felix snapped. "Make sure she's clean and then find out who's on the other end of that communicator. I want this thorn clipped soon."

"Let's go." Ivan shoved her hard from behind.

Serena held her composure, making check marks in her mental notebook. When the time came, he'd be the first to eat a bullet.

He escorted her back to her barracks on Level One. She expected him to leave. Instead, he blocked the door. "Strip."

An icy chill ran down her spine. "I beg your pardon?"

"You heard me, strip." His tone said he wouldn't repeat himself.

Serena's defenses went back up. This wasn't part of the plan. "You going to rape me to teach me a lesson?"

Ivan moved in closer, chuckling all the while. He caressed her cheek and moved his fingers through her hair. Serena whimpered, but she held her ground. His hand closed around a fistful of hair. He yanked back. Serena screamed and tried to pull away.

Ivan held firm, his hot breath only inches from her face. "I'm not interested in your body, only what it might be hiding. Let's get one thing straight. I haven't trusted you from the beginning. I don't believe for one second you're who you say you are. I think you're an undercover Consortium spy here to bring Felix down."

Serena ran her tongue across her upper lip and laughed despite her terror. "It's a good thing he doesn't share that opinion."

Ivan yanked again, eliciting a short yelp. "I'm going to find out what game you're really playing. Then we'll see who's laughing. Who knows, maybe then we can have a little fun." He shoved her hard against the wall and leveled his pistol at her. "Now, strip."

Serena undressed, her face passive. She tried not to focus on

Ivan's salacious grin. She closed her eyes and tried to picture it as a normal evening preparing for bed. Except, trembling in fear wasn't part of her typical bedtime routine. She stripped down to her underwear. The only thing keeping her upright was the pain she envisioned causing this son-of-a-bitch in the near future.

"Underwear, too," he demanded.

Serena hesitated, the humiliation almost too much to bear. She hated having to endure this to keep an operation she'd wanted no part of safe. If she lived through this, she was going to shove her fist down Logan's throat.

Ivan shook out every piece of her clothing while Serena hugged herself, covering up as much as possible. "Maybe this will teach you the consequences of stupidity. Next time, they'll be finding you in pieces."

He stormed out of the apartment and Serena buried her face in her hands, letting out a ragged breath. Even though Ivan hadn't touched her, she still felt violated. She felt the same when Harlon used to parade her in front of his friends like some piece of equipment up for auction. Her skin crawled at the thought of them undressing her with their eyes. No amount of showering would make her feel clean again. She stared at the pile of clothes in front of her. *What I wouldn't give for some gasoline and a match.*

Serena took a deep breath and wiped her eyes. She still had a job to do. Ivan wasn't the first man to see her naked. The marshal academy didn't segregate cadets. Except now it was personal. No matter what else happened, she'd destroy Ivan and Felix. She added Logan to the list for good measure.

Serena showered and dressed in plain black pants and a black tank top. The clothes matched her mood. What would her mother think of her if she saw her now? Perhaps it was better that she wasn't around to judge.

She jumped at the sudden knock at the door. The time on her wall display said 3am. Three hours since she returned to Land's

End. "Who is it?"

"Felix," an irritated response came from the other side.

Serena leaped from the bed, scrambling for something to defend herself. There was nothing. She calmed herself and considered her position. Killing her here didn't make sense. He'd have it done away from the complex, where he didn't have to witness it.

She opened the door to his scowling face. "I do not like to be kept waiting," he said.

She offered a nervous half-smile. "Sorry. I wasn't dressed."

Felix pushed his way into the room. "Your trust has been called into question, Olivia. I'm not sure the damage can be undone. Ivan wants me to get rid of you. Frankly, I see his point."

Serena leaned against the wall and crossed her arms. "He thinks I'm a Consortium spy."

"What if I told you I believed him? What if I told you I suspected it all along?"

Serena tensed, ready to defend herself. "I assure you Felix, I -"

He raised his hand, cutting her off. "Don't beg, Olivia. It doesn't suit you. Despite Ivan's reservations, I am not here to harm you. I have a better use for you. Consider it another test. One on which your survival depends."

"For the sake of argument, say you're right. You want to turn me. You think I can help bring down the Consortium Executive Order. I'll tell you right now. I don't know who they are and that's the truth."

Felix grinned. "Your intelligence is the reason you're still alive. Are you in agreement?"

The situation wasn't ideal, but she'd have to risk it. "I guess I don't have much choice. I'm rather fond of breathing."

Felix stepped to one side to let her pass. "We're going for a drive."

CHAPTER 25:
PROBLEMS

Rhea rubbed some of the tiredness from her face. They'd been at this for hours. What time was it anyway? Had to be well past midnight for sure. She pushed her chair away from the conference room table, cursing the day she accepted the appointment as mayor. "Grab some coffee or fresh air, everyone. We'll reconvene in fifteen minutes."

Sarah came to sit at the edge of her desk as the rest of her team filed out of the office. "You look like you used to on the Mondays after our wild university benders."

"Ha," she cackled, thankful for her personal assistant and dear friend. Rhea wouldn't be able to do half this job without her. Rhea may be the face of the government, but Sarah was the lynchpin. "I could use a stiff drink or six right about now."

Sarah grinned. "Can't help you there. You might want to try some of that coffee yourself."

"I'll be in the kitchen with my head in the coffee pot."

Rhea grimaced when she sipped the frigid bitter liquid. *Thank God for caffeine*, she thought. She brought her cup and the rest of the pot back to her office. She hoped to have evacuation plans to execute by sunrise. Getting millions of people out of the city with only the bridges turned out to be a logistical nightmare. Those that were willing to go, that was. Many had decided to ride it out. Rhea didn't know whether to call them dumb or brave.

Fighting over resources had increased in the past few hours. Then there were the shootouts in the Financial District. As if there weren't enough bodies to deal with. Never mind that many up there were her major campaign contributors. They wouldn't be happy with her over this.

Sarah appeared at the open door. "A bunch of Fed Sec transports just landed in the courtyard, and you have a visitor."

"I don't have all night, Mayor Waters." Logan Marks, Consortium stronghold and head of Marks' Security pushed his way into her office. He glared at Sarah. "Leave."

Speak of the devil. Rhea didn't want to deal with this man, but knew she'd have to sooner or later. Rhea nodded to Sarah. "I can't say I'm surprised to see you, Mister Marks. I assume you're the one who called Fed Sec. That decision should've been run by me first."

Logan snorted and leaned back in the chair. He put his foot up on her desk. "I'm running out of patience, Mayor, and your permission isn't required. Prepare yourself. You'll be shocked by some of what I have to say."

His arrogant expression grated on every fiber of her being. Rhea didn't have the energy to fight him. He could make her life a living nightmare. Not that the day hadn't been already. "Well, since they're already here, we might as well use them."

"I thought you'd see it my way. They're setting up in your main conference room."

They entered the conference room to find Commander Demitrius Solomon already moving with a cold efficiency. No platitudes. All business. Within minutes, they were set up with tablets on the conference table linked in with their Fort Bragg network. Each tablet had a section of the map of San Francisco open on it. Those sections were marked with symbols showing where the marshals and Logan's teams were. "Put this up on the big screen."

"I appreciate you helping out, Demetrius," Logan said. "We're running out of time."

"It's what we do. I'm a little surprised you couldn't handle this one on your own. Give me a full sit rep."

"It's pretty simple," Logan said. "Cyber-attack causing rolling blackouts, high explosive detonations in strategic sectors of the city, and all around general chaos. They've turned the Financial District into a combat zone. Our servers have been compromised. We've tracked the attack to Land's End and a man named Felix Nash. He is stealing all of our data and using it to target several high-level citizens, as well as power centers, water collectors, roads and bridges."

"I don't follow," Rhea said. "Felix Nash is a businessman, not a terrorist."

"A businessman, as you put it, who managed to build an underground bunker without anyone knowing. An underground bunker that would've required permits." His voice rose and spittle flew from his mouth as he spoke. "Not to mention, he's bleeding dry our reserves. How do you suppose he got that?"

Rhea didn't appreciate this cretin's implication. "You're crazy if you think someone from this office is helping him."

Logan leaned forward slowly and folded his hands on top of the table. "I'm pissed off, Mayor, not crazy. And when I find out who helped Felix, they're going to wish I was crazy." He switched on the monitor on the wall. Disturbing images of marshals herding people into transports and beating anyone that didn't comply. The caption across the bottom of the screen read: 'The marshals are not your friends. The Consortium doesn't care about you. They live in luxury while you languish in poverty.' "Where did they get those images, Mayor?"

"How should I know? You people own the media. Maybe you should talk to them."

Commander Solomon held up his hands, stopping everyone. "None of this helps the current situation. Those images are meant as a distraction. They're roadblocks. Reacting to them plays into their hands."

"I have reason to believe his motives are related to the dross lakes, but the security overrides have been disabled."

Rhea pressed her fingers to her eyes and slumped her head. She felt the beginnings of a massive headache building at the base of her skull and down through her neck. "No wonder we can't get into our servers. Can't risk exposing the Consortium's dirty laundry."

Logan snickered. "This isn't us. Whatever Felix is doing has shut us all out. We need that information as much as you do."

Yeah, so you can erase it. "A lot of families were none too pleased about being displaced by those lakes. Maybe Felix belongs to one of them and wants a little payback."

"The files are useless to Felix unless he can decrypt them, and he hasn't gotten that far yet."

Commander Solomon waved to one of his subordinates. "Get some algorithms on that. See if you can wrestle back some control. Tell me about Land's End."

"It's an underground complex with six levels and a lot of firepower. I'm convinced Felix has connections to a black-market group called the Underground Network operating out of the Mission District. They've been a pain in my ass for years and recently hit a truckload of our Synthetic Liquid."

"That's not your grandfather's TNT. What are you doing with that much Ice Water?"

Logan smirked. "Construction."

Solomon made a notation on the map at Land's End. "Mental situation? Demands?"

"No demands," Logan replied. "No contact of any kind. They are planning an assault on the Pyramid sometime soon. My employers believe this is a direct assault on their interests. I have an asset working on acquiring more intel, but Felix is playing everything close to the vest."

"Asset?" Rhea choked on the words she really wanted to say to this arrogant ass. "You sent a civilian into a potentially dangerous situation? I was wrong. You're not crazy, you're stupid."

"Insults aside, Mayor, this asset is very good, though she doesn't know it yet. I'd trust her with my life."

"How reassuring," Rhea replied. Insulting her benefactors' security chief probably wasn't a good idea, but her white-hot anger overrode any sense of self-preservation.

Again, Solomon put himself between them. "When is she due to check in again?"

"Couple hours. She's trying to shut it down from the inside. Something for her to go on makes our jobs easier."

Solomon turned to one of his soldiers. "Get me everything on Felix Nash, right back to when he crapped his first diaper." He turned back to Rhea and Logan. "How are you currently deployed?"

"Our efforts thus far have been directed at rescuing stranded citizens and controlling the looting," Rhea said. "Those that can be saved are given priority."

"We don't have the resources to police the city and take on terrorists," Logan said. "We've moved some of our people into hiding."

Solomon activated the communicator headset he wore. "Launch the birds. I want real time images in ten minutes. We can start putting together an assault solution."

Logan was shaking his head before Solomon finished speaking. "An overt assault would be a bloodbath."

Solomon cocked an eyebrow at him. "My team's pretty good."

"Good enough to overcome someone familiar with your tactics? Their security chief is former Fed Sec. Ivan Hess. They're well-armed, well organized, and don't mind getting bloody. They likely know you're here."

"Well, shit."

Rhea leaned across the table. "You know this guy?"

"Ivan Hess is a ruthless son-of-a-bitch that chases the money. When he left the agency, he started a gun-for-hire mercenary group. Poached some of our best operators. He's efficient. If you have a shot at him, don't hesitate." Commander Solomon called another one of his colleagues over. "Take a recon team to Land's End. I want to see what's going on there. Do not engage anyone. If things heat up, pull back. Watch your six. Hess is there."

Rhea tapped one of the tablet screens and the power generation center near Lands End appeared on the main screen. "What about a covert assault on their power grid? Without power, they lose control over the city's infrastructure. Not to mention their ability to generate breathable air."

"Not feasible. My intel indicates there are triggers embedded in the code that will go off if tampered with. Cutting the power could blow the whole thing sky high."

Solomon leaned over the table, eyes darting from Rhea to Logan. "Okay, so what are our options? Take out Felix? Snake dies without a head."

"Killing Felix doesn't turn the power back on," Rhea said. "Once he restores the network, you can do whatever you want with him."

"Taking Felix alive would be ideal. I intend to make him give me a list of everyone who helped him." Marks held up a hand, stopping Solomon's response. "There's more. My asset has made contact with a thief many believe to be somehow involved."

"I've seen his face on the news," Solomon said. "A sneaky son-of-a-bitch you can't seem to hold onto."

"He's insisting he's not responsible and is trying to shut down the cyber-attack. He's already failed at hacking Felix's network once."

Solomon snickered. "You're taking the word of a criminal accused of mass murder?"

"No, I'm taking the word of my asset. Besides, I have some history with him. He's dangerous with a keyboard, but heavy violence?" Logan shook his head slightly. "It doesn't fit."

"We need him in custody to find out what he knows," Rhea added.

"Let's handle the most pressing stuff first," Solomon said. "I'd like to coordinate with your marshals to take advantage of their resources."

"Chief Marshal Renaude Thiraro is leading the rescue effort. I'll have him report in when he is free."

"I also want all the evidence gathered from the bombings. I brought the whole setup. Field lab, facial rec. We can identify the ass end of a mosquito if necessary."

"I'll have it brought over," Rhea said. "Perhaps you can send one of your people to escort it?"

"Is that really necessary?"

Logan pulled Solomon to the far side of the room. Rhea followed. "The truth is, Commander, I'm questioning the chief marshal's loyalty," he said. "I'd rather not trust him with something this important. The thief has escaped his custody twice already."

Rhea's head dropped forward. Why did this idiot have to open his mouth? Rhea wished she could drop him and his whole organization. Yes, they'd saved the city after the Great Quake. That didn't make up for the festering cancer they'd become. "I'm not convinced Renaude is a traitor," Rhea interjected, "but Logan is right, until we know more, caution is prudent."

Solomon was confused. "What would drive him to turn against his own city?"

Rhea shrugged. "He's been edgy of late. Who knows what's in those pills he takes? He may not be in his right mind."

"Pills?"

Logan cut her off with a glare. "Renaude takes pills for an old knee injury. The result of a previous encounter with our thief friend, from my understanding. I'm assured there is nothing in them to turn him into a lunatic."

Commander Solomon held up his hand, silencing Logan. "This is all fine, but we're only a small team. I can't fight terrorists and the marshals too without calling in more resources. What about sub-commanders? There must be someone you trust."

Rhea's voice hitched in her throat. She didn't really know who to trust. Outside of perhaps Sarah. "We'll have to make do with what we have."

Rhea didn't miss his glance at Logan. Under different circumstances, she'd pay to hear the history between those two.

"I know you, Logan," he said. "What aren't you telling me? I expect full disclosure. If you're keeping things from me, I pack up my team and go home."

Logan took a deep breath. "During the encounter with my asset, the thief received a call on a locked communicator. The same type the marshals use. He also claims he didn't escape."

"You think Renaude let him go?"

"I find it difficult to believe one person could overcome even one trained marshal, let alone several. He also had information that somebody had to give him."

Rhea braced herself against the table, trying to make sense of it all. "Why would Renaude do something like that?"

"We'll be sure to ask him when he comes in."

"Renaude personally set up the transport that supposedly killed the thief." Rhea had to consider that Renaude staged the whole thing. "What if he wasn't the only criminal from that transport to survive?"

"I didn't think Renaude was stupid enough to get involved with something this big, but I've been wrong before."

"Maybe he didn't realize how far Felix would take it. Now, he's trying to back out."

"You should probably check those transport logs," Solomon said.

"They'll be coming over with the rest of the evidence," Rhea replied.

Solomon removed his head dress and swiped his sleeve across his forehead. "Okay, let's recap so I have this straight. You're sitting on a powder keg with a couple of wild cards out there doing their own thing. I remember you being smarter, Logan. Be warned, my people will shoot first and ask questions later. It'll end badly for anyone in the wrong place at the wrong time."

"I'll keep that in mind," Logan replied. "What's the next step?"

"Deploy everything the marshals have. No one lifts a finger unless it comes through me."

"I can help with the manpower," Logan said, "My security teams are already deployed."

Rhea groaned to herself. The Consortium and Fed Sec running roughshod around the city. "I'd appreciate it if you didn't bathe the streets in blood. You're not the one answering the questions afterwards." From the reporters and his bosses. Rhea would be lucky if she wasn't skinned alive.

"I make no promises. If the UN gains control of the city, Mayor, the consequences will be dire…for everybody. I, for one, will not see that happen. Do you want your city back or not?"

"Is it really my city, Mister Marks?" Rhea didn't care about the Consortium or their money. She did at one time, when she believed in what they were doing. Then the greed and corruption grew like an insidious weed. Most of their power was extorted from citizens anyway. Her whole body shook with rage. "You should've come to me this morning with all of this. The Consortium has no right to take the law into your own hands. We have marshals for that."

Rhea winced as soon as the words were out of her mouth.

Perhaps she should filter her thoughts a little more carefully. There was no taking them back now.

"Please, Mayor," he replied, "save your vitriol for the terrorists. It's wasted on me. I will do what is necessary to ensure our investments are protected."

"The extra men will help, Logan," Solomon said, cutting off another potential outburst, "but understand, like the marshals, they make no moves without my say-so. This situation is going to be hard enough to control as it is."

Logan scowled. "Fine, you can relay your orders through me. My guys don't like strangers."

Solomon raised his hands. "Whatever works for you." He turned to the mayor. "Call the chief marshal in. We can use him without letting on that we suspect something. Maybe he'll reveal what he's up to while we keep an eye on him."

He then turned to one of his lieutenants. "Organize a strike team to go into the hot zones. Non-lethal force only. Dead men can't speak. Send a couple guys to the Mission District to confirm Logan's suspicions."

"Your men should be careful, Commander," Logan said. "They don't like us too much down there. Now, if you will excuse me, I have to relay my report to my superiors."

Rhea approached the commander after Logan left. *I likely won't get another opportunity.* "Listen, Commander, I know you have a history with Mister Marks, but frankly, his shoot first, ask questions later methods make me uncomfortable. Not to mention his complete lack of a moral compass. I suspect he's purposely keeping information from me. He will leave me with a mess of bodies lining the streets."

"Subtlety was never his strong suit. We'll try to limit the collateral damage, but to end this quickly, we're going to have to bloody some knuckles."

"A few dead terrorists, I can explain. Dead citizens will go over about as well as a day old Synth burger. That stain won't be washed away with their money and it will likely cost me my job."

"I hear you, Madam Mayor. For what it's worth, I never liked Logan's style much myself, though you can't argue with his results. We'll keep an eye on his teams. We'll intervene if things get out of hand."

Rhea nodded. "Thank you, Commander. I'm here if you need anything."

She left the conference room buoyed by her new ally, but the feeling was fleeting. She fought a new round of indigestion as she wondered what the hell Renaude was up to.

CHAPTER 26: CHOICES

Felix brought Serena to a place she didn't want to go. A place she'd left only a couple hours earlier. She purposely stared at her feet. She didn't want to see the church, or the decrepit buildings, or the burnt-out cars. Even after all these years, it still brought too much pain.

"I must apologize for Ivan's treatment in the apartment. He is overbearing at times."

The apology surprised her. He didn't seem like that sort of man. "It doesn't matter," she lied. "It's not the first time a man has seen me naked."

"The first time it wasn't by choice, I'd imagine."

She forced herself to look out the window then. Darkness enveloped everything so she couldn't see much. The only ones out at this hour were kids with dirty and dejected faces. Some had mothers clutching them tight against their side. They all should be asleep in warm, comfortable beds. Most didn't have warm, comfortable beds. They watched Felix's fancy car drive past with a mixture of fear and anger. Such an arrogant display of wealth.

Nothing here gave anyone any hope for a brighter future. Despite Felix's grandiose ideas, she didn't see it. "Why are we here? I escaped this place once. I wasn't expecting to come back."

"To remind you that you have a right to go home," he insisted. "You have a right to have a home to go to. Yes, I see the agony in your face. Whether you want to admit it or not, that pain is born of desire to repair the damage."

Maybe that was true once upon a time. Most of her pain now was born of guilt. She burned the bridges with people she cared about. She realized that earlier. "There is nothing left for me here." *But it wouldn't be for me,* she thought. *We're in this mess because of selfishness. If I'm going to do anything, it has to be without reward.* "I doubt I'd be welcomed. As a marshal I helped put away several high-profile UN operatives. Most people here worship the UN."

"Organizations like the UN and Consortium, they're byproducts of fear. They prey on it. I don't blame you for joining the Consortium. What choice did you have? You did what was necessary to survive. The oppression has gone on long enough." He slowed the car and rolled down her window. "Look at the buildings, Olivia. Look at the people." When she didn't adjust her gaze, he screamed. "I said look! Why should they be any different than the people in Nob Hill, or the Tenderloin? Districts like this one go ignored while the elitists continue to pamper their useless lives, leaving disasters like the dross lakes for others to clean up. Soon everyone will see the truth of it."

Serena didn't give a damn about the dross lakes. Not unless it showed her a way out. Still, she felt a little guilty at the truth in his words. She had a nice apartment in a nice neighborhood. What was wrong with enjoying a little luxury, especially when you grew up in poverty? Her breath hitched. Janik said those very words earlier. "Perhaps I don't deserve your trust, but you told me I could make a difference. I can't do that if you won't tell me what's going on."

"You're a smart girl. Your passion is why I did not grant Ivan's wish. I should've seen it from the start. You've figured some things out. That is why your interference with the thief is such a delicate matter. Things are moving quickly and I can't afford detours."

Serena cast sidelong glances at him. "I don't understand."

"The call I received at dinner was from someone concerned

with the thief's presence. They requested I deal with the problem."

"I'm not sure I can help. I doubt I'll be seeing him again."

"Ah, but you can." Felix studied her curiously, trying to read her. Serena doubted she hid her emotions well. "I cannot tell you everything. The less people that know details the better. I need this person dealt with and the thief brought to me to decrypt some files. Ivan is too busy to handle it himself."

Serena couldn't have asked for a better break. "That might be a bit difficult. We aren't exactly on a first name basis."

Felix's face took on a grave note. "I'm sure you'll figure something out."

"I'll have to earn his trust. Make him believe I am helping him. That will take some time. Enough time for you to finish your preparations."

Felix nodded. "Do we have an arrangement?"

Serena locked eyes with Felix. "I'll drag him back by his neck if I have to."

Felix pulled over at the corner of Market and Valencia. He handed her a communicator and a pistol. "You won't shoot me if I give you this, will you?"

She ejected the clip from the gun. Fully loaded. He must've been really confident in her decision. She reassembled the weapon and tucked it inside her jacket.

"Very good," Felix said with a nod. "Your target has a ponytail and is at a club called the District. There is an alley behind the club. I suggest starting there."

"Never thought I'd become an assassin," she muttered. "Not that a piece of UN scum is worth losing any sleep over."

"Call me when you find him. I'll send a car to pick you up. Do not disappointment me, Olivia, or I will grant Ivan his wish."

"Don't worry. I know exactly what I have to do."

The buildings around her, the ones that weren't piles of

rubble, still showed cracks and broken brick from the Great Quake, now twenty years in the past. She remembered the bodies trapped beneath them as if it were yesterday. The image of her father's hand sticking out flashed in her head, making her flinch.

Did she really want to come back here? Did she belong here anymore? Serena allowed herself a brief moment to picture the district if Felix succeeded. Bright streets, fresh brick on houses that stood upright with painted walls and shiny cars parked out front. Smiling people. Her old house whole again. And the music. Once again, the music would play. Most importantly, no UN peddling their ill-begotten wares in the back allies and bathroom stalls.

For some, everything they owned, their whole lives, was here. They deserved hope. Her guilty heart hung heavy. No matter how hard she tried to forget it, this place would always be a part of her. Why had it taken Felix pointing it out for her to realize that?

Her newfound purpose left her in a bad spot with Logan. His corruption knew no bounds. He wanted Janik's UN contacts. If he got them, he'd sweep away this whole district. Surprisingly, he hadn't done it yet.

She tucked the gun and communicator in her pocket and made her way to the district's lower west side. Stripped out cars and leaning, burnt out street lights lined both sides of the road. Serena didn't fight the memories anymore. Alleys she used to play in as a girl were now filled with broken brick and glass, their darkness likely hiding a few homeless. If she had stayed, she'd be one of them.

Maybe that's why she hated Janik so much. She was just like him. As was Harlon, who only ever wanted her to use her. She felt a little guilty for knocking Janik over the head, but he deserved it. She'd tell herself that again when she killed him.

Serena leaned against the side of the building across the street, hands jammed firmly in her pocket. One of them was wrapped around the pistol grip. She watched the door for any suspicious traffic, but only observed drunken party-goers trying to shut out the chaos happening a few short miles away.

A motorcycle pulled up to the alley next to the club. A slender man got off and removed his helmet, releasing a long brown ponytail. He surveyed the street in both directions and disappeared into the alley. Serena inched her way down the sidewalk.

Serena stopped briefly to check out the bike, careful to stay quietly in the shadows. Serena checked the alleyway behind her. Muffled voices drifted from a cracked open window halfway up the wall. Serena couldn't make out the words. Her only option was the dumpster next to the window. She climbed up, using the rough, brick wall for support. She brought the back of her hand to her nose against the unbearable stench, but the motion almost threw off her balance. She clutched the windowsill and steadied herself. Some assassin she was. She should just knock on the window and get the inevitable over with.

She hauled herself back up to the window and strained to see through the dirty glass. Ponytail paused at the door when his communicator went off. He hit one of the buttons and set the device down on his desk. He threw his jacket across the back of his chair and poured himself a drink from a bottle in the liquor cabinet.

Ponytail took a sip before flopping down into the chair. "Wasn't expecting to hear from you for a few more days. Figured you'd have your hands full until then."

"I have another job for you." That was Felix's voice. "It involves a person of mutual interest. He has become a nuisance that requires handling."

"Not sure I can help you. I was planning on staying in hiding until this whole thing blows over. Perhaps I can put you in touch with an associate of mine."

"No," Felix replied. "You will handle this personally. I'm prepared to pay a premium for a quick resolution. Once I have Janik Brynn, you can crawl back to your slimy hole."

Felix didn't trust her fully to do the job so he doubled down. She admired the play. If Serena delivered Janik, it meant he could trust her. If Ponytail did, he'd know her intentions for sure. He'd still end up with the decryption codes and Ponytail dead.

"Why do you need him? He was supposed to be nothing more than bait that you were supposed to eliminate after you were done with him."

"There were complications with the procedure. He's carrying a tablet with some decryption codes on it. Bring both to me in good working order."

That wasn't good. If Ponytail got that tablet, she was finished.

"That may be a little complicated. I don't think he trusts me anymore."

Gee, I wonder why, Serena thought.

"I'm paying you well enough to uncomplicate it. Do this and I will overlook your interference with the Consortium warehouses. Don't bother denying it. You're about as obvious as a corrupt politician."

"I figured it was a fair trade for the Ice Water shipment that my people risked their neck to acquire."

Logan had been right about the explosives. The UN had been behind it all along. Janik suspected someone of setting him up. Serena now knew who it was. Logan would be real interested in knowing that.

"I told you once my work was complete there would be plenty of spoils for you to reap."

"Yeah, well, maybe I'm not the patient type."

"Do we have an accord?"

"He's got a house in Pacifica. If he's not there, I'll make sure to leave him a message."

Serena hoped Janik wasn't stupid enough to go back to his house. She jumped down from the dumpster. She lost her balance and stumbled back and slammed her elbow into the dumpster. It sounded like someone pounded a drum next to her ear. Everything stopped inside and Serena's stomach clenched.

She bolted for the front of the alley, putting bullets into the motorcycle's tires as she passed. She sprinted across the road and back into the darkness. The assassin came out of the alley and screamed. She didn't look back to see for sure, but she assumed he had found his bike.

Janik had clued in that Ponytail supplied the explosives. Serena had to find him before Ponytail did.

CHAPTER 27: INTERROGATION

Rhea stomped around her office, tearing at her hair. Blood pounded in her ears, and she'd barely heard the rest of the report on the epically stupid attempt on Ivan Hess's life. "What the hell were you thinking? You should have let my marshals go after him. You had no right to take matters into your own hands. Now more people are dead, and you have nothing to show for it."

She'd laid down on the couch in the corner last night to try to get a couple hours sleep anyway. It had been a futile exercise. Now, they were into the second day of a major terrorist attack and this asshole had gone and made things worse. For once, Rhea wished she weren't opposed to the death penalty.

Logan stood; hands folded behind his back. Anger seethed below the outward calm. Dirt coated his suit and his hair looked as if he just got out of bed. "I warn you, Mayor Waters. I'll only put up with your lack of respect for so long."

Rhea stalked up to him. She wanted to put her fist through his face, but that wouldn't end well. "To hell with your threats. Kill me if you're going to or get the hell out of my way."

Logan grabbed her by the throat and pinned her against the wall. He panted heavily, ejecting spittle into her face. Rhea clawed at his powerful hands, gasping for breath. "If I squeeze my hand a little harder, I'll snap your pathetic little neck. Beg me for your life, Mayor."

Two of Solomon's men pulled him off her. Rhea sucked in

gulps of air as she clutched her throat. Trembling, she sunk to the floor. She held back the tears threatening to spill over the rims of her eyes. She'd show him no more weakness.

"Let's get one thing straight, Mayor Waters," Logan seethed. "The Consortium owns San Francisco, not the people. Consider this your termination notice."

"Back off, Logan," Solomon snapped. "You agreed to play by my rules. Pull something like that again and I'll shoot you myself." Logan's face twitched nervously. "What the hell happened out there?"

Logan's white-hot glare remained on her. "Last night, Ivan did the rounds himself. He usually stays out of sight, which is why we didn't know he was here until recently. We had a few minutes of viable strike time. By the time we got into position, conditions were less than ideal. I took the shot anyway. I only grazed him before he made it back inside."

"What happened to 'an overt assault on the complex would be a bloodbath'?" Rhea demanded. "Your arrogance is going to get everyone killed."

Growling, Logan lunged towards her again. One of Solomon's men blocked his way, sidearm half out of its holster.

"Shut up, the both of you," Solomon snapped. He listened to his communicator. "Okay, track him, discreetly." He turned his attention to Rhea and Logan. "Renaude just left his mobile command unit carrying a duffle bag."

Rhea pressed her fingers to her eyes. "That idiot is only going to make things worse."

"Things can't get much worse," Logan said. "This is an opportunity to find out what he's up to. If things heat up, we can take him down."

Solomon held up his hand, stopping the angry retort she had on her lips. "We have bigger problems at the moment. Your little skirmish got someone's attention. One of my men put a fifty-caliber slug into the engine block of a delivery truck loaded with Ice Water heading for this building. My demo guy is dealing with the truck. Your boys are bringing the driver up now."

"Will he make it here alive?" Rhea spat. "Maybe you'd like to take a shot at him, too."

Stop it, Rhea, she scolded herself. Solomon won't be here to protect you forever.

Logan's stare felt like daggers in her chest. "Corpses can't talk, can they, Mayor?"

Rhea didn't flinch. "I want to be there when he's interrogated."

"Not a chance," Logan said. "I'm not letting your weak sensibilities interfere. This will be done by trained professionals."

"We will share what we learn," Solomon added.

Rhea held up her hand. They'd only give her enough to shut her up. She refused to be played like that. "I don't care. I want to hear what this bastard has to say from his lips, not disseminated from you two. Nothing gets left out."

"Suit yourself," Logan said after exchanging glances with Solomon, "I hope you're not squeamish."

Rhea watched the interrogation via video feed from the room next door. Her stomach turned every time Logan's fist landed. *This is the price of getting your city back.* Not to mention they'd stopped another bomb in the process. Even that silent reminder didn't completely ease her guilt.

She rubbed her throat, still feeling Logan's meaty fingers digging into her flesh. Logan Marks was a thing of nightmares. This was retribution, not an interrogation. Logan's anger shook foundations worse than any quake ever could.

Once they regained control, and they would regain it, Rhea vowed to do everything in her power to put the Consortium in their place. The insidious corruption had gone on long enough.

Flecks of blood dotted the floor like some sick abstract

painting. Logan slowly circled the prisoner like a shark circling chummed waters, rubbing his hand and smearing blood over his knuckles. He was enjoying this way too much.

She felt Commander Solomon's eyes studying her as he stood next to her. "You were warned, Mayor."

Yes, she had been. It didn't mean she had to like it. Rhea turned away as the prisoner's screams penetrated the walls. "This has nothing to do with explosives. Logan was embarrassed. This poor bastard is the unfortunate recipient of his revenge."

"Where are the other bombs?" Logan growled mere inches from his bloody face. "How many more are there? What are your other targets? Where did the truck come from?" Logan fired the questions in rapid succession.

"I don't know." The prisoner cowered away from Logan's imposing figure. He sobbed like a frightened child. "I only know the next mission. I don't remember anything before yesterday."

Logan's fist paused in mid-air. "Come again."

"I woke up in a hospital bed, was handed a key to the truck, and told to drive it here. The headaches were so bad I couldn't remember my own name."

Logan leaned in close to the prisoner, hands on the table. His nostrils flared as he studied the terrified prisoner's face. "How stupid do you think I am?" He grabbed the prisoner by the hair and yanked back. "You expect me to believe you can't remember anything beyond yesterday? That you've somehow had your memory wiped?"

"It's the truth. The only thing that mattered was getting that truck to this building. I had no impulse control. I didn't even know it was bombs."

A spark of recognition glimmered in Logan's eyes. "Where is this hospital? Who was the doctor? Give me names."

"I don't know," the driver wailed. "I don't know. Please, stop hurting me."

Surprisingly, Logan released his hair and backed away from the table. "What do you remember before you woke up?"

"Almost nothing. Everything is fragmented, confusing. It's like I went on a three-day bender. I have these weird burn marks on my forehead, but the headaches are the worst."

Logan stared at the prisoner for a long while, then pulled out his pistol and shot him in the head. "Deal with him," he ordered the guard. "I'll be back shortly."

Rhea gaped in dumbfounded horror. She thought the people blowing up the city were the monsters. Logan Marks was the real monster. She had to find a way to deal with him permanently.

A few seconds later, he entered the observation room. "I think I know what's going on, but I have to make a call."

Commander Solomon cocked an eyebrow and smirked. "Care to throw us a bone?"

"Cerebral Impulse Transplant," he replied and walked out of the room.

Solomon gawked at Rhea, a thick coat of confusion painting his face. "What the hell is that?"

Rhea took a deep breath and leaned against the wall. "A theoretical research program commissioned by members of the Pharmacy to study synapse reprogramming. Think electro-shock therapy on steroids."

"Why would anyone elect to go through something like that?"

"I don't know all the medical stuff, but it was meant to address certain mental illnesses. I didn't put much stock in it. A person's mind is a delicate thing to play with. More people died than lived. I questioned the ethics of it. Cost overruns eventually shut the program down. It appears Felix found a way to weaponize it."

Rhea had to accept some responsibility. She signed off on several of these questionable programs with next to no clinical data. In turn, she got to stay mayor. It turned her stomach now thinking on some of the things she overlooked to further her political career. No more. There had to be something she could do to make this right.

Solomon stared at the dead prisoner. "How much research did they do?"

She pictured the wheels turning in his head. *Don't get any ideas, buddy.* She wouldn't wish this on anyone. She didn't answer. She had no answer. After approvals were granted, the researchers went away, and she heard nothing else on it.

They returned to her office. She went to pour a cup of coffee, but the pot had only dribbles left in it. She threw the carafe back onto the side table and checked her watch. How was it 1pm already? "Sarah." Her assistant appeared in the doorway. "Can you make more coffee please, and see what's left in this building for food? I think I'm about to pass out."

"Of course, Mayor Waters. I'll be back shortly."

Logan came in right after Sarah left. "We have a big problem. The doctor that spearheaded the CIT research must have copied it and sold it to Felix."

"Who is this doctor?" Solomon asked.

"Neuroscience genius Doctor Mauro Barron. He's done decades of research in impulse transplants and synapse reprogramming. After the CIT program was shelved, he dropped off the radar."

"How did Felix get his hands on a doctor supposedly under Consortium observation?"

Logan shrugged. "That's a question for our Pharmacy partners. The company running the program was supposed to be containing the doctor. If Felix doesn't kill him, the Consortium will."

"Didn't you say a Pharmacy exec was killed at the Promenade? There has to be a link in there somewhere." Rhea asked. "Maybe this Doctor Barron didn't like being shut down."

"So those brainwashed citizens are probably planting more

bombs anywhere in the city," Solomon said. "I don't have to say that's not good, do I?"

Logan strode to the video monitor with his hands in his pockets. The guard had just finished zipping up the body bag. The blood stains would take a little longer to remove. "I suggest we start looking for connections to our friend in there. Find out where he's been. It might tell us how he got mixed up in this."

"Kind of hard to question him when his brains are splattered against the back wall," Rhea replied.

"Felix is going to know something's up when this building doesn't explode," Solomon said.

"He probably already knows. I think that truck bomb was meant to slow us down."

One of Solomon's men came in and handed him a tablet. His eyes narrowed in confusion. "Apparently, our forgetful friend in the other room was dead before Logan made it official. Died in a transport crash yesterday morning."

"Let me see that." Solomon handed her the tablet and a chill swept through her body. "It's the same transport the thief was on."

"Felix must be using your cerebral transplant thingy on the survivors of this phony transport crash."

"Begs the question what went wrong with the thief."

"I may have an answer to that," Logan replied. "Doctor Barron was never able to make the process one hundred percent reliable. It's part of the reason he was shut down. Too much money being spent trying to perfect a procedure impossible to perfect. Some of the subjects died, some went insane, and some reverted to their original state."

"How do you know all this?" Solomon asked.

"There were security threats with some of the subjects, so I was read into the program in the event drastic action was necessary."

Rhea rubbed her temples. When would this nightmare end? "Who else was on that transport, I wonder, and are they really dead?"

"We can compile a list of prisoners in holding about the same time as this fellow. It should give us an idea on how many operatives Felix has."

She looked back at the tablet screen. "If Felix reprogrammed all of those prisoners, that's a lot of bombs."

"Didn't you say the Renaude takes pills?"

"Logan did, but what does that hav-" Her eyes went wide with recognition. "Son-of-a-bitch. He thinks CIT can cure his addiction."

CHAPTER 28: COIT TOWER

The shaking had stopped by the time Janik pulled into old Mission Dolores Park. He sucked in one breath after another. He didn't understand what was happening. One minute everything was fine, the next, he couldn't even remember what day of the week it was.

As Janik continued the breathing exercises, his heart rate slowed, and his thoughts came back into focus. It didn't get any better.

Grisly images played over and over, like a bad song on repeat. The first thug he shot died before hitting the ground. The other two were not quite so easily dispatched. The remaining one was probably still tailing him.

Janik turned his attention from the thoughts he could no longer bear to his surroundings. The park had gone from the lush green grass of his youth to splotchy brown patches and a rundown playground with rusty monkey bars. Strange how he could remember the park, but not one specific time he'd been here.

Sitting here provided too much time to dwell on his encounter with Patricia. It went as well as expected, though, he sure as hell wasn't expecting to get shot at. He didn't see what happened to them after he started shooting. As long as they made it out alive, he'd live with never seeing them again.

He didn't have to wait long for Renaude. The chief marshal tossed a duffle bag at Janik's feet. "We don't have a lot of time. I am certain I was followed."

Janik paused as he stripped off his jacket. "Do they suspect you of working with me?"

"Most likely, but the situation has changed."

"How?"

"Fed Sec has taken over the investigation. My authority has been revoked. Also, there have been assaults on Land's End and a short time ago on City Hall. The driver was captured." Janik shivered. "I suspect they tortured information from him."

I could've been the one being tortured. Instead, he was putting on a marshal's uniform and agreeing with Renaude. This night kept getting stranger. "Should've expected it, I suppose. I've had a change of plans as well. We're not going to City Hall anymore. We're going to Coit Tower."

"Why? There's nothing there."

"Yeah, except a secret server farm where major Consortium members store their most sensitive data. There are some files there I'm interested in seeing. I'd hoped someone in your ops center was still online. Going after them from multiple sides increases our chances significantly."

"That's not going to happen," Renaude replied, his voice solemn. "There may not be anyone left alive in there."

Janik paused in buttoning the shirt. "I'm sorry, Renaude. Those guys didn't deserve that."

Renaude snapped out of it quickly, returning to his normal cantankerous self. "Are you sure this is necessary? Seeing you in that uniform turns my stomach."

Janik stopped dressing. "I can take it off if you want. You can't have it both ways, Renaude. I can't get into Felix's network without being detected. The only thing better than doing it this way is doing it from inside the complex. Unless you've got some invisibility serum, that's not happening."

Renaude spun away from him. "Hurry up. We're wasting

time."

Renaude didn't know how right he was. If things kept going the way they were, it wouldn't be long before Janik forgot everything he knew about computers.

"Before we go, I have a little information that might interest you. Call it a little peace offering, if you want. I know someone who I'm pretty sure is involved, though I don't know how yet." It hurt to turn on him like this. They'd been through a lot together. But, if Kirox wouldn't help him, Janik wouldn't keep protecting him.

"I'm listening."

"Kirox Sintha. He's a major exporter with the UN. I'm sure you have a file on him. He operates out of the District at the corner of Valencia and Sixteenth. I believe you're familiar with the establishment."

Renaude failed at keeping the excitement off his face. "This better not be some ploy to sidetrack me. We've found nothing on any of our countless raids."

Janik snorted. "Trust me, he's there. When Kirox doesn't want to be found, you won't find him no matter how hard you try and he's too smart to leave any incriminating evidence lying around."

"I'll see what I can dig up. Now, let's go end this."

Janik followed Renaude to Coit Tower, the oily stench in the air thickening as they closed in. The distant sound of gunfire pierced the silence. The assassination raids were still going on.

The grounds were blocked by a ten-foot high security fence and armed security patrolled out front. Hardly surprising this was where they'd keep a top-level server farm. Janik hadn't tried, but he suspected the building was well-protected against electronic attack as well.

Security met them at the front gate. "This is a private facility. Security clearance is required to access."

Renaude tugged down on his uniform tunic and stepped

forward. "Sir, I am trying to put an end to a major terrorist incursion, which we believe to have a direct link to this facility. You can either let us in or I can arrest you and everyone inside on obstruction charges. I have brought one of my best cyber-crimes officers to help get you back online. We think we may have found a way in. Show us to your control room."

The guard spoke into a shoulder mic and after a brief moment, waved them forward. "Follow me, please." He led them to a small waiting room and left.

A short time later, a tall lanky man came in with a sour disposition. Sweat gleaned on his forehead beneath his disheveled hair. He reminded Janik of what he looked like after those all-night study sessions. "I'm Director Compton. No one called to say you were coming, Chief Marshal. This is a closed facility."

"You're a server farm storing top-level Consortium data," Janik said. "So, let's dispense with the subterfuge, shall we?"

Director Compton clenched his jaw. "Since you know what we do here, you understand why I can't let you in. Our clients count on us to keep their data confidential. My own people don't even know what's stored here."

Janik handed him Stephen's security access card. "I have direct authority from Stephen McIntosh to access their servers. I'd suggest calling him, but I don't think he's home right now."

"I do not wish to debate merits of jurisdiction with you, Sir," Renaude said. "You will give my officer access to the system, or I'll pull every hard drive from this facility and hand them over to my forensic team. I doubt your clients would like that very much, would they?"

The director huffed. "Very well. Follow me."

Janik understood the Director's reticence. Once his Consortium handlers found out the cops accessed their data, he was as good as dead.

The room he brought them to filled Janik with memories.

Monitors lined the walls and six terminals dotted various parts of the room. The McIntoshes had a room like this. Janik counted fifteen other people in the room. Only about half were needed to run this facility. The rest were probably gifted their jobs. Janik sat at one of the empty terminals and started typing.

"What exactly are you looking for?" Renaude asked.

"Bill McIntosh was feeding Felix data I believe to be related. I'm interested in seeing what it was."

"How long will this take?" Renaude asked.

Janik shrugged. "Depends on how much security I have to defeat." Hopefully, it was before the trained killers showed up.

Janik never made it into the main network. Felix had hacked the system and disconnected it from the network. "That's unfortunate. Felix is not only stealing your data, he's completely disconnected you from it. Someone is monitoring your system through an open port somewhere." A major downside to having everything in one place. One well-placed hack could lock down the whole damn thing.

"Can you restore access?" Renaude asked.

"If I can find the lockout algorithms."

He scanned the code scrolling on the screen. "I found it," he announced suddenly, throwing his arms into the air. "It's in the messaging network on one of the terminals in the offices. Whose office is that?"

Renaude and the director looked over Janik's shoulder.

"Mine," the director replied. "I have some system controls from there, but my terminal has more security than Fort Knox."

"Well, they found a way in," Janik replied. His fingers danced over the keyboard. "Let's see what this does."

"What about the logic bombs?" Renaude asked.

"That's a real concern, but there's no time to go through all the source code."

Renaude hesitated. "We don't have a choice. Close it down."

"The system is rebooting," a controller called out a few seconds later. The murmurs became louder. "We're coming back online. Data download has been interrupted."

The excited buzz couldn't quell the sinking feeling in Janik's stomach. Any first-year programmer could have found that lockout algorithm. Everyone in this room was a pro. *This ain't over*, Janik thought. "Something's wrong, Renaude. This doesn't feel right."

"What are you talking about? You've put a major dent in Felix's attack. As much as it pains me to admit, you've done well."

Janik pursed his lips and blew a breath out through his nose. "Listen to me. Finding that algorithm would've been child's play for any one of these monkeys. Why didn't they?" Janik's gaze settled on the director's bone white face watching them suspiciously. "He seemed really insistent we not intervene and it was his terminal compromised. He'd have no trouble introducing a subroutine into the system giving Felix control. Ask yourself why this facility hasn't been hit yet. They don't need to hit it if they have someone on the inside."

"We've got a problem here," someone called out.

Renaude rushed to his side. "What is it?"

The programmer pointed at his screen. "The downloads have resumed. I'm locked out again."

The monitors on the wall switched to a clock counting down from one minute. "We should probably go. I don't think that timer is for a microwave warming a burrito."

The director glared at Janik. "What did you do?"

"I deleted the lockout protocol that should've given you back control. The question is what did you do? You knew it was there all along. There's some kind of worm in the system that you put there, isn't there? What does Felix have on you?"

The director's eyes popped, and his mouth dropped open. Janik snatched his credentials from his shirt. "Please," he begged.

"He vowed to destroy me if I didn't help him. He has control over my money and my family."

"How did they get that?" Janik asked. "Isn't the Consortium supposed to be protecting you?"

"The Consortium doesn't care about us as long as we keep their data secure. Some of us have sick kids and spouses. The meds companies like McIntosh Corp prescribe is laced with so much crap, it's making things worse. We still have to pay, and they can't get off it. I would've helped Felix without the threats."

"Do you know what's on those servers? Do you have access?"

"No. It's all encrypted prior to upload. These servers add more. All we have to do is keep the servers and chilling towers online. In the event of a breach, we're supposed to wipe everything. Obviously, I disabled that feature."

"I assume that timer is connected to an explosive device," Renaude said.

"Two. Next to the chilling towers in the basement. They're big enough to bring down this whole tower."

"Everything else Felix is doing is nothing more than a diversion to get what's on these servers. This has been his target all along."

"We'll deal with you when these people are safe," Renaude said. "Get them out of here."

The director slapped a large red button on a nearby panel, activating the emergency alarm. "Evacuate!"

The cacophony in the room shot up like a cannon as fifteen people pushed chairs over and scrambled for the door all at once. Some wept in fear, others prayed as they pushed against each other, trying to get out.

Janik counted in his head. They had about twenty-five seconds to make it down the long corridor and outside. Never mind making it far enough from the building to avoid the blast. Janik lost sight of the director in the chaos.

When the bombs blew, Janik was transported back to the Promenade. Hot, stinging shockwave followed almost instantly by the deafening roar. Once again, he was thrown to the ground, broken and bleeding. Like the Promenade, not everyone made it out. More death, more destruction. Only this time, it was his fault.

He thought of the little boy and his mother. He did this for them. They weren't the only ones to die at the Promenade, never mind the other places that were attacked. But he hadn't looked at the faces of those others, hadn't seen the terror in their eyes like he had with the boy and his mother. Maybe it reminded him too much of his own vulnerability and needed to change that. Except everything he did backfired. Maybe he wasn't meant to clear his name.

Renaude lay a few feet away, unmoving. Janik felt for a pulse. Still alive. *Can't believe I'm happy about that.* The marshal moaned and rolled over, opening his eyes. He slapped Janik's hands away when he tried to help him up. "Give me a minute."

"I don't have a minute. If I'm found here, there'll be questions neither of us wants answered." *Never mind the questions I need answered,* he finished silently. Accessing those McIntosh servers would've cleared a lot of things up.

Renaude nodded. "Go. Leave the questions to me. I'll check in when I gain control of the scene."

"Find that director, Renaude. Make him tell you what he knows. I have to find some way into Felix's complex." Janik disappeared into the darkness. Knowing his luck, the director died in the explosion. He might be the lucky one. If he was a turncoat and the Judiciary got to him, his death would have been slow and painful.

CHAPTER 29: CONFRONTATIONS

The fire's heat reached Rhea a block away. She purposely ignored the burned bodies as she walked by. She covered her nose with the back of her hand and quickened her step. Coming here wasn't necessary, but she had to see it for herself. Breath came in spurts, drying her throat. *I'm going to kill Renaude.*

Coit Tower was gone and several buildings in the immediate area had suffered significant damage. There should've been more fire fighters and paramedics on site, except they were handling crisis in other parts of the city. They had no choice but to let this one burn.

"Don't stray too far, Mayor," Solomon warned. "There's no telling who'll try to kill you."

Rhea scoffed, though she glanced over her shoulder for Logan. "When I find Renaude, I might be the one doing the killing."

Solomon stopped her with his hand on her shoulder. "Renaude is smart and not easily intimidated. Let me deal with him. I've handled his sort before."

Rhea appreciated him trying to ease her burden, but she wasn't in the mood for it right now. She pointed at the inferno. "My city is burning, Commander Solomon. I'm done with the games. I'm going to wring his neck until his pimply little head pops off."

"Rash behavior serves no one, Mayor. Least of all, your citizens. If you let me handle this, I can probably even save your job. Not to mention your life."

Rhea sighed. The job was one thing, but Logan wasn't going to forget her challenging his authority. Once Solomon was gone, she'd be vulnerable.

She pushed that aside for now to deal with Renaude. She'd make him tell her everything before she skinned him alive. They found him at a makeshift triage unit receiving medical treatment. He bled from several gashes and the edges of his clothes were singed. He'd gotten goddamn lucky.

"I wondered when you'd show up," he said. His voice was emotionless, robot-like.

"Hard to miss a giant tower blowing up, don't you think?" Rhea seethed. "What were you doing here?"

"Janik believed this was a storage facility for Consortium data. He wanted access to files associated with McIntosh Corp."

"Let me guess. Cerebral Impulse Transplant."

Renaude's face drained of color. "I don't know. Felix has everything locked down. He couldn't access it."

Logan appeared beside her. Where the hell had he come from? He'd beat Renaude just for the fun of it. He raked his hand through dingy hair and straightened his loose tie. "I can be a reasonable man, Chief Marshal, but if you lie to me, things will not go well for you."

Renaude glared at Logan, having about as much use for Logan's threats as she did. In this case, though, they were warranted. One of Solomon's officers came and whispered something in his ear. He touched her arm, and she backed off. "Where is he now, Chief Marshal?"

Renaude eyed the Fed Sec commander. "He fled right after the explosion."

"You can find him though, can't you?" Rhea said. "I'm sure you're tracking that communicator you gave him."

"Janik is a genius code scriber. That communicator is merely a toy to him. Frankly, I'm surprised he hasn't dumped it yet."

"You said Felix has everything locked down." Logan asked. "How do you know that?"

"Janik found a lockout algorithm in the source code. He deleted it and we thought it worked. Obviously, it didn't."

"Deleting that algorithm triggered the bomb," Solomon said. "We may still be able to trace it back to its source. My people are searching the grounds for bomb fragments."

"That's what Janik said. He also said anybody could've detected it. He suspected the facility director- a Director Compton, I believe, as an inside man. Don't bother looking for him. I doubt he's still alive. He was behind everybody else when the tower blew. The bombs were planted where they'd do the most damage. They'll be sifting through the rubble for weeks."

The veins in Logan's neck popped. He was like a volcano about to erupt. "Compton. I knew him. A slimy little worm always whining about sick kids or a sick wife or something.

Renaude laughed. "Felix is using the Consortium's own people against them."

"Tell me about the prisoner transports. How many did you provide the doctor for CIT?"

Renaude's cheeks reddened, then he shrugged. "Three or four. The exact number escapes me. Each one had maybe twenty to twenty-five prisoners. I doubt all survived though. The first one was several weeks ago. The doctor contacted me, promising to help me with my condition if I provided him with test subjects. Criminals were overrunning our jails. I saw opportunity to solve two problems at once."

Solomon rubbed the back of his head and cursed under his breath. "That's potentially up to a hundred different bombers running around the city and who knows how many bombs each one planted."

Renaude's head snapped up. "What are you talking about?"

Rhea hauled him up by the front of his jacket. "Those prisoners are the ones planting the bombs around the city. Felix was using CIT to plant the orders that are forgotten a few hours after carrying them out. There's nothing tying them back to Felix. The thief was one of the subjects."

Renaude's jaw worked for a moment. "The doctor said the research was personal. I had no idea he was working for Felix."

Rhea released him and he stumbled back. "Now you understand the scope of what we're dealing with."

Renaude's stance stiffened. "I make no apologies."

Rhea crossed her arms. "Why, Renaude? Tell me why."

"It's so simple for you, isn't it?" Renaude sneered. "To walk around without pain, without thoughts of your next fix screaming in your head. To not have to rely on pills to make it through the day. You judge me, yet you have no idea what I deal with."

Rhea sympathized, but being right didn't justify his actions. "CIT won't save you, Renaude. It'll likely kill you."

"You don't know that. Janik lived, as have others. These prisoners obviously survived if they're the ones planting the bombs. Besides, death is better than continuing to live this way."

"Your mind could end up worse than it is now. That poor bastard is lucky to remember his own name. What do you think is going on inside his head right now?"

"That's not my concern. I willingly took this risk."

"But you had no right to sentence others to the fate." Rhea leaned against the side of the ambulance, somewhat surprised she was still standing at all. It was well past time for this nightmare to end. "The sad part is, Renaude, help was there if you'd asked for it."

"The Consortium doesn't help people, Mayor. They use people and dispose of them when they're done. You and I are no different."

You're not wrong. She planned to do something about it. Right now though, her problem was Felix.

Logan's hands balled into tight fists. "Remember your place, Renaude. You hold your position only because the Consortium allows it."

Renaude burst out laughing and, for a moment, Rhea thought he had finally snapped. "It's funny that you think you are any more important than I. You are as much a puppet as the rest of us."

"You're wrong, Chief Marshal. I am the one pulling the strings."

"Kill me if you're going to. Otherwise, shut the hell up. I'm done talking to you."

Rhea held out her hand, stopping Logan's advance. "What else do you know?"

"Janik said the only way to shut down the attack is from within the complex. Felix made it impossible to do it any other way."

"That's only possible if he has people who know Consortium networks inside out," Logan said. His teeth gritted. "Our own damn people are helping him."

Renaude laughed again. "Welcome to the rebellion, Mister Marks."

Thick booms interrupted their interrogation. Muzzle flashes slashed the darkness on the far side of the lot. Bullets struck the ambulance inches from her head, blowing apart the flashing lights on the roof. The windshield and side windows disintegrated in a shower of razor-sharp glass. Rhea pulled her head down against the deafening chaos.

"Take cover," Solomon screamed and pulled her to the ground. Those still able bolted across the lot towards them to escape the gunfire. Solomon pulled her behind the ambulance to avoid being trampled. He keyed the mic on his communicator. "Get the gunships over here now! Concentrate fire on the west side of the lot."

Rhea snapped her head around. "Where's Renaude?"

Solomon shook his head. "He must have joined the stampeding crowd. We can't stay here."

Rhea held onto the commander as they joined the rest of the scattering crowd. His reaction completely contrasted her own. She winced with every staccato pop of gunfire. Solomon barely blinked. Her heart ached for him a little. How much action had this man seen to completely steel him against the carnage? Logan trailed behind them somewhere. Fed Sec and Consortium officers returned fire to cover their escape.

Rhea wasn't sure what happened. One minute they were running, the next Solomon howled and clutched the back of his leg. She stumbled as most of his weight landed on her hip. Both of them fell to the ground in a heap. Blood seeped through his fingers.

Two gunships soared overhead, a maelstrom of gunfire leading them in. Somewhere on the west side, more explosions rocked the parking lot. The gunfire subdued somewhat. The battle had been quick and merciless.

Rhea struggled to her feet. "Can you walk?"

Solomon nodded "I can manage."

Logan crouched behind one of the vehicles as Rhea and Solomon staggered up. "You two alright?"

Rhea leaned over with her hands on her knees. "Never better."

"Yeah," Solomon replied wiping his bloody hand on his uniform. He didn't argue as a medic went to work wrapping his damaged leg. "We're having a blast."

"I know you're in charge here, Dem," Logan said, "but I've had enough. I'm taking my forces to Land's End. Feel free to come along if you want."

"Had the same thought. It's time we knocked on Mister Nash's door."

"We can't leave these people here like this," Rhea said. "I'll stay here to help emergency services. I'll join you when I can."

"Take care of yourself, Mayor," Solomon said and limped away after Logan.

CHAPTER 30:
CONNECTIONS

Serena rested her head against the headrest as she sat at the end of the street outside Janik's house. No Ponytail yet. For all she knew, he'd already been here. The hour she wasted hiking back to Old Buena Vista Park to pick up her car hadn't helped any. Checking the house risked exposure. Sinking lower in her seat, she started to drift off when her communicator beeped. "Yeah, Logan."

"Where are you?" he snapped impatiently. Why did he sound out of breath?

His misery provided a small bit of satisfaction. *Now you know how I feel.* "Outside Janik's house waiting for an assassin."

"Assassin? Sounds like your evening has been as eventful as mine."

She rubbed her hands over her face. "That's one way of putting it. Apparently, pissing people off is another one of his many skills."

"Any idea who this assassin is?"

Serena debated for a minute whether to tell him what was really going on. "I don't have a name, but he has a ponytail and frequents a club called The District in the Mission District." Serena counted on Logan wanting to find this person. Hopefully, they'd kill each other and save her the headache. "He's the one who hijacked your explosives."

Logan's nostrils flared. "I want this ponytail person dead."

So did Felix, but she wasn't about to tell Logan that. "Where are you? It sounds like a war zone there."

"It might as well be. I'm at what's left of Coit Tower. It exploded right after Renaude showed up with the thief."

Serena wasn't surprised. She figured Janik would find some way to cause trouble again. "It confirms our suspicions of them working together."

"Which is why you need to find him before he disappears. Renaude said the only way to shut down the cyber-attack was from inside Felix's complex. Go handle it."

"Why can't you handle it?"

"Right after we showed up Felix's men attacked us. I think Ivan is still a little pissed I shot him. I'm taking a team to knock down the front door."

Serena sat up, suddenly wide awake. "You went after Ivan? Are you crazy?"

"We can't wait for your intel anymore, Serena. Felix is distributing the explosives using subjects affected by cerebral impulse transplants. Half of them probably don't remember their names, much less planting those devices."

That had to be what the ten thousand volts to the temples had been about. "Dare I ask where he got the subjects?"

"Prisoner transports supplied by Renaude. The thief was one of them. I've sent you the list, along with a present from Nelson. It's the video you asked for. Don't worry. I asked nicely. The lab and other subjects are in Felix's complex somewhere."

She knew exactly where. They had mistaken it for the explosive's lab.

"You're the only one who can get inside to shut this thing down. I want that doctor alive. He has some explaining to do. And I want all of his files."

"Anything else? Would you like me to end global warming too?" Serena winced as soon as the words were out of her mouth. She couldn't help it. Her jittery nerves made her snippy.

"Shut your smart mouth, Serena, and do what you're told. Or don't bother coming back to the Pyramid."

Serena's stomach lurched. Despite his callousness, Logan had never spoken to her with that much vitriol before. "Felix still doesn't trust me enough to grant me full access to the complex. Beside, I'm supposed to be keeping an eye on Janik. Questions will be asked if I show up at the complex without orders." She left out the part where she had a keycard granting her access and that she needed Janik's scripts to unlock the Pyramid data.

"He left here less than an hour ago. He may be injured. He can't have gone far."

Serena caught movement a little further down the street from her position. "The assassin is here."

"I told you to forget about him. There are bigger things on your plate. Find the thief and get inside that complex."

"It's Ponytail. I thought you wanted him dead."

Ponytail strolled casually down the street, metal briefcase in his hand. She stuck the pistol out the car window. One shot, that's all it would take. She led the target like they taught at the academy. Of course, this was nothing like shooting metal targets on a motorized rail. The pistol bucked each time she pulled the trigger. Unfortunately, none of her shots came close. Ponytail dove to the ground as the bullets kicked up puffs of dirt from the street. Marksmanship was never her forte.

"Goddamn it," she swore, pulling her arm back in. Not going to get another clear shot now.

"What's happening?"

She'd almost forgotten Logan was there. "I missed."

"Get out of there now," he ordered. For once, she didn't argue. Ponytail had already rolled back up to his feet with his weapon clutched in his hand.

Slamming the car into gear, she sped away as Ponytail shot at the back of her car, taking out a taillight and smashing the window.

I haven't seen the last of him.

She took a steadying breath. "That didn't turn out the way I'd intended."

"Maybe next time you'll listen to me. Check in when you have the thief." Logan's voice faded from the car as the line went dead.

Serena headed towards the Coit Tower, her mood significantly worse. Flames and thick black smoke licked into the air. Glass and metal littered the streets. She maneuvered her vehicle between the debris and panicked people. Fed Sec gunships screamed overhead, firing at something in the distance. She slowed as she approached a man in a marshal's uniform. Except he was no marshal. She rolled down the passenger window as she rolled up beside him.

Janik rubbed the back of his head. "I didn't think I'd see you again, given the way we parted."

"I'm full of surprises. I see you've made your presence felt. Get in."

Janik snickered. "Sorry, left my helmet at home and my insurance doesn't cover repeated blows to the head."

"If you want to live long enough to find your answers, you'll get in. Ivan is probably still in the area. I don't have all night." If those gunships had anything to say about it, Ivan and his goons were already dead and she wouldn't have to worry about him anymore. Fed Sec usually didn't miss. She was a little disappointed she wasn't the one to end Ivan's miserable existence, but as long as he was dead, she'd live with it.

A mixture of smoke and sweat crossed her nose as Janik settled into the passenger seat. He adjusted the seat so he was almost lying down. "I don't know who smells worse, me or you."

"Definitely you," she replied without hesitation. She turned around and headed south towards Pacifica again. "Care to tell me what happened in there?"

"I deleted a lockout algorithm Felix used to access their system." Janik wiped his bloody hands on his shirt. "There was a logic bomb linked to timed explosives planted around the tower. That's not the most disturbing thing." He blew out a tired breath and pressed his fingers to his eyes. "Felix threatened to bury the facility director if he didn't help him. He fessed up as soon as I confronted him. He said he would've helped Felix anyway. Seems like the Consortium is losing its grip on its own people."

"What's so important about Coit Tower anyway?"

"It's a server farm for high level Consortium data. I'm surprised you didn't know about it. Or, maybe you did and don't want to admit it."

That's what Logan was trying to protect. She hated when people she was supposed to trust kept things from her. "It is time for you to come clean, *Ladron*. People died in that explosion, and this time, it *was* you."

Janik's head shot up. "You think I don't know that? What choice did I have? I didn't ask for any of this. These people came after me. I was ready to retire. I couldn't walk away with everyone thinking I killed all those people, especially kids." He swiped away soot and tears with his sleeve as he gazed out the window.

"I'm sorry," Serena whispered, a little surprised she actually meant it. "What is your connection to the chief marshal? I know he got you into Coit Tower and gave you that communicator."

"He has a file on me that he promised to make disappear if I helped him turn the power back on. It's a list of all the cars I boosted. He can't prove any of it, but they're all my jobs. Ever notice how he walks with a limp? He got that jumping onto the hood of one of my jobs. We came to a mutual arrangement."

"You're doing all this for a stupid file?" she asked in barely a whisper.

"That stupid file used to be the end of the world for me. Every car I stole I thought I escaped without a trace. I was supposed to be a ghost. It was a point of pride for me. Turns out that wasn't the case."

Serena tapped a finger on the steering wheel. "I'm still waiting for a point."

"The point is that file doesn't matter anymore. That little boy and his mother from the Promenade, their family is shattered. All those people on the overpass. The people from Coit Tower. They didn't choose that, Felix did. I have to live with my chosen path. Whatever happens to me is worth it if I can give them some justice. I'm not giving up until that woman understands exactly what happened."

"So this is about easing your guilty conscience? You're the first person I've met from the UN to have one of those."

"Partly. I somehow feel responsible for all of this." A cold awkward silence followed. "We both have our reasons for fighting. As different as they are, we have to live with them."

"I guess the reasons don't really matter anymore."

"They matter to me. You think I'm same as Felix and your bosses. I want you to understand I'm nothing like them."

Serena went quiet, not wanting to continue a conversation that laid open so many demons and regrets. He glanced over at her. "I don't blame you for hating me. I hate myself a little. I've sacrificed lot to live the way I have. More than I ever realized."

Serena sighed heavily. "I don't hate you. I thought I did. I wanted to see you as a heartless criminal. That's not really true. I realize I was scared I'd end up like you. I've ended up as something much worse."

"You're doing what you have to in order to save the city. It's not pleasant, but it's necessary, and it sure as hell doesn't make you heartless. You're right. I'm a bad person. I took advantage of people, I hacked computers, and I did it for money."

She regarded with a little more sympathy than before. "You can still run away, you know. I can't, but you can. Renaude's offer isn't worth dying for and that mother will learn the truth eventually. I promise you that. Regardless of how this ends, changes are coming to San Francisco. The Consortium Executive Order has been exposed. Their days of hiding are numbered."

Janik pulled out a crumpled photograph of Patricia and Stephen from his wallet. "My sister and her husband. He ain't so bad for a McIntosh and she loves him. They're in danger unless we stop this. I'm not going anywhere."

She studied him for a long while before speaking. "That was hard for you, admitting that. I can see now that I've misjudged you badly. You don't talk about them not because you're selfish, but because you want to protect them from what you do."

"They don't deserve to be caught up in my decisions. Their life is better without me in it."

Serena rubbed the steering wheel with her thumb and stared out the front window. "Don't you miss them?"

Every damn day. "They've disowned me. They want nothing to do with me."

"I hope someday you find a way to see them again."

"Unless I fix whatever is going wrong with my memory, that'll never happen. How did you know I was here?"

"A colleague called me. He told me some things you might be interested in. I also have something I think will interest you." She held up her tablet screen with a distorted image. "It's the Promenade footage."

"I've been asking Renaude for that all day."

Serena smirked. "Renaude doesn't have my connections."

"Take me home. I have to get out of these clothes, and I lost all of my equipment in the explosion. That gives us enough time for a conversation. No more games. You're going to tell me who you are, who you work for, your involvement with Felix. You're going to tell me everything, agreed?"

Serena let out the breath she'd been holding. She figured it would come to this sooner or later. "Agreed."

CHAPTER 31: UNMASKED

anik lay back with his eyes closed, waiting for her to speak. Something told him he was in for more than he bargained for.

"My name isn't Olivia Benitez," she said after a drawn-out silence, "and you were right about who I work for. I'm a data analyst for the security arm of the Judiciary. I was hired to help take down the UN. Though, recently, I've come to regret it."

"We all have regrets." He had his fair share. He knew that much. "What's your real name?"

She took a deep breath. Janik understood. She was about to strip away layers of defense to reveal a truth about herself, leaving her vulnerable. "Serena Abel."

"How did you become involved with the Consortium?"

"My story is not a whole lot different than yours, except in reverse. My mother got sick not long after the Great Quake killed my father. I'd heard stories about the new Consortium and how this underground network was fighting them. I went to the UN for the medicine for my mother, but they wouldn't give it to me unless I did certain things for them. The guy I was with at the time only cared about how to use me. When I realized no help was coming, I approached the Consortium. By then, it was too late. My mother died anyway."

Her eyes held the same sadness he felt. "I'm sorry."

"I thought joining them would make things better. If I'm being totally honest, I wanted revenge on the UN for trying to use me the way they did. I helped the Consortium take down the cell my former friend worked for. Last I heard, they brought him to the Hall of Justice. He never came out."

"You and I understand each other far better than you realize."

"The Consortium was no better than the UN. They were only interested in exploiting where I came from. My mother warned me of their corruption before she died. She'd been right all along. I've been so blind to everything. They don't care who they hurt so long as they get what they want. Sometimes I can't tell the difference between the criminals and the cops in this city."

Janik laughed sardonically. She just described exactly what working for the McIntoshes was like. "The draw of power is too big a temptation to resist for most. Where does Felix fit into all this?"

"I went undercover to infiltrate his network. My orders were to shut down the cyber-attack."

Janik grunted. "I see you've been about as successful as I have. What else did you find out?"

"Felix's grudge against the marshals and the Consortium has something to do with the dross lakes. I think he's searching for who ordered them in the files he's stealing."

"The Consortium locked all that stuff down. They didn't want people knowing their ugly truth. Before I joined the UN I worked for McIntosh. He was having a problem with another hacker who was threatening to expose all their dirt. I was supposed to stop her, but she ended up showing me the truth of what I was involved with. I decided then I would no longer be a party to their corruption."

The clarity of which that memory formed when so many others didn't terrified Janik. He wasn't sure what it meant. He just knew he had to find some way to fix his short-circuited brain.

"Felix released a media packet with some images that are pretty damaging to the Consortium. There's probably more on those files you've encrypted."

"He's turning the city against the Consortium. Smart play." That meant Patricia and Stephen were still in danger, given their connections. Hopefully, they made it out of town.

"That's not the whole of it. Renaude supplied prisoners to a doctor for something called a cerebral impulse transplant."

"Kind of figured as much. Explains why he didn't want to tell me about the crash." Janik gazed out the window. Still no sign of those gunships. *Maybe my luck is beginning to turn.*

"Renaude didn't know the doctor gave the subjects to Felix. They're the ones planting explosives around the city."

"I was supposed to blow up the marshals' building. That one would've been fun." Maybe he did plant the bomb. Maybe the text from Kirox wasn't for the Bentley.

No. He wouldn't believe it. He couldn't. The Promenade footage would tell him for sure.

The fact of the matter was Janik wasn't sure if his memory problems were the result of the constant trauma or cerebral impulse transplant. His life before the Promenade bombing was nothing more than a blurred haze, fragments that felt like they belonged to someone else. He feared what he'd have to do to put it back together.

"I have a list of other prisoners that may be involved. The lab on the map we thought was the explosives lab is actually the CIT lab."

"Why would Renaude be involved in a banned procedure? The Consortium would crucify him if they found out."

"They know now. He believed the doctor was close to a cure for his pill addiction."

"Makes sense." Janik sighed. He should've seen Renaude's selfish goal sooner. "I'm assuming you know who this doctor is."

"Doctor Mauro Barren. He fell in with Felix after the Consortium shut him down. I also know where Felix got his explosives.”

Janik's stomach fluttered. He needed to hear her say what he knew was coming.

“A club in the Mission District and I believe a friend of yours. I don't know his name, but he has a long ponytail. He's been ordered to bring you to Felix with the decryption codes, but I'm pretty sure he's planning to kill you and blackmail Felix.”

Janik's head dropped forward. “His real name is Kirox Sintha and he's ever the opportunist. Kind of disappointed he wants me dead though.”

“He's Felix's direct contact. My boss thinks that truck was a UN sanctioned job.”

The news just kept getting better and better. “I'd like to say it wasn't, but I don't know. With Kirox involved, anything is possible.” Janik tried to remember back to specific times with Kirox but kept coming up empty. He knew the man; knew they were associated. Beyond that, he drew a blank.

“My boss is planning to bury the Mission District. He wants to eradicate the UN. He wants the names you have. If he goes into the Mission District, more innocent people are going to die. We can't let that happen.”

Janik rubbed his hands over his face, wincing at every stab of pain jabbing his beat-up body. He was tired. So, so tired. He wished he could lie down, but he still had work to do. “You said you infiltrated Felix's network. That's how you knew I tried before.”

“We were in the middle of dinner when you did it.”

“Did he tell you to follow me from Land's End?”

“No, he didn't know you were there. That little stunt almost got me killed.”

Janik grunted. *Now you know how I feel.* “What else have you told him?”

“Nothing, except the phone call in the ravine. I had to

convince him I was helping him. Your wellbeing was the lowest on my list of concerns."

"Fair enough." He ran his hand over his head. He winced as he flexed his shoulder. That was going to hurt for a long time. *I should consider myself lucky*, he thought. *I should be dead.* "I doubt he believed you. I know his type. He only trusts himself. Did you go back to him after you knocked me out?"

"After I met with my handler. His sec chief wanted to kill me after making me strip, but Felix stopped him."

Janik felt a little vindicated. "What promises did you make to save your life?"

"I'm supposed to bring you to him with your decryption keys. Nice touch with the locked screen too, by the way. I should've expected that you wouldn't make it easy."

"I've been in this game a long time. I know how to protect myself."

Janik stared out the window silently. Perhaps he should let her. Though, it'd likely end in his death. If that's what it came to, so-be-it. He'd made peace with the likelihood of an early death a long time ago. There was no going back now.

He locked eyes with Serena and there was only truth. No lies, no hidden agenda. No hate. "I don't know who's right or who's wrong. Frankly, I don't care. I don't like being caught in the middle, so let's end this."

CHAPTER 32:
UNTANGLED

Janik felt a little better when they turned onto his street. "What are you doing?" he asked as she drove past his only bastion of safety.

"Kirox may still be hanging around."

They circled the block twice. Nothing seemed out of the ordinary. Still they approached the back of the house cautiously, Serena staring at the ground. "What are you looking for?"

"Trip wires," she replied.

Janik grunted. "That makes me feel confident."

"It's better than your body parts fertilizing your backyard."

Janik peered through the small window in his front door. "Odd place for a suitcase. Especially one that doesn't belong to me."

"I don't think that one's packed with underwear," Serena said. "The front door is probably wired."

"The side window is low enough to crawl through. Kirox had to get in somehow."

Sure enough. The side window was smashed and had no foreign objects attached to it. They were inside in minutes. They tiptoed up to the case, fearing a vibration trigger. Janik didn't even chance wiping the sweat from his forehead. "Why plant a bomb in my house if he wanted me alive?"

"Maybe he wants to hit you where it hurts. Your wealth."

That sounded like something Kirox would do. He was never one to pull any punches. Janik's communicator dinged. 'Bring me the decryption codes and everything you have on Felix. I'll trade it for the deactivation code to the bomb in your house. Oh, and Janik, I hope you're not inside…'

"That answers that question."

"There's no reason for us to touch that thing. Get your gear and let's get out of here."

"Easy for you to say. It's not your house."

"We'll send someone back to disarm it, I promise."

Probably better that way. He stopped on the stairs on his way to his office. "That thing is stable as long as we don't touch it, right?"

"Yeah, in theory…" Suspicion crossed her face. "What are you getting at?"

"With enough time and the computer power I have here, I can clean up that Promenade footage and access Felix's network. This might be our only chance."

"Really don't like the idea of staying here with that thing, but you have a point." She sighed. "Get to work. I'll watch the street from the bedroom window."

Janik resisted the urge to follow her. He'd spent his whole life trusting exactly one person. Himself. Changing that now was difficult. She was probably still keeping things from him. For her own safety, no doubt. He had to trust her for now. He had footage to recover.

Progress was slow. He recognized some of the scripts Felix used, but they'd been altered. Eventually he had a glitchy, pixelated version of the Promenade footage. All of the emotions from yesterday morning flooded back. A lump formed in the back of his throat and his lip quivered. The little boy's face flared in his mind.

Serena came back into the room. "The street's still quiet. How's it going in here?"

Janik quickly swiped a sleeve across his eyes. "I've managed to recover the video." The wide-angle shots showed a happy crowd enjoying breakfast on a beautiful day. He felt like he'd seen this in a movie somewhere rather than experienced it. Janik scanned the data stream around. "That's me right there," he said, pointing to the far side of the Promenade. "Right before I crossed to the parking lot."

They watched the bomber slide the hard metal case under the table after hitting the timer. Janik zoomed a little closer. The bomber entered something on his communicator before his gaze settled on the giant billboard monitor. He left the Promenade seconds later.

"It's one of the prisoners from the missing transports."

Janik zoomed in on a table with a chess board. A woman sat across from a young boy. "That's the mother, and her son. I'm trying to find out who they are."

"After you crack the network."

"Do you still have that keycard?"

Serena retrieved the card. "How is this going to help you find out who she is?"

"They would've scanned everyone's fingerprints at the Promenade and uploaded them to the hospital network. Maybe I can find some kind of back door in. It's worth a shot."

He tapped a few more buttons. Hospital records flashed on the screen. "There." His fingers flew over the keyboard. "Ella Cobb. She escaped almost unharmed. Her son Matthew, however, took a piece of shrapnel in the side. He died before I got to him."

"This isn't your fault, Janik. Even if you had gotten to him, the damage was too extensive."

Now she knew the truth. She knew he wasn't a monster. It shouldn't have mattered as much as it did. "They sent her home after her examination. Probably nowhere to put her with all the incoming casualties."

"What are you going to do?" she asked hesitantly.

Janik shared her worry. "Like I said before, I have to tell her what really happened."

Serena sat on the couch and stared down at her fidgeting hands. "I feel bad for her, I really do, but we don't have time for this. Felix and Renaude are coming for us."

"It's important that I see this woman, Serena. I can't force you come, but I'm going."

A sympathetic smile touched her lips. "Alright, Janik. We'll go. After we see what else is on Felix's network. Deal?"

Janik launched his encryption program. Data immediately scrolled rapidly across the screen, none of it useful. "The program will tell me when we hit the juicy stuff."

Serena went to peak out around the window curtains. "How long will that take? That bomb downstairs is making me nervous."

"No idea," he replied. "Depends on how deep we have to go. My program runs pretty quickly though so it shouldn't take too long."

The tablet trilled suddenly and Serena was beside him. "What is that?"

"A couple of ghost drives. Could be back doors into the network." Unfortunately, after several minutes of searching, they didn't find any sort of master kill switch. He did find something useful though. "The marshals should have the traffic cams back."

"That's a start. Anything else?"

"The main communication network is back up, though, I wouldn't plan on making any long-distance calls for a while. Oh, this is interesting. Let's see how well he can breathe without the ventilation system. That's the best I can do without being on site."

Janik moved around the network. They didn't have long before Felix sent one of his kill squads after them. He removed the encryption from a few of the Coit Tower files Felix stole. The screen filled with unfamiliar folders and files.

Janik keyed in one called 'Bill McIntosh'. He clicked on it, expecting to see files of bribery, and fixed programs and government collusion. What he got instead stole his breath. There were two files of particular note. 'Gina Hendrix' and 'Janik Brynn'.

"Who's Gina Hendrix?" Serena asked.

"She was the hacker I told you about," he replied. He wouldn't elaborate. It still hurt to think about her.

"You were in love with her, weren't you? I can see the pain and regret written all over your face."

He could feel Serena's eyes on him, and he wanted to be anywhere but here at the moment. "I'd prefer not to talk about it, if you don't mind."

He clicked on the folder with her name. Her picture popped up next to a series of text messages.

"I can see why you'd be attracted to her," Serena said. "She's beautiful."

Janik took a deep breath. There was no way he could escape this part of the conversation, so he had to suffer it, like ripping off a band-aid. "Probably the only woman I've ever had feelings for in my life. I thought I lived a privileged life, but she showed me what it really meant to be alive. And then Bill McIntosh had her killed."

She put a hand on his shoulder. "I'm sorry."

"It is what it is," he replied with a stiff shrug. "I can't change it, so I have to live with it. Let's figure out what else is on this drive while we have the chance."

Janik went through more of the folders, not really seeing anything of use.

"What a minute," Serena said suddenly. "What's that? Go back." Janik complied. "There. That folder called 'Dross Lakes'."

Janik cocked an eyebrow. "I don't think that's going to shut down their network."

Serena reached around him to hit ENTER. Janik didn't argue. He'd done that enough already. Images of the dross lakes and decrepit homes filled the screen.

"That's right after the Great Quake," Serena whispered, the crack in her voice unmistakable.

"That's a Pacifica neighborhood."

Serena shook off whatever dark thoughts had consumed her. "Open the next one."

The screen filled with news articles about the quake, the Consortium and the dross lakes. Many of them detailed violent protests that involved the Consortium shooting unarmed citizens. This was the Consortium Executive Order and what the UN wanted to expose.

"This is who you're working for," Janik said as he played a particularly violent video.

"Not anymore," she replied. "I bet Felix's house was from the neighborhood that was leveled to put them there."

Janik opened a news article. "Those lakes were never very popular, but the ones with the money had more influence than they deserved. The residents wanted to keep the neighborhood. Some families, including Felix's, had to be removed by force.

Several more articles popped up. One caught Janik's eye in particular. Outside city hall where a bunch of protestors waved signs. 'STOP THE DROSS LAKES'. 'LET US GO HOME'.

"There," Serena said, pointing at one face in the crowd.

Janik zoomed in. "Now this is interesting. The name doesn't match the face." He zoomed in further on the caption below the picture. "Felix Nash is really Leland Preston."

"He would've only been about twelve years old when they leveled those neighborhoods. That's why he's so obsessed with them."

"He blames the city for taking away his childhood home. I can almost sympathize."

Serena read a few words from the article. "He spent his teenage years protesting in front of City Hall, arrested multiple times for disturbing the peace. Nothing more serious than that.

How did he go from that to hacking the power grid and blowing the hell out of everything?"

Janik leaned back in his chair. "I think that's where my pal Kirox comes in."

"Felix or Leland or whatever the hell his name is, is no savior. He's a goddamn mercenary."

"Maybe he has a lot of blame to go around. Between the companies, the government, the people. No one listened. I bet they're all ears now."

Poking around a bit more, Janik found a folder with a bunch of call logs between Renaude and Doctor Barren. "The Consortium even bugged communicators. It was only a matter of time before Renaude was caught."

"Download everything from that file," Serena ordered. "I want to make sure this information doesn't disappear."

"Then what?"

"We shut the whole thing down."

An alarm sounded on Janik's terminal. "They're onto us. I'm surprised it took this long."

"Hurry up and copy those files I have this thing about getting shot at."

"I'll let the elves inside the computer know. In the meantime, how about you start packing some of this gear into my case? I'm sure it'll come in handy."

Serena rushed around the room while Janik kept an eye on the download. The last bit of information on Leland was his release from jail after firebombing one of the construction crews working on the dross lakes. Curious that the Judiciary let him walk away instead of making him disappear in their normal fashion.

"I've got it," he said snatching the wafer from the tablet. "Let's get out of here."

They took the stairs in twos. Janik had almost forgotten about the suitcase of death sitting in his front hall.

Serena moved towards the window. "Hurry up, but go slow. I kind of like my body in one piece."

"To be perfectly honest, since we're probably about to die anyway, I kind of like your body in one piece too."

He swallowed the giggle at the astonishment on her face. She wanted to say something, but words failed her. He would've never associated speechlessness with this woman.

Janik's case hit the floor with a *thunk*. He froze. The little green light on the bomb went out and Janik let out a breath of relief. The red light next to it turned on and the small display lit up with a five-second timer. *I wonder if immolation is painful.*

CHAPTER 33:
THE FINAL TRADE

Janik grabbed the case and bolted for the door. "Run!"

They were at the end of the driveway when the bomb went off. The blast threw him down the street like a scrap of paper in a windstorm. The hard landing on his back knocked the wind from him. Skin peeled from his arms. His head spun. His stomach churned. His ears rang like church bells.

Janik rolled over and pushed himself up to his knees. The heat from the bonfire would've been almost pleasant if it hadn't been his house burning. Flaming debris and ash floated to the ground around them. This was really going to piss off the Home Owners Association.

Serena lay nearby, unmoving. Thick blood matted the side of her face. Her eyes were closed, her chest still. He crawled over to her and rolled her onto her back.

"Come on. You can't be dead. I was just starting to like you." He alternated between chest compressions and mouth-to-mouth. Still, she wouldn't breathe. "Come on, Serena. Get your ass back here. We're not done yet." He repeated CPR again. And again. And again.

Time seemed to stop. Tears dropped from his eyes as he pressed down on her chest. He wouldn't give up. He buried his face in her neck and sobbed. Another person dead because of him. His strength waned as he resumed CPR. He'd have to tend his own injuries soon or share her fate. Janik kept going.

One more time he performed mouth-to-mouth letting his lips

linger on hers for a second longer. When he pulled away, he heard the low wheeze of Serena breathing on her own. Her eyes blinked open, and she nodded slightly. He slipped his hand behind her back. "Go slow. You have a nasty scrape on your head." Janik cradled her gently until she could support herself.

Her head drooped forward between her knees. After a few moments, glassy green eyes shifted towards the fireball. "I was always partial to fireworks." She then looked at him. "You saved my life. Why? You could've left me."

This feeling in the pit of his stomach hadn't been felt in a long time. "I have this thing against dead people," he grinned. "They're kind of boring."

Her face was a mash of blood and confusion. "I don't know what to say."

Was it so hard to believe he didn't want her dead? "I'm not a monster, Serena. I don't want to see anyone dead any more than you do. Although, I think Kirox has earned his ride on that particular train." He helped her to her feet. "Careful, you probably have a concussion."

A number of the neighbors wandered out of their homes, looking around, surveying the destruction. Some had hands over their mouths in shock. One man, an elderly fellow, approached Janik with a bit of stutter step. Janik put his hand on his shoulder to help steady him. "You okay, pops?"

"Yes, I think so. What happened?"

"Gas leak, I think. I'm gonna try to find some help. You make sure everyone else is okay. Can you handle that?"

"Of course. Of course. I'm surprised rescue services aren't already here."

"I think they have their hands full up north."

Another woman approached as Janik retrieved his case from the neighbor's lawn. Outside of a few scorch marks, it was in one piece. She regarded him with an odd mix of fear and recognition.

She wagged a finger at him like an angry schoolteacher. "I know you. You're the one from the news. You blew up your own house? You almost blew up my house."

"Calm down, lady. I didn't do anything. I don't have time to explain right now."

She tried to block his path, but he went around her. "I'm calling the marshals."

Janik laughed. "Go ahead. I'll be sure to come back in a few hours when you get through."

Janik helped Serena stagger back to the car at the end of the street. The blast radius was small enough to leave it untouched. He eased her into the passenger seat. "I have to confront Kirox. He stabbed me in the back. He turned the UN against me. I can't let that go."

"Didn't think you could," she replied. "One good thing about the Consortium is they provide the best toys. Have a look in the trunk."

Janik popped the hatch to reveal a small arsenal of weapons and other tech. Sniper rifle, a shotgun, a couple pistols, and a half dozen fragmentation grenades. "I think this stuff might come in handy."

He closed the trunk and slid into the driver's seat. Serena's head rested against the side window. She looked haggard, spent, defeated. They weren't done yet. They still had some cards to play.

He pulled onto the main road. The physical damage from the explosion was an afterthought as emotions took over. He loved that house. Kirox was going to pay for this. After everything Janik did for that slimy worm. He punched the steering wheel. He should've walked away.

The trip back to the Mission District didn't take long. There was no one around to stop them. They were close enough to the District where ambush was a real possibility. Janik hated being out in the open like this and the pain from the explosion made focusing difficult. He sank lower in the seat, trying to ease the throbbing in his shoulder, and to make himself harder to spot.

"What's the plan?" Serena asked as she pulled out her pistol.

"Kill Kirox, blow up the District." His heart hurt having to do that. The club had been a second home to him. He'd spent countless hours hiding out there after he turned on McIntosh Corp.

"Sounds simple," she said dryly. "He's probably got Felix's goons hiding in the shadows to take you and your decryption keys in."

Janik tucked the data wafer with the network recordings into his pocket. He set the timer on the grenades at ten minutes. That should give him enough time to get Kirox to fess up. The bastard owed him an explanation, and not one that included the words 'It was just business'. "You plant the grenades while I deal with Kirox. I've kept a couple to put by the front door in case he gets any bright ideas."

"You're not giving us much option to escape."

"I never expected to live this long anyway."

They approached the District cautiously, staying in the shadows tight to the buildings. "Cocky bastard is probably leaning back balancing a drink on his knee."

"I'll go around back to make sure there are no blood thirsty assassins waiting for us."

Serena disappeared again. He tucked the gun behind his back, and after straightening his jacket on his shoulders, started for the door.

Janik dropped the pack with the ticking grenades next to the door and walked in. He hadn't been wrong. Kirox sat alone at a table near the stage with a half-empty bottle of bourbon and two glasses.

Kirox grinned widely as he brought the amber liquid to his lips. "Come on in, Janik. Have a drink. Where's your sexy Spanish friend?"

Janik scratched the back of his head. "Dead, I think. Took a shot from a marshal."

"Come now, Janik. Let's make a rule to be honest with each other, shall we?"

"Were you honest with Felix when you told him you'd bring me in?"

The grin disappeared from Kirox's face. "I told him you weren't stupid."

Janik laughed as he sat across from Kirox. "You think you know anything about Felix. That isn't even his real name. He's playing you like a trumpet."

"Felix and Ivan are too arrogant for their own good. They didn't listen when I told them at the beginning to get rid of you." He downed another shot of bourbon. "You've left me a giant mess to clean up, Janik, but I'm willing to cut you a deal. Hand over the decryption keys and you walk out of here officially retired, no questions asked. I'd even be willing to cut you a slice of whatever extra I can squeeze from Felix. Of course, I'd hoped you'd reconsider staying on. There aren't too many around with your particular skillset."

"I didn't make the mess. I didn't cut the power. I didn't blow the hell out of the city. I didn't volunteer to have my memory fried. I'm not the one blowing up my friends' houses."

"Details, details," Kirox replied, waving his hand dismissively. "I should have killed you when you showed up at the club the first time. I didn't give you enough credit."

"I didn't think you would turn your back on the UN, so I guess we both misjudged. I wondered how Renaude knew I came to talk to you. You were the anonymous phone call. Let me ask you something. Was the Promenade job legit or a setup all along? Nice touch, by the way, with that whole valuable intel on the cellphone. I should have expected there was nothing to it."

Kirox downed another drink. "Someone high up in McIntosh Corp needed a favor and you were the one loose end from the Gina Hendrix days they could never tie up. You were Felix's fall guy to buy him some time. The payoff was too good to pass up. You were supposed to be in jail. I had no idea that screw up Renaude would let you escape. What was I supposed to do when you went on your little crusade?"

"You were supposed to help me," Janik shouted. "I guess our history means nothing."

Kirox touched his tongue to his lip and spread his hands out to his sides. "I'm the Trader. I trade things. I saw an opportunity. Besides, you said you were done. Did you actually think I'd let you walk away without consequence? Nobody walks away from me."

Janik poured a shot of bourbon and gulped it down. "Did you know about the cerebral impulse thingy on prisoners Renaude sent them? I can barely remember my name half the time. At one point, I thought I bombed the marshals' building. Turns out, Felix used this mind scrambling procedure to plant mission parameters in my brain."

Kirox peered down at his empty shot glass. "I didn't know you were one of the subjects. I'd assumed, like everyone else, that you were dead. Not that any of it matters now." Kirox brought a pistol up from beneath the table. "Give me the codes. I'm due for a business meeting with Felix in an hour, and well, there's really only one thing he wants."

"You're fooling yourself if you think they're going to let you live. You're as dead as I am."

Kirox waved the pistol back and forth. "I don't think so. I've got my spot already staked out as Felix's exporter. He may run the city, but I own it. Not even the UN will be able to touch me."

The man was delusional. "How's that?"

"Having the power out only increases my business opportunities. Gasoline generators, food, and meds. The city is full of people with money willing to pay. Once the Consortium Executive Order is dealt with, it'll be a free-for-all. Felix is in for a bit of a shock if he thinks people will flock to him. I've already started to relieve the Consortium of their inventory. Soon, we'll control their other assets." Three sec officers came through the front door, each armed with assault rifles. "You're early. I told Felix I'd bring him the tablet within the hour."

The officer on the far right stepped forward, rifle raised. "Felix is tired of waiting. He wants the thief and the decryption keys now."

"Good thing you boys showed up," Janik said. "My old friend here was about to kill me and keep the keys for himself. Something about a bigger piece of the pie, I believe."

"He's lying. Felix knows where I stand."

"Shut up. You're both coming with us. Felix and Ivan can sort this mess out."

Kirox's gun dipped at a noise from the back. "Go check it out," he ordered the sec officers. "I'll watch him."

One of the sec officers split off from the group and went to the back door. Gunshots erupted, followed by a scream. *Good girl, Serena.* Janik dove to the floor. Kirox's first salvo hit one of the two remaining sec officers before he was forced behind cover.

"Don't kill him, you idiot," the remaining sec officer shouted. "Felix still needs him."

"I'm not going to kill him," Kirox spat. "Just maim him."

Janik heaved up on the table, sending everything crashing to the floor. There was no way to get to Serena without eating a bullet or two.

"I should have known you had something up your sleeve," Kirox called. "You always did go into a job with a plan."

"And your arrogance has always been your weakness. You always considered yourself untouchable here." Heavy shots struck the table, pushing him back. His return fire missed.

"Time to wrap this up, Janik," Serena called urgently. "Clock is ticking."

"Working on it."

"Keeping you from your date, am I?" Kirox mocked.

"As a matter of fact, yes. Got seats for a real explosive show."

"I'd ask for a rain check." The table scraped across the floor towards him.

"Hey, lowlife," Serena called. "Over here."

The District echoed with gunfire. Serena screamed. It all happened so fast. Janik stood up, disregarding his own safety. Serena lay near the back corridor, squirming in obvious pain, blood seeping from her shoulder. Just above her heart.

The last sec officer lay dead near the front door. Two red splotches dotted his chest. That left the three of them and the ticking timers on the grenades.

Kirox shifted his aim. "Lose the gun."

Janik dropped his gun as the lump got bigger in his throat. His legs felt like they were about to cave in beneath him.

Kirox followed Janik's gaze to Serena's supine form on the floor. "Ivan said she was hot. He wasn't exaggerating. Her death is on you." Kirox aimed his gun at Serena while staring at Janik with an arrogant smirk.

Rage threatened to overwhelm Janik. "You're the one who pulled the trigger."

"If you had gone away, I wouldn't have had to. Where's the tablet? Give it to me now." Kirox cocked the hammer on his gun. "I'll only ask once."

Janik removed the tablet from his jacket pocket. "Let her go and it's yours."

Kirox pulled the trigger and the room boomed. The bullet splintered the floor inches from her head. "The next one won't hit the floor."

"Alright, alright, Kirox. Take it easy. Here, take it." Never in a million years did he believe he'd be willing to sacrifice everything for someone he'd met less than a day ago.

"No, Janik, don't," Serena mumbled.

"Unlock it," Kirox screamed. "Now! Hurry up."

Janik pressed his thumb to the tablet scanner and the screen flickered to life. With a trembling hand, he entered the codes to run the decryption program. "All you have to do is plug it into the system."

Kirox waved his hand for Janik to come closer. "Slowly. No sudden movements."

Janik inched closer, keeping the tablet just out of Kirox's reach.

Kirox's gun dipped as he reached for the tablet. Janik lowered his shoulder and barreled into Kirox as he pulled the tablet back. Both crashed to the floor. The gun jarred loose and slid across the floor amongst the shell casings. Janik almost blacked out from the pain shooting through his chest.

Janik grappled with Kirox, going for his eyes, but the Trader slapped his hands away. Janik shifted in time for the knee aimed at his ribs to glance off his side, but now he was underneath Kirox and vulnerable. Kirox's fingers wrapped around Janik's throat.

"Time to say goodbye, Janik."

Janik was close to blacking out when the room boomed again. Kirox's fingers loosened and he slumped forward. Janik coughed and panted in several deep breaths. Slowly, his vision and heartrate returned to normal. Janik pushed Kirox aside and sat up. Serena stood at the back of the club holding the Trader's gun. Janik let his head dangle between his knees for another minute, allowing more of his strength to return.

"Looks like the UN needs a new supplier."

Janik retrieved the tablet tucked into the inside pocket of Kirox's jacket. The one he never let go of. It held the whole San Francisco black market network. It probably had details of the Ice

Water hijacking.

From the corner of his eye, he saw Serena eyeing it longingly. Maybe he should give it to her. It would ruin the Underground Network and prove Janik was as much a victim as anyone. No, that wasn't good enough. It had to be public. Everyone had to know. The UN had left him to rot. They deserved it as much as the Consortium did. "Time to make ourselves scarce. Unless I forgot how to count, we have about twenty-five seconds."

"What is that?" Serena asked, pointing at the tablet.

Janik pocketed the tablet for now. "Proof."

CHAPTER 34: COMPLICATIONS

The grenades exploded, raining hot shrapnel down all around them. Serena eased herself down onto the curb, wincing at the stabs of pain throughout the various parts of her body. She kept one eye on Janik and one on the destroyed building. He didn't move, his face frozen in stoic resolve.

"And so my life as I know it ends," he said with a resigned sadness.

She felt the same, though for different reasons. Given what she'd learned, she couldn't go back to Logan, and Felix would most likely grant Ivan's wish to kill her. "You said you were ready to retire anyway, right?"

"Not quite how I envisioned it. Thought there'd at least be cake."

Serena stood, with some difficulty, and went around to face Janik. She took his head in her hands and inspected the cuts and bruises. For the first time, perhaps, she didn't see a criminal. She saw a man, a haggard and beat up man. She leaned in and kissed his cheek. "I never properly thanked you for saving my life."

Janik brushed his fingertips over the spot where her lips landed. "You would've done the same for me."

She locked eyes with him for a moment before pulling away. Her head told her to do one thing, her conscience told her to do another, and her heart…that confused her all together. She dabbed at a particularly nasty gash over his eye with the corner of her sleeve. "These need stitches."

"We don't have time for that," he replied. "This place will be crawling with UN sympathizers soon, wondering what happened. We shouldn't be here when they arrive."

She didn't argue. It was time to finish this once and for all anyway. Janik didn't fight her when she took the keys from him. He was in no condition to drive. His eyes closed the minute he settled into the passenger seat.

Serena drove away from the flaming District, checking her mirror one more time before turning towards her old neighborhood. No one would look for them there. Only she knew where 'there' was. It gave Serena time to think. And it made what she had to do all the more difficult.

Felix's idea had been a good one. His execution had been over the top. You didn't use a hatchet to cut away diseased tissue. You used a scalpel. Remove the sickness so the body can heal. She'd be the scalpel.

The majority of the Consortium's power ran through the Consortium Executive Order. Now that she knew that, she could do something about it. All she needed was a plan.

She had wanted no part of this battle, but Felix was going to kill her when she didn't hand over the scripts. Logan was going to kill her when he realized she'd turned her back on him. Serena glanced at Janik snoring softly in the passenger seat. *What will you do when the time comes for me to do what I have to?*

She climbed out of the car, leaving Janik to sleep. She kicked chunks of broken brick, sending them skittering over the ground. Her heart ached at the sight before her. Her childhood home reduced to a pile of nothing that had been picked through and pillaged, and then left to rot. *I wish I could stay here.*

She moved through the remains of the kitchen, her hand tracing along the length of the grimy cracked countertop. Broken glass crunched under her boots. She pictured the room whole and her mother standing at the stove, stirring her Pozole. Serena hated the soup. She'd give anything for her mother to cook it again. Once the Consortium was dealt with, she'd set up a soup kitchen to help feed the hungry. Maybe she'd have a tiny music shop as well. It had been too long since she'd heard the music.

"You shouldn't have come here. Harlon Cruz still has friends in this neighborhood. If they catch you, they will torture you."

A man she hadn't seen in many years stepped into the meager light, sadness marring his weathered face. "I had to, Bruno. I had to see it again."

"I figured as much. I've been keeping an eye on this place, just in case. There isn't much left to see. What the Great Quake didn't destroy, apathy did."

Serena shrugged. "I guess there were bigger problems."

Bruno strolled forward, hands in his pockets. He still wore his apron, grease stains and all. The man never stopped cooking. "Or maybe they needed someone to fight for them."

"I know what you're getting at. No one could replace my father. My mother was too frail, and the others didn't have his strength."

"Maybe there's someone with that strength now."

Maybe, she thought. That was the hope anyway. "I tried calling you. There was no answer."

"There were marshals crawling all over the neighborhood. I couldn't risk being exposed."

"You never did tell me why you agreed to help me. After the way things went down with Harlon, I figured you'd never want to see me again."

"Simple. You're your father's daughter. I have no love for the Consortium, but I thought with you there, you could change things."

"You put your faith in the wrong person."

"Fight's not over yet, Serena. Speaking of which, what are you doing with Janik Brynn? He's a good man, but a UN operative is the last person I expected to see you with."

Both eyebrows popped up. "A good man? He's a criminal."

"That word is not as black and white as it used to be. People do unsavory things when backed into a corner."

"Janik isn't one of those people. He has as much money as anyone in the Consortium."

"No, you're right, but he does the things he does so the really desperate ones don't have to."

"What about Harlon? Was he desperate too?"

Bruno laughed. He saw through her attempt to trip him up. "Of course there are exceptions. Not all criminals are desperate. Harlon and Kirox Sintha were one and the same in that regard."

"Janik is a means to an end. Once this business is done, so is he." She wondered if her voice betrayed the disappointment that statement created.

"I'll leave you to your thoughts," Bruno said. "I'll keep an eye out, but you shouldn't linger here too long."

The network data was in Janik's pack along with the scripts to decrypt the Pyramid data. She only had to bring it to Felix. She hesitated to call him though. Once he had what he wanted, her usefulness ended. There had to be a way to guarantee her safety.

Janik wanted to release the data on Kirox's tablet to clear his name, but if Fed Sec got their hands on it, it'd be useless to her. She couldn't allow that. Her whole plan hinged on no one knowing she existed.

She returned to the car where Janik still lay unmoving in the front seat. She opened the rear door where the packs were. Pausing for a moment, she watched him sleep, haunting pain evident on his face. She'd misjudged him. He wasn't as selfish as she expected. She couldn't deny her guilt knowing he likely wouldn't survive the night.

She froze when he shifted. He settled and she flipped open the cover of the pack. Her hand trembled as she stuck it inside.

Only a few more seconds. Once she had the decryption keys, she'd disappear. Her next moves required careful calculation.

Janik bolted straight up in the seat, screaming. Serena jumped back, smacking her head off the top of the doorframe. She bit her lower lip to keep from crying out as tears of pain welled up in her eyes. The tablet still sat in the bottom of Janik's open pack.

"Where - where am I? What's going on?" he stammered as his head whipped around.

Serena rushed around to the other side of the car. Before she could explain, he brought his gun up. "Who are you? What are you doing here?" The gun shook in his hand. His finger pressed against the trigger.

She made eye contact, hoping he recognized her. His eyes were glazed and unfocused. Distant. She had to get through to him. "It's me, Janik. It's Ser-"

He thrust the gun out in front of him. "How do you know my name?"

She ducked away, though at this range, it wouldn't matter. *Not a good time to lose your mind, Janik.* "It's Serena, Janik. Settle down and listen to me. We don't have a lot of time."

Janik backed deeper into the car, shaking his head rapidly. "I don't believe you. You're here to kill me. Renaude sent you, didn't he? Renaude sent you. He had my brain fried and now he wants me dead."

Serena raised her hands reflexively. Had the trauma of the past two days finally pushed him over the edge? "No, no, Janik. Renaude didn't send me. Let's calm down and talk for a minute. Let's talk."

The gun dipped and his eyes seemed to focus a little. Serena circled slowly towards the back of the car, hands out.

"I can't remember anything," he said, pressing the heel of his palm against his temple.

Serena smiled sympathetically. "I know. Let me help you." She inched her way forward. Perhaps if she touched him, let him feel her, he'd recognize her.

His head snapped up and so did the gun. "What do you mean? How can you help?"

Serena stopped. His eyes revealed a man lost and afraid, full of regret. All of the cockiness, the self-assurance was him protecting himself. From himself. "Let me show you."

"No!" Janik waved the gun towards the back seat. "Sit down over there. You're going to show me what you're talking about or I'm going to end you."

She complied. "Okay, Janik. Just relax. I'll show you." Serena kept her eyes on him as she retrieved the tablet from his pack. "You're not a killer, Janik. You're a good man trying to make things right. Let me show you."

Serena inched out of the back seat and crouched outside the car in front of the door. "Everything is explained on this tablet. Use your thumbprint to unlock it.

Janik reached out nervously. Serena lunged. She grabbed his wrist with one hand and wrenched the gun away from him with the other. She let him go.

Janik pressed his back against the car door, covering his head with his arms. "Don't shoot me," he babbled. "Don't shoot me."

Serena unloaded and tossed the weapon away. "I'm not going to shoot you. Relax. Let me help you. Please."

Janik, still unsure, babbled like a frightened child. He shied away when she reached for his head. "Close your eyes. Deep breaths. In through the nose, out through the mouth." She cradled his face in her hands, letting him feel their warmth. "Keep breathing. In through the nose, out through the mouth."

The tension melted from his body with each breath. His pulse slowed. Serena didn't let go. "Okay, open your eyes. Focus on me, on my voice." Recognition returned.

His eyes locked onto her face, and after a moment, he placed his hand over hers. "Serena? What happened?"

"Your memory lapses are getting worse. You lost your mind and almost shot me."

"I'm glad I didn't."

Serena's face heated and she pulled her hands away. He wasn't making her decision any easier.

"I can't go on like this," he finished. "It's driving me insane."

"Use the breathing exercises. They help."

Janik followed her direction and sat in the front passenger seat. "Did we get attacked again?"

"Yes. We were at the District. Kirox tried to kill us."

"How did we escape?"

"We blew up the club after I shot him."

"Seems like everyone is trying to kill me. Are you?"

Serena chuckled, thinking he was playing with her. When he didn't return the mirth, her face darkened. "Are you serious?" It hurt that he didn't trust her, despite having ample reason not to.

"I don't know," he replied as he stared out the window. "You have secrets. You work for the Consortium. I'm sure there are still things you're not telling me. Like what happens to me after I unlock that tablet with the decryption keys."

"I'm not going to kill you, Janik." She couldn't face him as she spoke. "Unless we get you some medical attention, I won't have to."

Her own physical condition wasn't much better. Her whole body ached and there was the small matter of the hole in her shoulder. She wished she could forget all this undercover spy stuff. In a way, she had Logan to thank. If he hadn't shown her his true colors, she'd still be blindly working for him.

Her communicator chirped. That'd be Felix ordering her to bring Janik in. Serena threw it to the ground, smashing it into pieces. "Telemarketer," she shrugged as Janik stared at her with a slack jaw. "What's our next move?"

"I'm going to see Ella, then I'm going to see Fed Sec, then I'm going to find Renaude. Any one of those will likely get me killed so I'll understand if we part ways here."

She swallowed the sudden lump in her throat. She didn't want to kill Janik, but their paths were about to split. Since her first days at the academy, she swore never to let her personal feelings get in the way of her duty. *The job always comes first. Personal desires don't matter.* The way Harlon treated her only reinforced that feeling.

Now, that had all changed. She couldn't deny her feelings. She wasn't sure she wanted to. That weakness had put her on the path she was on so many years ago. Her gaze fixed on the pocket holding Kirox's tablet. So much power in such a tiny device. Once she had it, nothing would stop her from making the difference she'd always hoped to. Bruno's veiled suggestion played in her head. She had the strength. She'd have to. She drew her pistol. *Don't think about it. Just pull the trigger.* Simple.

"So this is what you've been hiding." Janik crossed his arms. "You intended to kill me all along."

"No. This was a recent development." Her voice held a surprising amount of detachment. "It's not personal. That tablet and those scripts are my best chance at putting things right."

"And killing me is what? Bonus points?"

Pull the trigger, Serena. Janik was never going to survive this. He admitted as much himself. "I realize now that Felix isn't wrong. Only his methods are. Once Fel- Leland and Logan are dealt with, nothing will stop me from destroying the UN and the Consortium. I'm resetting San Francisco back to the way it was before the Great Quake. People deserve to live free from corruption."

"You're as insane as they are if you believe that. Logan and Leland are puppets. As much as they like to think so, they hold no real control. There'll be others like them. As long as the Consortium Executive Order, the ones with the money hold the strings, this will never end. Kill me if it'll make you feel better, but it won't change anything. There will always be someone greedier, someone crazier, trying to use you. Even your friends will have an angle."

She tried picturing him as another faceless man, but she'd have a better shot at convincing Ivan to like her. *He'll only hurt me.* The words rang hollow. All of her hesitation boiled down to one simple fact. She cared about this man. As crazy as it seemed, and despite all of his numerous flaws, she cared about him. "What about you? How will you use me?"

He inched his way towards her. His hot breath tickled her forehead. "I have never hidden my true intentions. I only want my memory back and my name cleared. Though, I think I'd like to add a third thing to that list." She didn't resist him pushing the gun down. "You can have the scripts and Kirox's tablet when I'm done. God knows both the UN and the Consortium deserve to be wiped off the map. I have no interest in getting in your way."

He wrapped his arms around her, and perhaps for the first time since she left home, she felt safe. Janik was right about all of it. She'd been infuriated with his nobility. Criminals weren't supposed to be noble. She told him before she didn't hate him. She wasn't exactly sure what she felt. "What do we do now?"

"That's up to you. Are you still planning on using that gun?"

She grinned widely. "I haven't decided yet. Depends on how angry you make me." Her gaze dwelled on him a moment longer. "You're a self-centered, egotistical man," she said before kissing him.

"And you're a stubborn, vindictive tyrant," he replied after pulling back.

She didn't care that her mind was jumbled chaos. This felt right. That's all that mattered. To hell with the consequences.

CHAPTER 35: EXCHANGES

Janik checked the address on the tablet again. Ashbury Heights. Another swank neighborhood in the heart of Consortium territory. He didn't care. Everything he'd done since the Promenade was with the purpose of talking to this woman.

They skulked between the parked cars down the dark, narrow street. Only the occasional siren in the distance, or the rumble of heavily armored Fed Sec vehicles, broke the eerie silence. They'd been lucky to avoid them so far. Most of the action was likely still over by what was left of Coit Tower anyway. They wouldn't push it by sticking around too long.

"Just my luck," he murmured. "The house is halfway down the street." No time to prepare an escape route. He hated working on the fly like this. It led to mistakes.

Janik felt Serena's nervousness. "If she screams, we'll have to subdue her."

"She won't scream." Janik came up a little short on confidence. "I'll make her see the truth."

Serena laughed. "She's lost her son. That is the only truth she will see. Do you think it matters whether you were the one to kill him or not?"

Janik stared straight ahead. "It matters to me."

A Fed Sec rover shone a search light from the far end of the street. Janik bolted for the cover of a large delivery van on the other side. Thankfully, Serena followed. Having her here with him eased his mind a little. He settled against the side of the van and covered his face with his dark jacket. The rover rolled past agonizingly slow, its spotlight sweeping both sides of the street. A Fed Sec officer leaned out the passenger window, his rifle following the light. Their communicator chattered over the engines' rumble. They were setting up a final assault on Land's End at a parking lot at Forty-Fifth and Point Lobos. Janik's next stop once he finished here.

He inched from behind the truck once the rover was well past. His stomach lurched when Renaude's communicator chirped in his pocket. Hearing from him now was a little unexpected. His hand shook as he pulled it out and activated the view screen.

"I knew you would find her eventually. I've always admired your resourcefulness, if not your employment methods." The screen panned out to reveal Ella bound and gagged. "As you can see, I have taken Miss Cobb into custody. For her own protection, of course. I know how eager you are to speak with her and I'm happy to oblige you. I know you're having some memory troubles lately, so I think you'll approve of the meeting place. You're a smart man so I'm sure I don't have to spell it out. Oh, before I forget, I'll have another surprise waiting for you when you arrive. Don't keep me waiting, Janik."

The screen went black, leaving Renaude's evil grin imprinted on his brain. Janik smashed the communicator against the pavement. "He's taken her to the lab in Felix's complex."

"You'll be walking into a death trap."

"You're right," he said, his voice shaking as he shrugged his shoulders. "Let's be honest. I was never meant to walk away from this anyway."

They drove to Geary and Fortieth Avenue to see the mayor before going to Land's End. Janik took Kirox's tablet and the tablet with the decryption keys from his pack. He copied the Dross Lakes and Call Logs folder onto a blank wafer, as well as the files on everything McIntosh Corp was doing to the medications they pushed on people. He encrypted it with a simple key Logan's scribers would have little problem figuring out. He then copied some of Kirox's tablet over to a separate encrypted wafer. He left a little surprise for them though. "As soon as they unlock this one, this virus will wipe it clean."

He handed the originals to Serena. "Unfortunately, this is only the tip of the iceberg of Felix's network. We didn't have time to copy any more. If you want the rest, you'll have to get it directly from him. I'm sure you'll find some data on the Consortium Executive Order as well. I don't need any of it. Once I deal with Renaude and free Ella, I'm gone."

Wetness rimmed the bottom of her eyes. "I don't want you to go."

Hearing her say that was odd, yet comforting. "That's why I have to. I'd be getting in the way. Now, go deal with Felix. I'll handle Logan. I'll try to bring help as quickly as I can."

"Be careful, Janik."

She kissed him again and he savored the moment. He knew at the Promenade he was ready for an exit. Perhaps, deep down, this was one reason why. Nobody would ever love a thief. She got out of the car, and he drove away before temptation forced him to drop everything and head for the city limits with her beside him.

Heavily armed officers met him at the Fed Sec blockade, positioned to get a clear shot through the windshield. He stepped out with his arms raised. Three officers approached cautiously. "On your knees," they ordered and Janik complied.

"My name is Janik Brynn," he said as they cuffed him. "I'm here to see the mayor. She'll want the information I have."

They confiscated the data wafers, as expected, and escorted him to a staging area where the mayor and Serena's friend, Logan, were waiting, along with the Fed Sec commander.

Logan regarded him coyly. "We finally meet. Serena has told

me so much about you."

"Yeah, she's told me some things about you as well. First time I've seen a snake walk on two legs."

Logan surprisingly refrained from ripping his throat out. "You may be surprised to learn this, but we have history. I didn't realize it until recently."

"What are you talking about?"

"Gina Hendrix," he replied with a smirk. "Bill McIntosh hired me to deal with her when you couldn't handle it. You were supposed to be the bonus catch, but everyone thought you were already dead. I must say, that was well-played."

Janik's chest tightened, and he couldn't breathe. His voice came out hoarse and low. "Gina told me once that she was sure there was an assassin after her. That was you. You killed her…"

"No, Eldridge Row did that. I was too late to take credit."

"I'm going to kill you," Janik said, having found his full voice again.

"Please," Logan replied. "That's water under the bridge. With Bill McIntosh dead now, there's no way I could collect on the contract. You win some, you lose some. We have other, more immediate business to discuss. Did you get into the network?"

As much as Janik wanted to strangle the life from this piece of crap before him, Logan was right. Personal vengeance would have to wait. "Of course I did. What kind of code scriber do you think I am?"

Logan grinned coldly. "Obviously, one to whom I didn't give enough credit. What did you see?"

"Everything. Including how the Consortium Executive Order terrorized those families in the neighborhoods where the dross lakes now reside. Not to mention the extortion they continue to use to keep people in line. Healthy people don't need your medicine, nor the crap you put in it to keep people hooked." Janik raised his hand, stopping Logan's expected denials. "Don't bother.

I've seen the files. You know, I'm almost tempted to let Felix succeed. It's high time someone knocked you clowns down a peg."

Mayor Waters glared at Logan. "You son-of-a-bitch. You never gave a damn about saving the city. Only about saving your own ass."

Logan's nostrils flared. "Where is Serena? I expected her to be here."

"She's taking care of some unfinished business. She asked that I deliver her resignation in her absence. She wasn't happy with the benefits and the overtime was murder."

"I'll discuss that with her personally, if it's all the same to you."

Janik shrugged. "She did say that if you want the power restored, you'll send her some backup, preferably before she's killed. I think she's considering doing something stupid."

"My team is ready to move," the Fed Sec commander said before Logan interrupted.

The mayor held up her hand, stopping everyone. "You said you had information for me."

Janik held his hand out to the officer who had taken his gear. "My data wafers?"

The officer put the device in front of him. He tossed one to the Fed Sec commander. "That one's the Promenade footage from yesterday. It proves I didn't plant the bomb." He held up the other wafer in front of him. "Before I play this, we're going to conduct a little negotiation."

Logan crossed his arms. "I don't negotiate with filthy UN thieves."

Janik laughed. "Suit yourself. Do you have the encryption keys for the wafers?" Despite the danger, he enjoyed watching Logan slowly steam like a kettle. Still, he pressed on. "Good luck shutting down the UN. It's larger than you think. You have Kirox, who's dead, by the way, but he's small time. By the time you figure out who's running things, everything will have changed." Serena would see to that.

Logan cracked his knuckles. "I can be rather persuasive when I have to be."

"Oh for god's sake, Logan, shut up," the mayor snapped. "Okay, Mister Brynn. You have us at a bit of a disadvantage currently. Name your terms."

"Lucky for you I don't want much. You're going to forget you ever knew me. You're going to let Serena walk away and forget you ever knew her too. Once I have my memories back, you'll never see my face again." Janik held up the data wafer. "I'll transmit the encryption codes to this when I'm safely away. It contains everything on the UN. Major players, locations, how they're moving stuff around, how they're hitting your shipments. That sort of thing. You'll understand if I ask you not to reveal how you acquired it."

"What if you end up dead before you transmit the codes?" Logan asked.

"That's a risk you'll have to take."

Mayor Waters snatched the wafer before Logan got to it. "Why so quick to sell out your friends?"

"Presumptuous of you to assume they were ever my friends. They abandoned me long before I considered returning the favor. They didn't like the fact I was retiring. They were expecting me to not make it out of this alive. Still fifty-fifty on that one."

"I find it hard to believe that all you want for this is to walk away?" the mayor challenged.

Janik leaned back, confident they'd agree to his terms. "I gave you the means to turn the power back on. I gave you Renaude. I figured out who Felix Nash really is. Without me, you'd all be eating by candlelight for the foreseeable future. I asked for none of this and don't want the blood of children on my hands. My freedom is a fair price to pay for your city back, agreed?"

"Make the deal, Logan," the mayor demanded. "I'm tired and

want to go home."

Logan's hands were balled into tight fists and if his jaw clenched any more it would crack. Serena said he was used to getting his own way. Not this time. "Fine, but screw me over and I'll hunt you down. You will know pain before I kill you."

Janik would be long gone before Logan figured it out. He'd have his hands full dealing with Serena anyway. "Fair enough. I believe that concludes our negotiations. Now, would you all like to know what your beloved chief marshal and one Felix Nash have been up to recently?"

"About bloody time," the Fed Sec commander said.

Janik slid the remaining data wafer across the table. The Fed Sec commander plugged it into a terminal as the mayor looked over his shoulder.

Her mouth hung open in shock. "These are the files Sarah was supposed to get for me. How did you get them?"

"I downloaded them from Felix's network after he stole them from the Coit Tower server farm. There's a lot and since time is short, I suggest you go through it a bit later. Suffice it to say, it'll all make sense when you see it. The stuff in the Call Logs folder, on the other hand, will be very entertaining."

The commander activated the recorder.

"This is Renaude."

Mauro Barron's excited voice echoed through the room. *"Marshal Renaude, I need more test subjects. I am close to a breakthrough."*

"Impossible, Doctor. This business with the cyber-attack is demanding my attention. How are you able to conduct tests with the blackout anyway?"

"That is not your concern. If I don't continue my research, you will not get what was promised. My clients have committed a tidy sum of money to you as well as the procedure for your cooperation."

"I refuse to live under the thumb of the Consortium and their pills any longer. Still, I find it distressing that you refuse to tell me who these clients are. For all I know, they're the ones behind the attacks."

"*My clients are capable of many things, Chief Marshal. What of the test subjects?*"

"Renaude wasn't lying about not knowing what the prisoners were for," the mayor said.

"*It will take some time. I have to arrange a transport. I have someone special in mind for the procedure. He has been a particularly nasty thorn in my side for quite some time.*"

Logan regarded him with some amusement. "I assume he means you. I can relate."

"*Do not take too long,*" the doctor's voice continued. "*My clients grow impatient.*"

The recording ended and Janik didn't know if the mayor's face could get any more ashen. "There's more."

Mauro Barron's synthesized voice came from the speaker again. "*I thought I told you not to call me. What do you want?*"

Renaude's voice sounded strained. "*There is an issue with the thief.*"

"*What are you talking about? The transplant failed. He's dead.*"

"*No doctor, Janik lived. I thought you knew the difference between the two.*"

"*How much does he know?*" the doctor asked after a brief pause.

"*I don't know. I have him contained for now. When are promises made to me going to be fulfilled? I grow weary of these delays.*"

"*I am not sure. The power outage is affecting my schedule. As soon as it comes back on, you will be the first one I call.*"

"*That could be sooner than you think, Doctor. I have my best man on the case.*"

There was a hesitation in the recording, as if the doctor hadn't expected that response. "*I must go now, Chief Marshal. I have work to do.*"

"*Remember your promises. We both know how important your research is to you, despite its illegality. I would hate to have to shut it down.*"

"I never thought Renaude would sell out his uniform for

revenge," Mayor Waters said. "Where is he now? He has to know now that it's over. He'll never get that procedure."

"That brings me to my next reason for stopping by. He called me earlier. He's at Land's End with hostages."

"How the hell does he think he's getting inside there?"

"We put a significant dent in their sec force," Logan said. "It's a lot easier now than before."

The mayor turned on the Fed Sec commander. "I want every available unit inside that lab within the hour. No one goes home until I see Renaude in mag-cuffs or a body bag."

Janik cleared his throat, getting their attention. "Renaude isn't stupid. If he sees anyone other than me approach the lab, he'll kill everyone one and destroy the lab. That means I lose what I want. Let me go in after him."

The mayor shook her head. "I'm not letting one criminal go after another."

"Please, Mayor," Janik chided. "Park your sense of morality for a minute. Felix is expecting me to decrypt the files he stole. He won't kill me until that happens."

"How do you plan to avoid capture?" Logan asked.

Janik gave him a sly wink. "I've managed to avoid it up to this point. I have a few tricks up my sleeve."

"He has a point," the Fed Sec commander said. "Renaude is teetering on the edge. One wrong move and the body count climbs. I'm not keen on losing good men to a maniac with an itchy trigger finger. Let him go in. If he comes out with Renaude, we win. If not, we can still send everything and take him down that way. We'll have our hands full dealing with Felix anyway."

A Fed Sec officer approached, leading a man Janik thought he'd never see again. Stephen clutched his side and blood seeped through his fingers. "What are you doing here? I thought you were on your way out of the city."

"Renaude shot me," he stammered. "He has Patricia. He's

going to kill her, Janik. You have to stop him."

He rounded the table and grabbed Stephen under the arm. He didn't fight him. Janik's worst nightmare had come true. "You'll have to shoot me to stop me, Mayor. He'll let my sister go if he has me. I'm nothing to you. If I die, so what? I have to save Patricia."

The mayor stared at him for a long moment. "Get out of here. Don't come back without Renaude."

CHAPTER 36:
DEAD WEIGHT

Serena crouched next to a tree on the western edge of Land's End. Although far from a sure thing, the factory loading dock was her best entry point option. Logan's assault had drawn much of Felix's force to the front of the complex. Or they were all waiting inside. She drew her gun and started down the embankment. *No point in waiting for them to come kill me.*

A mercenary lay dead inside the unlocked loading dock door. Renaude's handiwork, probably. *One less for me to shoot.* Serena relieved him of the communicator he wouldn't need anymore.

"Multiple contacts at the front gate," the voice on the other end said. "Units responding."

A few more out of her way. In the far left corner of the loading dock, three plain delivery trucks sat idle. *Explains how Felix moved the explosives.*

If she remembered the map correctly, the stairwell down was hidden behind a false wall in a small closet off to the right. The door was splintered from its hinges. Seems Renaude knew about it as well. The lack of an ambush made her nervous. Ivan wasn't dumb enough to send everyone to the front gate.

Serena squeezed through the door into the empty stairwell, holding her breath, listening for sounds below. Pressing her back against the wall, she took the stairs one at a time, past Level One, and Level Two. The real fun started on Level Three.

Several closed doors ran down the length of the hallway and

the beginnings of an idea formed in Serena's mind. One of these rooms was likely the server room with all the breakers for the complex inside.

She crept down the corridor until she came to a door with an electronic lock and a thumbprint scanner. A lot of security for one small door. She shot the lock twice and let out a sigh of relief when the door swung silently inward.

She paused inside the door to let her eyes adjust to the darkness. There was a light switch on the wall, but she wasn't that dumb. As expected, the room was filled with servers and chilling fans whirring at high speed. She could start pulling cables out, but no. She didn't want to destroy the data. She still needed it.

The back wall was lined with breaker panel after breaker panel. Serena didn't have time to shut them all off. She had to find the mains. She opened the first panel. It was everything for level one. She flipped breakers, not entirely sure what she was shutting off.

She got halfway down the row when she came to the one labeled 'Lab'. She hesitated. Janik was there trying to get his memory fixed. If she shut these off, she took that away from him. Shutting them off also forced Renaude out into the open. Serena knew what she should do. Instead, she left the breaker room unsure of the difference she made. If it gave Fed Sec a small advantage, it was worth it.

Well-lit corridors stretched straight ahead and to the right. The control room was on the far side of the level, guarded heavily by Ivan's goons. Her training officers liked to refer to these as 'kill zones'. Death was almost guaranteed. *Should've kept a couple grenades from the trunk.*

"Fed Sec is inside the complex," someone's communicator squawked. "We're being overrun."

"Take the others," Ivan replied. "Kill anyone in a marshal or Fed Sec uniform. Lead them here if you can't kill them."

Serena's jaw dropped a little. She didn't expect Ivan to be on this floor too. She thought he'd be down below with Felix. It changed nothing about her mission. She was getting inside that server room one way or the other.

"What about the girl? Surveillance picked her up coming in through the loading dock."

"Felix wants the pleasure of killing her himself. After I have a bit of fun. Felix won't recognize her face by the time I'm finished."

Her grip tightened on her weapon. Not if I kill you first, you son of a bitch.

With no way to take him by surprise, Serena shuffled to the left side of the corridor, her boots thudding a little too loudly on the floor.

"Give yourself up, bitch." She pictured the salacious grin on his ugly face. "Perhaps I can convince Felix to kill you quick."

"You seem to think you have the advantage," she mocked. "Well, I know something you don't know. Fed Sec has hacked into the network. Once they deal with your little militia, they're coming for you, and they have bigger guns."

Ivan hesitated before answering. "Let them. I'll kill them, too. Hopefully your boss is with them. I owe him a painful death."

Serena laughed. "In that, we have a common desire. Where's Renaude? I hear he's around here somewhere."

"Probably in the lab with the doctor. Those two peons can kill each other for all I care. They've been nothing but a pain in my ass anyway. You're my only concern."

"I'm flattered. Most guys only want me for my body."

Gunfire slammed into the corner, tearing away chunks of glossy tile. She retreated towards the stairwell to reassess her options. Two bad guys popped into the corridor in front of her, and Serena fired without hesitation. Ivan hadn't sent them all to the top after all.

She leaned out a little farther and opened fire with renewed vigor. She leaned out a bit too far and a bullet grazed her left arm.

She screamed and dropped her gun. She had to stop letting people put holes in her.

"Did that hurt?" Ivan mocked. "That sounded like it hurt."

Serena clutched her arm, sticky blood seeping through her fingers. She slid down the wall to the floor. She couldn't run away, though the situation had become less than ideal. Ivan stood between her and the server room halfway down the corridor. She only had to kill him to be in the clear. She drew her dagger and held it against the inside of her forearm, the tip pointed toward her elbow. "I've had worse. In fact, staring at your ugly face is about all the agony I can bear."

Ivan strolled casually towards her. "You have some fight." He kicked her in the kidney with a grin. "I'll give you that much. But you had to know you were doomed right from the start."

Serena doubled over, pinning the blade against her belly, and squeezed her eyes shut against the agony. She coughed and retched, trying to regain her breath. Once she regained her composure, she spat a bloody gob on the floor between Ivan's boots. "What choice did I have? You and Felix were destroying the only home I have."

"None really."

Ivan dragged her up against the wall by the front of her shirt. She managed to keep her tenuous grip on the dagger. Ivan hadn't even looked down at her hands. The arrogant fool thought he'd already won.

He pressed his thumb against her injured shoulder. "Consider yourself lucky. If I had my way, you wouldn't have left Felix's office alive. You see, I'm a businessman. Pragmatic, you might say. I don't let emotion cloud my judgment. So, when Felix got a little love struck and blocked me, it became personal."

Serena bit down on the building scream. Ivan threw her against the far wall. Her head smacked against the wall and black spots danced in front of her vision. She struggled back to her feet and back-pedaled out of Ivan's reach. The dagger was no longer hidden. Not that it mattered anymore. She whipped it around, slashing at his stomach.

Ivan jumped back out of the blade's reach and tossed his gun aside. He drew a short dagger from behind his back. "I was hoping you'd put up a fight. I'm going to make you bleed."

Serena reversed her swing, stabbing at his throat. "Can we skip that part? Red's really not my color."

Quick punches to the face and stomach had Serena back on the floor bleeding from her nose and mouth. Felix only said to bring you to him alive. Conscious never entered the conversation."

Serena started laughing.

"What's so funny?"

She swiped the red mess from her face and stood again. She wouldn't let him break her. "It's cute that you think his name is Felix."

"What are you talking about?"

"Felix is actually Leland Preston, an angry little boy out for revenge. The Consortium and the marshals stole his home and he's making them pay."

Ivan snorted. "I'm not surprised. I suspected there was more to him than he let on. Not that it mattered. He could've called himself God as long as I got paid."

"Typical mercenary," Serena sneered.

"A man's got to make a living, doesn't he? Law enforcement wasn't paying the bills." Ivan launched a fist into her belly. "Not entirely sure what Felix ever saw in you."

"Maybe he needed someone with balls to actually get stuff done. I killed the UN trader. I'm delivering the thief with the decryption codes. I'd say that makes you pretty useless. Once the Consortium Executive Order is destroyed, we're gonna live happily ever after."

Ivan's hand shot out at her face like a striking snake. Serena stumbled back, slashing across his arm with her dagger.

"That's the spirit," Ivan hissed as he licked the blood from the back of his arm.

She had only one chance to end this. "Come on, Tinkerbell. Show me how much of a man you are." Ivan attacked again, rage burning like wildfire in his eyes. Serena ducked under a punch aimed at her face and thrust her dagger upwards, burying it deep into his inner thigh.

Hot blood poured from his severed artery over her hand. She pulled the dagger free, plunged it into his stomach, all the way to the hilt. She reefed up, making sure it did the maximum damage. Serena held his limp form in her arms. She wouldn't let him go until every last bit of life faded. "Not so tough when you're bleeding out, are you?" She grabbed his balls and twisted, but all that came out was a low grunt. "Still want to have some fun? I'm sure there's a nice quiet room we can use. Or would you rather do it right here?"

He struggled to get words past the blood gurgling in his throat. His eyes bulged with a mixture of shock and fear. Serena figured he never expected his life to end this way.

Serena pulled the knife free and wiped it clean on Ivan's shirt. She slumped against the wall for a moment to catch her ragged breath. Her face throbbed and a stream of blood ran down her chest from her wounded shoulder. She tore a strip of Ivan's shirt and stuffed it against the wound. If she didn't regain control over her racing heart, she'd end up like Ivan.

She used the wall for support to help her stand. She retrieved her gun and staggered along the corridor to the server room. She used her keycard to open the door, and shot the only sec officer on duty in the room. Then she turned the gun on the two techs controlling everything. Both wore wrinkled t-shirts, one with mustard stains on the front. These guys needed Janik to teach them how to dress. "You're it? You're all Felix has bringing the city to its knees?"

"We had no choice," Mustard Stain said. He held his hands up in surrender. "Ivan's men grabbed us and brought us here. Wherever here is. We were blindfolded when they brought us in. We haven't been outside in three weeks."

Serena flopped down into an empty chair and flexed her damaged shoulder gingerly. She'd be months recovering from these injuries. If she lived. "Grabbed you from where?"

"Coit Tower," the other one replied. "We handled accounts for multiple Consortium divisions."

"You knew exactly where to point Felix. Everything else was a smoke screen."

"He threatened to kill our families if we didn't help him," Mustard Stain added.

"Felix is after the Consortium Executive Order."

Mustard Stain's eyes narrowed. "What the hell is that?"

"We told Felix when he brought us here that we didn't have access to any of the data. He needs access codes from the clients to even get into the server. You have a better chance of reuniting the continental United States than getting those codes."

That explained why Ivan's people were hunting the city's elite. Serena chuckled at the poetic irony. Leland was using the Consortium's own people to destroy them. "Shut it down," she ordered. "Now."

"We can't," the first one said. "Once things started going wrong, Felix commandeered control remotely. The only thing that can shut it down now is the tablet he's carrying."

"What do we do? The Consortium will kill us for helping Felix."

"Stay here and lock the door. I'll come back for you once I've finished a small bit of business. You work for me now."

Felix, no, she had to think of him as Leland, waited, tucked away in his little apartment. She was sure of that. She was less sure of the likely unpleasant surprises waiting for her. Either way she was walking into a trap and if it meant her death, she'd take the bigger prize.

CHAPTER 37: NEW BEGINNINGS

Leland sat calmly behind his desk with his tablet in front of him. All the power in the city in such a tiny device. He didn't look up when the sec officer shoved Serena through the door. "Hello, Olivia. Or should I say Serena?"

She should've expected him to find her true identity. And to have someone waiting for her when she came for him. "Hello, Leland."

He smiled broadly. "I guess it's only fair you know who I am since I know who you are."

The sec officer placed her weapons on the desk, along with the tablet and data wafer Janik gave her. "She was carrying these, sir."

Felix tutted and shook his head. "Such crude weapons."

"I guess next to bombs and network hacks, they would be."

"Those are not weapons. They are tools to affect necessary change. I had hoped you'd see that, but you're no better than the rest of them." He tapped the screen on the tablet. Good thing she remembered to lock it. "Clever girl."

"How did you find out who I was?"

Leland pushed his chair away from his desk. "I suspected what you told me about your father and the Mission District was partially true. The emotion was too real. I had Ivan check it out. Then we found your profile in some recently acquired files. Your father was a great man and I truly am sorry about your mother. She didn't deserve to die that way."

Serena's throat constricted. "Leave my parents out of this. You don't know anything about them."

"I was expecting Ivan to deliver you. Where is he?"

"Lying in a pool of his own blood on Level Three. Your control room is shut down. Clever how you used the Consortium's own people against them. I guess you were right. They really were motivated. Oh, and I'm pretty sure you're not getting anymore data from Coit Tower since it no longer exists."

Leland's jaw tightened, and his eyes narrowed. "I wasn't expecting the logic bomb to be triggered so soon. The download wasn't finished. I should've made sure the thief was dead myself." He moved slowly from behind his desk, never taking his eyes from her. "You disappoint me, Serena. I thought you understood what I was trying to accomplish here. Turns out you are all lies."

Serena dropped her eyes. "Not all of it. I share your feelings, but blowing the hell out of the city won't move the dross lakes and bring your neighborhood back. Revenge won't bring back your mother. Trust me, I know."

"You're right, of course. Part of it is vindictive, perhaps most of it. They stole the one thing I couldn't get back - my childhood. All so they could put a filthy lake of slop there. The Consortium doesn't care about the city. They didn't step in to save it after the Great Quake. They took advantage—continue to take advantage—of desperate people to satisfy their insatiable greed. People can't see that this city is rotting from the inside out."

Serena stepped forward, keeping her hands out in front of her. "Holding the city hostage sure as hell won't damage the Consortium enough to make a difference."

Leland threw his head back and laughed. "Oh, I'm not going to damage them. I'm going to destroy them. I'm sure you know by now that those files contain links to every member of the Consortium Executive Order. Ghost drives with every filthy backroom deal, every filthy detail extorted for money and power.

I own it all. This city will be whole again. Under my terms." He retrieved a pistol from his desk, picked up Serena's tablet and gestured towards his apartment. "Let me show you."

The monitors on the wall in the apartment instead of showing various views of the city now showed one large map spotted with red dots. "As you can see. Though I have lost the traffic cameras, I still control the grid. Nothing moves in this city unless I say so. Soon, I will know all of the Consortium secrets and they will be choked off little by little." He squeezed his free hand into a tight fist to emphasize his point.

"You're dreaming if you think people are going to sit idly by while you devastate the city. They've taken control of the upper floors of this complex already. Stop this so we can all get on with our lives. You've made your point."

Leland held up a small control panel and flipped open the plastic cover on the trigger switch. "My point will be made when I say so." He motioned to the sec officer. "Wait outside."

Behind all of his anger, lay immeasurable hurt. The same hurt marred her mother's face when their house collapsed. Serena would never forget that image. She knew better than anyone what it was like to have a home torn apart.

"I could use a drink. Nasty business, all this killing. I will be glad when it's over." He poured a large measure of whiskey from his well-stocked liquor cabinet. "I was twelve the day the marshals showed up at the door. They said the area wasn't savable because of earthquake damage. They wouldn't even let us try. They said the coastline had sunk too much into the sea. Unstable they called it. The worst of it was seeing the tears streaking down my mother's cheeks. They had no regard for how we felt, how others felt. Powerless. That's how I felt."

He tucked his vulnerability behind his steel mask again. "Only after we were gone did we realize they wanted the natural bowl created by the earthquake. Less digging meant less money required for the dross lakes. There were miles of desert to the east. No one would've complained if they had put it there. They could've made a deal with the Federals. But no, they insisted on destroying a whole neighborhood. The air smelled so sweet then. Of flowers and grass. Of pine and oak. Of all things natural. Nothing synthetic. Now, it stinks."

Serena realized they were fighting for the same thing. The same principle. The city took something he cared about. He wanted it back. "You're making an entire population suffer for the actions of a few. So you were forced out. No one argues that. But this is not the way to get people to listen. Half the people in this city don't even know the history of the dross lakes."

"Ignorance is no defense," Leland screamed. "I tried it their way. They wouldn't listen. They didn't want to know. The Consortium coddled them and they continued their pitiful existence as if nothing was wrong." He spun away. "Well, they'll learn firsthand those emotions when their homes are destroyed. Fitting, don't you think?"

"You're a maniac," she said, her voice barely a whisper. "The Consortium will kill everyone in here before you get the chance."

He waved the control panel at her with a grin, "I don't think so. Killing me would be a really bad idea. I happen to be the only one with the encryption key to restore the network and deactivate the remaining bombs." He motioned to the sofa. "Have a seat. It is time for the announcement. It's time to get the city on my side. I'm sure they will understand what I am trying to do. After they see more images, they will understand. You can still help me. I will ease your passing if you unlock the tablet with the thief's encryption keys."

"Not much of an incentive."

"I'm afraid it'll be my only offer, but you can ensure you leave the city better for those still to come."

Serena flexed her injured shoulder, wincing at the stab of pain.

"If you want them, come and get them."

"All in good time, my dear. Now, please sit while I finish my business."

Serena sat as instructed, although, she doubted there'd be wine this time. After a few seconds of working on the tablet, Leland's synthesized voice came from the apartment's speakers. Another video played on the monitor. Horrific images of marshals beating helpless men. Women and children being herded into transports. How many of them were still alive, she wondered.

"The time has come to take this city back from the corruption and greed. I have confiscated the government, removing the cancer masking itself as leadership. The Consortium Executive Order is no more. I have isolated the city from outside interference. No longer will heartless people neglect whole neighborhoods. No longer will they take what they have not earned. Resources will be regulated so there will be enough for everyone. Non-compliance will be severely punished. No one else has to die. Your lives will improve if you follow my direction. Ignore me and suffer the consequences." Leland smiled and sat next to her when the recording ended. "How did you like my performance?"

Serena was horrified. "You don't give a damn about this city. You are as bad as the Consortium and the UN. You're just wearing a different mask."

Leland launched a fist into her face. Blood splattered the fine leather seat as her head snapped to one side. He rubbed his knuckles. "That is but a sample of the pain coming to you. Your end is almost near."

Serena pressed her hand against the wound and worked her jaw gingerly. "End this, Leland. Your bombs are being defused. Fed Sec is at your front door. I doubt even your doctor friend is still alive. There is nowhere to run."

"It doesn't matter. The balance has been shifted. People have woken up. More will fight." He brushed her cheek with his fingertips. "And it hasn't been a total loss. I still get to kill you."

Serena snorted through the blood running down her face. "Don't I get a vote on that?"

"Afraid not," he replied. "The jury has already rendered its verdict."

Serena shook her head. "I feel sorry for you, Leland. So much pain, so much agony. I understand. I know what it's like to lose people close to you. I still see my father's face every time I close my eyes."

He stood and raised his pistol. "It is time to unlock the tablet."

"No, I don't think so." Serena shot forward off the couch into him, knocking the tablet and the pistol to the other side of the apartment. "I should thank you," she said as her fist connected above his left eye. "You've saved me the trouble of having to track down the Consortium Executive Order."

She reefed on Leland's shirt with all her strength, intending to throw him against the wall. Instead, her injured shoulder gave out and she lost her footing. Leland landed on top of her and pressed his thumb into her wound. Serena screamed and clutched at his hand, unable to find enough purchase to break free.

"What do you think you'll accomplish that I haven't?" he sneered as he dragged her towards the sofa. "Do you actually think you'll make any more of a difference?"

Serena's laugh came out as a hiss. "You've blown up a few buildings and killed a few people. You've accomplished nothing. The Consortium is still intact. I know how to find them. I know how to hurt them."

"I won't let you steal my vengeance. I've waited twenty years for this. I deserve closure. Tell me what you know, and I'll end your suffering."

Time seemed to slow to a crawl. "Is that what your mother would want? Would she want a genocidal maniac for a son?"

Leland growled and came at her full of aggression and determination, like a bulldog to a bone. "Imagine how ashamed she'd be."

Pain cascaded down her back as her shoulder slammed into the floor. Serena rolled, trying to pin Leland underneath her. Her marshal's training served her well against his superior strength though Leland still ended up on top of her. She punched him in the kidney and heaved up with her legs. Leland flipped over her head, but he was on his feet again almost instantly.

Rage gripped him as he attacked again. "This whole plan was her idea! My only regret is she never lived to see it come to fruition."

Serena struggled to stay out of his reach, any glimmer of hope he could be reasoned with gone. "I doubt she wanted you to become a cold-blooded killer, a monster."

She slapped his hands away as they went for her throat. Weaponless and desperate, she pedaled back. The self-defense techniques that came naturally were of little use against his rampage.

Leland lunged and Serena stepped to the side and jammed her shoulder into his back sending him careening into the wall. She punched the back of his head over and over. She spun him around and drove her fist into his nose, the cartilage collapsing beneath his skin.

Leland fell backwards, bleeding from his shattered nose. Another punch, to the jaw this time, dropped him to the floor. Serena scrambled for the gun near the far wall. When she turned back, Leland was up on his knees.

"You've only damned the city to a horrible existence. The Consortium will never stop. The people will continue to suffer."

Her whole body shook. Her vision blurred momentarily. "Not if I can help it. Give me the codes to restore the network."

Leland wiped a sleeve across his mangled face. "It doesn't have to end like this. We want the same thing."

Serena filled her lungs with air trying to calm herself. "You had your chance." She hammered on his face with her balled fist. "Now it's my turn. The codes."

He grinned at her. "You think either one of us is going to walk out of here alive? They'll kill me for attacking them, and you for betraying them." He leaped for her.

Sidestepping, she pulled the trigger. She regretted having to do this. "Under different circumstances, we could have done something. This wasn't the way."

Leland coughed as blood bubbled up between his lips. "I wanted to save the city."

She knelt beside him. "I know. Unlock the tablet and let me finish what you started. I promise I will see it through."

"Why should I believe you? You've lied to me from the beginning."

"We all lied, Leland. I'm sorry I had to. The Consortium's power blinded me until recently. No more. Things will be different now." Serena retrieved the tablet. "Unlock this for me and I will see that you are remembered properly."

With trembling hands, Leland typed a single word into the tablet's prompt. Gabriela. His mother's name. His hands fell away, and his eyes closed for the final time. Now her real work began.

CHAPTER 38: LOGAN'S LOSS

Serena fell back against the couch and wiped some of the blood from her face. A proper cleanup would have to wait. With Felix's tablet, she could turn the power back on for Janik. She owed him that much.

Kissing him probably hadn't been wise, but since she expected both of them to die, what did it matter? He wasn't a bad person. He had some morals. He stayed to fight for someone who couldn't fight for themselves. The words he said to her, that not all people were as bad as she thought still rang in her head. As did her own. She had to deal with Logan.

She retrieved Felix's gun from the floor and found a communicator. She called Nelson's direct line in the ops center. "How's it going, kid?"

"Could be worse. I could be trapped six floors underground with a madman."

Serena laughed. "That madman won't be a problem anymore, but there are ones far worse still with a pulse."

"What are you talking about?"

"Do yourself a favor, Nelson. Leave the Pyramid right now and don't ever look back. The good work I thought we were doing, it's all a lie. Now's your chance to get out."

"Don't think I like the sound of that."

"The cyber-attack may be over, but the real battle's just beginning. I'd hate to see you get hurt."

"I figured as long as I stuck with you, I'd be fine."

"Who knows? I may have a job for you if you're willing. I'll be in touch."

She called Logan but didn't give him the chance to speak. She fired the gun, screamed, and threw the communicator against the wall. She doubted he'd believe she was dead, but it was worth a shot. Maybe she'd get lucky and one of Leland's remaining mercenaries would shoot him.

Serena went into Leland's office. The guard had fled, either to the upper levels to fight Logan and Fed Sec, or if he was smart, into the night, forgetting this whole mess.

Serena sat at Leland's desk and flipped through some of the data on the tablet. One small break she got was by the time Coit Tower blew, much of the data had already been downloaded. The download had taken hours. *I don't have that long.* There were several ghost servers similar to the ones they found earlier. The useful stuff was there. She copied them and uploaded the virus Janik gave to wipe the drives clean. *Let's see them reconstruct the government now.* Maybe she could work something out with the mayor, if she were still alive.

There were several more videos as a part of media packets Leland intended to release. Video of the marshals clashing violently with the people of Leland's neighborhood. Videos of government officials accepting payoffs from corrupt businesspeople. Leland had the whole city under surveillance for a while.

It wasn't enough though. The figures on these videos were middlemen, messengers. The ones with the real power, the Consortium Executive Order, were smart enough to stay out of the public eye. Those were the ones Serena had to go after. They were the ones inside the Pyramid. It'd take her a while to identify them all, but they had to pay.

It wouldn't stop there though. The UN was bigger than Kirox. They had some things to answer for as well. It was time for someone to cut out the rot. All of it.

There were a couple other files that had appeared after the decryption keys did their work. Permits, forcible removal orders, demolition contracts. All issued from the same place. The Office of City Management. *Was John Barks one of the Consortium Executive Order?* She chuckled. Mayor Waters had one of the top Consortium players right under her nose and didn't even know it.

Not everyone in city hall was loyal to the Consortium though. Someone had to grease the wheels to help Leland build this place. Find them and she'd have a major ally. Nelson could help her too if she could convince him of what was going on. But not now. She had to lay low until the city cooled down.

Serena had one thing left to do before she disappeared. She entered the codes exactly as Janik showed her. The terminal changed as the uploaded subroutine took effect. It didn't take long for things to happen. She went back into the apartment where the monitors still showed the map. One by one, the red dots turned green. The power was coming back on. Traffic lights shown on various monitors flared to life, all of them flashing red. Logic bombs that Leland embedded in the power centers and water collectors were being wiped out.

The whole system had been returned to city control. For now. Serena allowed herself a tiny smile at her success, but that's as far as it went. Janik deserved the real credit. She hoped he was still alive. Not something she would've thought this morning.

She lifted Felix's tablet, its physical weight paling in comparison to the weight of its power. Janik had been right about the need for change, but the cost had been great. She tucked it inside her jacket at the sound of footsteps outside the office. Any happiness she felt disappeared when Logan came through the door. *Damn. I'd hoped to have a little more time.*

His eyes went to her injured shoulder. "You look a little worse for the wear."

"Barely a scratch," she replied coolly.

"What happened? I thought you were dead."

You were supposed to, she said silently. "I tried calling for help. Leland smashed the communicator. I'm lucky to be alive. You'll be happy to know that I've shut down the cyber-attack. Networks should be coming back online throughout the city."

"A lot of people will be happy when the sun comes up. They can get back to their miserably boring lives."

"Nothing will ever be normal again." Not for her anyway. "There's a lot of damage to undo."

"We've cleaned up the mess once. We'll do it again. Though, the loss of Coit Tower will be challenging to overcome. I expect the next few days will be spent in boring meetings."

I'll make sure it goes differently this time.

Logan had a bit of a sideways smirk on his face. "You don't look too happy to see me."

Serena raked a hand through her sweaty and matted hair. "It's been a long day. I'm not happy to see anybody."

He poked his head into Leland's apartment. "I expected more from someone who brought this city to its knees."

"Physical strength isn't a requirement to be dangerous. Leland was smart and motivated. Not to mention angry at a lot of people. And he had every right to be."

Serena struggled to remain calm. Her stomach did somersaults. Fighting Leland was bad enough. She didn't want to fight Logan as well. She'd definitely lose that one. She kept Leland's gun tucked under the desk out of sight.

Logan snorted as he sat down across from her. "Not smart enough, apparently. What did you find?"

"Nothing," she replied, painting on her best dejected face. "I was too late."

"You expect me to believe that? What about all the files he stole?"

Serena shrugged, hissing at the stab of pain in her shoulder. "Believe whatever you want. Leland must've had another failsafe that wiped the data should he be compromised. Everything is gone."

Logan sighed and his shoulders slumped. "I'm disappointed in you, Serena. I thought I could count on you. I had hoped you could go far in our organization."

"That makes two of us." It shouldn't have taken this for her to realize how screwed up this city was. "I didn't expect you to be a conniving worm complicit in protecting monsters and keeping a city hooked on whatever drugs you're pushing."

Logan wagged a finger at her as if she were a naughty child. "I gave you everything necessary to complete the mission. You got distracted. You let Felix and-"

"Leland Preston. Remember that name."

"I don't give a damn what his name is," he roared. "You've let this maniac and the thief fill your head with nonsense. You took your eye off the ball, Serena."

"You hung me out to dry like you do to everyone who works for you. You don't give a damn about anybody, including me. You never have. You'd rather destroy the Mission District than build it up. People you cannot control are nothing more than obstacles."

"The thief told me of your decision to end our relationship. That requires a little further discussion. Your skills are hard to replace."

"Somehow, I can't see myself beating someone to death for not doing what you tell them."

"Actions have consequences, Serena," he said as he cracked his knuckles. "I thought you understood that when you left the Mission District the first time."

"You're a son-of-a-bitch, Logan," she spat. "A despicable son-of-a-bitch."

Logan massaged his forehead and let out a slow breath. "I will overlook your disrespectful insubordination as acute stress. Let's go back to the Pyramid for a drink. Talk things over."

Serena pushed the chair away from the desk, still keeping the gun out of sight. The longer she stayed here, the more opportunity Logan had to do something stupid. "The only place I'm going is to find Janik."

"You're too late." Logan's hand snaked inside his jacket to the gun Serena knew he always kept there. "There's nothing you can do."

"Like I'm going to take your word for it."

"He's not worth it, Serena. He's a filthy UN thief. The data he gave me contained a virus. We lost everything. Both him and Renaude deserve shallow holes in the ground."

Serena strained against the rage building up within her. "You don't know a damn thing about him. You don't know anything about anyone because we aren't people to you. We're pawns on a chess board."

"There have been enough people killed in this mess. I'm not about to throw away a valuable asset. I've invested way too much time and money in you to allow that."

Serena glared at him openly. "My point exactly. An asset. Not a colleague, nor a peer." She took a deep breath. "Never someone you respected. A tool to use and discard as you please. You fit right in with the Consortium."

Logan shook his head and pressed his fingers to his eyes. "There you go bringing emotion into things again. I thought we were past that."

"You thought wrong," she snapped. "We're nowhere near past it. You're wrong, you know. Janik is worth it. If there's anyone who isn't, it's you. I'm done being used."

Logan twisted his neck and rotated his shoulders. His free hand clenched opened and closed. "This is the thanks I get after taking you in. I groomed you, Serena. I gave you power. Security to do what you want, go wherever you pleased. I'm the only reason that community center Felix blew up existed in the first place."

"I told you his name was Leland. You can have it all back. It's not worth the price. Find yourself another protégé."

He slammed his hand down on the desk, and she jumped. "It doesn't work like that, Serena. Nobody walks away from me." He brought his gun up. "Give me what Felix stole and maybe I won't kill you."

Serena tightened her grip on her own pistol. "Go ahead. Pull the trigger if that's what you want. I'm not giving you anything."

Logan squeezed off a round that whizzed a few inches past her ear. "Last warning, Serena. You work for me, or you don't work. Understand?"

She stood, preparing to head for the door. The roar of an explosion swallowed everything. Glass and mortar from the ceiling showered them with sharp, hot shrapnel. Logan dove to one side and she dove under Leland's desk. She squeezed her eyes shut against the blinding dust. *What the hell did you do, Janik?*

Serena opened her eyes after a few seconds of silence. Blackness engulfed her like a tomb. This had to be what her father experienced when their house fell. She kicked away some of the debris and crawled from beneath the desk, picking her way by feel. Sharp debris sliced into her hands and knees. The acrid stench of scorched wiring and mortar dust choked her. She coughed into her sleeve, trying desperately to get a clean breath.

The floor above her was gone. Janik was there. No way he survived that blast. Serena fell back against the desk, swallowing the pang of hurt. Perhaps it was for the best. With what she had to do; she couldn't afford to worry about him. She couldn't afford to love him.

Emergency lights blinking near the top of the walls led her to the exit. A pile of rubble sat in the place where Logan had been standing. Was he really gone? Knowing her luck, probably not. She checked to ensure she still had Leland's tablet and climbed towards her freedom.

CHAPTER 39:
THE LAB

The elevator door opened to an empty, brightly lit foyer. Janik was a little surprised the lights and elevators still worked, but he really shouldn't have been. Leland had been smart enough to avoid capture all this time and build an underground complex without anyone knowing. He wouldn't back himself into a corner by leaving his power source vulnerable.

Janik held back a moment, anticipating an ambush that didn't come. He stepped out and the door closed behind him. No going back now. He'd either leave here with the hostages and his memory intact, or in a body bag. The odds leaned towards the latter.

There was no reception desk or nurse's station like in a normal doctor's office, no tables stacked with reading material in the corners. One corridor led left and one led right. Renaude was down one of them, waiting to kill him.

Leading with his weapon, Janik went right. He feared what he'd find in the rooms down here. *I have to know.* He fumbled his decoder from his backpack. "I hope this works."

The door slid back, revealing a hospital room. Janik's stomach turned. "This is where they're keeping the brainwashed prisoners," he mumbled as his mind flashed with sharp familiarity. "I was in one of these."

The unconscious form in the next room confirmed his suspicions. Wires and tubes ran from his arms and chest like tentacles. Attached to machines beside the bed, it was the only thing keeping him alive.

Janik couldn't leave them like this. *I'll probably kill them if I touch anything.* He wouldn't chance it. Shutting down the lab was the best way to save these people. They may have been criminals, but they didn't deserve this. He found six more unconscious people in the other rooms, "I'm going to kill the doctor right after I kill Renaude."

Janik breathed deeply. As satisfying as that would be, he couldn't harm a hair on the doctor's head until he reversed all the damage he'd caused.

Janik tapped into the control panel near the elevator. Shutting down the ventilation system didn't have the desired effect. On top of the complex's layout, he found the power control system and shut down the main input. There'd be redundant backup power sources, but they wouldn't be enough to run everything. "Let's see how you work in the dark, you bastard."

Janik used the tablet's screen backlight as a flashlight as he inched down the corridor. Unfortunately, he couldn't do anything about his boots clicking on the tiled floor. The doors on this side were all closed – except one. The lab and Renaude.

"I know you're out there, Janik." Renaude unhinged voice squeaked. "Come out now, or I blow the whole floor."

Janik almost questioned how he got his hands on enough explosives for that, but remembered the onsite bomb factory. The whimpering hostages gave him little choice. Renaude wouldn't be reasoned with, and Janik couldn't shoot him before he detonated the bombs. "Okay, Renaude." He tucked the pistol behind his back. "Let the hostages go, and we can talk."

"You are in no position to make demands, thief. Show yourself or I blow it."

Janik stepped through the door. Ella and Patricia sat in chairs against the right-hand wall. Perhaps Renaude's arrogance gave Janik a small advantage. Renaude held the remote trigger in one hand and a gun in the other.

"Where are the bombs, Renaude? You got what you wanted. There's no reason for this."

"When I let go of this trigger, there will be nothing left of this floor or the one above us."

"Not a great escape plan, if you ask me."

"Oh, I have no illusions of escape, but I will be whole when I die."

Great. Suicidal maniac was the only one missing for his terrorist Yahtzee.

Lights flashed on a control terminal sitting behind Renaude. Electrodes dangled from one side of it. There'd be more blinking lights if Janik hadn't shut off the power. A stranger in a lab coat, Doctor Barron, Janik assumed, prepared to use the machine.

The doctor slammed his fist down on the table next to the control panel. "This will not work without power, Renaude. Even with power, your chances are not good."

"Not to worry, doctor. I believe Mister Brynn here can help us."

"Wouldn't count on it," Janik said. "I deal with computers, not power lines. You should check with Fed Sec. I think they're around here somewhere."

Janik's breath hitched when he saw the gurney on the other side of the room. White, taut sheets with a single green blanket on it triggered something dark in his mind. He'd been on that very gurney yesterday.

His eyes locked with Ella and Patricia. "Don't worry," he said. "I'll get you out of this." Renaude paced a few feet behind, trembling. The man teetered on the edge of psychotic meltdown. "Let them go, Renaude. It's me you want."

Renaude stopped pacing. "It's too late for that. So many already dead. A few more don't matter." His maniacal grin sent chills down Janik's spine. "I must applaud you. You've made it farther than I ever anticipated."

"You're not the first to underestimate me. You should've never set me up for CIT, but you had to have your pound of flesh. Now see the mess we're in?"

"Did you expect anything less? You stole my life the day you ran me down. The surgeries, the rehab, the meds. I couldn't survive without it. I became hooked on pain killers."

"You can blame the Consortium for that. They're ones pushing the pills."

"You're the reason they're necessary. I was forced to give up the freedom of working the streets for a desk. As much power as it has given me, I hate that desk."

Keep him talking, Janik. There had to be a way to disarm him. "You're insane, Renaude. Kids are dead, families destroyed. You want that on your conscience? All because you hate a desk?"

Janik had no room to talk, he supposed. His motivation for helping Renaude in the first place involved getting rid of his rap sheet. Not the whole motivation, but a big part of it.

"I belong in the streets with my officers, helping old ladies cross the street and arresting car thieves. I was making a difference. You made me a different person. Less of a cop, less of a man. I wanted my mind fixed. I wanted my life back. Do you have any idea what it's like to live with nothing but chaos inside your head?"

There was irony in those words somewhere, two broken men trying to fix the unfixable. "You're kidding, right?"

"Yes, I suppose you do. Still, you do not know my pain. If my memories were yours, you wouldn't be so glib. You'd understand. You would have compassion."

"Compassion is not a word I associate with you, Renaude." Janik took another tentative step forward. "There is still time for you to make this right."

"Oh, I'm going to make it right. And you're going to watch."

Janik looked from Patricia to Ella to the doctor standing at the terminal. "I pity you, Renaude. Your life has been one pathetic misguided notion of getting back at me. You failed to live the life in front of you. I do understand better now. I've recently learned the error of my own choices."

"Normally, I'd applaud the repentant, but somehow I doubt your sincerity."

"Believe it. Once I'm done here, I'm gone. I'm sure you know by now that the doctor here had no intention of ever helping you. I'm not convinced he could have. Why do you think they shelved his program in the first place? It's unreliable. The Consortium doesn't keep things they can't use."

Renaude's expression faltered. Janik had found a chink in the armor. "With a little more time he would've figured it out. He would've been able to fix me."

"Do you actually think the Consortium intended to let CIT and synapse reprogramming gain a foothold? They're making too much money, and have too much control from their drugs. Losing that market reduces so much of their power. I'm surprised they let the good doctor here live after they shut down his research."

"I went into hiding," Doctor Barron said. "They couldn't kill what they couldn't find."

Renaude spread his arms apart in mock surrender. "What are you looking for? Remorse? Apology? It'll be a cold day in hell before that happens."

"Like you, Renaude, I only wanted my mind fixed and to prove I wasn't a child killer. I don't care about anything else. Let Ella and my sister go. We can die together."

From the corner of his eye, Janik saw Ella's lip tremble and tears stream down her face. How terrible it must be for her to have to relive her son's death over and over again.

Renaude circled slowly to his left. "Well, you've done that." He dragged Ella to her feet, followed by Patricia. "The time for chatting is over. I know you had something to do with the current power situation. Fix it."

We're all dead whether I help him or not. "I don't think so, Renaude. Not this time. Too many have died because of us as it is."

"Perhaps you require a more personal stimulus." Renaude shot Ella in the arm.

Janik fought the urge to rush between them. He couldn't handle watching either of those girls hurt. "Fine, Renaude, don't hurt them. I'll turn it back on."

His hands shook as he accessed the internal systems. Serena hadn't uploaded the scripts yet or this wouldn't be necessary. "It's done," he said after a few minutes. The main lighting came back on. Both Ella and Patricia sobbed.

Renaude moved to the gurney. "It is time to reprogram my synapses."

CHAPTER 40:
MEMORIES REMAIN

The doctor shook his head emphatically as he tried to back away. "The procedure is still flawed, Renaude. My research isn't finished."

Renaude grabbed the doctor roughly by the hair. "Well, you better 'un-flaw' it, Doctor. Quickly." He hauled Patricia up by the arm. "And just to be sure you get it right we'll test it on your sister."

Janik jolted forward. "No, Renaude, don't. Use me instead."

The gun came up. Renaude's wild eyes stared back, empty of all reason. Sweat poured down his face and the gun shook violently. "Stay back, Janik."

Ella surged past him, knocking Renaude off-balance. Patricia slammed her fist into the crazy cop's face and scurried to the other side of the room. Renaude wheeled around and pulled the trigger wildly. Bullets slammed into the wall above Patricia's head.

Janik pounced, knocking the gun from Renaude's grip. He wrapped his hands around Renaude's throat and tried to squeeze. The chief marshal was stronger and uninjured though. Within minutes, Renaude had him on the ground, kicking him. Patricia wailed.

The beating stopped. Janik stared up into the face of a madman.

Renaude spun on Ella, her ashen face streaked with tears. He retrieved his fallen weapon and slid it back into its holster. "If you as much as twitch, I will kill you." He grabbed Janik by the collar and pulled him over to the gurney. "I thought my greatest pleasure would be having my mind fixed and seeing you a broken shell, but no, my greatest pleasure will be seeing you dead."

"I'm sorry," the doctor muttered as Renaude forced him to connect electrodes to Janik's temples and chest. It was a little late for remorse.

"Make sure they are in the correct positions, Doctor. No mistakes this time." He crossed the room, dragging Patricia with him. He flipped the switch on the detonator trigger and forced it into her hand. "Would you be so kind as to hold this for me, my dear? Be careful not to let your finger slip off that button. We wouldn't want any accidents now, would we?"

Janik couldn't move. His chest burned with every breath. His shoulder felt as if someone had ripped his arm from its socket. Blood dripped from several open wounds.

The doctor worked at a laptop for a few seconds. "The program is loaded. We're ready." There was no enthusiasm in his voice. Only fear.

"Begin," Renaude ordered.

Janik braced himself as the doctor reached for the switches. This was going to hurt. As a thief, Janik never expected to die of old age. A violent mark catching him in the act, a fiery crash after a high-speed chase. He never dreamed he'd face his final judgment strapped to a madman's gurney.

His mind raced through all of the people he hurt throughout his life. Only a few of them truly mattered. He hoped they found it in their hearts to forgive him.

The doctor cranked the dial slowly. Jolts of electricity shot through his temples and down through his chest. His back arched as every muscle contracted. His jaw clenched shut, legs and arms bounced up off the gurney.

"Turn it all the way up, doctor," Renaude commanded. "Make sure he's all the way dead this time."

The doctor looked at Renaude with unreserved shock. "Too much power will overload the system. It could kill us all."

Renaude wordlessly shot the doctor and cranked the dial all the way up.

Debilitating electricity surged through Janik's body once again. He groaned through clenched teeth and rose off the table. Images crashed through his head in waves. Cars, Renaude, Kirox, the Promenade. The marshals' building, delivery trucks, cases full of Ice Water. His head felt like Renaude had it crushed beneath his boot.

Gina kissing him. Patricia slapping him. Stephen punching him.

The images wouldn't stop.

The pressure. Oh god, the pressure.

More memories.

The prisoner transport, the lab, the doctor, giant needles piercing his veins.

Janik squeezed his eyes shut. The air crackled with electricity, building to the breaking point. The machine whined and hummed. The stench of burning wires choked off his airways. Through blurry vision, Janik saw Renaude shaking the machine, trying to coax every ounce of power from it.

His mother's tears, his father's anger. Overwhelming loneliness. Serena's warm hands on his face.

One of the control panels in front of Renaude exploded, throwing him back against the wall. The electricity hadn't stopped. Why hadn't the electricity stopped? Janik couldn't move his arms to rip the wires off. He couldn't move anything.

Another panel exploded. Janik collapsed to the gurney, his whole body shaking. Tension slowly melted away. He only faintly felt the pain of the burns left by the electrodes on his skin. An odd calm washed over him. The final descent into death. He welcomed it. Darkness was his friend.

Patricia was beside him then, undoing his bindings and still holding the detonator. "I'll take that. You get out of here," he mumbled. "Run now."

Janik threw up before he accepted the trigger, then retched again. Acidic bile stung the back of his throat. He sucked in ragged breaths. His heart pounded like a drum at a heavy metal concert. He rolled onto the floor, ripping wires from his chest. He was too numb to feel anything close to pain.

Through tears, Janik watched helplessly as Renaude sat up. Blood ran down his face from open gashes, some with shards of glass and plastic still sticking in them.

"I should've killed you sooner," Renaude said as he stumbled to his feet. "I won't make that mistake again." The voice sounded as if it came from the other side of a wall. "You have left me with so many bad memories, Janik. You owe me at least one good one."

"Leave him alone," Patricia screamed.

Janik shoved her to the side as Renaude came at him. He slapped at Renaude as he struggled to maintain consciousness. His arms felt so heavy. Renaude's fingers wrapped around his throat. Janik's legs wouldn't support his weight. They tumbled to the floor, Janik beneath the monstrous man.

Janik slapped at Renaude's hands and twisted his head, trying to break free. He couldn't do it. As the tried to turn, he spotted Renaude's gun on the floor just beyond his reach.

Renaude's pistol.

Janik fumbled for it, his tingling, numb hand unable to reach it. He struggled to draw breath. Someone, Ella he thought, tackled Renaude to the floor. Janik flexed his hand once, then again, welcoming the intensifying tingle.

Renaude was on his feet again, stalking toward Janik.

Fingers wrapped around the pistol's grip. He aimed and fired all in one desperate motion. Renaude stopped. A red patch bloomed on the front of his shirt. Janik fired three more shots as

Renaude dropped to the floor, unsure if any of them hit. The gun fell from his grasp, and he let his head fall back against the gurney.

Fed Sec burst through the door, screaming for no one to move. Inside his head, Janik laughed. Move? Breathing was an accomplishment at the moment. Patricia crouched beside him then. "Please, Janik," she sobbed, shaking him. "We have to get out of here."

He opened his eyes and smiled. "I'll be right behind you. Give me the trigger and follow these nice men out. They'll make sure you're safe."

"I'm not leaving without you."

"Yes, you are. Stephen is waiting for you. He's going to need you to open his soup cans for the next little while." She wrapped her arms around his neck, and it was the most wonderful thing. He allowed her to linger for a moment. If this was the last thing he ever felt, he wanted to cherish it. Tell Mom I'm sorry for everything." Janik nodded to the Fed Sec officer who gently pulled her away. Janik tried not to hear her sobbing fade away.

Ella knelt in front of him. "Why did you do all this?"

Janik forced a smile past his trembling lips. "You deserve to know the truth. I didn't kill your son. I've done a lot of things I'm not proud of. It's important that people, especially the lady that just left, know that killing kids isn't one of them."

"Why did they want to hurt us? We did nothing to them."

"I suspect you're going to hear some things about the Consortium in the coming days that may change your opinion of them. Do me a favor. Think for yourself. Ask difficult questions. Don't let anyone else try to convince you of their truth." Janik took the black knight from his pocket and pressed it into Ella's palm. "I found it next to Matthew at the Promenade. It's not much, but you should have it."

"The knight was his favorite." Tears ran down her cheeks as she hugged his neck gently. "Thank you."

"I'd give anything to turn back time and bring him back." He returned the hug, then eased her away. "Maybe in a sense, I know what it feels like to lose someone close. You should go now. It's about to become really uncomfortable in here."

Another Fed Sec officer knelt beside him. "Give us a few minutes to find and defuse those bombs. We'll have you out of here shortly."

Janik shook his head. "Every floor is wired to a tamper trigger. The second you open any of those cases, they all go off. Leland's bomb expert was a smart cookie. Leland planned to destroy this place after he wiped out the Consortium. You can't defuse them. Get your boys out of here."

"All right then. We'll carry you out before you let go of that trigger."

"Good thought, except the cases will blow if they get too far from the transmitter. This bomber really thought of everything." Janik didn't know if half of what he said was true, but he needed everyone gone. This lab could not be left in one piece. "I'm a lowlife thief. My life doesn't matter. There's no reason for any of your people to get buried down here with me."

The officer's communicator crackled. "The bombs are on Level Three set against the support pillars. If they blow, this whole complex will collapse in on itself."

"Copy that," the officer said. "Clear the area. Move people back from the building. I'll be out in a minute." The officer refocused on Janik with a newfound measure of respect. Janik had never seen that from anyone before. "It wouldn't be right to leave you. I'm sure we can find something to keep that trigger pulled until we get far enough away."

"Do me a favor, man. Just go. It's for the best, trust me. You have thirty seconds, then I'm letting go." Janik started counting. He accomplished what he wanted to. He got his memory fixed. This was the price.

The Fed Sec officer pressed his lips together and reluctantly backed out of the room. "God speed, buddy."

A deafening roar and a cloud of stinging dust and smoke swallowed him. The overturned gurney didn't stop the overwhelming heat. The floor crumbled away from him. The air left his lungs as he landed hard on his back. He could do nothing about the mountain of debris falling in on top of him.

Janik gasped until he could breathe again. The pressure on his chest and legs kept him from moving. He was buried. He heaved up, jarring some debris loose. Maybe it was luck, maybe it was fate, maybe he was cursed, but much of the complex had survived the blast. How long that would last, he had no clue.

The pounding in his head eased a little. Dizziness threatened to turn his stomach again. *Can't believe I lived through that.*

Renaude's limp form lay a few feet away similarly buried. Janik dragged himself over to him and checked his pulse. Nothing. With all the strength he could muster, he punched the marshal in the jaw. Then he punched him again. It didn't make him any deader, but Janik felt better all the same. *Good riddance.*

Janik collapsed next to Renaude and took a deep breath. There was no way to get back up through the gaping hole in the ceiling and there was no other way out. The smoke had thinned, but dust still stung his eyes.

Janik looked up at the sound of shifting rubble above. Commander Solomon threw chunks of concrete and twisted metal to the side and lowered himself to Janik.

"I wondered when you guys would show up."

Solomon snickered. "Sorry, traffic was a bitch."

"Patricia? Ella?"

"Both fine. The power is coming back on. Slowly. Going to be one hell of a mess to clean up tomorrow."

Janik grinned. Serena had succeeded. He should've expected nothing different. "More than a few eyes have been opened, I imagine."

Solomon knelt beside him. "I don't suppose you'd be willing to provide a statement."

Janik let his head fall back against the rubble. "There was a bomb. It exploded."

"Honestly, more than I expected," Solomon said with a chuckle. "Would you take a hand getting out of here?"

Janik nodded. "That I won't turn down."

"How badly are you hurt?"

"I'll live. A few cuts and bruises, maybe some broken ribs." He inspected his current state. "Gonna need a new suit though."

Solomon laughed. "I can help with the injuries. You're on your own for the suit. You have any sort of plan?"

"Thinking about catching a shuttle to somewhere far away. Maybe I'll try to sneak into the Canadian Free Zone. I hear they have good bacon. I doubt I'll be back." He had no reason to come back.

"What about your family?"

"They're better off believing I'm dead. I'd only bring them trouble."

"If you saw their reaction to this explosion you'd think differently. Your sister hasn't stopped crying."

That only reinforced his decision. "Between the Consortium and the UN, I'll be the most wanted man in the city. They've been targets enough already. I'm hoping I can count on you to keep my secret."

"Hey, what you do is your business. As far as I'm concerned, there are nothing but corpses down here."

Solomon led him out through the loading dock where there weren't many marshals. It felt good to breath clean air again. "Any sign of Logan?"

Solomon shook his head. "He went in right after you did. Hasn't come out yet."

"Hopefully, he never does."

Janik thought of his sister, and Ella. They were safe. That would have to be enough. Then he thought about Serena. He wondered if she got out before the bombs went off. Probably, he told himself. She was too smart to be ambushed. He took comfort in that. Believing she was still out there and about to make the difference she'd always wanted was the only comfort he'd have for a long while.

***

Serena watched Leland's complex burn from the shadows near where her transport went down when all this started. That seemed so long ago. Another lifetime, almost.

She thought of Logan. She doubted he was dead. That man was like a cockroach. Lucky for her, she had a boot big enough to crush him.

Her thoughts then turned to Janik. She hoped he wasn't dead. That explosion should've killed everyone inside the complex. He was a remarkable man though, so there was always a chance. She walked away, clinging to that tiny sliver of hope.

THE END

ACKNOWLEDGEMENTS

Criminal Impulses is a debut from an author with enough self doubt to fill the Great Lakes. Honestly, even as I type this, I'm questioning every writing decision I've ever made. Writing is my passion, but passion doesn't get you much if it isn't harnessed. This book wouldn't exist without the support of so many people. Most notably, my writing group, 10 Minute Novelists. Katharine Grubb, Ian Hugh McAlister, and many others from that group have become a second family to me and I can't thank them enough.

My accountability partners Glenda Thompson and Emily Potter. When I didn't believe in myself, they did.

And lastly, my wonderful family. Heather, Dennis, Emmy, without you, I am nothing. You are my everything. I love you.

ABOUT THE AUTHOR

Born on the Canadian East Coast, Sandy R. Stuckless now lives in the 'big city' with his wife, two teenage children, and three cats. When Sandy isn't writing fantasy, sci-fi, paranormal, or anything else his twisted mind can conjure, he can be found at his day job in the traffic management systems industry.

In his downtime, Sandy can either be found watching the game with a plate of chicken wings, or during the summer, traveling the province of Ontario in his travel trailer, searching for a good burger and craft beer. His love for hiking, camping, and being outdoors keeps him on the move avoiding confined spaces at all costs.

Social Media:

Facebook: https://www.facebook.com/SandyRStuckless

Site X: https://twitter.com/SandyRStuckless

Threads: https://www.threads.net/@sandystuckless

Website: https://sandystuckless.wixsite.com/sandyrstuckless